LAVISH PRA[illegible]
DEEP SO[illegible]ANNEL

"*Deep Sound Channel* is a hell of a read."
—David Hagberg, author of *White House* and *Joshua's Hammer*

"An action-packed thriller that is all too real. Lots of action, lots of grit."
—Dick Couch, Capt., U.S. Navy (Ret.), author of *Rising Wind*

"Notable . . . formidable . . . mounds of high-tech detail."
—*Kirkus Reviews*

"A sobering look into the possible future of undersea warfare—the one environment where nuclear weapons can, and probably will, be used."
—P. T. Deutermann, Capt., U.S. Navy (Ret.), author of *Hunting Season* and *Scorpion in the Sea*

"A great premise . . . Buff knows weapons and warfare."
—*Library Journal*

"*Deep Sound Channel* demonstrates Joe Buff's intimate knowledge of undersea warfare. . . . Nonstop action!"
—Barrett Tillman, author of *The Sixth Battle* and *Warriors*

"Exciting battle scenes, fascinating naval maneuvers . . . suspenseful submarine action . . . [with] a satisfying, cliff-hanging ending."
—*Publishers Weekly*

DEEP SOUND CHANNEL

JOE BUFF

BANTAM BOOKS
NEW YORK TORONTO LONDON SYDNEY AUCKLAND

This edition contains the complete text
of the original hardcover edition.
NOT ONE WORD HAS BEEN OMITTED.

DEEP SOUND CHANNEL

A Bantam Book

PUBLISHING HISTORY

Bantam hardcover edition published July 2000
Bantam mass market edition / July 2001

Library of Congress Catalog Card Number: 00-24535.

ISBN: 0-553-58239-9

Published simultaneously in the United States and Canada

Bantam Books are published by Bantam Books, a division of Random House, Inc. Its trademark, consising of the words "Bantam Books" and the portrayal of a rooster, is Registered in U.S. Patent and Trademark Office and in other countries. Marca Registrada. Bantam Books, 1540 Broadway, New York, New York 10036.

PRINTED IN THE UNITED STATES OF AMERICA

OPM 10 9 8 7 6 5 4 3 2 1

In memory of the crews of USS Scorpion
and USS Thresher,
Cold Warriors who gave their lives perfecting the
nuclear submarines that helped the good guys win.

The announced public policy of the United States is to treat chemical and biological weapons as deserving of retaliation with nuclear weapons.

No one over fifty in Europe is entirely comfortable with seeing tanks bearing Iron Crosses. The degree of discomfort in Central Europe were Germany to be nuclear armed . . . would be very high.

It takes two sides to make peace but only one side to make war. By maintaining a ready and powerful force, the United States encourages others to choose peace.

—Rear Admiral W. J. Holland, Jr.,
U.S. Navy (Retired)

formerly director of Strategic and Theater Nuclear Weapons, U.S. Naval Institute Proceedings, *January 1999, pp. 46–47*

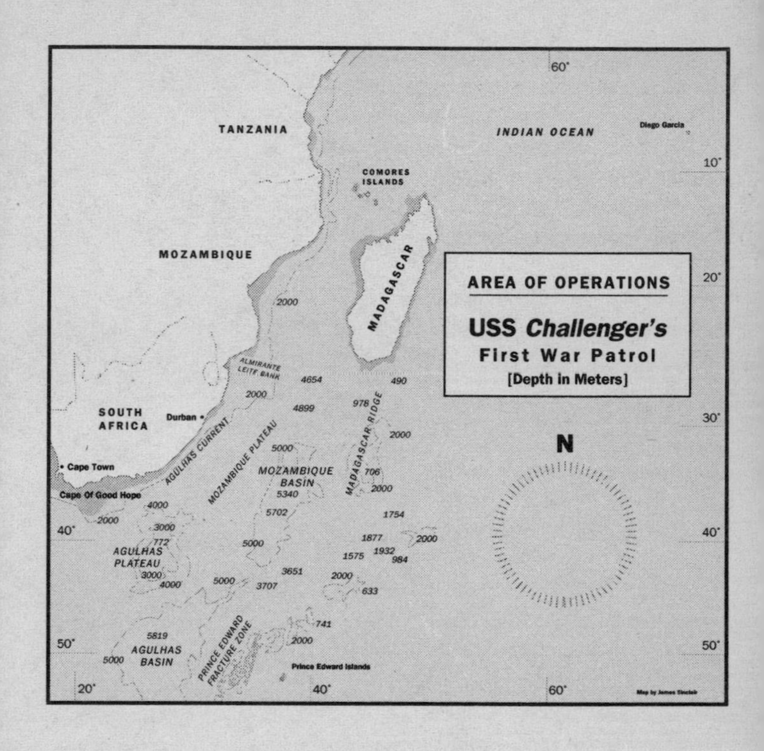

TANZANIA
INDIAN OCEAN
Diego Garcia
COMORES ISLANDS
MOZAMBIQUE
MADAGASCAR
AREA OF OPERATIONS
USS Challenger's
First War Patrol
[Depth in Meters]
ALMIRANTE LEITE BANK
SOUTH AFRICA
Durban
AGULHAS CURRENT
MOZAMBIQUE PLATEAU
MADAGASCAR RIDGE
MOZAMBIQUE BASIN
Cape Town
Cape Of Good Hope
AGULHAS PLATEAU
AGULHAS BASIN
PRINCE EDWARD FRACTURE ZONE
Prince Edward Islands
N
Map by James Sinclair

DEEP SOUND CHANNEL

PROLOGUE

TWENTY YEARS AFTER DESERT STORM, IN A DIFFERENT SORT OF WAR. OFF THE EAST COAST OF SOUTHERN AFRICA

Damn, the wingman told himself, this is something *else*. He grunted as he pulled back on the stick between his legs, giddy with expectation, jinking to evade the anti-aircraft fire from the Axis frigates below. He kicked his two F414-GE-400 turbojets into afterburner power, literally going ballistic. The acceleration pressed him hard into his ejection seat. His U.S. Navy F/A-18E jolted as he released the special ordnance, America's latest salvo in this limited tactical nuclear war at sea, a war that Germany and South Africa started by a giant ambush earlier the same year.

The wingman went for altitude and separation, and his g-suit squeezed his guts. His aircraft handled easily now, all its missiles and its cannon ammo gone, both 480-gallon wing-mounted fuel tanks long since jettisoned. He closed up in loose formation on the other Super Hornets in the four-plane element—their defense-suppression roles had been well played while they loitered, their electronic warfare pods had functioned perfectly.

His flight leader ordered them all to flee for safety on heading three two zero true. The wingman brought his head-up steering bug in line, then eyed the other data on the holographic plate and on his cockpit LCDs:

chronometer, airspeed and angle of attack, kinetic energy cue, fuel gauges and bingo point, engine temperatures and RPMs, chronometer again. His autopolarizing visor was already down, but he could still see well enough in the clear late morning air. Just about *now,* he told himself.

The sky lit up, it seemed from all directions, a quick violet-white stabbing glare. He looked back—like Lot's wife, he told himself, surprised that now of all times he'd think of the Bible. The high cockpit and twin tails of the F-18 gave him good visibility rearward.

A blinding orange-yellow fireball punched high into the air, tendrils of superheated plasma dancing on its crown, perched atop a widening column of smoke and tortured water, an obscene phallus whose warmth the flier felt right through his mask. A small atomic warhead, yet already he could see the tsunami begin to spread. He watched the airborne shock wave gradually overtake him as his formation built up speed, riding afterburners hot as blowtorches. He checked the sky around, checked his leader's position, glanced down at his hydraulic pressure and electric system amps, and watched again.

The sphere of ghostly condensation bloomed fast in all directions, much more swiftly than the tidal wave, quicker at first than sound. The aviator could see the overpressure's Mach stem piling up to punish the surface of the water. Then it hit his aircraft, a hammer and a hurricane. He struggled for control, avoiding a flat spin by just a whisker, pulled back in his fly-by-wire air brakes, and leveled off. Inside his nuclear-biological-chemical protective suit he dripped with sweat—his thighs seemed soaked and he wondered if he'd wet himself. He glanced at all his readouts, then at his flightmates. He smiled grimly. The other fighter-bombers looked okay, and his own mount was in good shape, all things considered. Those frigates had just paid dearly for nuking his carrier battle group's last E-2C Hawkeye AWACS and the midair refueling forces.

The wingman's leader signaled a turn due east and a lower airspeed. The wingman followed gladly. Today's battle, just the latest battle, had been long—the air and sea around were marred with thick black plumes, stale pyres of ships and planes and men. This was his diminished squadron's third sortie since sunup, and it was time to head for home. Not back to Jacksonville, Florida, of course, to his high school teaching job and family and duties as a weekend warrior. God knows when he'd do that again, get to see his wife and kids. Right now back to USS *Ranger* was enough, his home away from home, recommissioned out of ready reserve after the ultranationalist Double Putsch in Berlin and Johannesburg, the coups that were the setup for the ambush.

At this point aiming inward almost toward ground zero, from a hundred meters up the aviator watched the tidal wave his bomb had made come at him. It was easily sixty feet from crest to trough, a mountain of angry ocean boiling as it raced on by. Others followed, smaller only by comparison, foam and spindrift whipping backward off their peaks. His flight path cut the periphery of these concentric juggernauts, heading well north—upwind—of the blast. He double-checked that his cockpit ventilation system was sealed.

The wingman saw another flash beyond the earth's curvature, more southward and more pink, and assumed another strike had been made, more enemy vessels hit, more stragglers gone. Or maybe that was a defensive missile, to smack others of his air wing down. A mushroom cloud rose over the horizon, black with white intrusions capped by throbbing energetic red, silhouetted against the azure blue, delicate and vicious. Sooner than he expected the shock wave struck. His plane bucked in chaotic winds. The surface of the ocean chopped and writhed.

He scanned his instruments again. Three yellow caution lights but nothing major. His encrypted tactical radios still worked. They'd survived the electromagnetic pulses, though reception was shot to hell by the persisting TREE—transient radiation effects on electronics. The onboard shielding protected his avionics gear, but nothing could protect the very ether. His flight leader ordered one more course change, the last leg back to the carrier.

The wingman glanced down at the ocean—something caught his eye. Jesus, rocket motors. One, two, three, more and more, coming from deep underwater, leaving brownish trails of smoke till their sustainer jets cut in. His leader saw them also and warned *Ranger*. This sector had been sanitized repeatedly, but somehow an Axis submarine got through—were those Boer frigates a feint?

A dozen cruise missiles ripped the air, all aimed at *Ranger*, a full salvo from the modern U-boat's vertical launch array. *Bad news*, there go eight more, must be from her torpedo tubes. Again the flight leader sent a warning, but no one else was yet in interception range. The carrier ordered the four pilots to knock the vampires down. The overworked battle group's main line of defense hinged on the wingman and his flightmates now, and many lives hung in the balance.

The flight leader had some gun ammo left, and one of the other planes still had two Evolved Sidewinders. The whole flight headed for the deck, on afterburner again. These enemy cruise missiles were supersonic, almost certainly SS-N-19s, export-model Shipwrecks sold by a pseudo-neutral Russia to the Berlin-Boer Axis for hard cash. Shipwrecks did Mach 2.5, according to the briefings. Boeing's McDonnell Douglas Super Hornets topped out at 1.8.

The wingman's leader actually got two missiles before his M61A1 cannon ran out of 20mm shells. Debris went flying, winglets and fuselage sections mostly, splashing into the sea and then falling far behind. The pilot with the Sidewinders got two more. Chemical explosions flared—missile fuel and high-explosive charges—gentle caresses compared to the earlier atomic fireballs. Two other vampires malfunctioned on their own, hit the water, and disintegrated. That left fourteen. Some of these would be decoys really, mere conventional warheads, but Shipwrecks, the wingman told himself, were nuclear-capable platforms. The Axis had secretly built U-235 bombs to spare, then announced the fact by using them in combat.

Rapidly the four aircraft and the cruise missiles chewed up the remaining distance back toward *Ranger* and her escorts. Two older, smaller F-18Cs vectored in, also low on avgas and munitions. The wingman watched his own fuel gauges drop alarmingly. They were running out of time, and so was *Ranger*. He hit Mach 1.

Easing in toward one cruise missile, he tried to slap it with his vortex turbulence. He watched it stagger but then get back on course. He eased in again, nudged it with his wingtip. It flipped over and crashed. He saw his leader do the same to another missile. But rapidly they were coming up to speed, planes and vampires both, and soon the missiles would outrun the Super Hornets irretrievably.

One of the other aircraft also tried to flip a missile, miscalculated, and both went into the sea. No chute, just a giant drawn-out splash. At a thousand knots airspeed you died instantly. The reservist watched the fourth pilot in their element aim his aircraft at another missile, ramming it on purpose. Jet fuel and missile fuel went up in a sharp double explosion, silent through the wingman's canopy and earphones, unheard above his rumbling engines. No big high-explosive blast this time—that one had been atomic. Bits of metal and flesh rained on the ocean and were quickly left behind.

Inside his uncomfortable protective suit the wingman fought his stick, driving hard through the thick air right above the water. The sea swell rolled by in a blur. Behind him, he knew, his twin jets and his shock front would be making cockscombs on the ocean, but now he couldn't spare a moment to look back. He eyed his flight leader just in time to see him hit the surface, bounce once, and disintegrate. A split second's inattention, a wavelet slightly higher than the rest—it didn't take much.

Another, slower fighter, a late arrival, fired two AIM-120 AMRAAMs. Both missed, corkscrewing erratically, leaving useless trails of smoke—they must have suffered battle damage in some earlier dogfight. Flying on just vapors now, probably, that pilot pulled up and ejected. Good chute! The wingman called it in.

Another fighter rammed a missile, another harsh eruption, and the wingman was alone. He tried for one himself, using every ounce of thrust, his engine temps far in the red, happy to make the sacrifice for his 5,000 shipmates, surprised how easy it was to die. But his target was too fast. He watched the surviving missiles draw relentlessly ahead, arrayed in an arc in front of him. They left his Super Hornet to buffet in their jet wakes, spattering his windscreen with kicked-up spume.

With no other option the pilot gained altitude and throttled back and radioed in another warning. Ahead, hull down over the horizon, an Aegis guided missile cruiser opened fire. He guessed these were RUM-139B Updated ASROCs, in very short supply, antisubmarine rockets that dropped nuclear-tipped Mark 54 torpedoes, aimed to bracket the sub that launched the vampires.

Common sense told the wingman to turn north or south and flee, but loyalty kept him on course eastward. Running very low on fuel, running away from the ASROCs' impending nuclear detonations, heading almost certainly toward one more, he went for altitude again. Now he could see the whole battle group ahead, *Ranger* in the center, escorts spread around her in a circle foreshortened by perspective. They were well dispersed against atomic warheads, but at the cost of weakened interlocking antiaircraft fire.

White spray began to shroud the vessels as high-pressure nozzles started the washdown that was a basic defense against the upcoming heat and fallout. The ships seemed so tiny against the surface of the water, their wakes curving in coordinated Vs as the formation altered course. To buy a little time? To show the smallest profile? Blue-gray fumes poured from *Ranger*'s stack as her engineers squeezed every last knot from her aged oil-fired boilers. Steam billowed from her flight deck as F-14s catapulted into the air against the crosswind, and her combat air patrol did what they could.

One missile went for an *Arleigh Burke* destroyer, attracted by the rippling thermal signature of her gas turbine exhausts. There was a brilliant flash. Conventional high explosive but she went dead in the water immediately, shrouded in flames and dirty smoke.

The wingman tried to spot the Shipwrecks, aptly named he told himself, but from his lofty, slower vantage point the supersonic projectiles were invisible to the human eye. They'd be mostly unseen to crewmen on the ships as well, he knew, though not to their pulse-Doppler and phased-array air-search radars. He watched the fluffy booster trails from RIM-7P Sea Sparrows, which made Mach 3.5 themselves, but whose range was only eight nautical miles. Some scored hits with their fragmentation warheads, and he prayed none picked up his fighter; he put his Identification-Friend-or-Foe in squawk mode just in case.

Roiling black puffs belched from guns on every vessel now, throwing up a wall of steel, hoping for last-minute intercepts. Clouds of SRBOC chaff burst between the ships, and HIRAM decoy magnesium flares drifted on the wind—they showed up, too, amidst the chaos on the pilot's sea mode radar and on his forward-looking infrared. He pictured the ships' close-in-weapons systems slewing into action, firing 20mm nickel-cobalt-tungsten slugs at 3,000 rounds per minute. Some connected, and other missiles exploded or plunged into the sea.

But *Ranger* couldn't hide. Her thousand-foot-long bulk, her fifty-year-old most unstealthy lines, would draw the target seekers hungrily. The wingman altered course to northward, self-preservation taking hold at last. There was another blinding flash. Once more he looked back.

Off *Ranger*'s starboard side a supernova flared. Her island superstructure blew apart, antennas first and then her stack and other chunks of twisted steel. The flag bridge and the main bridge vaporized, as the aviator tried not to think of the men and women who'd been inside. *Ranger*'s remaining warplanes took off sideways, dissolving in midair, followed by her four big aircraft elevators, tumbling like leaves in an autumn breeze. The carrier's entire flight deck crew, traditional multicolored vests worn over rubberized jump suits and breather hoods, shriveled like ants under a magnifying glass and blew away in tiny puffs of soot. The carcass that was *Ranger* burned furiously from stem to stern.

The wingman felt the shock wave lift his fighter-bomber bodily, flung forward and yet almost in a stall. His moving map display, his head-up display, his helmet-mounted cueing system all went dead. Both artificial horizons failed, and he looked up to see the ocean, not the sky. He fought for control as more cautions and warnings lighted on his panels. From upside down he saw the Aegis cruiser take a tidal wave bows-on, pitching like a roller coaster, yawing frighteningly, white water thrown up higher than her masts, green water burying her weather decks.

Suddenly the wingman's port turbojet flamed out,

from the negative static pressure pulse of the nuclear detonation. Fighting the torsion of unbalanced angular momentum on a single turbine, the twisting from uneven thrust, he went through the relighting sequence on pure instinct. Blessedly it worked. He leveled off.

The wingman blinked repeatedly, the dazzling spots before his eyes now mixed with angry tears. He glanced at the DI-60P/D dosimeter clipped to his flight harness, wondering if he'd gotten lethal rads, whole-body penetrating gamma rays and neutrons. You needed a computer to read the thing, but he'd find out soon enough if symptoms showed—nausea would be first. Off his left shoulder the horizon flickered lavender, violet, pink, then new suns rose in mockery of Sol. In the cockpit his upfront digital touchscreen died.

The aviator reviewed the little clipboard strapped to his right thigh, then did the calculation in his head. He came to zero five five true—his inertial nav and GPS were fried, his radars and his forward-looking infrared were useless, but at least his backup mechanical gyrocompass worked. Some sixty miles away an Australian *Collins*-class diesel sub patrolled on lifeguard duty for emergencies like this, courtesy of America's wartime British Commonwealth allies.

The wingman read his fuel gauge one more time: just four hundred pounds of JP-5. He throttled back yet further, to a mere three hundred knots. His hydraulic system automatically switched into low-pressure mode, 3,000 psi, but then began to drop. He numbly tried to focus on just staying in the air. He'd barely make it.

CHAPTER 1

A FEW DAYS LATER, AT DIEGO GARCIA, IN THE INDIAN OCEAN

Lieutenant Commander Jeffrey Fuller looked up from his night-long labors at USS *Challenger*'s weapons loading hatch, wiped his dripping brow, and watched in morbid fascination. The crewmen he'd been working with did too, and for once he didn't urge them back to it. They've more than earned a break, he told himself, so let them look. Let them see what this is all about, this tactical nuclear war at sea with the Berlin-Boer Axis.

"Jesus," the submarine's chief of the boat said, looking east from under the lead-lined awning with its propane jets, radar and thermal antisatellite masking.

"Yeah," Jeffrey said. What else was there to say? The young seamen just stared.

The sun had breasted the horizon now, well past the first moment of nautical dawn, that special time of day that Jeffrey loved but rarely saw. The extra-yellow early light shone above the seventy-foot-high trees off in the distance, the long-abandoned coconut plantation on the other side of the lagoon. The light picked out the cloud-flecked sky, high scudding altocumulus over fluffy fractostratus blobs, and it illuminated the hideous procession in the foreground.

"Ranger," Jeffrey whispered.

The ATR(X) oceangoing salvage tug bore zero three

five relative, crossing the line of bearing to the lighthouse on Leconte Point. Her charge's stem could just be seen, slowly making progress past the anchorage. Gradually, like some obscene burlesque, the hulk came into view, dragged by the tow cable whose catenary curved beneath the water and then up again. Slowly, almost teasingly, she moved out from behind the looming steel-gray side of the submarine tender, USS *Frank Cable,* against which *Challenger* lay moored.

Instinctively Jeffrey did the target-motion analysis in his head. Angle on the bow starboard zero four zero, *mark*. Speed five knots, course one six five. Distance to the track, call it 1,200 yards.

Jeffrey noticed there was comparative silence now. Work topside had ceased on all the other ships as well. Only the incessant roar of jets and turboprops and helicopters persisted, off past his right shoulder at the airfield. Overhead, birds soared, oblivious.

Ranger's wake washed under *Challenger,* and she started pitching slightly as if in homage. The nylon mooring lines stretched, creaking softly. Thankfully the light breeze was from behind Jeffrey, from the west.

Ranger's island superstructure was gone, Jeffrey saw, except for a tangled mess of wreckage, a livid stump three meters high. Her flight deck, warped and twisted, was more or less still there, except for the aircraft elevators, which all were missing. Edge-on to the enemy cruise missile blast, Jeffrey figured, the flight deck was peeled upward as the atomic shock front's ground reflection diffracted over the vessel. Stress loadings of the incident wave, severe drag and compression forces, and explosive negative pressure gradients did the rest.

"My God," Jeffrey said out loud. "You can see right through her hull." He watched the sunrise glowing where the hangar deck had been, and in the other empty spaces lower down. Those once were all compartments, where her crew had worked and studied, slept and messed, written letters home. Tortured longitudinals were what remained of her first platform deck amidships, forward of engineering. Along her waterline arced the discharge from many pumps, undoubtedly P-250 portable gasoline-powered units, keeping her afloat.

"They're finishing the detailed decontamination," COB said, pointing out the little figures in nuclear-biological-chemical protective suits on the hull, busy with the scrubbing and the sealing. "Aging will have happened on its own."

"Iodine 131," Jeffrey said, continuing the idle shop talk in spite of himself, "radon 222, the shortest half-lived stuff."

COB nodded. "The gross washdown would have been completed after putting out the fires."

"The naval architects will claim her now, I think," Jeffrey said. "To improve their damageability models."

"It isn't right," COB said. "She's a tomb, not a pile of data."

Here and there patches of hull plating still clung to *Ranger*'s side. The plates were pressed inward against the frame members, whose outlines stood out clearly. The plates seemed plastered to her flank like sheets of canvas in the wind, a devil's wind. Everything was black, deep coal-mine black, except for splotches where the fires and ocean salt had oxidized her steel a matte pastel red-brown.

"She fought hard," a junior officer said with awe.

"A Presidential Unit Citation for sure," a senior chief said.

"Awarded posthumously," COB said, an obvious tightness in his throat.

"The larger battle won," Jeffrey said, "but at such cost." It was better if they talked, he told himself. It eased the pain.

Jeffrey saw two seamen wipe their eyes—maybe they'd had friends aboard, or maybe not. He watched as

Ranger moved on through the lagoon, toward its closed end at the south point of the atoll's miles-long V, toward shallow water and foul ground.

"Message from *Frank Cable*, sir," COB said when there seemed no point in watching further, being formal for the benefit of the enlisted men, all petty officers themselves. "Captain's due back in fifteen minutes."

A group of crewmen had been standing close together at the bow, huddling like at a funeral, near the dozen hatches for the Tactical Tomahawk cruise missile vertical launch system. The men got back to work, unbidden, at the torpedo loading gear.

"Last one, correct?" Jeffrey said, eyeing the lethal cylinder.

"Confirmed, last nuclear torpedo," COB said carefully.

Jeffrey initialed the checklist, then held out his clipboard for COB to countersign. The old chief would have his thirty years in soon, Jeffrey knew, but with this war the navy wouldn't let him go. Not that he would want to, and victory was much too tenuous to plan that far ahead. COB, whose given name was never used aboard, came from a clan of Latino Jersey City truckers. Black sheep of the family, he instead had gone to sea.

At least COB had a family who cared. Jeffrey sighed to himself, then stood up straighter. "Let me give you guys a hand."

They positioned the crane's long burden carefully, then eased the two-metric-ton weapon onto the loading cradle and secured it. Jeffrey watched the cradle first elevate to line up with the channel through the hull, then trundle down toward the transit rack in the torpedo room three decks below.

A variable-yield warhead, the cryptic markings on the fish's glossy green side said 0.01 to 0.1 kilotons. Maybe that didn't sound like much, till you remembered these were meant to go off underwater. "Up to almost one percent of Hiroshima," Jeffrey said, mostly to himself. The casing at the back for the fiber-optic guidance wire was labeled NO STEP.

COB cleared his throat. "The message said we have two guests. Passengers. No honors to be rendered."

"Very well," Jeffrey said. He shrugged. "Security, I guess."

"Cripes," COB groaned. "Please, no."

"Watch that," Jeffrey said, but smiling. He'd seen why COB had cursed. Captain Wilson was coming down the gangway from the tender, accompanied by two uniformed figures. One had a beard and one was female.

Jeffrey went to meet them at the brow, the portable aluminum stepway that led onto the hull. The brow was positioned at *Challenger*'s so-called quarterdeck, a flat space behind the sail.

The captain's male guest was a Royal Navy four-striper in summer whites, a full captain, not like Jeffrey's CO, who was actually a commander. The woman wore a khaki short-sleeved shirt and slacks, but from a distance Jeffrey couldn't make out her collar tabs. He watched the arriving threesome honor the national ensign at *Challenger*'s stern, then exchange salutes with the in-port duty officer.

"Commodore Morse," Wilson said, "let me introduce my executive officer, Jeffrey Fuller. . . . Jeffrey, meet Richard Morse." They shook hands. A commodore was a senior captain acting in the role of rear admiral, commanding more than a single ship. Jeffrey saw that Morse was qualified in subs—between the dolphins on *his* badge was a crown with inlaid rubies.

"Welcome to our island," Morse said, smiling. Then he added puckishly, "Of course, hardly anyone here's British." Diego Garcia was a U.K. dependent territory, in the middle of the Indian Ocean, in the middle of nowhere. Its strategic value lay in being on the way to or from so many other places.

"The commodore's with us as an observer," Wilson said. "He'll take command of a new undersea battle group when we get to the Cape Verdes."

"HMS *Dreadnought* will be my flagship to escort the Allied buildup," Morse said, "so I'm quite interested in how *you* people go about things. You know our troopship and tank transport convoys to Central Africa will be crucial. German and Boer land forces are still hell-bent on linking up there."

Morse's frame was compact, like Captain Wilson's, and his wan complexion seemed more so next to the CO's deep chocolate brown. Morse had erect posture by submariner standards, with slightly rounded shoulders that spoke of quiet power. Wilson's shoulders were squared off, always, conveying toughness and a not-so-quiet power.

"XO," Wilson said, "this is Ilse Reebeck. Miss Reebeck, Commander Fuller." A lieutenant commander was called "Commander" publicly, and as XO Jeffrey would have gotten the title in any case, a military courtesy. Now he could see Ilse was a civilian—no one had told her civilians don't salute.

"How do you do," Jeffrey said. Ilse was slim, close to Jeffrey's height. She had a good figure and a good firm handshake, but her eyes were angry, or maybe sad.

"Pleased to meet you," Reebeck said officiously in a not-quite-British accent.

"Anything vital still not loaded?" Wilson said to Jeffrey, never one to waste his time or words.

"How vital do you mean, sir?" Jeffrey said.

"We've got mission orders," Wilson said, holding up his bulging briefcase, "but first things first. An Israeli Type 800 diesel boat just reported an inbound hostile PROBSUB contact, then didn't have the signal processing power to hold on to it."

"The hostile's not nuclear-powered?" Jeffrey said.

"No, it's too quiet, that's the problem. Helos are being vectored now to help confirm and localize. We're tasked to make the intercept before the bastard gets too close."

"Understood, Captain."

"Tell Maneuvering I want to get under way in fifteen minutes. You take the bridge until we dive."

"Aye aye, sir," Jeffrey said. He knew *Challenger*'s reactor had been kept critical. With her steam throttles cranked open and proper control rod adjustments, the ship would answer all bells almost instantly.

"Weapons load-out completed?" Wilson said.

"Yes, sir," Jeffrey said.

"Everyone aboard? SEAL team squared away?"

"We struck their gear below first thing."

"Good," Wilson said, eyeing the flexible conveyor passing boxes from the tender. "Anything still waiting when we single up gets left behind. And once we're submerged, I want your recommendation on what goes in the torpedo tubes. So use your head."

"Understood, sir," Jeffrey said.

"You got grease on your good uniform."

"Sorry, sir," Jeffrey said, "I didn't have time to change after the meeting with Admiral Cook."

Wilson nodded. "Call me when we're ready to cast off." Wilson let the Brit precede him down the hatch behind the sail. COB followed, presumably to help Morse get settled in.

Ilse Reebeck lingered. She glared at the armed enlisted man who stood guard by the brow. He instinctively stepped back. "I'm South African," she told Jeffrey, making it a dare, not an explanation.

"I'm sorry," Jeffrey said. He thought she had nice hair. Light brown, like her eyes, straight and shoulder-length.

"You were with the SEALs," Ilse said, pointing to his Special Warfare qualification badge.

"Long ago," Jeffrey said. "I transferred to the SubForce. It's been more than fifteen years now."

"Miss it?"

"Excuse me?"

"Do you miss being in the SEALs?" Ilse pronounced each word distinctly, as if Jeffrey were retarded or slightly deaf.

"Frankly no."

Ilse pointed to his uniform blouse again, below the gold twin dolphins. She jabbed two of his ribbons. "Silver Star, Purple Heart. Somewhere in Iraq, the captain said. . . . Did it hurt much?"

"Yeah." Jeffrey wondered what this woman was all about. "It was months till I could walk again."

"Feeling all right now?"

"Yes," Jeffrey said too quickly. Times when he went short on sleep, his left thigh ached badly.

"Good," Ilse said. She looked him up and down. Jeffrey met her gaze. She responded with the coldest sneer he'd ever gotten from a woman.

Ilse walked to the hatch, then glanced back at Jeffrey as she started climbing inside. "I suppose nobody's told you yet," she said. "You're coming with me on the raid."

Jeffrey asked the junior officer of the deck, the JOOD, to stay with him up in the tiny cockpit on top of the sail, the conning tower, to watch and learn—maneuvering on the surface wasn't like underwater. Jeffrey glanced at the sky. The sun was noticeably higher. Today would be hot, in more ways than one.

"First question should always be, where's the wind?" Jeffrey said.

"Still light from off the stern, sir," the lieutenant (j.g.) said.

"Not that that matters much," Jeffrey said. "Subs ride so low in the water, and these days have such tiny, stealthy sails, wind's usually the last thing you have to worry about when getting under way."

"Just like I read, sir. Just like in the simulator."

"What's the latest fallout report?" Jeffrey gestured to the intercom. Of course, he already knew the answer.

The young man cleared his throat and pressed the button. "Control, Bridge. Radiology, how's the air?"

"Milliroentgens per hour and counts per minute well inside normal tolerances, sir."

"Very well," the JOOD said.

"Good," Jeffrey said. "*Frank Cable*'s met staff predicted that, but you should always check. Weather forecasts are still just weather forecasts."

"Understood, sir."

"Meltzer, you ever been to Diego Garcia before?" A rhetorical question, since Jeffrey had the night before reread young David's file.

"No, sir. This is my first time overseas, not counting summer cruises at Annapolis."

Jeffrey looked down from his vantage point atop the sail. He'd done Naval ROTC instead, at Purdue. "The tide's running out, from right to left. See the way that buoy's listing with the set?"

"Two knots maybe, sir. Not strong."

"The lagoon here's huge, but the opening at the north end's pretty wide. There's lots of room to ebb and flow without making nasty currents."

"Should we use our auxiliary propulsors, sir?"

"Nah. That makes things too easy." Jeffrey smiled. "We hardly ever get to ship drive on the surface, right? Besides, it's fun."

With his bullhorn Jeffrey had the deck hands take in two and three: the forward and aft breast lines that were crossed to keep the boat from sliding back and forth. Then lines one and four, the bow and stern mooring lines, were singled up. Jeffrey ordered four brought to the little capstan on the deck, the after capstan.

He asked for lots of slack on one and had four take a strain.

"From here it's mostly feel," Jeffrey said. "You get the hang of it with practice. We have all these extra visual cues on the surface, but the sea state has much more effect, sonar doesn't work as well, and there are only two degrees of freedom."

Gradually *Challenger*'s bow began to lever from the tender as she rotated against the aftmost deep draft separator. Before her stern parts could make contact Jeffrey ordered all lines taken in, then had the deck gang go below.

"Control, Bridge, rudder amidships," Jeffrey commanded into the intercom. "Ahead one third, make turns for six knots." He used the bridge horn toggle to sound a lengthy blast. He checked again that all the bridge instruments were working.

Water began to surge from *Challenger*'s shrouded pump-jet main propulsor, a design innovation first used by the Royal Navy. The turbine churned up a wake and the boat moved forward, quickly gaining steerageway.

"Subs are notorious for squishy directional control at dead-slow speeds. Know why?"

"Their rounded bows, sir, and rudders forward of the propulsor wash."

"Yup. We're moving now, so that's one less thing to worry about." Jeffrey leaned to the intercom again. "Control, Bridge. Rig for dive." He turned back to Meltzer. "That won't take them long."

"No, sir. We've been at material conditions ZEBRA and CIRCLE WILLIAM since we surfaced yesterday."

"And these signify . . . ?"

"Watertight doors and fittings shut, ventilation subsystems sealed or making overpressure, except when needed for reprovisioning and maintenance."

Jeffrey nodded. "The torpedomen'll be starting final assembly of the special weapons warheads now, and they'll insert the exploders in our conventional ADCAPs too. . . . Now I'm gonna check for conflicting ship traffic again. You have to let the lookouts know you're relying on them, but you also need to make sure for yourself."

"I understand, sir."

"If anything goes wrong, anything at all, it's the OOD's responsibility. Get that in your blood for when you qualify."

"Yes, Commander."

"Since we're at EMCON, we can't use the Sperry BPS-16." That was *Challenger*'s surface surveillance radar, shut down for electronic silence. "But visibility's good. Just remember *we're* very hard to see, 'cause of our low profile. Defensive driving counts."

Jeffrey watched Meltzer take a thorough look around, practicing for when his time came.

"*Frank Cable*'s in anchorage area A-3," Jeffrey said, "about as close to the exit channel as you can get." He leaned to the intercom. "Left standard rudder." He looked at Meltzer. "I'm judging by eye the advance in yards and lateral transfer you'd expect for our present speed and rudder setting. The assistant navigator has all the tables."

"I've studied them very carefully, sir. In training they said we shouldn't just rely on the computer."

Jeffrey watched as *Challenger* turned into the channel. "Observe the wake. See the way we rotate round our pivot point? It's about a fourth of the way back along the hull, so part of the boat always swings out as we turn. That happens underwater too, but you don't get to see it."

Meltzer's lips moved silently, as if repeating what he'd heard. "Quite so, sir."

"You have to make allowances for that yaw around our track. More than one promising young naval officer has come to grief against a pier or shoal."

"I understand, sir," Meltzer said.

"The worst is if you hit another vessel in tight quarters."

Meltzer swallowed.

Good, Jeffrey told himself, the kid takes this stuff seriously. "And . . . just about *now*." Jeffrey hit the intercom again. "Rudder amidships." The sub steadied up on heading three one five. Jeffrey smiled. "I think I timed that well."

"Very nice, sir."

"Good shiphandling," Jeffrey said, "that's the key. Nothing impresses your seniors more, or disappoints them faster."

Soon Jeffrey eyed the bridge gyrocompass again. "See, you want to keep your eyes moving constantly, take in everything, assume nothing. What's our course?"

Meltzer looked at the instrument. "Still three one five, sir."

Jeffrey glanced forward. "Straight down the outbound lane. Any nearby traffic?"

A pause. "Negative, sir."

"Very well. . . . Ahead one third," Jeffrey said into the mike, "make normal turns." The control room acknowledged.

Jeffrey watched with satisfaction as *Challenger*'s bow thrust the seas up on her foredeck. The water cascaded smoothly into standing wave depressions on both sides of the round black hull amidships. Some creamed up and around the curved juncture between sail forefoot and the foredeck. "That bit of streamlining's from the mid-nineties," Jeffrey said, "before your time."

"I know, sir. It reduces flow noise and helps our quieting submerged."

"I'd argue the Russians thought of it before we did."

"The *Akula* and *Typhoon* classes, sir."

Now and then Jeffrey and Meltzer caught some spray. "That *is* one disadvantage," Jeffrey said, wiping his eyes and laughing, "especially when you're in a heavy sea. Today's okay, though."

"It's refreshing, sir. . . . Think they'll ever come in on our side? Russia/Belarus, I mean."

"Doubtful," Jeffrey said, no humor in his voice now. "The Germans sent a message it would be hard not to hear, those two A-bombs in the Pripet Marshes on the Ukraine border. Then they backed that up with bribery, buying arms galore from Moscow."

"But what if things between us and the Axis escalate?"

"Let's just hope they don't. The Putsch leaders are coldly calculating, not insane." Jeffrey cleared his throat. "There's Eclipse Point." He gestured with his left arm.

"Downtown Diego Garcia," Meltzer said. "Such as it is."

Jeffrey gazed at the water tower and big antennas and all the low white buildings. For a moment he watched *Challenger*'s wake spread out behind, foaming steadily, also white.

"We're in the Main Pass now," Jeffrey said. "That's little West Island there to port, and Middle and East islands both to starboard. Notice how they're thickly wooded, and the big coral reefs."

"I see them, sir. We're clear."

"No swimming on the ocean side, by the way. Sharks." Jeffrey chuckled again. The submarine passed the last pair of channel buoys and entered open water.

Two aircraft overtook the boat, passing low on either beam, air combat missiles on their hard points. "F-14D Tomcats," Jeffrey said. He turned to Meltzer. "A-models flew before you were born."

The two-seat Tomcats both did barrel rolls in greeting, their engine noises deafening, little trails of vapor forming spirals off their airfoils. Jeffrey and Meltzer waved. The pilots pulled back on their sticks, their afterburners brilliant in the daylight. Each riding 56,000 pounds of thrust, the aviators swept back their wings and disappeared into the clouds.

Jeffrey glanced up at *Challenger*'s American flag, now shifted to a gaff behind the cockpit. He listened to it snapping briskly, and had to smile. Then he gripped the edge of the cockpit with both hands, facing into the relative wind off the port bow. He was way too tired to feel much emotion, just a kind of numbness and a sense of purpose.

"*Challenger*'s first war patrol," he said aloud. God knows when I'll get some sleep. God knows if I'll be alive this time tomorrow.

"It's exciting, sir," Meltzer said. "Now we get to do our part."

Then Jeffrey thought about what Ilse Reebeck had said.

He had a flashback, not his first the last few weeks. The concussion of grenades, the crackle of small-arms fire. The screams, the smells, the blood mixing with seawater. He shook his head to clear his thoughts.

It didn't work. He saw his old fiancée in his mind, looking down at him in traction, pity and revulsion in her eyes. He remembered the final time, struggling in his walker, when she just gave up and left.

Jeffrey chided himself angrily. "Duty, Meltzer," he said by way of cover. "Keep your mind on duty."

"Absolutely, sir."

"You can just make out the sea state reduction system," Jeffrey said, pointing south-southwest. "Use your binoculars, you'll get a better view."

The young man took a look.

"Disc-shaped barges," Jeffrey said, "anchored to the bottom. They knock down big waves caused by storms, or ones made artificially by the enemy."

"That's a euphemism, sir," Meltzer said.

"Damn straight," Jeffrey said. "What I really meant is

the tsunami from a nuclear explosion. Diego Garcia's average elevation's just four feet over mean high water."

A few minutes later Jeffrey tapped the bridge fathometer. "You been watching soundings?"

"Yes, sir," Meltzer said. "We went from fifty feet to fifteen hundred pretty quick."

"The bottom drops off fast here. It's already twenty-five hundred plus."

Jeffrey thought of *Ranger,* and of the airfield left behind him now. He thought of the 4,000 people on the base. Targets, he told himself. They're all juicy, sitting targets for nuclear warheads.

That PROBSUB was getting closer by the minute. It was time for *Challenger* to dive.

CHAPTER 2

"Clear the bridge!" Jeffrey ordered. The port lookout snapped the flag gaff off its mounting. The lookouts and bridge messenger went below, then the JOOD. Jeffrey inspected the hatch and followed last. He dogged the hatch, climbed down the ladder through the sail, and checked the next hatch. A petty officer sealed the second hatch after Jeffrey confirmed the bridge was clear.

Jeffrey took the ladder to the next deck down, walked past some computer banks, and strode into the Command and Control Center, the CACC. As was standard procedure when *Challenger* got ready to submerge, Jeffrey as officer of the deck became the diving officer now. Wilson had the conn.

Jeffrey sat down at the two-man desk-high Q-70 command workstation, to Wilson's right. In front of Jeffrey against the forward bulkhead was the ship control station, another part of Lockheed Martin's AN/UYQ-70 control room console suite. In its left position sat COB, as chief of the watch. To COB's right sat David Meltzer, still JOOD, now acting as the helmsman. Between them was the engine order telegraph, a four-inch dial. Jeffrey buckled his seat belt.

COB was busy with the ballast and the trim. His console had valve manifold and vent and pump and moisture trap controls, air and water pressure gauges, fill-level meters, and status enunciators. One of his screens showed a flow diagram of the entire pump and tankage system, and the ship's hydraulics.

On his own active matrix LCD Jeffrey called up a copy of the digitized ship status board. He studied it very carefully. Everything that was supposed to be open was open, and everything to be closed was closed. Reports from all compartments confirmed there were no leaks, fires, or critical equipment casualties, and all checklists for submerging were complete.

"Captain," Jeffrey said, "ship is ready for dive in all respects."

"Very well," Wilson said. "Make turns for eight knots."

Jeffrey picked up the 7MC microphone, a dedicated line to the men in charge back behind the reactor. "Maneuvering, Control. Make turns for eight knots." Maneuvering acknowledged. "Maneuvering acknowledges turns for eight knots," Jeffrey said.

"Dive the ship," Wilson said. "Dive, dive. Make your depth seven zero feet."

"Dive the ship, aye," Jeffrey said. "Make my depth seven zero feet, aye." Jeffrey hit the dive alarm, and an electronic tone sounded twice in the CACC. "Chief of the Watch, dive the ship." Jeffrey missed the loud Klaxon they'd used in the old diesel boats.

"Dive the ship, aye," COB said. He made the announcement on the 1MC.

"Helm," Jeffrey said, "make your depth seven zero feet." He knew seventy feet at the keel was *Challenger*'s periscope depth.

"Make my depth seven zero feet, aye," Meltzer said.

Jeffrey watched COB flood first fore and then aft ballast tanks. Meltzer used his split-yoke control wheel to put two degrees down angle on the bowplanes, helping get *Challenger*'s nose beneath the waves.

Jeffrey set a window on his main console screen to show imagery from one of the two non-hull-penetrating photonics masts. Starting with the fast-attack sub USS *Virginia,* ordered in 1998 and commissioned in '04, these took the place of traditional periscopes with their awkward straight-line optical paths.

On-screen Jeffrey saw *Challenger* blow spray just like a spouting whale as air rushed from the ballast tanks through big vents in the hull. Gradually she left that unnatural upper world where all stood naked, descending into the other world for which she had been made. A world of silent darkness, yet one that teemed with life and evanescent light.

"Bow's under," Jeffrey announced, then used the little joy stick to look aft. "Stern's under. Helm, make four degrees down bubble."

"Four degrees down bubble, aye," Meltzer said. In older boats—like the *Los Angeles*–class USS *Alexandria,* where Jeffrey did his own first tour—a pair of junior enlisted men worked the rudder and the dive controls: sternplanes for depth, bowplanes at low speeds for bank and angle of attack. These days, though the navy still used two-man piloting, those roles were combined with ballast/trim control in two more-senior jobs.

As *Challenger*'s propulsor, now well submerged, drove the boat down more quickly, Jeffrey saw their rate of descent increase on his display. "Chief of the Watch," he said, "blow negative to the mark."

COB fed high-pressure air back into the negative tank, emptying it to the point, the mark, he estimated would restore neutral buoyancy—the tank was flooded when the ship first rigged for dive, to get her down fast when the time came. Skillfully COB and Meltzer leveled *Challenger* off at seventy feet.

Next Jeffrey oversaw as COB altered trim so the boat would hold zero bubble, stay level. Then COB pumped seawater between auxiliaries one and two amidships so there was no list port or starboard. Jeffrey knew he'd made a first cut when they got under way, based on fore and aft ship draft measurements and weight calculations at the tender. It helped that the local seas were calm—the master chief was done in record time, and Jeffrey reported to Wilson.

Wilson took control of the photonics mast, scanning for surface visual contacts on wide angle, then high power. Jeffrey backed him up on his own monitor—a deep draft Military Sealift Command auxiliary could do fatal harm in a collision. Jeffrey confirmed there was nothing to be seen now, even on passive infrared, except for clouds and a KC-130T transport aircraft wearing Marine Corps camouflage.

"Make turns for four knots," Wilson said.

Jeffrey relayed the order to Maneuvering, then passed their acknowledgment back to the captain. The lower speed was to let COB fine-tune the trim and buoyancy.

"Navigator," Jeffrey heard Wilson say, "how's our GPS?"

"Way off, sir," the navigator said. "Bad guys still playing with the signals."

"Inertial navigation and gravimeter?"

"Ring laser gyrocompasses are all in order. No discrepancies or drift on ship's ESGN accelerometers. Tight agreement with seafloor gradiometry and the dead-reckoning plot."

"Soundings?" Wilson said.

"Two seven three five feet, sir, and increasing," the navigator said.

"Sonar," Wilson said, "any nearby contacts?" With increased automation and distributed data fusion, Sonar no longer had a separate room.

"Negative, sir," the sonar officer said, confirming what he'd sent to Jeffrey's screen.

"Very well, Sonar," Wilson said. "XO, I want to head

due south, take that incoming PROBSUB from the flank. Make your course one eight zero."

"Make your course one eight zero," Jeffrey formally relayed to the helmsman, who sat just feet away.

"Make my course one eight zero, aye, sir," Meltzer said. "Steering one eight zero, sir," he broke in thirty seconds later.

"Steering one eight zero, sir," Jeffrey repeated to the captain, continuing the age-old rituals of the sea, almost religious incantations. In ancient times, Jeffrey knew, they kept the idols on the quarterdeck.

"Very well, Dive," Wilson said. "Sonar, where's the layer?"

"One seven five feet, sir."

"I plan to stay above the thermocline till we take a better look around. Stream the port towed array."

"Aye, sir," Jeffrey said. "Chief of the Watch, stream the port towed array."

Jeffrey saw COB's hand was poised, anticipating the order. He acknowledged and flicked the switch.

Jeffrey pictured the half-mile-long TB-29 thin-line array streaming out astern. The starboard towed array, the fat-line TB-16D, gave a shorter aperture and wasn't as good at catching the very-low-frequency five- or ten-hertz noises of a diesel sub.

"Make your depth one five five feet," Wilson said.

"Make my depth one five five feet, aye," Jeffrey said. "Five degrees down bubble." Meltzer acknowledged, and with no sense of motion or vibrations the deck tilted down once more.

One thing Jeffrey liked when he was diving officer was its position facing forward. It let him feel more at one with the ship, sneaking or charging through the ocean. Since a submarine was just a long and narrow tube, and virtually every compartment doubled as passageway fore and aft, almost every station or console fronted a port or starboard bulkhead. Almost all the crew rode sideways, and some of them slept that way. Jeffrey played many roles in the course of a day, a week, a month at sea, and sometimes felt like he was going sideways too.

"Photonic mast's under," Jeffrey said, watching the monitor again. He took a quick look around underwater—no threatening shadows. "Chief of the Watch, lower the photonic mast and all antennas."

"Lower the mast and all antennas, aye," COB said.

"Passing one hundred feet, sir," Meltzer said.

"Passing one hundred feet," Jeffrey repeated to Wilson.

"Dive, we're under time pressure," Wilson said. "Make normal one-third turns."

Again Jeffrey palmed the 7MC. Again Maneuvering acknowledged. Again he relayed this to the captain.

"XO," Wilson said, "once we clear our baffles and do a thorough check for sound shorts, I intend to make the transit south by sprint-and-drift at fifteen hundred feet. . . . We'll slow up when we're closer to our target."

"Understood, sir," Jeffrey said, knowing Wilson would always share his plans as navy regs required. Jeffrey would be the CO's sounding board and punching bag, constantly preparing for the job.

"XO," Wilson said, "send the messenger of the watch to invite our guests to the CACC."

Ilse Reebeck sat alone in the tiny state-room they'd given her. It took just a minute to unpack, and now she was looking at a picture of her family. These little lulls were the worst, the times like this with nothing else to do.

She held the photo to her chest, rocking gently back and forth. She tried again to lock in all the memories, knowing they'd fade inevitably with the hopeless years.

Images flashed through her mind, and the sounds of voices now forever gone. Echoes, of everything she'd lost and of things she'd never had.

Someone knocked. With all her self-control she said, "Come in."

The messenger was very young, polite, and shy. Ilse rose to follow him and took her first good look around. The corridor was clogged with boxes now, mostly food. The walls had fake wood wainscoting, a pleasant touch, she thought. Certainly the decor in other ways was stark—a big fire ax and extinguisher gave the only real touch of color. Then she spotted the foot-sized Velcro-like red triangles on the deck, marking thin pipes with small nozzles labeled RESPIRATOR AIR LINE. Ilse and the messenger squeezed down the short corridor past various crewmen: enlisted, officers, chiefs. Most of them seemed friendly and surprised. Give them five more minutes, she told herself, and everyone aboard will know I'm here, if they don't already.

Ilse passed other state-rooms, marked XO and CO, and then she was in the control room. To her right were two closed doors, RADIO and ESM, posted with security warnings.

"Why is it so dark?"

"Ma'am," the messenger said, "we usually rig for red like this. It makes the screens and instruments easier on watch standers' eyes. . . . Some boats use blue."

Ilse looked at the ceiling, which was low. Excuse me, she told herself, that's the *overhead*. Pipes and cables ran everywhere—between them hung the coiled black cords for mikes. There were rows of computer consoles along both side bulkheads, mostly occupied, most with two large screens, one above the other. There was a digital navigation plotting table near the back. Every bit of available wall space was clogged with junction boxes, other gadgets, countless dials and switches, knobs and handles in every possible shape and size.

Keyboards clicked. Men seated or standing watched their screens or touched them or spoke in confident hushed voices. Occasionally someone called out, orders or information. Ilse smelled warm electronics and ripe male bodies. Where were the periscopes?

Captain Wilson and the executive officer came over.

"Miss Reebeck," Wilson said with a smile Ilse already knew was rare for him. "We have a few minutes till we're in firing position. We'll do a SEAL mission briefing with you once our present task's complete. We can use the wardroom later."

"Good," Ilse said.

"In the meantime Commander Fuller can get you started. He's in charge of training in the boat."

"How about this one?" Ilse said, claiming an empty position at a row of what were obviously sonar consoles along the port bulkhead.

The XO nodded. "Just what do you have in mind?"

"Commander, I'm an oceanographer. While I'm here, Captain Wilson wants me to help upgrade your ship's modeling of underwater sound propagation. I've got better data on the local seas."

"A-hah," Jeffrey said, as if things were starting to make sense to him.

"You should never have scaled back NOAA's research budget," Ilse said. "If your country hadn't cut defense spending so much, we might not all be in this mess. Think of the American lives it's cost already, to save some dollars."

Jeffrey winced, opened his mouth to retort, then seemed to think better of it.

Ilse pulled three rewritable three-inch CD-RWs from her blouse pocket. "Bottom geology and currents, salinity, water temperatures, and tides. Volcanic vents and their effects. Seasonal biologics at different depths and times of day."

"Super," Jeffrey said.

"I have a lot of experience in these waters and where we're going next."

"And where might that be?" Jeffrey said.

"Durban."

"The main South African sub base?"

"Not exactly."

"So what's the plan?"

"The usual commando op. Stab, kill, blow up things."

"You make it sound too glib."

"Commander, there's nothing glib about this. The Putsch hanged my brother, okay? He was one of the ones they showed on television."

"Jesus. . . . I'm sorry."

"I'm not interested in apologies."

"Um, how did you get out?"

"I was in the U.S. when it happened. At a marine biology conference."

Jeffrey cleared his throat. "You know how to use this thing?"

"It's a *Virginia*-class ARCI terminal, part of the onboard fiber-optic LAN. Each console can handle sonar, target tracking, or weapons control, depending how you set it up."

"Yup."

"It replaces the older systems in *Los Angeles*- and *Seawolf*-class SSNs."

"You're well informed."

"*Challenger*'s the fourth fast-attack sub built since *Virginia*," Ilse said, "a bit of a hybrid though with commonalities to *Seawolf*, seen by some as an unnecessary step backwards. *Challenger* has a *Seawolf*-sized hull envelope, a *big* propulsion plant, eight extra-wide torpedo tubes, all quite expensive."

Jeffrey nodded.

"She's got all-electric drive by Westinghouse," Ilse said, "with no reduction gears—that part's new, extremely quiet. Third-generation pump-turbine propulsor, like an underwater jet engine, extremely fast."

"Hull number 778," Jeffrey said.

"I know. They've been painted over for the war."

"Exactly what *else* do you know about *Challenger*?"

"I've been through SUBSCHOL in New London," Ilse said. "Flooding drills, fire fighting, escape tank swim, the works."

"What did they say about this boat?"

"Just that she's different, and controversial."

"That puts it mildly."

"I suppose I'll find out soon."

Jeffrey glanced away for a moment, then looked back. "You speak American English very well."

"I spent four years in San Diego. I got my Ph.D. from Scripps."

"Impressive."

"So I've been on lots of research ships. Diving is a hobby. And I dated a few navy guys, out of Coronado. . . . No, they didn't blab about your precious submarine. I've been briefed, on the way out here. Only up to a point, apparently, but by COMSUBPAC himself."

"Really?" Jeffrey sounded almost jealous.

"He said this boat's assigned to DEVRON TWELVE, as if that explained everything."

"It would, to a submariner. Development Squadron Twelve."

"And if you're wondering why they picked a woman, I wasn't their first choice. The other three they tried were men, but none of *them* had the guts for it."

Ilse wriggled her bottom to get more comfortable in the seat. She put the first CD-RW into the drive, worked the console's keyboard, and massaged the trackball with her palm. She called up a menu she knew by heart, then leaned over to talk to the sonar officer, a slightly plump lieutenant sitting to her right. Step one, she presumed, would be to enhance his ocean models, used to compute sonar detection and target counterdetection zones. That should keep her busy for a while.

"Anyway," Jeffrey said, "I'm going forward to talk to Weps." Ilse hardly noticed.

The smell of coffee began to fill the air as the messenger put up a fresh pot in a nearby pantry alcove. Then he came around. Ilse and the sonar officer both took their coffee black.

Sonar said his name was Robert Sessions. He looked in his mid-twenties. If war made people older, Ilse told herself, he must be very young. At almost thirty she felt ancient.

"Mmmm," Sessions said, drinking deep. "*Caffeine.* The drug of choice of the Silent Service."

Ilse couldn't help smiling. She had some coffee herself, very strong and hot. That's better. She'd slept badly on the plane.

She leaned over to examine Sessions' waterfall displays, which she barely understood. "Whose do you think it is?"

"You mean the other sub?"

Ilse nodded.

Sessions shrugged. "No whiffs at all yet. Doesn't matter much. They're the same designs, right? Same crew training, far as we know, Germany and South Africa."

Like many of the other crewmen, Sessions wore a baseball cap, with the ship's name and number and an emblem. On the emblem was a dragonfish, a black deep-sea creature with a distorted fish's body and a hideous face with long sharp teeth and a dangling luminous barb. The dragonfish was grinning, clutching in its stunted fins a torpedo and a missile.

Challenger? Of course! Ilse realized the sub wasn't named for the blown-up space shuttle after all. HMS *Challenger* was the first dedicated oceanographic research vessel, a British sailing ship in 1872.

Ilse liked the hat. She wanted one.

CHAPTER 3

4 HOURS LATER

"Captain," Jeffrey said, "the boat's closed up at battle stations antisubmarine. We are rigged for ultraquiet. Our course is one eight zero, speed six knots; depth is fifteen hundred feet."

"Very well, Fire Control," Wilson said. At general quarters Jeffrey as XO was fire control coordinator, overseeing Sonar, Weapons, and the TMA—target-motion analysis—team. The captain had the deck and conn as approach coordinator, grand strategist in the upcoming duel.

Jeffrey paced the three steps back to Sonar. "Still nothing, Commander," Sessions said. "We continue tracking Sierra 6, that convoy." Jeffrey leaned between him and Ilse, looking over Sessions' shoulder as he pointed to the wideband and narrowband displays.

"Those are the fast auxiliaries and escorts," Jeffrey said, "heading west to replenish the *Reagan* carrier battle group."

"Correct, sir," Sessions said. "These thick lines here're the battleship *Wisconsin*."

The display was labeled across the top like an unraveled helix, showing each bearing several times but from different incoming depression/elevation angles. Jeffrey hit a switch on Sessions' console, then read the screen.

"Blade rate on *Wisconsin*'s four shafts says she's doing thirty-one knots."

"She's so noisy we hold contact in the surface duct at a hundred nautical miles."

"Survivable as hell, though," Jeffrey said, "in this sort of war."

"Agreed, sir," Sessions said. "The main thing for big surface units is keep moving fast. . . . *These* two contacts are our ASW helos." He tapped a pair of thin lines slanting across the broadband waterfall. "They just relieved the first ones that were running low on fuel."

"They doing ladder searches?" Jeffrey said.

"Yes, sir," Sessions said.

"Dropping sonobuoys or dipping sonar?"

"Intermittent plopping sounds. No pinging yet, so the hostile can't steal echoes off our hull."

Jeffrey nodded. "No sign the helos have a passive contact?"

"Negative, sir, neither one is circling."

"That would be our cue," Jeffrey said. "Let's hope they hold their fire, on the off chance they pick *us* up. Them's the rules of engagement—no one wants a blue-on-blue."

Jeffrey glanced at Ilse, who looked up at him. She was busy rewriting some computer code. Jeffrey thought her lips seemed very sensuous in the subdued control room lighting. Her pupils were nicely dilated. Then he caught himself.

"I've traded e-mails with your onboard systems administrator more than once," Ilse stated. "This change will make better use of real-time surface temperature inputs and static-height anomaly data."

"More accurate water column density gradients?" Jeffrey said.

"Exactly."

"Um, great."

"Sir," Sessions said, "we also have Sierras 7 and 8,

Klakring and *McClusky*, the ASW frigates on the outer picket line. They're intermittent in the second convergence zone, some sixty nautical miles, as they zigzag in their sectors. But nothing submerged."

"We know the enemy's out there somewhere," Jeffrey said. "*Integrity*'s passive towed array heard him running on air-independent propulsion. The PROBSUB's been upgraded to a CERTSUB."

"After we picked up their data dump on EHF," Sessions said, "when we went back to 'scope depth, I looked at it myself. Faint but clear low-frequency tonals from the fuel-cell reactant circulators, looked like a German *Klasse* 212."

"They probably switched to batteries, at least for now."

Jeffrey knew *Integrity* was a SWATH—small waterplane twin-hull—a steel catamaran displacing 5,000 tons and "armed" with a twin-line passive towed array. Fully 6,000 feet long, that gear had 180 acoustic channels and was optimized for hunting diesel subs by their near-infrasonic tonals.

As Jeffrey and Sessions huddled, Wilson walked over. "Talk to me," he said.

"Sir," Jeffrey said, "allowing for possible variations in enemy course and speed, our target should be somewhere on an arc to the west of us, within striking distance of our weapons, but we have no datum for a shot."

"And why not, Fire Control?" Wilson said.

"Captain, it's the same old problem we always have with a diesel/AIP running off its silent storage batteries. We can't hear him except for flow noise when we're practically on top of the guy. And we can't go active without giving ourselves away."

"Now tell me something I don't know."

Jeffrey winced. "Well, sir, there's no way his sonar and signal processors can be as good as ours, 'cause his combat payload's small. We know we can run rings around the guy thanks to our nuclear propulsion. We know we can dive deeper."

"But we can't assume *he* doesn't know that, since they have boats that do that too."

Jeffrey hesitated. "We know he has to snorkel eventually and run his noisy diesels, and if we can force him to sustain high speed, his quiet fuel-cell fuel won't last long either."

"So what do you think his mission is?"

"Could be one of several things. To lob a nuke at Diego Garcia. To lay mines in the approaches."

"And . . . ?"

"Could be an anti-surface-shipping patrol, against our sea lines of communications. Could be intel gathering or a commando op."

"In other words, Mr. Fuller, it could be anything."

"Yes, sir," Jeffrey said. He watched Ilse's fingers delicately tap her keys. He noticed she wore no jewelry, though her ears were pierced.

"How long till he's in missile firing range of the atoll?" Wilson said.

"Er, those boats don't have vertical launch capability, sir. The land-attack missiles they fire from the torpedo tubes have a range of about seventy-five nautical miles."

"Sir," Sessions offered, "the Israeli datum combined with *Integrity*'s puts the enemy's mean speed of advance at sixteen knots."

"Right," Jeffrey said. "Since we're ninety miles from Diego now ourselves, that gives us about an hour."

Wilson snorted. "Sixty minutes till the base gets nuked?"

Jeffrey nodded. "If that's their intent."

"You want to count on D.G.'s antiaircraft defenses splashing all those missiles?"

"Of course not, sir."

"Should we request more backup? Just plain admit that we can't find the guy?"

"Not yet, sir," Jeffrey said. "We're the best platform to prosecute, and we're in the best position. The air assets have plenty else to do."

"So what's the call?" Wilson said.

"That's what I've been thinking about, Captain."

"Well, break it down. How do you think he got this far?"

"I'm guessing he's a lurker, snuck in past *Ranger* west of here. After she was hit, I mean."

Commodore Morse came over. "You're saying they *planned* it this way? Coordinated movements?"

Behind Morse's friendly manner there was a challenge to his tone. Morse had actually gone through the dreaded British Perisher, where they didn't just teach, they aggressively eliminated. The U.K. had fewer SSNs than the U.S.: ten compared to barely fifty—before war losses, that is. The Brits were nearly beaten by unrestricted submarine warfare twice in the last century, and they took the business seriously indeed. Jeffrey wished America had taken the business more seriously these past twenty years—when the U.S.S.R. broke up, the U.S. Navy had had *twice* as many SSNs as now, but far too many had been retired prematurely and not enough new ones built.

Morse was a foreign guest, Jeffrey told himself, but he was also the most senior man aboard. His interest here was not just academic. Everybody's life depended on it, and once again the U.K. was almost on the ropes. If this new Hot War went on much longer, the badly overworked attack-boat groups might not meet their commitments—the Allied fleets' initial six-month surge capacity was fast running out, the units badly needed maintenance and upgrades, and the Axis knew it.

Jeffrey met Morse's eyes. Morse's expression seemed to say, Go ahead, lad, impress me if you can.

"The problem, sirs," Jeffrey said, "is that the helos' air-dropped active sonobuoys don't have much power. If they ping while we listen for echoes, the detection probability would be low."

"That's true," Morse said.

"Their dipping sonar's better, but not by much. They just don't have the electrical capacity aboard. It would almost be better if we drew back, went deep so the dome wouldn't cavitate, and *we* pinged at max power, with the helos listening from closer in."

"Bipolar," Morse said, "but with the roles reversed."

"That's all fine in theory," Wilson said. "But . . . "

"But two things," Jeffrey said. "They can almost certainly hear the helos the same way we can, from the shock waves off their supersonic blade tips, and they don't know *we're* here, though they may suspect. Plus the helos don't have much lifting capacity either, so their lightweight torpedoes have a lower PK than ours. They just don't pack the punch."

Jeffrey knew that the kill probability, PK, of *Challenger*'s Advanced Capability Mark 48 torpedoes—called ADCAPs—was outstanding, but the Seahawk ASW helicopters simply couldn't lift the things and still have useful on-station time. Instead they each carried two air-droppable littoral-capable Mark 46 fish, whose warheads barely weighed a hundred pounds.

Wilson stood there, waiting.

"Do you mind if I look at the chart, sir?" Jeffrey said.

"Go ahead, you're the fire control coordinator." Wilson gestured for Sessions to join them.

Jeffrey walked to the navigation plotting table, where Morse and Wilson had been caucusing before. The others followed. The navigator, Lieutenant Monaghan, a tall and gaunt man, respectfully stepped aside, then looked on.

Jeffrey wasn't interested in finding deep water now. Quite the contrary. "This is really an old idea, Captain, but we could have a helo drop a weapon set to go off right away, like a depth charge. Not close to the expected target, but *here,* toward these shoals in the distance."

Jeffrey pointed to the digital nav display, to the East and Great Chagos banks, then continued.

"The explosive power might be enough to get an echo off the diesel, no matter how stealthy his hull coatings. Set the fish to blow at a hundred feet, and well astern of us to minimize our own signature. That would give two bearings, one from our bow sphere and another from the towed array."

"And the one," Morse said, "would solve that pesky ambiguity in the other."

"Exactly," Jeffrey said. "And their intersection would give the range." Unlike the bow sphere, Jeffrey knew, the towed array always showed a contact at *two* bearings on the wideband display.

"Captain," Jeffrey said, "doing it this way we'd also spare the helos the risk the target takes a shot at them, in case they get too close. Those Polyphem antiaircraft missiles they can fire from underwater have a nasty sting. A standard-sized torpedo tube holds four."

"Considerate of you to think of that," Wilson said.

"Then we can shift position *this* way," Jeffrey said, moving his finger on the chart again, "while waiting for the explosion's reverb to bounce back from the shoals."

"After a useful time delay," Morse said, "that reflected noise would hit the target from behind."

"He'll have moved," Jeffrey said, "and we'll now have him localized, so we get another set of bearings using our starboard wide-aperture array in hole-in-ocean mode. That'd be enough to give a complete firing solution, with target course and speed."

Jeffrey knew hole-in-ocean passive sonar detected

targets not by their radiated self-noise, but by their tendency to block the constant ocean sounds from farther off. The wide-aperture arrays were three widely spaced hydrophone complexes worn rigidly along the side of the hull like saddlebags, allowing electronic beamform scanning.

"Why not just go deep," Wilson said, "and use our ambient detection mode to watch him go by over us?" Ambient sonar was another form of covert active search—it used sea noise reflected from the target instead of own-ship pinging.

"Won't work, sir," Jeffrey said. "The water's deep enough to give a nice-sized look-up search cone, but the sea state locally's too mild to generate much surface noise and there're no nearby ships whose propulsion plants could act as sound projectors. Those diesel boats are small, barely half of our dimensions, so a quarter of our footprint."

"That's one of their strengths," Morse interjected.

"Exactly, sir," Jeffrey said. "Right here right now he wouldn't be acoustically illuminated well enough for us to see."

"And you're not worried," Wilson said, "with your helo torpedo bipolar thing, that this enemy boat could use active out-of-phase sound emissions to break up the echo, and active feed-through noise to plug the hole?"

"Captain," Jeffrey said, "first of all, those subs don't have that capability like we do, at least not to the degree they'd fool our signal processing algorithms. At a fifth of our displacement they're too small to carry the computers and the power supply."

"Okay," Wilson said.

"Secondly, what makes it even harder for them is that the explosion would be gray noise, not a coherent active ping, with *very* complex reverb coming back from off those shoals. . . . And thirdly, for hole-plugging emissions to do much good they need to know our relative bearing."

"What if we go through this rigmarole and there's no contact?" Wilson said.

"We should shift position and try again," Jeffrey said. "I'd head closer to the atoll, since in this case the greater risk exposure is underestimating target speed."

Wilson gave Sessions a piercing look. "And what do *you* think, Sonar?"

"Um, I concur with Commander Fuller, sir. We can also use the wide-aperture arrays to do synthetic instant range gating. The data would be soft, but it would help us validate the firing solution."

"Good," Wilson said. "That's what the ARCI's for."

"And I think the helos should stay here for a while," Jeffrey said, "keep working this same area. Have them drop a few more 46s now and then."

"Give the bad guys a false sense of security?" Wilson said.

"Affirmative, sir," Jeffrey said, smiling. He glanced again at Ilse Reebeck, who seemed to be taking all this in while pretending not to. He made eye contact and she looked away.

Jeffrey wondered if Morse and Wilson had intended this front/back bipolar trick themselves, all along. Maybe Wilson just wanted to see if Jeffrey could come up with it.

"Sonar," Wilson said, "how's wave action topside?"

"Long gentle swells now, Captain."

"Coming way up from Antarctica," Jeffrey said, "as you'd expect this time of year."

"Maybe three feet crest to trough," Sessions said.

"Period?" Wilson said.

"Four per minute, sir," Sessions said.

"Any contacts overhead?"

"Negative, Captain."

"Very well, Sonar," Wilson said. "Fire Control, we'll

use your plan." Wilson turned to Meltzer at the helm. "Bring the boat to periscope depth. Let's talk to those helos."

"Chief of the Watch," Jeffrey said to COB, "stand by to raise the UHF antenna." Then Jeffrey grabbed a mike and punched in circuit 22. "Radio, Fire Control, prepare to send on short-range airborne tactical."

"Sir," Sessions said to Jeffrey, "the helo's parachute-retarded torpedo has hit the water. . . . Unit has detonated, acoustic power spectrum confirms a Mark 46 conventional warhead."

"Very well," Jeffrey said. Since the explosion was dead aft and relatively small, he didn't hear it through the hull.

"Sir," Sessions said, "I have a submerged bipolar contact, bearings three two five and three two three on towed array and bow sphere! I designate the contact Master 1."

Jeffrey watched the bearing lines appear and intersect on his target-motion analyzer window, all relayed to him by the combat control technicians sitting to his right. The range was over 30,000 yards. A 3-D representation of the tactical picture came up on the CACC's wide-screen situation display, with a multicolored halo around the contact—the probability envelope of uncertainty.

"I have a *second* bipolar contact," Sessions said, "bearings three one nine and three two one! I merge and designate this Master 2!"

"There's *two* of them?" Jeffrey said.

"Affirmative!" Sessions shouted. "Shoal echoes put their speed at twenty knots!"

The odds just lengthened badly, Jeffrey told himself.

The enemy boats were at long range for him to make a good torpedo shot, and they were closer to Diego Garcia than *Challenger* was. They must be going all out now on batteries. Their endurance at that speed was short, clear indication they were up to something—something nasty—and it was coming very soon.

CHAPTER 4

"Flood tubes one through eight," Wilson said. "Equalize the pressure and open all muzzle doors."

They were still well away from the targets, Ilse knew. Was this so they wouldn't hear us?

"Sonar," Jeffrey said, "what's target depth?"

"Best estimate is six five zero feet, sir," Sessions said. "Miss Reebeck helped make our ray traces more precise."

"Good," Jeffrey said. "Very well, Sonar."

Wilson looked at Ilse and nodded, then he glanced at Jeffrey. "Your thoughts on firing tactics, Fire Control?"

"Sir, since we're in friendly waters, I'd recommend going shallow just before we fire, shooting from above the layer. That way if Master 1 and Master 2 stay deep, they're less likely to hear our ADCAPs till the terminal active-homing phase. I think we need to get much closer, though, maybe fifteen thousand yards, before we shoot."

"Even though the ADCAPs go almost twice as fast as we can?"

"Sir, the Mark 48s are fast but their propulsion system's loud. The longer the run, the more chance the targets have of a detection, and the more time the enemy has for using countertactics."

"You're right," Wilson said. "So how do you propose to halve the range unnoticed, given the clock's still ticking?"

"Well, if we go shallow and go fast, we'll cause a surface-wake anomaly and thermal scarring, which would be visible to long-range Axis airborne and spaceborne sensors, and any cavitation sounds would be worse from the lower water pressure. But if we stay deep and make a sprint, we'll be on the same side of the layer as Master 1 and Master 2. They're much more likely to hear us coming."

"So which of these wonderful choices is it?" Wilson said.

"Sir, my recommendation is to approach at top quiet speed at two thousand feet. Then we can come up to maybe one fifty carefully and open fire."

"Why move in so deep?"

"Sir, at the ranges involved, putting a wider chunk of the thermocline between own-ship and target depth might help shadow us acoustically. Because of temperature-induced sound wave diffraction, our radiated noise would bend down toward the bottom isothermal zone. Miss Reebeck's data suggest two thousand feet is optimum for us."

"Very well, Fire Control," Wilson said. "Helm, make your course three four zero and make your depth two thousand feet. Ahead two thirds, make turns for twenty-six knots."

Ilse listened to Meltzer repeat the orders, then she saw him working his controls.

She was almost used to it by now. The deck tilted forward uncomfortably, but there was no other sense of motion, no vibration. A sound on the threshold of hearing grew slightly louder, a kind of whooshing with an underlying visceral rumble. It wasn't coming from the air-conditioning ducts.

Ilse glanced aft. This is the closest I've ever been to a

nuclear reactor, she told herself, and I can't jump in my car and flee if something goes wrong. She fidgeted with the dosimeter on her belt, but no one else seemed worried.

Soon Ilse felt the boat leveling off, and she watched the digital depth gauge on her screen. It steadied at exactly 2,000 feet. Aren't there supposed to be popping, screeching noises this far down? Don't rivets start flying around the control room so close to crush depth?

Suddenly the danger of their actions hit. If we make a peep, they could hear it. They'll shoot atomic bombs at us for sure. We're too far away for a good attack, the captain and Jeffrey said so. We have to get in closer, before they fire at Diego Garcia. And even if they fire prematurely and their cruise missiles fall short, they'll stir up a fearful shock wave and tsunami.

But if we go in faster, they could hear us, and Captain Wilson said to go in fast.

I don't want to die, Ilse told herself, not like this so soon. I have something to do first, *dammit*.

"Time's running out, Mr. Fuller," Wilson said. "What do you think?"

"It would be ideal, sir," Jeffrey said, "if we could time our shots to hit them just as they come up through the layer to launch their missiles."

"Devoutly to be wished," Wilson said, "but unrealistic. By the time we got in close enough for a good attack, they'd almost surely make a counterdetection and get off a snap shot at us with a nuclear torpedo. So how could we tell they're going for the surface, assuming that's their plan, if we can't even hear them?"

"We couldn't, sir," Jeffrey said. "But if they rise above the layer prematurely, they'll hear our own fish coming in plenty of time to evade and counterfire."

"At close enough range they might even hear the

ADCAPs *through* the layer," Wilson said. "You know acoustic shadow masking's always an iffy thing."

"I'm starting to change my mind on something, sir," Jeffrey said.

"Oh?" Wilson said.

"I think maybe we should use a single weapon, a fission warhead. Set for highest yield, one-tenth KT. It's got a lethal radius big enough to catch them both, even if they run, even with some error in the firing solution." Relying on just two stale data points was *not* recommended practice, Jeffrey knew.

"Concerned that we're outnumbered?" Wilson said.

"Respectfully, sir, yes. The fuel-cell *Klasse* 212s are vulnerable with all that liquid hydrogen on board, but they have twelve torpedo tubes between them, to our eight."

"And taking potshots with our ADCAPs would just tip them off?"

"Affirmative, sir."

"Then what about going active, disguise our ping as biologic?"

"You know how I feel about that, Captain. Once we start, we'd have to keep it up. Shrimp don't click real loud just once. Whale songs go on for minutes, even hours, so they can stay in touch moving in and out of each other's convergence zones. The enemy boats would track the source, watch our maneuvers. The water here's too quiet."

"I concur, sir," Sessions said. "The range is a bit extreme for that tactic in any case."

Wilson gave Jeffrey a hard look. "Still don't want to call for help?"

"Sir," Jeffrey said, "our aircraft are heavily committed all along the front. If we suddenly vector in more stuff, including those two ASW helos we were working with, the 212s will know for sure we know they're here. We'll lose the element of surprise, and they'll fire off their missiles. The whole point of *Challenger* is we're invisible till we strike."

"What's range and bearing to the helos?" Wilson said.

"Twenty miles now, sir," Jeffrey said. "Bearing one seven five, crosswind from us."

"All right, then," Wilson said. "Debate's over. Assistant Navigator, let the rough log show that at . . . zero five two three Zulu this day, CinCPAC Theater Nuclear Forces rules of engagement were satisfied for a tactical nuclear launch against submerged enemy contacts."

"Assistant Navigator," Jeffrey said, "I concur." Jeffrey breathed a sigh of relief. Compared to this, Prospective Commanding Officers School would be a cinch.

"Sonar," Wilson said, "where's the layer?"

"One nine zero feet, sir," Sessions said.

"Helm," Wilson said, "ahead one third, make turns for four knots."

"Ahead one third," Meltzer said, "make turns for four knots, aye. . . . Maneuvering acknowledges turns for four knots, sir."

"Make your depth one five zero feet."

"Make my depth one five zero feet, aye," Meltzer said.

"Fire Control," Wilson said, "have Combat Systems warm up a nuclear Mark 88 torpedo. Same presets you put in the ADCAPs, to run above the layer. Load it in tube seven."

"Aye aye, sir," Jeffrey said.

"That way we'll slap them down real good if they stay deep," Wilson said, "and blow them to kingdom come if they've gone shallow."

Jeffrey relayed the commands and took the electronic acknowledgments. He eyed his weapons status screen as tube seven's outer door rotated closed, sea pressure was relieved, the water drained, and the inner door swung open. The weapons autoloader shuffled the units around on the racks, then presented a wide-bodied Mark 88 at tube seven's breach.

Lights in the CACC started flashing.

"General security alarm," Jeffrey said. "A special weapon has been shifted."

"Special weapon handling is authorized," Wilson said.

"Very well," Jeffrey said. "Disregard the alarm." The lights stopped blinking.

Next Jeffrey watched as the fire control technicians on the CACC starboard side worked their consoles, establishing the weapon presets—under current nuclear war-fighting protocols the combat systems officer himself, called "Weps" for short, manned a retrofitted station on a lower deck, for two-man positive control.

Jeffrey knew that overall authorization for tactical nuclear weapons had been handed down by the President after the war broke out. Final decisions were made on the spot by *Challenger*'s senior officers.

"XO," Wilson said, "take the conn. Messenger of the Watch, have Weps meet me in my state-room. Assistant Navigator, accompany me with the electronic logbook. I'm going for the special weapons enabler tool."

Ilse and Sessions spoke in undertones, their voices blending with the constant murmuring of CACC technicians.

"Ever seen a nuclear torpedo detonate?" Sessions said. He kept his eyes glued to his sonar screens.

Ilse shivered. "No. Have you?"

"Just on film. It's awesome. Surface units caught some footage when things first got hot in the Atlantic."

"What's it like?" Ilse said.

"Depends on warhead yield and depth when it goes off."

"How big do they get?"

"U-235, using just one critical mass, you can go up to maybe twenty kilotons."

"In this war that's pretty much a strategic weapon," Ilse said.

"Yup," Sessions said. "For comparison Hiroshima was roughly twelve. Nagasaki, they used a plutonium bomb, maybe twenty-two KT. Warsaw, when this war broke out, they think was ten."

"So what happens when one goes off underwater?"

"There's two things—really just like a regular depth charge, only bigger. Step one, warhead blows. That immediately lifts the surface of the sea, 'cause water's incompressible, and sends a suction wave back down."

"You get a big white fountain?"

"With a dot one KT explosion, could be a hundred yards across. Step two, blast of dirty water hits the surface from below, bigger than the first spout. That's the warhead burst itself. It pulsates as it rises."

"The bubble energy fights back and forth with the water pressure?" Ilse realized now that everyone said "dot" instead of "point" for decimals—less ambiguous?

"In this case that's the fireball," Sessions said. "It's buoyant, hot as hell, so it comes up *really* fast. There's a nasty airborne shock wave when it breaks the surface."

"How hot is it?"

"Try ten million centigrade."

"Ouch."

"It dissipates, cooling on the way, but being underwater doesn't help."

"How come?"

"Compared to air, the hydrostatic pressure confines the blast, concentrates the fireball. The water boils, of course, but that won't carry off much heat. Seawater's got poor transparency too, from all the stuff that's floating in it—"

"Suspended particulates, organic matter . . ."

"Yeah, Ilse, you would know. The whole photon flash

on detonation, the gamma rays and X rays, ultraviolet, visible and infrared, not to mention all the neutrons, they get held in close, strengthening the fireball. On the other hand, seawater does suppress the EMP, the electromagnetic pulse that fries unshielded circuits. . . . Anyway, first you have this giant burst of water, then you get the fireball. Timing between the two depends how deep the thing went off. There'll also be what's called the base surge, a kind of ground fog that spreads out like a fluid and evaporates, ocean surface atomized by the vicious shock wave through the water. You know an underwater blast's much more destructive to naval vessels than an airburst at a given distance. Water's much more dense and rigid, and sound travels five times as fast."

"How much fallout is there with a nuclear torpedo or, or a depth charge?"

"Nothing like an H-bomb used on land."

"But how bad *is* it?"

"Not counting any from the ships they hit?" Sessions said. "There're the weapon parts, of course, vaporized. Fish and plankton, what's left of 'em. And loads of radioactive steam, from carbon, sodium, trace metals in the seawater, by neutron activation."

"Tidal waves?"

"At least two surges," Sessions said, still watching his displays. "They subside eventually with the kind of warhead yield we're using."

"So they aren't like the big ones from an earthquake?" Ilse said. "Like that one in the Caribbean that wrecked your cruiser *Memphis* years ago?"

Sessions shook his head. "Then the thing's a meter high way out at sea, but moving literally fast as a jumbo jet, piling up murderously onshore. Nuclear tsunamis act more like ripples in a pond, except they're fifty, sixty feet from crest to trough. They die off, mostly, in a matter of miles."

"Can't big surface ships just ride that out in open water? I got caught on the edge of a typhoon once, on a research trip."

"Yeah," Sessions said, "assuming the enemy doesn't ripple fire or hit from several bearings at once. A ship's hydrophones will give some warning, if you don't receive it on the data links or see the fireball glow, and you can turn bows-on. Still one hell of a ride."

"I can imagine."

Sessions turned to face Ilse. "The worst is if you're close, caught by the blast itself, or lose propulsion from the shock and take a wave from off the beam that's any higher than you're wide. Busted open, capsized, either way you've had it."

CHAPTER 5

"Warhead locks are bypassed," Jeffrey said. "Special weapon loaded in tube seven."

"Very well, Fire Control," Wilson said. "I am relaying the permissive action link code."

"Green light in the torpedo room," Jeffrey said. "PAL code is accepted. Weapon is enabled, armed guard has withdrawn."

"Very well, Fire Control," Wilson said.

From here Jeffrey knew the procedures were the same as were used with a conventional fish. To be fully armed, the warhead had to first be surrounded by seawater, then get an electronic signal, then feel the g-force of launch, then run out for a preset safety distance.

"Make tube seven ready in all respects," Wilson said. "Tube seven, firing point procedures, area burst on Master 1 and Master 2."

"Solution ready," Jeffrey said. "Ship ready. . . . Weapon ready."

"Match generated bearings," Wilson said, "and *shoot*."

"Unit from tube seven fired electrically," Jeffrey said. "Unit is swimming out."

"Unit is running normally," Sessions said.

"Time to target?" Wilson said.

"Current range is fifteen thousand yards, sir," Jeffrey said. "We should detonate in ten minutes."

"Very well," Wilson said. "I intend to put some distance between us and our unit's track, but we'll do it stealthily and keep the layer between us and our quarry. Helm, make your course two six five, make your depth one eight zero feet."

"Aye, sir," Meltzer said.

"Captain," Jeffrey said, "since we're about to make one hell of a datum anyway, recommend we increase speed slightly to gain more track separation."

"Concur, Fire Control," Wilson said. "Helm, ahead one third, make turns for eight knots." Meltzer acknowledged.

"I intend to leave our towed array deployed," Wilson said.

"I concur, sir," Jeffrey said. "Sonar, there could be more enemy boats out there."

"Understood, Commander," Sessions said.

"Hull popping sounds on the towed array," Sessions said, "bearing three five five true! Assess the transient as coming from Master 1."

"Interpretation?" Jeffrey said.

"*More* hull popping sounds on bearing zero zero five! Assess both targets are rising!"

"They're preparing to fire," Wilson said. "Will our unit intercept in time?"

"It'll be close, sir," Jeffrey said.

Suddenly Ilse saw Sessions sit bolt upright. "Water slug transient on bearing three five five! . . . *Torpedo in the water! Incoming torpedo bearing three five five!*"

"They heard our weapon after all," Wilson said.

"In time to launch a snap shot back at us," Jeffrey said. "Sir, recommend we move away from our unit's track more rapidly."

"Concur," Wilson said, "but first, fire a brilliant decoy toward the incoming torpedo."

Jeffrey gave the orders.

"Helm," Wilson said, "take us back below the layer. Make your depth six hundred feet, make normal one-third turns and do not cavitate."

"Maneuvering acknowledges," Meltzer said.

"Chief of the Watch," Wilson said, "keep the foreplanes deployed—they enhance our maneuverability."

"Do not retract the foreplanes, aye," COB said.

"Lose the towed array. I don't want it tangling our stern and we don't have time to retract it."

"Shear off the towed array, aye."

"*Second* incoming torpedo," Sessions shouted, "bearing zero zero four!"

"Master 2 just fired at us," Jeffrey said.

"Chief of the Watch," Wilson said, "on the sound-powered phones, prepare for radical maneuvers. Helmsman, make a knuckle. Hard left rudder, make your course one six zero."

Ilse braced herself against her console as *Challenger* banked into the turn. Meltzer called out their course every ten degrees, finally announcing, "Steering one six zero, sir."

"Very well, Helm," Wilson said.

"Incoming torpedoes drawing left to right," Sessions said. "They're in passive search mode, sir."

"What kind are they?" Jeffrey said.

"Modified Russian propulsion systems, their export model VA-III Shkvals."

"Nuclear-capable platforms," Jeffrey said.

"We'll try to sneak away fast as we can," Wilson said, "see if our decoy draws them off. Helm, top quiet speed. Ahead two thirds, make turns for twenty-six knots and do not cavitate."

Wilson gave Meltzer a moment, then picked up the

7MC. "Maneuvering, Conn, this is the captain. Stand by for high-speed operations."

Ilse watched two bright lines cascade down Sessions' waterfall displays, gradually getting thicker. She could see a third line run between them, thinning out. Those are the torpedoes, she realized, theirs and ours.

"Unit from tube seven has detonated!" Jeffrey said.

"Did those contacts launch their missiles?" Wilson said.

"Not yet, sir," Sessions said.

"Chief of the Watch," Wilson said, "on the sound-powered phones, collision alarm." COB acknowledged.

But there was nothing, and Ilse was confused. Then she understood. The fiber-optic signal, through the wire, came at the speed of light. The shock wave traveled at the speed of underwater sound—

Challenger rocked, shaking Ilse against her seat belt. A thunderous blast pummeled the ship, heard right through the hull. The mike coils jerked crazily from the overhead, and navigation instruments flew. A heavy brass divider crashed to the floor, one sharp point sticking in the fleshy part of Commodore Morse's ankle. Snow danced across the sonar screens.

"Loud explosion bearing three five nine!" Sessions said.

"No kidding," Ilse mumbled.

"Status of incoming torpedoes?" Wilson said.

"Impossible to tell."

"Navigator," Wilson said. "Sounding."

"One three five zero zero feet, sir," the navigator said.

"Helm," Wilson said, "doctrine for our steel-skinned boomers says run shallow, but I want to take her deep. Make your depth ten thousand feet smartly." Ilse thought she'd heard wrong.

"Aye, sir," Meltzer said. "Thirty degrees down angle on the diveplane functions."

Ilse gripped her armrests as the deck nosed down. Meltzer called out the numbers every hundred feet. They kept coming faster and faster and started getting much too large.

"Relax," Sessions said. "More depth helps squelch the blast."

Ilse caught her own reflection in a console screen—her eyes were popping and she couldn't make them stop.

"Our hull's ceramic-composite alumina casing," Jeffrey said. "We're designed for this, Ilse. I guess now you need to know."

But knowing didn't help much, Ilse thought.

"Chief of the Watch," Wilson said, "disengage shallow water valves and pumping hardware, line up abyssal suite."

Another shock wave hit, not as hard but more drawn out.

"The surface echo from our weapon," Sessions said. Then another one went by, sharp but weaker still. "Bottom echo that time."

A third concussion hit, this one soft but snappy. "Fireball throbbing," Sessions said, "hydrostatic oscillation, damping coefficient is dot nine."

"I want to make another knuckle," Wilson said. "Keep those inbound torpedoes on our quarter, starboard side instead. Let's confuse them with some bearing rate. Helm, hard right rudder, make your course two zero zero." Again the ship banked hard.

Sessions whispered, "That'll force their seekers to keep leading us. They can't just ride up our wake turbulence and then we get it in the ass."

"But aren't we blind that way," Ilse said, "without the towing sonar?"

"We've got partial baffles coverage from the wide-aperture arrays."

"Fire a noisemaker," Wilson said. "Fire another decoy onto our previous course."

Jeffrey relayed orders to Weapons Control to launch the decoy in tube six.

"Fire an acoustic jammer, starboard side," Wilson said. "Reload tubes five and six, more brilliant decoys."

"Reverb is clearing somewhat," Sessions said. "One incoming torpedo, bearing three four five and constant, depth three thousand feet. It's ignoring the countermeasures. Doppler says it's gaining on us."

"What's the range?" Jeffrey said.

"Fourteen thousand yards."

"Fire Control," Wilson said, "fire two more noisemakers."

"Sir," Jeffrey said, "we're too deep now for noisemakers."

"Then fire another active decoy, shallow running on a reciprocal course. Program hull-popping and cavitation sounds, with a ten-decibel step-up from nominal."

Once more Jeffrey went to work.

"How close is too close?" Ilse whispered.

"*If* it's dot one KT like ours," Jeffrey said before Sessions could answer, "at this depth and with our hull, at two thousand yards of lateral separation we're a mission kill for sure, outright dead if you believe the pessimistic calculations."

"Time to lethal range?" Wilson snapped.

Sessions punched more keys. "Eight minutes if we can't lose it, less if it's a larger warhead. . . . It's got passive lock, *it stopped wigwagging*!"

"Locked on us or on the decoy?" Jeffrey said.

"On *Challenger,* I think. . . . Yes, confirmed, our initial decoy's failed, a machinery implosion."

"How's that torpedo tracking us?" Wilson said. "Do we have a sound short?"

"Negative, sir," Sessions said. "It must be catching reverb off our stern. It's still incredibly noisy out there. . . . Torpedo's first-stage pump-jet has switched to *end-game speed*!"

"Then we're committed to a dead heat now," Jeffrey said.

"Helm, ahead flank smartly," Wilson said.

Meltzer reached for the engine-order dial and flicked it several times. More transients appeared on the sonar screens, making Ilse jump.

"That's us," Sessions told her as he forced a smile. "The reactor coolant check valves just slammed into their recesses."

"Chief of the Watch, flood negative," Wilson said. "Add some weight to pick up speed."

The ship continued diving. Ilse eyed her screens. Fifty-one knots downhill through the water. Fifty-two. The ride was rough.

"Sonar," Wilson said, "did we get those two 212 boats?"

"Can't tell yet, sir. No flooding or implosion sounds were heard above the blast."

"Captain," Jeffrey said, "recommend we go active, search for metallicity inside the bubble cloud."

Wilson nodded. "One ping, maximum power. The whole sector knows we're here."

Ilse heard a double buzz, and several crewmen held their ears. Then there was a sharp and high-pitched *eeeee,* deafening, not at all what she expected. Yet the sonarmen in headphones once again seemed unconcerned. Automatic amplitude filters?

The echoes came back in several seconds. Sessions put the data through his signal algorithms. "Commander Fuller! We have two distinct clouds of falling matter, diffuse, well separate from each other. I assess both targets as destroyed!"

"Status of incoming torpedo?" Jeffrey said.

"Range twelve thousand yards, depth decreased but now it's diving again. . . . It went right past the latest decoy."

"The blue-green laser target discriminator," Jeffrey said. "It's even better than we thought."

"Concur, sir," Sessions said. "Axis hardware's good."

"And we can't use our antitorpedo rockets this far down," Wilson said. "We *could* go the rest of the way to the bottom, try to twist and turn inside the canyons, and risk being buried alive when the warhead blows. Or we could head up toward the surface, shoot some underwater rockets, and gamble the depleted uranium buckshot'll have the range."

"Commander," Sessions shouted, "the torpedo's going active. . . . It's in range-gate mode!"

"Put it on the speakers," Jeffrey said, "and filter out our flow noise."

Ilse heard a hard and eerie *dingggg,* above a constant whining.

"Depth of the weapon?" Wilson said.

"Steady at three thousand feet."

"That must be its limit," Jeffrey said, "or its preset floor." The *dingggg* repeated, slightly louder.

Wilson frowned. "Can't we actively suppress?"

Sessions hesitated. "It's not working, sir."

"We must have damage to our aft transducers," Jeffrey said, "and we're so deep the piezo-rubber hull coating won't function from the pressure."

"Torpedo booster rocket's firing," Sessions shouted as a not-so-distant rumbling came over the speakers. "It's gone to supercavitating speed inside the vacuum bubble! . . . One hundred knots and accelerating!"

Jeffrey eyed the sonar console. "Can we outdistance the weapon's final sprint?"

"Negative, sir," Sessions said. "We'll be in lethal radius when the warhead blows at end-of-run."

"And we can't hit something that small with an ADCAP," Jeffrey said. "Captain, recommend we fight fire with fire."

"Concur," Wilson said. "Load tube eight with another Mark 88. Set it for low, repeat *low*, yield, dot zero one KT, a snap shot on the incoming torpedo's bearing."

Ilse watched as Jeffrey watched his console screens. Again lights blinked as he replayed his special weapons litany. "Security alarm!"

"Handling authorized," Wilson snapped.

"Armed guard is in position," Jeffrey said, talking faster and faster. "Electronic locks are bypassed, mechanical locks are broken. Weapon loaded in tube eight. A-wire is connected, special weapons enabler tool connected."

"I've relayed the PAL code," Wilson said.

"Green light!" Jeffrey said. "Breach door closed! Recommend a preset running depth three thousand feet."

"Concur," Wilson said. "We'll command-detonate through the fiber-optic cable."

"Sir," Jeffrey said, "we'd better launch bows-on. We can't afford to lose the wire."

"Concur," Wilson said. "Cut the wire, tube seven. Close muzzle doors and drain the tubes, tubes one through seven. Shore up the inner door tube eight."

Jeffrey confirmed and then relayed the instructions, his voice clinical and clear. "Sonar, we need your absolute best estimate of that torpedo's range and speed. This is going to be close."

"I'm passing them to Combat Systems now, sir," Sessions said, "but that thing's hard to model. It's still accelerating, now *two* hundred knots!"

Wilson grabbed the 7MC. "Maneuvering, Conn. Stand by for severe control surface movements. Lock down the hydraulic ram relief valves." Wilson paused for the acknowledgment. "Expect a sudden back flank engine order. When it comes, give me everything you've got, but for God's sake don't trigger a reactor scram." He paused again. "Yeah, that's good, take it to a hundred eight percent."

Wilson hung up the mike. "Helm, hard right rudder, make your course zero two zero. Make your depth three thousand feet smartly."

Challenger pitched up and banked into the turn, trading velocity for altitude. Ilse was pressed into her seat. Her console showed their speed was dropping fast, as their heading swung through 180 degrees. The visceral rumbling from aft got louder.

The rumbling over the speakers got louder too, as did the awful dings. A relentless robot's coming for us, Ilse told herself. Those men we killed are reaching from beyond the grave.

"How many?" she said out loud.

"What?" Sessions said.

"How many did we kill?"

"Two dozen on each boat."

"XO," Wilson said, "when should we fire?"

"The sooner the better, Captain," Jeffrey said. "The Mark 88s are rated to our test depth."

"We can't risk a failure," Wilson said.

"Six thousand feet, then, sir?"

"Four thousand," Wilson said. "Let's make really sure." Wilson glanced at a depth gauge. "Chief of the Watch, pump negative. Pump variable ballast to bring the boat up faster."

Ilse felt a repetitive labored clunking from below. Their rate of climb increased but only slightly.

"Sir," Jeffrey said, "recommend retract the foreplanes—they might snap off or jam from shock."

"Helm," Wilson said, "retract the foreplanes."

"Recommend we level off at three thousand feet before our weapon detonates," Jeffrey said. "It's best to take the blast bows-on, show a minimum profile, protect our side arrays and pump-jet."

"Concur," Wilson said.

"Three thousand's the depth of minimum danger this close in," Jeffrey said, "the tight part of the hourglass. Higher up the blast cone spreads as it lifts the surface; deeper down the counterpressure widens as it hammers toward the bottom."

"Concur," Wilson said.

"Depth six thousand feet," Meltzer said. Ilse looked at a pressure gauge: a metric ton for each square inch of hull.

"Range to the incoming torpedo?" Jeffrey said.

"Five thousand yards," Sessions said. "Too close," Ilse heard him mumble.

"If it's got a proximity fuze," Jeffrey said, "it's set real tight."

"Back full," Wilson said.

"Back full, aye," Meltzer said. "Maneuvering acknowledges back full."

"Watch the trim as we slow down!" Wilson said. "The blast catches us from off the level, we'll be knocked out of control."

"Adjusting the trim, aye," COB said. Ilse heard pumps gently whirring.

"Back flank," Wilson said.

"Back flank, aye," Meltzer said. "Maneuvering acknowledges back flank."

Ilse watched their speed mount up again as they fled in reverse from the enemy torpedo. Meltzer was sweating in concentration, his fingers bloodless white as he worked the control wheel.

"Make tube eight ready in all respects," Wilson said, "including valve lineup for a punch-out with a water slug. Tube eight, firing point procedures on the incoming torpedo."

"Solution ready," Jeffrey said. "Ship ready. Weapon ready."

"Chief of the Watch," Wilson said. "On the 1MC, rig for depth charge."

"Rig for depth charge, aye."

Ilse saw Jeffrey glance at Commodore Morse. The Brit winked back and gripped a handle on the overhead.

"Depth four four zero zero feet," Meltzer said.

"Very well," Wilson said, "match sonar bearings and *shoot*."

"Unit from tube eight fired electrically!" Jeffrey said.

Sessions tried to clear his throat. "Unit is running normally, sir."

Jeffrey looked up from his console and again met Ilse's eyes. "Thirty seconds to intercept! Incoming torpedo should exhaust its fuel and blow any moment!"

Jeffrey turned to Captain Wilson. "Unit from tube eight has—"

With a deafening *wham*, pile drivers slammed the bottom of Jeffrey's feet and spine. His entire skeleton rattled. *Challenger*—still moving in reverse—lurched sternward violently. Jeffrey was thrown against his seat belt, his skull bouncing off the headrest. Commodore Morse went flying.

Red shadows shifted wildly as the CACC's spring-loaded fluorescents jiggled crazily in their mounts. But the lights and shockproof monitors didn't flicker once.

Then Jeffrey's ears registered a painfully loud *sssss* and the air began to fog. He ran his tongue along his lips and blinked. Good, it wasn't the blinding salt spray of ambient-pressure seawater. Instead a compressed air leak, cold as it expanded through some failed pipe joint or valve, was condensing the moisture in the CACC atmosphere. The force of the leak blew dust and papers everywhere. Jeffrey saw COB work his panel, bypassing the fault.

"Nav gyros have tumbled," the assistant navigator called. "Reinitializing now."

Another shock wave hit as the giant gas bubble of the fireball fell in upon itself and then rebounded hard, trading kinetic and potential energy back and forth. Jeffrey eyed a depth meter. The boat was falling slowly, rocking badly in the disturbed water all around.

"Chief of the Watch and Helmsman," Wilson said, "watch our buoyancy but do not let her broach. If we can play dead now convincingly, it'll make our next job easier." Wilson grabbed the red handset for Damage Control, located back in Engineering.

"Fire, fire, fire in the ESM room," a sound-powered phone talker said. Probably a short in one of the electronic support measures consoles, Jeffrey told himself, or maybe one of the multiband receivers kept warmed up on standby. That might impair *Challenger*'s intelligence-gathering ability later, and her detection of enemy radar.

As fire fighters hustled along the after passageway, someone opened the ESM door from inside. "It's out, it's nothing," the technician said, holding up a CO_2 extinguisher. Thin smoke drifted out of the small compartment and was sucked into the overhead vents.

Jeffrey, now standing, was doubly relieved: the air-conditioning meant the boat couldn't be in such bad shape. The Enj wouldn't run the fans on batteries, he wouldn't waste the power. So the reactor and heat exchangers had to be okay, along with at least one ship-service turbogenerator. The speed log on Jeffrey's digital display told him both steam sides survived and *Challenger*'s propulsor jet still worked.

Then Sessions shouted, "Flooding sounds! We're taking water somewhere!"

"Localize it," Jeffrey ordered.

"I'm getting flooding forward!"

"Phone Talker," Jeffrey said, "have all compartments near the bow check in."

"Sir," the phone talker said a moment later, "torpedo room does not respond."

"No feeds from the torpedo room," Jeffrey stated, studying his screens.

"We're taking water forward," COB confirmed.

A messenger arrived. "Sir," he said to Jeffrey, "Weps reports torpedo room is taking water. We looked through the hatch port. It's impossible in there."

COB stopped juggling the variable ballast and safety tanks, reaching instead for the fore and aft emergency blow handles. He flipped up the protective plastic covers and looked meaningfully at the captain.

Wilson nodded. "Chief of the Watch, emergency blow on high-pressure air, do *not* use the backup chemical gas generators." There was a great roaring sound. "Start to vent again at four hundred feet. I don't want us surfacing a leaky boat right under a pair of mushroom clouds."

"Vent at four hundred, aye," COB said.

"How bad's the flooding?" Jeffrey said. The enlisted talker relayed the question on his big chest-carried mouthpiece, then listened on his headphones as the damage control party reported back.

"Bad, sir. Water's gaining on the bilge pumps fast, rising over a foot a minute. The spray's still taking paint right off the bulkheads."

"XO," Wilson said, listening on the damage control handset, "that's our biggest problem now. You head down there and take charge, get Weps in here as Fire Control." Wilson picked up the 7MC with his left hand. "Maneuvering, maintain back flank. We need speed for depth control and the pump-jet's got lousy pickup in reverse." Wilson turned to Meltzer. "Helm, how are the waterfoils?"

"Sir, foreplanes will not deploy. All after control surfaces are nominal, but functioning is awkward going backwards."

"Make your depth one hundred feet and try to hold her steady there. That'll reduce the outside pressure and give us some protection from the fallout."

As the boat came up, she began to roll and pitch. "Captain," Meltzer said, "we're too unstable!"

Wilson held the mike open as he continued, "Right standard rudder."

"Right standard rudder, aye, sir. No course specified."

"As our bow swings left to two seven zero," Wilson said, "steady her there and stop the shaft. Then go ahead to one third smartly. I want us clearing datum upwind, just in case. The lower speed'll relieve some of the force of the water on the bow. Use down-angle on the sternplane function if we get too heavy forward."

"Understood, sir," Meltzer said.

"XO, tell me if you can't stop the flooding. Besides the radiation problem, I'd hate to surface and make a datum for some overflying satellite."

"I concur, sir," Jeffrey said. He started for the ladder aft of the CACC, the one leading down to the weapons spaces.

On the way he grabbed a portable radiac—radiation, detection, indication, and computation. This one measured alpha particles, the heaviest and slowest-moving—thus least penetrating—fallout emission by-product. But alpha sources were the most carcinogenic if inhaled, lodged in the alveoli of the lungs. At another locker Jeffrey donned a self-contained Scott air pack. He sealed the mask very tightly, drawing in the metallic-tasting oxygen from the heavy tank. He put on thick work gloves.

When he reached the torpedo room lower level, the damage control parties were inside. Jeffrey quickly sized up the situation.

Challenger's eight torpedo tubes, her war-fighting business end, were grouped vertically in sets of four, starboard and port of her centerline. The tubes were located abaft the bow, canted outward nine degrees to clear her sonar sphere—gantries between the four tall weapons racks created an upper mezzanine. Tube eight was on the lower left of the port-side, even-numbered group. Water gushed from around its inner door, blasting harder than a fire hose.

By the time Jeffrey climbed through the hatch and dogged it shut behind, the boat was trimming noticeably by the bow from all the weight of added water. The lowest pair of three-foot-wide gleaming titanium inner doors was half submerged. The next pair up, tubes five and six, wore small signs, WARNING WARSHOT LOADED.

The water was tinged with red and flecked with bits of plastic and raw flesh. Shoved out of the way behind one weapons rack were the remains of the torpedomen who manned the room at general quarters. The force of the incoming spray at depth had battered them beyond recognition. Electronics cabinets near the tube-eight door were smashed as if hit by cannon fire. The fore-ends of the weapons in direct line to the door had all been shredded, their blue protective covers and fiberglass nose caps gone and their guidance packages in tatters. The conventional Mark 48 highest on the inner port-side rack teetered menacingly, its support clamps knocked asunder by seawater jetting in at a thousand psi. Jeffrey wondered what state its arming circuitry was in.

He sloshed forward through the thigh-deep freezing water, his head just clearing the gantry overhead, his shoulders brushing the weapons racks on either side. He wriggled past the damage control party, then bent over and took a good look at tube eight, which projected from the forward bulkhead through a mass of pipes and fittings. Thick wooden beams pressed against the damaged door, placed there before the concussion by the now-dead crewmen. The sea spewed out all around the edges of the interrupted-screw breach, ricocheting off the bulkheads and hydraulic loading gear.

"The balks won't hold it," the local man in charge yelled in Jeffrey's ear, above the constant roaring of the water. "The outer door's jammed open!"

"We tried driving in more shims!" a leading petty officer said. "It didn't do much good!" The LPO held a sledgehammer with both hands.

Jeffrey nodded. The balks, hastily fitted when Wilson ordered the door shored up, had kept the door from being blasted inward by their own Mark 88. But the shock wave of the detonation had driven into the tube—kept open so they wouldn't lose the fiber-optic wire—and like a water hammer, it warped the inner mounting frame.

Jeffrey eyed the door once more. "We'll have to knock those off first," he shouted through his mask, pointing to the balks, "then fit a lock-down collar on!" He glanced at his radiac and didn't like what he saw. *"Everybody without a respirator get out of here!"*

The LPO read Jeffrey's unit, a proportional counter that caught radioactivity from the unfissioned uranium or plutonium scattered in a low-yield burst. "Sir, four millirems a minute's *nothing*!"

"The guidelines say—"

"Screw the guidelines, Commander! We helped build this boat!"

"Okay," Jeffrey shouted back, "belay the order." He'd transferred on as *Challenger*'s exec after the war started, and wasn't about to argue with a motivated plank owner, especially one who'd just lost friends.

Besides, everybody was already soaking wet and breathing hard. Ordering them to put their masks on wouldn't make much difference now. Instead Jeffrey told the local phone talker to have COB pump in high-pressure air—at least that would slow the flooding. The man kept flicking water from his mouthpiece as he bellowed each word carefully, then listened. He caught Jeffrey's eye and nodded hard.

Jeffrey glanced at a depth gauge as the bow suddenly whipsawed vertically, sloshing water everywhere, knocking crewmen off their feet. The boat was going down, getting too hard to control.

"Sir," the man in charge yelled hoarsely, "that topmost ADCAP's shifted more! We can't get to it with this spray, and if it falls, the thing could blow!" And if they surfaced now, the A-bomb-ravaged seas would toss them more.

But the torpedo room's rear bulkhead wasn't very pressure-proof. Jeffrey knew that if this compartment filled at depth, the seawater could get into the battery bank in the bilge spaces just aft. Broken batteries would short, giving off hydrogen and chlorine gas, and then explode. Jeffrey's ears began to ache as the atmospheric pressure rose. He swallowed hard to ease the pain.

"All right!" Jeffrey shouted. "We have to do this all at once and fast!" He positioned several crewmen next to the leaking door, ready with the heavy ceramic repair collar. Another half dozen men stood by to get the massive beams out of the way.

On Jeffrey's command the LPO whacked the shims loose with his sledgehammer, freeing the beams. The water inflow got much worse, and now they used hand signals because of the noise.

Jeffrey helped wrestle the two halves of the repair collar, hinged at a joint, to fit the collar around the door, fighting hard against the bruising spray. He grunted when one of the beams rammed him in the calf as it was hastily moved aside. An electrician's mate slipped, cracking his jaw against a protruding autoloader cam. The man got up, lip and chin bloodied, hair and denim jump suit soaked, and resumed his place. A severed arm floated by and Jeffrey batted it aside.

The crewmen crouched into the rising water to get more leverage. Jeffrey and two men wearing respirators put their heads under to better see what they were doing. Pink water pressed the improvised scuba masks against their faces, but at least down low the built-up water helped soften the incoming spray. They rammed the collar flush.

Muscles bulged as the men gradually forced the halves of the collar together against the flow, then cranked it closed. Someone brought a metal tool, a long valve extension rod, and the work gang used brute strength to tighten each of the collar's ten giant wing nuts, squashing the door the rest of the way shut. The LPO gave the mating crank one more solid heave, seating the collar decisively.

"Pretty good, guys," Jeffrey said, admiring their handiwork. He noticed the flood in the compartment was already going down, as submersible pumps passed the water to main bilge pumps aft whose motors were still dry. Jeffrey pulled off his breather mask and picked up a mike hanging from the overhead. Taking a breath, he smelled the heady odor of machine oil mixed with sweat, and the blood-and-sewer stink of mangled corpses.

"Control, torpedo room lower level," Jeffrey said. "Flooding secured, three fatalities."

"Who are they?" Wilson said over the intercom.

Jeffrey gave the names, feeling sad and humbled as crewmen put them into body bags. The LPO opened a first-aid kit and tended to the injured crewman's jaw, irrigating the cuts thoroughly with disinfectant.

"Material condition?" Wilson said.

Jeffrey cleared his throat. "Depot-level equipment casualty, inner door tube eight. I count six weapons damaged beyond repair based on gross visual inspection."

"What else do you need down there?" Wilson said.

"Request a freshwater decontamination washdown, machinery and personnel. Request a corpsman's radiological exposure assay, all affected personnel."

"Sir," a torpedoman suggested, "we'll start checking all the weapons right away. Hopefully the rest of them still work."

Jeffrey nodded, looking around at the four dozen

close-packed missiles, mines, and torpedoes. Emergency battle lanterns cast harsh shadows—the compartment's power had been isolated when the flooding started, to eliminate shock hazard in the highly conductive seawater. Now two auxiliarymen eyed the ground readings and cross-checked the switch lineup on a control panel, reset some breakers, and the regular lights came on. Jeffrey saw the air still held a pungent mist, saltwater atomized. Everything dripped.

A machinist's mate restored hydraulic pressure, dumped earlier so an errant piece of equipment wouldn't maim or kill. He raised the pressure slowly while companions checked for leaks, after first isolating some obviously damaged autoloader machinery. They gave up immediately—fluid still oozed everywhere.

As Jeffrey studied the devastation wrought by the incoming sea, he tried not to think about the tons and tons of high explosives and self-oxidizing fuels stacked all around him here, and the atomic warheads. Fire and water, he told himself, the elements that own all submariners. Buoyancy and crush depth, nuclear furnaces and steam, they make us go and make us die.

Another worry crossed his mind and he spoke into the mike. "Captain, XO. Request permission to cycle the outer doors tubes one through seven to verify their function."

CHAPTER 6

NEAR THE ANTARCTIC CIRCLE, FAR SOUTH OF DURBAN

Captain Jan ter Horst grinned as another blast of frigid water hit him in the face. "Just like the good old days, Gunther," he shouted over the southeast gale. "The way it used to be, when sharks of steel drank diesel fuel and wolf packs ruled the seas!"

Gunther Van Gelder eyed his skipper, more than ever convinced the man was mad. "None of this is really necessary, Captain," he said through chattering teeth. "Can't we just dive and get it over with?" He gripped the edge of the bridge cockpit with gloved hands, trying to steady himself against the roll, the pitch, the shudders of the hull.

"Never!" Ter Horst laughed as his vessel bounded and punched through the waves. He sneered at the surface ship in the middle distance. "I *want* them to see *Voortrekker*! I want them to try to run!"

Van Gelder ducked as more green water broached the cockpit, then drained away. Ice rime was already two centimeters thick on the ESM antennas and photonic masts. "We'll freeze, sir, before much longer, and this is dangerous." He tried to close his parka tighter but it was zipped high as it would go.

"Don't be silly, Number One," ter Horst said. "There aren't aircraft anywhere near here. She's been running her radar at full power since she spotted us—and we keep stealing echoes. Besides, their low-observable fighters don't have the range, and if they did, we'd pick them up on passive infrared."

"But sir, that's just line of sight."

"The latest satellite pass showed nothing in the area. . . . So *let* them call for help. That's the whole idea!"

"But they might attack us!"

"Pah. She's unarmed except for some machine guns. Our unmanned aerial vehicle told us that. Probably worried about a special boat squadron takedown, not a sub."

Van Gelder watched the supertanker morosely, barely visible as it labored through the blowing fog. Half a million tons displacement, laden with priceless crude. Liberian registry, U.S.-owned and -manned. They'd known that much about the target for hours—*Voortrekker* had sonar tapes of all the big ships that plied the Persian Gulf.

"I suppose we could have used a missile," ter Horst said half to himself, "but we fired the last of them up north. . . . I wonder if the Americans know it was *my* vessel that sank *Ranger*."

Van Gelder felt too frozen to wonder about much of anything. "We're not supposed to waste nuclear warheads on single merchant ships, Captain." He huddled by the bridge instrument panel, gaining scant shelter from the forty-plus-knot wind. The cockpit crew's bright orange protective clothing gave the only color to the scene of blacks and leaden grays.

Ter Horst nodded curtly. "What I don't understand," he yelled in Van Gelder's ear, "is why she's here at all."

"Greed, sir?" Van Gelder spat out bitter seawater as more spindrift hit his face. He shifted position and frozen glaze crackled on his coat front.

"Arrogance, more like," ter Horst said. "They think they can run the blockade. To reach America's Gulf

Coast refineries by crossing the Pacific instead would take four times as long."

"Maybe they hoped to hide against the ice pack." Van Gelder stamped his feet to keep his legs from getting numb.

"Idiots!" ter Horst shouted. "Did they really think their engine tonals would be masked against the floes?"

"They must not realize, sir, what modern sonar can do."

"Fools! *Our* merchant marine masters would never make that error. The Americans are soft, Gunther, I'm telling you, and desperate. Putting this tanker on the bottom will show that to the world, and it will show the world we're strong."

"But, sir! *Here* of all places? It'll be an ecological catastrophe."

"Exactly! A test of will, a monument to our determination. The Southern Ocean current will carry the oil slick round and round, till the whole Antarctic coast is mired. Fifty million gallons loosed! From every longitude, from every nation, they'll look south and see our power."

"Couldn't we just trail her till she makes for the Atlantic?"

"In God's name, why? We have other work to do!"

"But the penguins, sir. The seals, the whales. They'll be wiped out!"

"Birds, Gunther? You worry about fish and *birds*? You're not *backsliding*, are you?"

"Sir, no, of course not. Of course not, sir."

"Good. Remember what happened to the others. It took some of them five minutes to die! More stiff-necked, I suppose."

Seasick already, Van Gelder rolled his eyes at the dull overcast. He swallowed bile.

Ter Horst laughed again. "Relax." He pounded Van

Gelder on the shoulder. "I trust you implicitly, my friend."

"Target aspect change, sir," Van Gelder said, grateful for the distraction. He pointed. "I think she's started zigzagging."

Ter Horst leaned to the intercom. "Weapons, Bridge. Disable torpedo homing packages. Use zero gyro angle, set running depth seven meters."

A muffled acknowledgment sounded on the speaker.

"Her draft is four times that, sir," Van Gelder said. That's why the tanker couldn't use the Suez Canal, he told himself, not that they'd ever make it through the Med.

"I know," ter Horst said. "I want to blow her sides out. She'll go down fast that way. . . . Infrared binoculars, please."

Van Gelder took the strap from around his neck, gulping at the grisly association, and presented them to his CO.

"I can see her load," ter Horst said as he peered intently. "It's a kind of X-ray vision, you know, infrared."

"Yes, sir."

"Good German optics, and good electronics too. Look at that, I can even see the crewmen on the bridge . . . and a few more in the deckhouse on her forecastle."

"Can't we give them a chance to surrender, Captain?"

"Don't be ridiculous. What do you think this is, World War *I*?"

"It's just that—"

"Yes, I know. With the best survival gear in creation they'd never be rescued from the sea in time. Whose fault is that, *hmmm*? Certainly not ours."

A rogue wave struck from aft, and *Voortrekker*'s bridge was under for endless seconds. Van Gelder felt the suction begin to lift him from his feet. He fought to hold his breath, praying that his lifeline held. Then the water cleared.

Ter Horst shook himself off and leaned to the intercom again. "Weapons, use target speed eighteen knots. Our angle on her bow is starboard zero four zero, mark."

"May I see, sir?" Van Gelder said, badly needing something to do. It was so cold with the wind chill that his speech was getting slurred, and his face had lost all feeling in spite of the woolen ski mask and fur-lined parka hood.

Ter Horst handed over the binocs. "Sonar," he called, "go active. What's the range?"

"Thirty-nine hundred meters, Captain," came back a few seconds later.

"Weapons," ter Horst said, "target bearing, call it two four five relative, mark!"

Van Gelder heard the acknowledgment as he studied the doomed tanker. Their own boat pitched to an especially nasty following wave. The sub heaved upward in the swell and he could see the endless choppy seas. The horizon was a dusky blur beneath a dark and glowering sky, the sun a lifeless coppery orb low to the north. He watched the wave roll past the bow, completely covering *Voortrekker*'s foredeck. The massive supertanker, four hundred meters long or more, seemed to barely feel the storm.

"It's a little approximate," ter Horst shouted, "doing this by eye, but she's so big we can hardly miss."

"I know, Captain."

"We've pulled ahead. Time to set up the shot. Helm, Bridge, port ten degrees rudder. Steer one nine five true." The sub slid down the back of one tall wave, bore up into the next, and a wall of water slammed the sail. Now the seas came from broad off the port bow, slowing *Voortrekker* down, and the wind seemed more intense.

Van Gelder ran the infrared binoculars along their quarry's hull. The huge laden cargo tanks stood out clearly in the enhanced imagery, the warmth of the crude petroleum radiating through the vessel's cold steel sides.

"Weapons," ter Horst called, "she's turning away. . . . She handles like a pregnant bathtub. . . . Angle on the bow now starboard zero five four. Bearing three two zero relative. Make the range thirty-six hundred meters, mark."

Again a tinny acknowledgment came back, barely audible above the howling of the storm and the water surging, slapping the cockpit.

Van Gelder stared at their target. A heavy bank of fog spoiled his view, then passed. "Sir, I don't understand something."

"Weapons," ter Horst called impatiently, "final bearing, three two four, angle on the bow now starboard zero six one. Range closing to thirty-four hundred meters, mark. . . . What is it, Gunther?"

"Her tanks aren't quite full. In fact I'd say they've only got three quarters of capacity."

"Helm," ter Horst said, "increase speed five more knots. I'm getting cold." He turned to Van Gelder. "The way she's altered course away from us makes it more challenging, you know. Not that she can keep it up. Icebergs calve in that direction this time of year."

"I know, sir. We're inside the mean limit of pack ice for December as it is."

"Bergy bits off the starboard quarter!" a lookout called. Van Gelder watched the cottage-sized translucent obstacles bob and tumble. The sub quickly left them behind.

"We have our prey in the snare for sure," ter Horst said. "She's embayed against Princess Ragnhild Coast. . . . We should change that name. Kruger Coast, or something."

"Sir, these waters are getting hazardous, and something doesn't make sense."

Ter Horst leaned to the intercom again. "Weapons, make tubes one through four ready in all respects. Open the outer doors. . . . What is it *now,* Gunther?"

"If she's running the blockade, why wouldn't her tanks be full?"

"Let me see that," ter Horst snapped. He grabbed the binoculars. "Hmm. I see what you mean."

"Sir, I don't like this."

"What's there not to like? We're alone with her out here."

"I know, sir, it's just that—"

"*Look.* We've used her noise to do an ambient sonar search, and we checked twice for anything backlit against the grinding of the floes. We patrolled under the ice shelf on our way over here, remember?"

"Yes, sir, I know."

"I inspected her bottom myself using an unmanned undersea vehicle probe. There's nothing that's a threat."

"Something just doesn't feel right, Captain. The bridge crew, they never move."

Ter Horst chuckled. "Talk about frozen with fear."

"Bridge, Sonar," came over the intercom.

"Sonar, Bridge, aye aye," Van Gelder shouted.

"Mechanical transients, wide-field directional effects, mean bearing one five seven true. Range matches the tanker."

"Near her stern," ter Horst mused. "Engine room noises?"

"Bridge, Sonar, negative. They sounded like muzzle doors opening."

"Muzzle doors?" ter Horst said. He hesitated. "*Scheisse!*" He turned in a circle and pounded the cockpit windscreen with his fist. "Now it all makes sense. *Seawater.* I'll bet her tanks are filled with fucking seawater!"

Van Gelder nodded. "Crude's lighter, sir." *That's* why the tanks were partly empty. Saltwater took some 80 percent of the cargo volume for the same weight and hull displacement.

"Torpedo in the water bearing one five seven!"

Again ter Horst cursed. "Fire an antitorpedo rocket!" He glanced at Van Gelder confidently. "They'll never go nuclear, Gunther. Not while we're this close."

There was a violent explosion halfway between the submarine and tanker. Dirty water soared into the air, and soon the acrid fumes made Van Gelder choke.

"Intercept successful," Sonar said.

"She's a *verdammt* Q-ship," ter Horst sputtered. "Torpedo tubes jury-rigged below the waterline."

"Yes, sir," Van Gelder said.

"How *dare* they? The whole thing's a bloody trap!"

"Second torpedo in the water!"

"Destroy it!" ter Horst shouted.

Again rumbling water fountained and a shock wave raced across the sea. The torpedo and antitorpedo's twin concussion hit Van Gelder in the gut.

"Sir," he said, "she's turning toward us."

"With that deep draft they'll try to ram. . . . Helm, port thirty rudder *now,* steer one six five true."

Ter Horst winked at Van Gelder as the sub's sail heeled into the turn, putting the two vessels on a collision course. "We'll still do this *my* way." He leaned to the intercom. "Weapons! Firing point procedures on the tanker, tubes one through four."

Van Gelder looked through his binoculars, his ears ringing from the explosions, his forehead aching from the cold. "The crew still haven't moved. I think they're heated dummies, sir."

Ter Horst grabbed the binocs. "It's robotic," he said at last. He looked up at the sky and shook his fist. Van Gelder wondered if the satellite could see.

"We can't stay here, sir," Van Gelder said. "They'd

gladly sacrifice an empty tanker to get one of our nuclear-powered boats."

"Fire tubes one through four!" ter Horst screamed. Then, "Port thirty rudder! Clear the bridge! Dive! Dive! *Emergency deep!*" The lookouts, stiff and awkward in their bulky garb, unclipped their soaking harnesses, then latched open the bridge hatch and dashed below.

Van Gelder went last. As he glanced fearfully over his shoulder, *Voortrekker*'s conventional torpedoes hit home. Four bursting eruptions marched along the tanker's starboard side. Wreckage flew up higher than her superstructure aft. Entire sections of her waterline gaped open to the sea, and even above the driving wind Van Gelder thought he heard the ocean rushing in. Thick black smoke and dazzling flame began to spread amidships—there must have been some oil left in her auxiliary tanks and pumping systems. Machine-gun ammo cooked off vividly, red tracers jabbing into the sky.

Mist and foam sprayed as *Voortrekker*'s ballast vents first sighed, then screamed, then roared. Van Gelder stood transfixed as the sub's bow started nosing under. The tanker seemed dead in the water now, her keel beginning to sag, overstressed metal moaning and screeching. But what if she bore an atomic warhead, or maybe more than one?

Van Gelder climbed through the massive bridge hatch, made a quick inspection, and yanked it shut. He twirled the wheel to lock it as fast as he could. The Americans would wait for the tanker to be well underwater, to maximize the blast effect submerged. They'd probably use some kind of timer, or a pressure-sensitive switch. The world's biggest nuclear depth charge, Van Gelder told himself, with *Voortrekker*'s name on it.

There was a terrible drawn-out detonation and Van Gelder cringed. *Voortrekker* rocked but that was all. It must have been the tanker's red-hot boilers, rupturing from thermal shock as frigid seawater reached the engine rooms. But the next explosion wouldn't be from chemicals or steam, and it would be Van Gelder's last. He clung desperately to the sail trunk ladder as his boat dived hard and turned away.

Van Gelder saw the lower sail trunk hatch pop open. Ter Horst looked up from below. "Gunther," he said with exaggerated politeness, "would you care to come down, please?"

As Van Gelder dropped into the control room, a messenger handed him a flask of genever, a high-proof gin. He gulped some gratefully, then shed his outer garments. The deck was tilted steeply and his boots squished as he walked.

Van Gelder took up his position at the conning stand next to the captain. The warmth of the genever spread throughout his body. He flexed his fingers as the circulation returned. "Helm," Van Gelder said, "report."

"Steering zero zero zero, sir," the helmsman said. Due north. "My speed is ahead flank."

"Diving Officer, report."

"Making emergency deep per captain's orders, thirty degrees down angle on the planes. Passing through six hundred fifty meters, no maximum depth specified."

"Navigator, soundings."

"Water depth fifty-eight hundred meters, sir."

Van Gelder made eye contact with ter Horst.

"They fooled us, Gunther," ter Horst said. "They won't fool us again."

"Sonar," Van Gelder said, "range to the tanker?"

"Four thousand meters, sir."

"Sonar," ter Horst said, "put it on the speakers."

Roaring and burbling echoed in the control room, seawater and air bubbles in vicious foregone conflict. A continuous noise like breaking glass told of steam pipes bursting endlessly. Van Gelder heard the rapid-fire pops of rivets failing, the sharp bangs of ruptured welds. The tortured screams of frames and plating punctuated the giant tanker's death, steel groaning in final torment.

"Sonar," ter Horst snapped, "target depth?"

"About two hundred meters, sir, increasing fast. She's tearing apart in the middle, still in one piece so far."

"Target range?"

"Now forty-seven hundred meters, Captain."

"I'm afraid to go any faster," ter Horst said. "I don't want to overpower the reactor. . . . Damned Russian nuclear engineering."

"I agree, sir," Van Gelder said. "Even with the Hamburg firm's enhancements we could lose the boat."

"We still might," ter Horst said. "If that tanker's rigged with an atomic warhead, we'll know it very soon."

It was. The initial shock was so hard it made Van Gelder's vision blur. A gigantic rolling *boom* hammered through the hull and over the sonar speakers, strangely stereophonic. Half the control room screens imploded, ground glass flying everywhere. Crewmen's arms and legs and heads flailed wildly as *Voortrekker* lurched and lurched. Then the speakers all went dead but the nerve-rending thundering continued. Van Gelder's limbs and ass felt pins and needles from the impacts. He waited for the hull to crack, for the inrush of the icy crushing sea, for the sudden compression of the atmosphere that would set his clothes and skin afire.

Instead *Voortrekker*'s stern reared up, higher and higher, lifted by the blast, throwing Van Gelder and ter Horst forward against their workstations.

"Fifty-two degrees down bubble!" the helmsman shouted. "I can't control the boat!"

A soul-piercing alarm bell filled the air. "Reactor scram!" came over an intercom. "Excessive trim reactor scram!" The overhead lights dimmed immediately, switched to batteries as *Voortrekker*'s turbogenerators wound down. Then Van Gelder heard the inevitable: "Control, Maneuvering, we've lost propulsion power!" The sub's vibrations changed in character, nastier than before.

"We're in a jam dive!" the helmsman screamed. "Cruise by wire's inoperative! Backup hydraulic system's failed!" He and the diving officer twirled their control wheels uselessly.

"Fire in the forward fan room," came over the intercom. "Flooding through the main shaft packing gland."

"Diving Officer," ter Horst said, "pump all variable ballast. Pump out the safety tanks."

The intercom began to hiss and squeal, becoming unintelligible. Ter Horst tore a sound-powered phone rig from a crewman lying on the deck. The man's neck stretched like rubber and Van Gelder realized he was dead. The body slid downhill.

"Silence on the circuit!" ter Horst snapped, then, "Engineering, engage sternplane manual overrides. Can you give me back full revs on batteries?"

Ter Horst listened, frowning. "Then lock the shaft and use the propulsor as a water brake. We've got to stop this dive!"

Van Gelder glanced at a depth gauge. They'd just passed 2,500 meters, rate of descent increasing fast. This far down even *Voortrekker*'s ceramic hull compressed, reducing their buoyancy further.

"Captain," Van Gelder said, "our momentum's much too high. Recommend emergency main ballast blow while we still have the chance."

"That was a three-KT warhead out there," ter Horst said, "if not more."

"I know, sir. But we're too heavy now with the heat and gas bubbles around us." The ocean's supporting density had just dropped out from under them. "Our crush depth's coming up fast!"

"Surfaced into those tsunamis, we could turn turtle

easily," ter Horst said, "spill air from the bottom of the ballast tanks and sink, even do a full three-sixty, smashing everyone and everything inside."

Van Gelder nodded. Which was the better way to die?

"Engineering," ter Horst said into the bulky mouthpiece, "status on the diveplanes? Can you shunt past the bad main motor breakers?" He paused for the response. "They need more time."

"*Captain!*" Van Gelder urged as he watched the depth gauge. "We've got barely sixty seconds till the hull implodes!"

"Very well," ter Horst said, sighing, "it's the lesser of two evils. . . . Diving Officer, emergency-blow the forward main ballast group."

High-pressure air screeched like a strident harpy, forcing its way into the tanks outside the pressure hull. Enough leaked through the distribution manifold to pop Van Gelder's ears.

"Number One," ter Horst told him, "lay forward and steady the damage control parties. See to that fan room fire."

As Van Gelder stood up awkwardly, the control room began to fill with wispy smoke. He ordered the crewmen into respirators. Some cursed in pain as they put masks to bruised and bloodied faces, then aided unconscious or stunned neighbors who flopped sideways strapped into their chairs. Van Gelder reached for a walk-around breather set stowed under his console.

"We're still going down," ter Horst said. "Diving Officer, give the forward ballast tanks more air."

"Sir," the senior chief said, coughing, "it'll expand too much as we go up and we'll lose bubbles through the bottom vents. They'll make a datum topside."

"Christ, man, that doesn't matter now!"

Van Gelder staggered as an aftershock hit. The deck tilted even further in spite of the bow tank blow. He reached out desperately to avoid a long fall down the forward passageway. He grabbed a stanchion on the overhead and lunged to safety, dropping his air pack on the way. He wound up pinned by gravity beside the diving officer and helmsman. He heard his respirator crash against a transverse bulkhead somewhere forward. That could have been my skull, he told himself, then wondered how the fire fighters were making out.

"Emergency-blow stern ballast tanks," ter Horst said. "Use all the air you've got." Van Gelder's ears hurt more, but nothing happened.

"Dammit," ter Horst said, "it's not enough. Fire the hydrazine gas generators." Van Gelder knew the one-time-use chemical cartridges were a last resort. He heard them igniting in the ballast tanks, like missile engines on a hot run in the vertical launching system.

The boat shuddered, then seemed to stop and think about it, still with a frightening down-bubble.

The helmsman shouted that the sternplanes had been freed. He put them on full rise but then they jammed again. *Voortrekker* started coming up. The helmsman called out their depth every hundred meters, then every two hundred as the boat kept on accelerating, driven now by massive and increasing positive buoyancy.

"Sonar," Van Gelder said automatically, holding on for dear life, "any surface contacts?"

The sonar chief gestured helplessly. "Sir, it's impossible out there." His voice sounded distant, muffled through his breather mask.

"Collision alarm!" ter Horst said into the sound-powered phone. "Talkers relay to all hands: Emergency surface, stand by to broach. Rig for fallout, do not open air induction valves, do not man the bridge."

Van Gelder eyed the speed log. The boat moved in reverse, rising by the stern.

"Raise the photonics mast," ter Horst said. Still strapped in at his console, he activated the viewing screens that hadn't been blown out. He used the 'scope joy stick to look aft and upward.

Van Gelder stared at a screen. At first there was nothing, then he saw an image-intensified dull glow. Quickly the picture brightened, showing the greenish underside of waves, getting closer and closer. Van Gelder realized the waves were very large, churning and breaking horribly, not like normal windblown swell. Suddenly *Voortrekker* burst through, and ter Horst worked the joy stick.

Van Gelder watched their stern uncover, white water swirling off the hull, *Voortrekker* a massive projectile thrusting up into the sky. He could see the control surfaces and the cowling of the pump-jet, exposed naked in the air. Van Gelder's stomach rose to his throat as the sub topped out in her trajectory, halted, then smashed back down. She thrust the chaotic seas aside, water spraying from beneath her, then plowed under, reburying the hull. She seemed to stagger, then came up again, fighting against the violent ocean, settling on an even keel. At once she started to badly roll and pitch, steerageway gone, visibly stern-heavy now.

"Do not counterflood," ter Horst ordered.

Van Gelder struggled to his feet, his attention glued now to the monitor, taking in the scene with a practiced sailor's eye. Foam sprayed off the frenzied wavetops, streaming away beyond the stern.

"My God," he said, "the wind's blowing to the south."

Van Gelder knew that thanks to planetwide air circulation driven by the sun, the winds of the Southern Ocean were the steadiest on earth. They roared down off the high mountains of central Antarctica, spreading northward toward the coast in all directions. To conserve angular momentum while moving farther from earth's axis of rotation, the air had to lose ground to the planet's spin, veering left: the Coriolis force. The wind at this latitude always blew to the *northwest*, Van Gelder told himself. *Always*.

Ter Horst shifted the periscope head, searching. He switched to wider angle, then found what he was looking for. "Five thousand meters tall already, maybe more."

The overcast had dissipated from the heat, and the base surge had mostly cleared: the mushroom cloud thrust higher as they watched. The golden-yellow fireball cast shadows north along the wavetops, canceling the sun.

"Air's being sucked in toward its base," Van Gelder said. A satanic low-pressure front, he told himself, driven by staggering thermal forces. The superheated air formed nitric oxides, like in smog, adding a reddish-orange tinge.

"Look at that," ter Horst said. "The entrained steam's condensing now. . . . It's giving the pillar a nice fluffy white appearance."

In a mockery of normal weather the man-made cirrostratus cooled.

"It's started to rain," Van Gelder said. He knew droplets falling against the pillar's updraft would add their static charges to the massive ones created by the blast.

"Lightning," ter Horst said. "Wow." He actually smiled as the monitor flashed again. Each discharge's *crack* resounded through *Voortrekker*'s hull.

"Navigator," Van Gelder said, "get a radiation count."

"Working on it, sir. It takes a minute for the detector modes to integrate."

"Captain," Van Gelder said, "we're probably best off like this for now, with that thing facing toward our stern." His eyes were stinging from the smoke.

"What?"

"The slant angle, sir, from the fireball back aft. It makes the hull seem thicker."

"Yes, I think you're right. . . ."

"That way our sail and the reactor shielding give us more protection too, at least in forward compartments."

Ter Horst nodded. Finally tearing himself from the screen, he spoke into his mouthpiece. "All nonessential personnel evacuate the engineering spaces. Do *not* use the aft escape hatch, come forward through the reactor tunnel." He reached beneath his seat and gave Van Gelder his own air mask, then grabbed a spare stowed in the overhead.

"Sir," the navigator shouted through his respirator, "not much gamma radiation's getting through the hull, but it's murder topside. Strontium 90 all over the place, iodine 131, cesium 137, krypton 85. . . ."

The boat rolled into the trough of an especially lofty wave, the confluence of several others that had melded in a rogue. Van Gelder braced himself as the backup mechanical inclinometer plumbed toward sixty-five degrees, then recovered as the vessel yawed almost broadside to ground zero. The working of the ship seemed heavier now—she must have spilled some air and hydrazine fumes. Van Gelder glanced nervously at the overhead to starboard, toward the south, knowing what was out there. Another strong wave hit. Again the boat rolled mercilessly.

"We've got to get propulsion back," ter Horst said. "We need directional control. But a fast scram recovery will take them ten or fifteen minutes."

"Sir," Van Gelder said, "if we start the emergency diesel now, we'll draw in outside air."

"I know. And the batteries won't take us far in so rough a sea either, plus then we won't have the amp-hours to regain reactor power."

A breathless messenger arrived from aft. "Captain, the engineer reports wrecked main motor breakers bypassed now, but forward DC buses impaired by overheating from the fan room fire. Only trickle current available from the forward batteries."

"Enough to lift a control rod group and give us criticality?"

The man shook his head. "We need the after battery to pressurize the fire mains. Sir, we need to keep running the bilge pumps too. We took a lot of water through the main shaft packing gland."

"How bad's the flooding?" Van Gelder said.

"They tightened the peripheral bolts as far as the threads can go and the inflow stopped at shallower depth. The seawater's clearing, sir, but slowly, and the free surface hinders our stability."

"That fire's the key, then, Gunther," ter Horst said. "We've got to put it out, and quickly. Messenger, have Engineering deenergize the forward bus bars."

"I'm going down there now," Van Gelder said. The smoke was growing thicker and it was getting very warm. The boat took another violent roll to starboard, still facing sideways to the mushroom cloud.

CHAPTER 7

Van Gelder hurried down two ladders, through a dogged hatchway, along a companionway, and through another hatch. It felt like he was walking toward an oven. When he finally arrived, two charred corpses lay along the deck, wearing what was left of fire-fighting gear. One seemed to stare up at Van Gelder, its black and bloody face all melted, broken teeth in a now-lipless mouth, air mask fused to flesh. Above the acrid stink of smoke, even through his sealed respirator, Van Gelder smelled burned flesh and hair.

Hoses twisted everywhere, men crouching to stay below the heat, leaning into the recoil of the lines. Freshwater sprayed and white foam sloshed, making the deck treacherously slippery. The hoses roared, the fire roared and crackled.

"It started at the back," a senior chief shouted through his mask, straining to project his voice—already badly hoarse—above the constant noise.

"I can't see a *blery* thing," Van Gelder shouted back.

Just then another fire fighter was carried past, his face bright red, down from heat prostration. The chief turned to the stretcher bearers as they went through the hatchway aft. "Helmet!" A seaman understood, took off the fire fighter's headgear, and tossed it to Van Gelder.

Van Gelder donned the helmet, fastened the chin strap tight around his breather mask, and then flipped down the special visor. He activated the switch near his right temple. Immediately the infrared oculars gave him a false-color image through the smoke.

A hose team was crouched in the doorway to the fan room, another farther back, keeping the first team drenched to cool them down. Others aimed fog nozzles toward the overhead, letting the hot gases of combustion vent their energy by making steam. Already Van Gelder was sweating from the heat and the humidity. As he watched, flames licked out through the fan room hatchway, subsided, and then came back redoubled.

"What's burning?" he yelled to the chief.

"Christ, sir, everything. We think it started when a hydraulic line ruptured from the shock, then got set off by some sparking from a damaged motor."

Van Gelder nodded. Hydraulic fluid burned like gasoline.

"We dropped the pressure and sealed the line real quick, but it was too late. Mostly now the fire load's grease and lube oil in the machinery, plus all the insulation, and rubber, and the acoustic isolation pads."

"Scheisse," Van Gelder said. "They're full of PVCs, those vibration isolators. Make sure no one breathes that stuff."

"Right, sir. We know. The worst was some aluminum ignited. We couldn't reach it from the trim."

"What happened to those two?" Van Gelder said, pointing to the corpses.

"Both pitched in headfirst, right into the burning metal, when we caught that aftershock. We pulled them out with boathooks."

"Jesus."

"It's far from burning out, sir. The Class D metal fire, I mean. We just keep pouring on the water, best we can, with foam around the edges for all the Class B stuff."

"Your team's done well," Van Gelder shouted, "but you've got to keep going."

"Yes, sir. We've got auxiliary lines covering the exposures, hosing down each bulkhead from the other side."

"Good."

"Not good, sir. The bus bars from the batteries are right underneath."

"Can't we cool them down somehow?"

"Not while the fire's still going. It's just too hot. They're insulated against shorts and arcing, not a thermal overload."

The hotter the bus bars got, Van Gelder knew, the greater their resistance. It was like the opposite of superconductivity: chaotic outer electron shell paths from the overexcited molecular motions.

"So what are you suggesting?" Van Gelder said.

"The problem's getting in there, sir, to get at the seat of the fire. Our longest foam applicators only reach four meters, and the water isn't going where it should."

There was a sharp *thump* and a fireball blasted into the passageway. Everybody dropped fast to the deck. Van Gelder thanked the Lord when the flaming vapors went the other way, then he felt shame over his selfishness. At least the other crewmen have their fire-retardant Nomex suits, he told himself.

"That was hydrogen, probably," the old chief shouted, "from the metals that are still on fire contacting the water."

"How much freshwater do we have left in the tanks?"

"Less than half, sir. We have to get this thing under control. We take in seawater now, or use the forward trunk to ventilate, we'll pollute the ship."

Again Van Gelder nodded. Again an injured fire fighter was carried aft, screaming in pain, writhing on the stretcher.

"Someone has to get inside," Van Gelder said.

"Sir, it's a thousand centigrade in there! We can barely keep the blaze from spreading as it is!"

"We have to," Van Gelder shouted. "This heat builds up much longer, we'll be forced to abandon ship. . . . A steam entry suit! It might hold long enough to let someone knock down the worst hot spots."

"In among the *flames*?"

"I don't see any other way," Van Gelder said. "We can't just stay like this, there's too much fallout topside. We start up the diesel now, the NBC filters will be overwhelmed." Both men ducked as something else exploded. Orange sparks flew into the corridor.

A messenger arrived from the control room. Van Gelder withdrew to meet him a safe distance from the fire, both men down on hands and knees. The messenger was gasping, trying hard to catch his breath. He struggled to draw air from his respirator, straining the demand regulator to the limit.

"Sir," he finally panted, "Captain says reception's coming back. The satfeed downlink shows many inbound aircraft."

"British?"

The messenger nodded.

"How far from here?"

"Sixteen hundred kilometers, sir. Halfway from the Falklands."

"They're supersonic?"

"Yes."

"How much longer do we have?"

"The navigator says maybe half an hour, then we'd be too tightly localized to get away."

"All right," Van Gelder said. "Listen to me." He tried to make eye contact, but through his IR imagers the man appeared a spectral aura in pastel blues and pinks. Instead Van Gelder put a hand on the seaman's shoulder. "Get back to Engineering. Have them send me three steam entry suits."

"Yes, sir. Three steam entry suits."

"And on the way, tell the captain I recommend to hold off on the diesel. We might still restore the batteries in time."

"Hold off on the diesel, might still restore the batteries. Aye, aye, sir."

"We pull in the outside atmosphere," Van Gelder said, "the whole crew will end up with leukemia and lung cancer."

The messenger dashed aft, and another enlisted man approached Van Gelder, a fire fighter resting between bouts. Van Gelder flipped up his visor. Beneath his mask the crewman's eyes were watering and his nostrils dripped black phlegm. Both men braced themselves as the vessel rolled once more. The seas were dying down somewhat, but the inside air was getting much too hot.

"Sir," the crewman said, "why don't we just dive? At least we'd get below these waves."

"We'd never get back up again," Van Gelder said. "We're all out of high-pressure air and hydrazine."

A crewman brought Van Gelder a Nomex suit and he quickly dressed. He finished debriefing the senior chief on his manpower dispositions and fire-fighting tactics just as the messenger and two other men arrived, lugging the bulky steam suits. The messenger helped Van Gelder put his on over all his other gear.

"Sir," the young man shouted between breaths, "the engineer told me to remind you. Xenon's building up in the reactor core. It's been too long now since the scram. If we don't restart soon, we won't be able to for hours."

"Yes," Van Gelder said, "I know." The iodine 135 from the uranium fission was breaking down to xenon, which had a huge cross section for thermal neutron capture. With their pre-owned ex-Russian-SSBN core, the xenon

135 would poison the chain reaction until it in turn decayed, making it dangerous to regain criticality in a hurry. Van Gelder knew that was one of the things that went wrong at Chernobyl.

"All right," Van Gelder said. "Tell Engineering and the captain we understand. Ask them to hold off as long as possible."

"You understand, hold off as long as possible, aye aye, sir."

The messenger lowered the big steam suit hood over Van Gelder's head. Van Gelder peered out through the heat-resistant window. The chief fire fighter and a leading seaman finished donning theirs. They looked like men from space, garbed in the silvery reflective costumes.

Van Gelder found it hard now just to walk. With all the insulation and the built-in cooling system, each suit weighed forty kilos. The messenger and his companions checked that the suits were properly sealed, then ran aft. The others signaled they were ready.

"Let's go," Van Gelder shouted through his hood.

Using his thick gauntlets, he gripped the nozzle. His partners backed him up, shouldering the uncharged hose. Another hose team wearing simple Nomex—seeming now so vulnerable in comparison—started spraying them with water. Van Gelder moved into position.

For the first time he was close enough to see into the room. In infrared he watched the huge fans and motors, piping, ducting, cables, all sheathed in leaping flame. The steel of the bulkheads, the deck, the overhead were warped and bulging—even through his protective gear the heat drove him to the floor. He led the others forward, crawling on their bellies, sloshing through the filmy foam.

"Left!" Van Gelder shouted. "Let's go left! That near corner!"

From there he saw a mass of aluminum ducting actually on fire, fallen from the overhead, piled against the back of the room, twisted and distorted. The burning sheet metal was bright white in his visors.

"There! There!" he yelled. "That's the hottest point!"

Bracing himself on all fours, Van Gelder jerked back the nozzle actuator. The high-velocity water stream fought him viciously. Behind him the other men gave their support. They crawled farther into the room.

Van Gelder drenched the ducting, over and over, working his hose stream back and forth. Then he started at one end, pouring and pouring the water, until the flaming ducting in that spot died down. He manhandled the stream along, pushing the flames backward, forcing them toward the far bulkhead, denying them their metal fuel. Steam hissed so loudly he could hear it even through his hood and helmet and his respirator mask. Boiling water sprayed back at his face. He flinched instinctively, then drew courage as his steam suit did its job. He advanced another meter.

The water roared and roared and so did the fire. Gradually Van Gelder's arms grew sore, his back ached badly, but still he aimed his hose at the relentless flames. He inched farther into the room, feeling the radiant heat of a big electric motor casing close to his right thigh, its insulation and lubrication totally involved. In his peripheral vision, past the edges of his visor, he saw flames leaping toward him, yellow and vicious red. He watched their tendrils bathe his thigh, feeling a gentle warmth there, a surreal caress.

The senior chief gestured with his hands to urge Van Gelder onward. Van Gelder's digitized goggles told him the same thing as his eyes: the burning motor was relatively cool compared to the burning aluminum. The motor fire would have to wait.

Van Gelder shifted his hose stream yet again, aiming at the center of the aluminum, and the force of the water burst the duct's remains apart. Immediately the temperature grew less, and Van Gelder extinguished the fragments one by one.

"Switch to foam now," the chief shouted. "There's too much oil and grease!"

Van Gelder handed off the straight-stream nozzle, then took the foam applicator attached to another line. Two freshwater hose teams assumed position in the door, one to cool Van Gelder's group and protect their path of egress, the other to drench both overhead and burning equipment to help put out the fire. Working from the back of the room slowly toward the front, Van Gelder applied the penetrating detergent-soapy foam. It wasn't recommended for use on electrical equipment—it ruined what it touched—but by now the fan room was a total loss.

Van Gelder aimed the applicator into every nook and cranny, blanketing the burning apparatus, cutting off the conflagration's air. His faceplate now was stained with yellow soot. Inside his gear he dripped with sweat, and his breath came fast and ragged.

After what seemed endless minutes of brutal toil Van Gelder realized the teams were working at cross-purposes. "The water from the doorway crews is forcing back my foam!"

The chief ordered the other teams to change their tactics. One nozzleman concentrated on wetting Van Gelder's line so it wouldn't burn right through. The other aimed at the overhead to cool the superheated gases. But that just meant less water on the fire, making Van Gelder's job much harder. He started feeling dizzy, and his mouth was very dry.

"Look out!" the chief shouted, pulling Van Gelder to the side. In slow motion a big fan housing toppled to the deck. Immediately more flames reared up as the housing's innards broke wide open. Unburned aluminum threatened to reignite. Van Gelder's team was losing ground.

"Now!" Van Gelder shouted, and he stood up, bending low. His partners saw his intent and joined him, and they all rushed in among the flames, pouring forth their foam.

Shimmering sheets of ignited gases danced and beckoned all around, leaping up from crinkling debris that dwindled as Van Gelder watched. Plastic melted, dripping, running, and bubbling, then disappeared. Jagged wires wilted, twisted, sagged. Compressors and air circulators slumped within their mountings, cracking and distorting from heat stress and failed supports. Corkscrewed pipes and cable fragments hung down from the overhead, swaying weirdly in the thermal drafts. Air filters quickly carbonized, and their remnants then collapsed.

More soot began to build up on Van Gelder's faceplate, now brownish black, making it almost impossible to see. Everywhere equipment was consumed and everywhere he sprayed.

Once more Van Gelder's foam stopped for a moment, turning to plain water, then resumed as someone changed the foam concentrate cans. Onward Van Gelder worked, blind to his companions, hypnotized by the inferno, battling with it endlessly, all sense of past and future gone.

Another quick pause in the foam, another can, then all at once the heart went out of the blaze. Piles of rubble still burned here and there and cremated wreckage smoked and steamed, but the contest had been won.

Van Gelder handed off the applicator, not even seeing who took it, and he staggered from the fan room. A crewman played some water on the outside of his suit.

The senior chief followed. "We did it, sir! We saved the ship!"

Van Gelder tried to smile, but his parched lips cracked. He simply nodded.

The chief leaned closer. "We'll send more men to the

bilge space now, to start hosing down the buses. We'll have to draw from the reactor's secondary coolant loop main holding tank, but distilled water's a decent insulator."

"Good," Van Gelder said. "I'll tell the captain we can do a restart soon."

"We'll lay some dams to keep this foam from spreading, sir, then leave what's there in place. It'll protect against a flare-up, and we can clean the mess in a few more hours."

Van Gelder felt a dreadful weariness set in. He trudged aft along the passageway, leaving the damage control parties to their work. At a safe distance from the remnants of the fire he pulled off his steam suit hood, just as the cooling system's battery ran down.

He borrowed the microphone from a talker in the next compartment, then lifted his breather mask long enough to report to the captain. He refastened the mask, but lingering fumes had gotten in. They made him choke and cough. He still felt awfully hot but for some reason couldn't sweat. As a medical corpsman approached, obviously concerned, Van Gelder sagged against the bulkhead and slowly slid down to the deck. He wanted nothing more than a nice cold glass of water and a breath of natural air. The corpsman bent over to say something, but Van Gelder only heard a rushing in his ears as he passed out.

CHAPTER 8

ABOARD *CHALLENGER*

Jeffrey knocked on the CO's state-room door. The clean uniform he'd put on after a thorough decontamination washdown was already stained with sweat and grease from his walk-around inspection of the boat.

"Come in, XO," Captain Wilson called.

Jeffrey wondered how the CO always knew when it was him. "Sir," he said after entering, "I have the after-action battle damage overview report."

Wilson looked up from his little fold-down desk, covered with files and naval publications. His laptop was open too, a map of Africa on the screen. Enemy territory was in red, Allied-controlled in blue, the vast cruise-missile-dominated no-man's-land in amber.

"Let's hear it," Wilson said.

"Aside from the three fatalities, sir, personnel injuries were light and the rem exposures are pretty trivial."

"Good. What about equipment casualties?"

"Sir, the foreplanes are inoperative."

"Not too serious," Wilson said. "We can manage depth-keeping with the afterplanes at anything over dead-slow speed."

Jeffrey nodded. "Sonar's finished with an autocheck. Sessions says the wide-aperture array's fine after all.

That enemy torpedo's pinging must have picked up the stators at the back end of our pump-jet."

"I'm impressed," Wilson said. "It's not easy getting echoes off the edges of those blades."

"Agreed, Captain. The other side's technology outdoes ours in some respects."

"Their signal processing algorithms are supposed to be the best. Those math guys at Frankfurt scared me even before the war."

"Our bow dome took a beating, sir," Jeffrey said. "Sessions says the cover's cracked and dimpled."

"Not just at the tip?"

Jeffrey shook his head.

"So we're getting additional flow noise?" Wilson said.

"Yes, sir. Any chance we can stop back at the tender? For emergency repairs?"

"Out of the question, XO. We've got an awfully tight window to bring this SEAL mission off, and we're behind schedule already. Not to mention we're trying to play dead."

"Understood, Captain. . . . About the torpedo room . . . we have to load the weapons manually, and we're down to just four tubes."

"The other outer doors won't open?"

"No, sir. All the port-side ones were belled in badly."

"The starboard ones are working?"

"The blast was asymmetric, Captain. At fine scales of reference they always are. . . . It's a dry-dock job."

"Mmph." Wilson's tone was sour. "I'm not happy at our weapons expenditure."

"The ones we lost to damage?" Jeffrey said.

"The nuclear torpedoes. Those things are scarce. There're tons of fissile metal in the arsenals of democracy, just not enough goddamn delivery systems to go around."

"We still have four, sir."

"We've barely started our patrol. We wasted two just stopping a pair of diesel boats."

"Did we have a choice, Captain?"

"No. That's what bothers me. The Axis claims the initiative too often, in big things and in small. This is no way to fight a war."

"It's not *that* bad, sir, is it? Look at the latest fleet action in this theater, off Madagascar and the African coast."

"Sure, we control the Comoro Islands for now," Wilson said, "what's left of 'em, so the German and Boer armies won't be linking up by the east coast route any time soon, but at what price? Ten thousand KIAs, half of them on *Ranger*."

"Sir, D Day cost twenty thousand Allied casualties."

"We're a hell of a long way from another D Day, XO, in Africa let alone in Europe. The other side claims this one as a victory themselves."

"That's ridiculous," Jeffrey said.

"Not to some nonaligned countries it's not. They're better at propaganda than us, this Berlin-Boer Axis. They know many developing nations are secretly glad to have them break the back of American unipolarism. And since they intimidated the Russians into a false neutrality, they're still getting arms shipments courtesy of Moscow across the safe land bridge of eastern Europe."

"I know," Jeffrey said. "It's like back in the 1920s, sir, the Wehrmacht in bed with the Soviet Union, even long before Hitler."

"The deutsche mark is stronger than the dollar," Wilson said, "and entire continents are waiting to choose sides. So fine, the Germans didn't get to grab any of France's H-bomb stocks. But a few Hiroshima-sized cruise missiles aimed at London and New York are proving a pretty equal deterrent against our megaton-sized MIRVs. . . . And lately there've been rumors the

Germans are working up a Mach 8 liquid-H_2-powered cruise missile. A Mach 8 ground hugger's basically unstoppable."

"I didn't realize things were that serious, Captain."

"And keep it to yourself. Maybe I'm just bellyaching. . . . Miss Reebeck told me you know you're going with her."

"Yes, sir," Jeffrey said. "What's going on?"

"It's a nuclear demolition raid against a Boer biological weapons lab. She'll cover that part at the briefing. Since the mission's in a populated area, with hostage camps and innocent minority civilians, as my XO you're *it*. The independent command authority, on site, required for lower formations to use atomic munitions on land."

"So I'm supposed to be the sober head," Jeffrey said, "along for the ride to validate the rules of engagement in real time, since SEALs do so love blowing up things. . . . How long do we have to prepare?"

"The time it takes to sneak over there and get in position. Five days, roughly."

"Jesus, sir."

"Look, I understand your feelings. But I can't send the other officers, I need them here. *You're* my backup, my alter ego on policy and doctrine."

"And I'm expendable."

Wilson sighed. "Jeffrey, I was an XO too. You need to be there. These guys can't just phone home for instructions like in Desert Storm. The enemy homeland has continual surveillance for clandestine comms, *extremely* sophisticated defensive signal intelligence and jamming."

"I'm sorry, sir. I must sound unprofessional."

"Any other questions?"

"Why is Ilse Reebeck going?"

"She knows the territory, and her expertise will be of use."

"How do we know we can trust her, sir? She's one of *them*."

Wilson tossed Jeffrey an unlabeled videocassette.

"What's this, sir?"

"Since the war broke out six months ago, the Axis have been staging executions of their own dissenters. Her brother's part of the third batch in, next to his girlfriend. They made them take their clothes off first. Play it on your state-room VCR."

"No thanks, Captain." Jeffrey tried to hand it back.

"No, I insist. It's in color, with dramatic close-ups while they hang. Good camera work, anatomically explicit."

Jeffrey blanched.

Wilson looked right at him. "We can't have anyone going to Durban with the slightest doubts. The outcome's too important."

Jeffrey inhaled deeply, then let it out.

"Watch the tape *now*," Wilson said, "before the briefing."

"I will, Captain."

"Just remember, you and the SEALs at least are legitimate combatants under international law."

"You mean that if we're captured we're POWs?"

"Miss Reebeck, her they'll string up by her neck from the nearest tree or lamppost . . . after the troopies are done with her."

Jeffrey swallowed, feeling angry and protective . . . and manipulated.

"Anyway," Wilson said, "ask COB to see the crew gets fed. I know we've got repairs to do, but work with him on mandatory rest breaks for all hands."

"Aye aye, Captain."

"That applies to you as well. How long have you been up?"

Jeffrey eyed his wristwatch, a waterproof old Rolex that he'd blooded in Iraq. "Thirty-two hours."

"Get some sleep, after the briefing."

"Yes, sir."

"Ask the mess management chief to have lunch ready in the wardroom at thirteen hundred local. Department heads, the SEAL team leader, Sonar, and our guests. You make the invitations."

"Yes, sir."

"Have him lay on something special. We just survived *Challenger*'s first real taste of battle."

"I forgot how hungry you get after combat, Captain. It isn't like the drills."

"We'll hold a memorial service for the three dead crewmen in the morning." Wilson paused. "Morning, mourning. Sorry for that awful pun."

"It's macabre having them in the freezer, sir."

"Life goes on, Mr. Fuller. Someday you might just have my job. Then you'll understand."

Jeffrey realized now the captain's eyes were red, and he sounded slightly nasal.

"I'll talk to COB about the arrangements," Wilson said, "so add that to your Plan of the Day."

Jeffrey nodded, then moved toward the door.

"Oh," Wilson called after him. "And, XO." Wilson gestured toward the head that connected their two state-rooms, the boat's executive john. "You're awfully odorous. Take another shower, please."

Ilse wiped her lips with a linen napkin as the steward cleared the china. The sonar officer, young Sessions, turned off the Mozart on the stereo.

"So, Miss Reebeck," the CO said, "what's your impression of our table?"

"Very nice, Captain Wilson. I've always heard that navies serve the finest food."

"There was nothing fresh or frozen at the tender," Jeffrey said. "*Frank Cable*'s priorities don't cover haute cuisine, Miss Reebeck."

"Everything was good, Commander, even if it came from tins and boxes. . . . And I wish you'd call me Ilse."

"Good," Wilson said before Jeffrey could respond. "Let's all be on a first-name basis. You can call me Captain." The others laughed politely, and Ilse sensed they *liked* knowing their exact place in the hierarchy.

The steward came around and filled everybody's coffee cup. He brought tea for Commodore Morse, who tugged idly at his beard.

"Sorry our navy's dry," Jeffrey said.

"Let's hope for a speedy passage," Morse said.

"Hear, hear," Wilson said. The others chuckled, more heartily this time. Ilse tried to imagine what it was like to spend long weeks at sea without even a beer. I guess I'll find out soon, she told herself. She didn't smoke, but she'd seen it was permitted in certain areas. Right now the smoking lamp was out—men were servicing the weapons.

The steward brought a silver tray of fresh-baked cookies, chocolate chip. Ilse *loved* chocolate chip cookies. She'd expected to crash emotionally after the battle, but instead she still felt high. This dessert would be the perfect capstone to her first half-day of war.

The smell of the warm chocolate filled the air. Wilson passed the tray around, not taking one himself. He cleared his throat.

"Again, gentlemen, congratulations on a well-done job so far. Please pass that to your departments." The men all murmured thanks.

"As some of you have heard, we'll hold a memorial service tomorrow. But I see no better way to honor our deceased comrades than dedicating our efforts going forward in their honor."

There were murmurs of assent.

"I do not say that lightly," Wilson said. "Our next task,

if we succeed, will strike a crucial blow for freedom, neutralize a very dangerous threat. Ilse, maybe you should give your summary now."

Ilse sat up straighter. She'd noticed the captain and the others had grown more formal in their manner. Navy rituals, she told herself. Through all the easy lunchtime chitchat between the men, she'd felt like an invader in a very private world. Turbine-blade erosion rates, radiological spill drill reaction times, speeding up the new guys' progress on their quals.

I want to be a part of what they're doing, Ilse told herself. I want to know my efforts matter here, that they accept me. She tried to make her voice sound deep and confident.

"Our objective is to destroy a Boer bioweapons lab, at Umhlanga Rocks."

"That's in Durban?" Jeffrey said.

"Kind of, sir," said Lieutenant Shajo Clayton, the SEAL team leader. "It's ten miles north of the downtown area, but still well inside the city's main defensive zone."

"So it's germ warfare," Jeffrey said. "Like Saddam again. What is it this time, anthrax? Pneumonic plague? Botulinum toxin?"

"Not germs or viruses, Commander," Ilse said. "Archaea."

"The stuff that lives in hot vents? Those black smokers on the ocean floor?"

"Yes," Ilse said. "Primordial microbes. A new domain, technically. They're usually benign. They have industrial applications."

"Like cleaning oil spills, right?" Jeffrey said.

Ilse nodded. "But South Africa has done genetic engineering, with help from German scientists. We think they've made a killer strain, one that seeks out humans."

"How do we know this?" Jeffrey said.

"They didn't tell me everything," Ilse said. "Others like myself, who got out and know something, gave hints. Satellite imagery too, of bunkers being built in isolated areas, next to fenced-in trailer parks of captured U.S. tourists, bunkers meant for keeping something *in*. Suspicious movements of black children where we're going."

"Huh?"

"The Natal Sharks Board," Ilse said, "on a hilltop overlooking the shore at Umhlanga Rocks, did oceanographic research for many years before the war. They had daily shark dissections for school kids."

"Like a science museum?" Jeffrey said.

"They used sharks caught and killed in the big nets that protect the swimming beaches. That stopped with the war, but then it started up again. Black youngsters, the same group every day, are bussed in and out, except now and then a kid goes in and we don't see him come out."

"Human experiments?"

"Your government thinks so," Ilse said. "The real clincher is the air filtration. The basement at the Sharks Board has a positive-pressure NBC system. That's strange enough, for what should be a low-priority installation. Somehow your NSA learned half the filter banks run backward. The air goes through the micron-level catchments coming *out* of the facility."

"So there's a negative-pressure inner sanctum," Jeffrey said. "Probably a spy bird caught the infrared gradient of the air exhaust going the wrong way, on an especially hot or cold clear night."

Ilse nodded. "The school kids *might* be circumstantial, but this is a clear-cut signature of a biosafety level four containment."

"Not level three?" Jeffrey said.

"No," Ilse said, "the output volume's much too great. It's a whole lab, not just suction hoods."

"What does this stuff do to you?" Jeffrey said.

"The species they've been using digests sulfur."

"So?"

"Sulfur's in acetylcholine, the human body's neurotransmitter. It's also found in cystine, a key amino acid. Disulfide bonds in cystine form a polypeptide, collagen, the basic building block for our connective tissues."

"So?"

Ilse wiped a loose strand of hair back from her forehead, then looked right at Jeffrey. "If something eats your sulfur, your brain stops working and your muscles turn to goo."

Jeffrey frowned. "How do we defend against it?"

"Archaea's such a simple life-form our immune systems don't respond, so no vaccination's possible. A hybrid could be designed to spread through water, soil, the air, and through any intermediate host or carcass, making it appallingly contagious in a room-temperature nitrogen-oxygen environment."

"Antibiotics?" Jeffrey said.

"Archaea are *not* bacteria, which lack internal organelles, and they have a different cell wall chemistry, so once they're in your body, drugs won't work. Tetracycline helps conserve the collagen—that's one of its side effects—but not enough to save you."

"And they must think a sterilizing autoclave's some kind of health spa," Jeffrey said.

"That's right," Ilse said, "they're so-called extremophiles. Archaea thrive at temperatures of a thousand Fahrenheit, they're found at pressures of a thousand atmospheres or more, they can be resistant to alkalis like bleach, and they simply *love* acid, so there's no good way to decontaminate."

Lieutenant Clayton leaned forward. Like Captain Wilson, he was black—African American, Ilse reminded herself. Even through his uniform she could see he had a perfect swimmer's body. He looked almost thirty, more mature than Lieutenant Sessions somehow, must be more time in grade. To Ilse this reemphasized the importance of the mission—a lieutenant in the navy equaled a captain in the army.

"We have to stop this at the source," Clayton said. "There's evidence they'll soon disperse the R&D, then go into mass production. They use blackout curtains at the lab, of course, and carpooling to save gas, but we can still tell that the research staff's been working very late, like they're on the verge of a breakthrough. There's just one thing we know will do the job. An atomic demolition."

"You're taking in the warhead from one of our Mark 88s?" Jeffrey said. "You didn't bring your own—I'd have seen the guards and paperwork."

"We're getting a bit ahead of ourselves now," Wilson said. He looked at his watch, then asked the steward to send a messenger to fetch COB and the navigator.

"The navigator must be running late," Jeffrey said, "preparing his part of the briefing."

Wilson nodded. He poured himself another cup of coffee, then sat back. Ilse saw this was some kind of signal. People relaxed again.

"This infiltration should be stimulating," Jeffrey said, reaching for a cookie. "The facilities around Durban are virtually impregnable."

"That's where we like to be," Clayton said.

"We're looking at interlocking arcs of fire," Jeffrey said. "Nuclear-tipped cruise missiles, supersonic, atop the skyscrapers downtown and on the bluff outside the bay. More launch points on the escarpments up and down the coast, *and* on the top floors of those big resort hotels, the ones they haven't knocked down to make beach landing obstacles. Constant ASW patrols, using every type of sensor. And minefields, channeled into local SOSUS bottom-listening nets."

Captain Wilson nodded. "Then there's the bigger picture, the Axis hostage strategy. Using innocent people as their shield, which makes it hard for us to act decisively at every level everywhere. They play to Third World fence-sitters—that if we nuke 'em, it's our fault."

"This two-phase coup was brilliant," Shajo Clayton said. "We fell for it at every step."

"South African reactionaries stage a take-over," Jeffrey said. "They claim they're *liberating* the country, for God's sake, from malicious outside interference. They declare martial law, then put down the inevitable riots with modern nonlethal weapons. They say it's the only way to stop the social chaos—crime, terrorism, and AIDS—all forced on them by ending their apartheid, a system they claim worked."

"They fortify the Prince Edward Islands," Clayton said, "their own territory, halfway between Cape Town and Antarctica. The U.N. orders trade embargoes, enforced by a blockade. In retaliation the Boers close the Horn of Africa to what they call hostile shipping. The busiest maritime choke point in the world."

"They sink some American and British merchant ships," Jeffrey said, "using high-explosive rounds. So NATO mobilizes, like in the Gulf War and with Yugoslavia. Coalition forces drain from Europe and put to sea, where all those tanks and troops are vulnerable as hell."

"But due to pacifist demonstrations, the German deployment lags," Clayton said. "Except Namibia, the colony they lost in World War I, just to South Africa's northwest. *There* they go in first and meet no Boer opposition."

"Then there's the Berlin Putsch," Jeffrey said. "And then they launch the European ground war. Nuking Poland's how they got the French to cave."

"Restoring the kaiser," Wilson said. "Finishing the

work of Bismarck. Giving all of Europe the unity it needs, without all the disorder. . . . A new German reawakening, *my ass*."

"But the U.S. and U.K. and Germany were big financial allies," Ilse said.

"Ilse," Commodore Morse broke in, "in 1914 the U.K. and Germany were each other's foremost trading partners. That didn't stop the slaughter then."

"It was a dangerous myth," Jeffrey said, "to think Germany needed another recession to go on the warpath again. In 1914 they were very prosperous, and that gave them *ideas*."

Morse nodded. "The underlying enmities go back a century or more."

"That's true," Ilse said. "The old-line Boers *hate* the British, starting when you took Cape Town in 1795. Shoving them aside, plundering their natural resources, building concentration camps when they resisted. They'll fight you very hard, like in the old days. They think God's on their side."

The conversation paused. Ilse glanced at the oil painting hanging on the wardroom bulkhead, the corvette HMS *Challenger* in full sail, the odd fittings at her stern for the special trawls and dredges. Eighteen seventy-two, Ilse told herself, the same year that the Franco-Prussian War was winding down. The same time as the diamond rush in Kimberley was booming, and the gold rush in Transvaal—ten years before the first of *those* two Anglo-Boer wars.

"While we're waiting for the others," Jeffrey said, "let's take a rest room break."

CHAPTER 9

"Thanks for letting me go first," Ilse said after everyone got back. "I don't mean to be an inconvenience."

"We do have women riders now and then," Jeffrey said. "Contractor representatives, scientists, journalists . . . and congresswomen of course."

"Crew members?"

"Maybe someday." Jeffrey shrugged.

The navigator, Lieutenant Monaghan, arrived. COB showed up a moment later. COB had to lean against the sideboard—the bench seats around the wardroom table were completely full. The steward left and closed the door into the little pantry.

"Back to work," Clayton said with relish. At the slightest movement of his fingers, Ilse noticed, muscles rippled on his arms.

"Where are all your men?" she said while Monaghan wired his laptop to the flat-screen wardroom monitor.

"Squashed in a compartment forward," Clayton said. "You'll meet them soon. Right now they're sharpening their combat knives, holding high-stakes one-arm push-up contests, and practicing garroting one another."

"We can carry up to fifty SEALs," Jeffrey said, "in the torpedo room, but for that we need to off-load weapons."

Clayton smiled ferally. "One boat team's enough for what we have to do." Then he added, *"Een boot groep is genoeg voor wat wij mooten doe,"* which was the same in Afrikaans.

"You're fluent," Ilse said, surprised but then delighted.

"I practice all the time," Clayton said, switching back to English. "I also speak six native tongues from that part of the world."

"I missed something," COB said. "The CO told me we're hitting a bioweapons plant. Miss Reebeck, what's *your* role?"

"My job's to quickly spot the key lab notes and records, so we can bring them out, and to eyeball their progress and approach."

"You're an expert in the subject?" COB said.

"That's how I got my Ph.D., *peaceful* archaea applications, industrial uses of their enzymes, hyperthermozymes, as catalysts for chemical reactions."

"Are you grabbing any samples?" COB said.

"That's much too dangerous," Wilson said.

"To find some way to fight it," Ilse said, "we need their recipe, the genetic code and how they engineered it. We want the data, not the bug."

"Once weaponized," Clayton said, "there'd be no lower limit to *this* stuff's mass and bulk, unlike a briefcase atom bomb. No corresponding close-range gamma ray signature either, to be picked up at border crossings or shipping nodes. You could transport archaea dried—an aerosol can, a water-soluble lipstick, almost anything would do, and sniffer K-9s would be useless. Chemical weapons and biotoxins don't reproduce. Archaea does."

"And with bio warfare," Jeffrey said, "in place of Axis H-bombs, say, our infrastructure's left intact across the battle space or continental U.S. . . . Plunder, and *Lebensraum*—living room."

Sessions raised his hand. "I have a stupid question. Once it's been let loose, what stops this thing from wiping out the world? You know, including all the Germans and the Boers?"

"Archaea can multiply by budding like amoeba," Ilse said, "or sexually. We expect the killer strain's design builds in a generational life-span, after which the colony dies out. These days that's nothing special, from research on aging and recombinant DNA."

"What about this A-bomb we'll be using?" Jeffrey said.

"We'll destroy the lab by setting off the warhead in an enemy missile," Clayton said. "There's one dug in right there next to the Sharks Board. It'll look just like an accident, or sabotage within. The blast itself will hide our tracks. Three kilotons, we think."

"The zone of total sterilization," Ilse said, "the fireball and just beyond, would extend about a thousand feet across."

Jeffrey inhaled deeply. "Okay. And that's why you need a Boer bomb. A discrepant fallout isotope mix would show we'd brought in ours. . . . But I thought they couldn't go off by mistake—the safety interlocks and codes."

"We only need the physics package," Clayton said.

"You're bringing detonator gear," Jeffrey said. Ilse saw him start to grin as comprehension dawned.

"Cool, huh?" Clayton said. "That's how we'll fire the krytron switches, bypass their arming hardware altogether. They use a lightweight uranium implosion design now, by the way, well beyond South Africa's crude gun bombs in the eighties. With new dual-laser refinement methods, U-235's a lot easier to work with than plutonium. . . . I'm an expert in nuclear demolitions."

"If all this works," Wilson said, "there'll be a crucial bonus for us. The Boer regime will start a witch-hunt."

"*Another* witch-hunt, Captain?" Jeffrey said.

"Public hangings get habit-forming," Clayton said. "We saw that with the Nazis toward the end."

"The Joint Chiefs," Wilson said, "hope the Boers'll think someone on the inside set off the bomb long-distance, through their automated command and control net. They'll purge their senior systems staff, probably, even if they only *think* there might have been some treason."

"Their systems group has been too tight," Jeffrey said.

Wilson nodded. "But we have moles, I've been informed, less senior people waiting in the wings. Freedom fighters like Ilse, ready to move up."

"That might give us a way in, in the future," Clayton said. "Information warfare at its best."

"A back door to a landing," Jeffrey said, "airborne and on the coast."

"This raid's a big first step to that," Wilson said. "You all can see how critical this is. We absolutely have to get it right."

"We're good to go," Clayton said. "Commander Fuller, we'll work up with you and Ilse while *Challenger* makes transit. We have a few new tricks since you were with the teams."

"I can just imagine," Jeffrey said.

Wilson turned to Monaghan. "Last part of the briefing. Navigator, you're on."

Lieutenant Monaghan tapped some keys. A map of southern Africa came on the screen.

"I'll start with the basics for clarity. Durban's a major port, fronting the Indian Ocean. It can handle large oil tankers, up to eight hundred feet. Bigger ones moor outside and pump their cargo through a floating terminal southwest of the entrance channel."

"The harbor's artificial, isn't it?" Jeffrey said.

"The Bay of Natal," Monaghan said, "nestled behind a bluff along a promontory, was dredged years ago. Now the bluff, two hundred and fifty feet high, acts as a breakwater to south and east. Durban's a major city, an important commercial center."

"And it's their leading submarine base," Jeffrey said.

"That's correct," Monaghan said. "Back under the *old* Union, First Apartheid, their navy serviced diesel boats at piers on Salisbury Island, inside the port. That continued with the Republic, the post-racist democracy regime."

"With all the troubles of the last few years," Jeffrey said, "like India and Pakistan, North Korea and Japan, they dug into the bluff, then reinforced it from below with layered composite armor, to stop ground-penetrator rounds."

"That's where their subs go now," Sessions said.

"Yup," Jeffrey said. "Good cover, even from tactical atomic weapons. A little Cheyenne Mountain."

"The advantage of Durban to the South Africans," Monaghan said, "is the harbor mouth is very narrow, only two hundred and fifty yards from pier to breakwater, and the continental shelf there drops off quickly. The thirty-fathom curve is barely a mile offshore. Submarines can stay deep coming in or out, even go into the bluff submerged, thanks to the latest excavations."

"The iron oxide they keep sprinkling stops our long-range LIDAR scans," Jeffrey said. "Rust. Now it's a weapon."

"It causes phytoplankton blooms," Ilse said. "The water's surface transparency drops to almost zero."

Monaghan called up another map, the Durban coast.

"Another problem is the winds, which affect the distribution of the fallout. The shoreline here for many miles is straight, except for minor bays and headlands, and runs along a bearing north-northeast. Ninety percent of the time the wind blows up or down the coast; the rest, it usually blows inland."

"That whole coastline's heavily populated," Commodore Morse said.

"That's true," Ilse said. "It was a big resort attraction before the war, with perfect beaches and lots of coral reefs. Swimming and surfing, diving, golf, nature preserves, everything."

"Sounds like Hawaii," Jeffrey said.

"Yes," Ilse said, "except there's even more to do. Umhlanga Rocks was part of that. Tourism was a growth industry for us."

"It might someday be again," Morse said. "If . . ."

Monaghan went on. "Inland lie more suburbs of Durban, with millions of black South Africans and close to a million minorities of Indian descent. Fallout from a nuclear blast, of any size, is a serious concern."

"That's why the weather factor's crucial," Wilson said. "We have a window coming up in which the winds will blow offshore, because a major storm is on the way. There was a big convoy-versus-wolf-pack battle two days ago, with heavy use of atomic warheads by both sides. That created a cyclonic depression in the South Atlantic Ocean, in an area that's almost always calm."

"The winds and lofted moisture from the fireballs got things started," Monaghan said. "They formed the vortex, one that's especially intense. The result was a true man-made hurricane, as the sun pumped in more energy. Now it's drifting east across South Africa."

"Mind-boggling," Jeffrey said.

"Fortunately," Monaghan said, "most of the fallout came down at sea. Our arrival at Durban is timed for the few hours when this disturbance passes through, blowing itself out. Heavy precipitation is expected then, with—most importantly—winds to south or east."

"And built-up ground moisture," Clayton said, "plus rain and occluded skies. All of which should help limit collateral damage outside the lab itself."

"There's just one thing, though," Jeffrey said. "*They'll*

know about the weather too. They might be on alert, all up and down the coast."

"We're counting on that," Clayton said. "Stricter curfew means less chance of witnesses, and more of the sentries will be outside where we can get to them. Few bystanders if any in line of sight of the thermal pulse, and their precautions against the storm should hold down blast-wind drag force injuries."

Captain Wilson made eye contact around the room. "The team goes in at night four days from now."

"If we make top quiet speed to start with," Monaghan said, "then slow as we draw near, we'll *just* be in position to lock out the SEALs on time."

"We'll need to get some updates," Jeffrey said, "particularly on the weather."

Wilson shook his head. "Not if that would compromise our hard-won stealth. If we're lucky, the Axis think we're dead, killed by those 212 boats."

"But wouldn't there be wreckage on the surface?" Ilse said.

"All that floated up from *Thresher* was a rubber glove," Jeffrey said.

"What about your own headquarters?" Ilse said. "Won't they be worried?"

Jeffrey smiled. "They'll know we're okay when they see our flaming datum, the mushroom cloud at Umhlanga Rocks."

CHAPTER 10

ABOARD *VOORTREKKER*

Something jarred Van Gelder wide-awake. He tried to move but couldn't. He saw he was restrained in bed, on oxygen and packed in ice. He squinted but his vision was too blurred, and it made his splitting headache worse. He thought this was his cabin, on *Voortrekker*. His mouth was dry. He felt so hot. There was an intravenous in each arm.

He sensed more than heard the next concussion. It shook his bones and made an ice bag fall onto the deck. Someone entered.

"Just stay like this, please, sir," the sweating first-aid corpsman said.

Van Gelder tried to speak. It sounded like a croak. The corpsman took a washcloth from a bucket of cold water, then squeezed it out to drip some on Van Gelder's lips and tongue, holding the oxygen mask aside for just a moment.

"How . . . ?"

"Heatstroke, sir. A nasty case. You've been out for almost two hours."

Van Gelder tried to rise but felt awfully nauseous.

The corpsman gently pressed him back. "Your temperature was forty-two Celsius."

Van Gelder frowned. Now he remembered everything. He could have died.

"Good thing you were healthy, sir. . . . You sure were a sight, though, lying in the passageway. First thing we did was put a fire hose down your suit. Cooled you off real good that way." The corpsman laughed.

Another hard shock hit.

"We're being depth-charged, sir. Big atomic ones."

Another blast, but this one was different: a growing roar that built to a crescendo, then died out.

Van Gelder cleared his throat. "That one was far away," he whispered. "The multipath . . . the multipath effect."

The corpsman nodded as he took Van Gelder's pulse. "Just like Mozambique Channel, sir. Someone told me how that works, with distant contacts. I forget exactly what he said."

"The longest ray paths curve down through the deepest water. The sound speed's higher there, from the added pressure, so they reach us sooner, but with more attenuation loss." Good, Van Gelder told himself, my brain's okay. He knew severe heatstroke sometimes caused permanent dysfunction.

Another roar, heard more than felt this time. Like the others, it seemed to come from everywhere outside the hull at once. Surface and bottom reflections echoed eerily, and bubble-rebound shock waves thumped.

"They don't know where we are," the corpsman said, checking Van Gelder's blood pressure. "Fast-movers, worst thing for ASW. Those jets are shooting blind."

"What's our course?"

"Once we got propulsion and the sternplanes back, the captain headed west, right at them, but at modest speed, he said."

Van Gelder smiled. "The planes would bomb a circle, thinking that we'd run."

"They dropped one where we dived too, in case we just lay doggo. That must have been what woke you." The corpsman coughed. "The air's still pretty foul." He undid the BP cuff.

Another roar, not as loud, and then the reverb.

"Farther off," Van Gelder said.

"Or a smaller warhead?"

"No, the impulse was too extended. We'd need Sonar to tell the bearing."

The corpsman nodded. "Our ears can't sense direction underwater very well. Sound moves too fast. A safety diver told me that one time." He put a disposable thermometer in Van Gelder's mouth, then changed the ice bags. "Captain said that once these jets are gone, we'll go back to Durban. Resupply, more mines and missiles, and a quick turn in the dry dock. . . . And crew replacements, too."

Van Gelder turned his head to face the corpsman. "How bad were our losses?" He tried not to chew on the thermometer, a flimsy plastic thing.

"Just the three dead that you know about. We were lucky. Plus a dozen badly wounded. Compound fractures, class three concussions, things like that to keep me busy. No one senior. They'll all recover, more or less."

"How long?"

"To get to base?"

Van Gelder nodded, his head back on the pillow. He was feeling weaker now.

"I know, sir, we're all homesick and tired. . . . Horny too." He elbowed Van Gelder gently in the ribs, then read the thermometer. "*Much* better."

There was another distant rumbling, with a crackling overtone.

The corpsman glanced up at the overhead. "Must have hit the ice pack that time, in case we went under there. *Guess again, Tommy.*" He made a rude gesture toward the south.

Van Gelder swallowed, with difficulty. "How, how long?"

"Till you're out of bed? A couple of days."

Van Gelder shook his head, then felt himself begin to drift away.

"Oh. Durban. Sorry, sir." The corpsman's voice was fading, coming from the bottom of an oil drum. "We'll be inside the bluff three days from now. . . . Once we're fixed up some, we go hunting *Challenger*."

Van Gelder jerked awake. "She's been spotted?"

"Easy, sir, easy. . . . At Diego Garcia, eight thousand klicks from here, just a little while ago. On the surface first, then a battle underwater. Two well-spaced detonations, both atomic. Wreckage from our boats, then heavy bubbles farther off and aircraft searching for survivors. Intel in Pretoria thinks she's dead."

"*Challenger* destroyed?"

"The captain won't believe it—says see the beating *we* just took, forget about Pretoria. Says he knows her CO too, they met before the war. He's sure that they're still out there. Somewhere."

ABOARD *CHALLENGER*

When the briefing wrapped up, Jeffrey walked Ilse through a twisting maze of compartments and then up a ladder back to her state-room. Well, make that my *closet,* she told herself. It was barely two meters on a side, and like everywhere else on *Challenger*, the ceiling was very low. Good thing she had Jeffrey as a guide—on her own she'd be utterly lost.

"Three people usually live in here?" she said.

"Junior officers," Jeffrey said. "I've had to shuffle them around. Some are hot-bunking."

"Sharing beds?"

"We call them racks. The youngsters are in different

watch sections. Different shifts. A few of the junior enlisteds hot-rack too, but it isn't very popular. SSN crew size keeps shrinking, thanks to automation, but they keep installing new gear, so we're actually more crowded than ever."

"Um, how big's your crew?"

"One hundred twenty, counting me and the captain. That's down about a dozen from the *Seawolf*s and *Virginia*s, and the 688 (I)s need over one forty. . . . You can put your things in that middle drawer."

The so-called drawer was less than two inches high. "What's this?" Ilse said, lifting the little curtains, pointing to the boxes, secured with nylon strapping, that now filled the top and bottom racks.

"Just what the labels say. Xerox paper, printer toner, pens and pencils, scratch pads."

"*Scratch* pads?" Ilse tried to imagine what 120 *men* might do, left to themselves at sea, without even fish or birds for witnesses. An image of Cape buffalo rubbing their butts on tree stumps came to mind.

"Writing tablets," Jeffrey said. "Our manuals and charts are all on-line, but we still go through a lot of paper."

"Oh," Ilse said. It's like sleeping in a warehouse. She'd noticed that throughout the parts of the boat she'd seen so far, storage cabinets were recessed in every conceivable nook and cranny.

"You're all set for toiletries, and, um, you know, other stuff?"

"Yes, Commander," Ilse said. "The supply officer on *Frank Cable* made me up a package. She was very helpful."

"Yeah. There are things we don't stock on submarines."

Ilse had to look away. He was so coy about it. Men always were.

"There was one other thing," Jeffrey said.

Ilse looked directly at him. "Oh?"

"Laundry."

"That's right." She hadn't thought of that. "My clothes are filthy."

"Did you bring a change?"

"Just what I have on. At Pearl Harbor they made me travel very light. Before I got on the plane they even took my hair dryer."

"Home appliances don't mix well with seawater and steel," Jeffrey said. "We can fit you out. *That's* not a problem."

"I like those denim jump suits some enlisted men were wearing."

"I'll take care of that," Jeffrey said.

"Also, besides these khakis, those blue shirts and pants are nice."

"No problem," Jeffrey said. "There's, um, there's one other thing."

"Yes?"

"Could you, um . . . do you mind . . . doing your own underwear?"

Ilse laughed. "Don't your laundrymen have wives or sisters?"

"Oh, no, it's not that. It's just that, um, well, the machines are rough on delicate things."

Ilse pointed to the little metal sink, where a pair of panties and a bra were soaking. Jeffrey blushed.

Ilse chuckled. "We Boers are self-sufficient people. I take it you're not married."

"No."

"I thought you might not wear a ring. Safety or something. You know, machines and radiation. *Electricity*."

"That's true," Jeffrey said. "Sometimes jewelry can be dangerous. But no, I'm single. . . . You just called yourself a Boer."

Ilse sighed. "It's still what I am. Murdering my family hasn't changed that. There are many of my generation who want to stop what's happened—older people too. It seems to me sometimes that we live *just* to try to stop it. But that can't change who we are, Commander."

"It must be hard for you."

"Have you ever been to South Africa?"

"No . . . never."

"The mountains, the coastlines, the vineyards, and the veld. The cheetahs, the lions, the flowers, and the birds. The native art, the deserts, the Valley of Desolation, the Valley of a Thousand Hills." Ilse stopped to draw a breath.

"It all sounds very nice."

"I've been many places, Commander. Research trips, and travel just for . . . just for *fun,* I almost said. Nowhere compares to home. I want that back. We'd come so far in recent years, and now we've lost it all. We're shamed before the whole free world for what a few of us made happen. Or let happen. Can you understand?"

"It's like Cuba going communist, or France with the Resistance."

"Both of which you read about in books."

"Yeah."

"Well, this is *happening* to me. You have your ship, your crew, your relatives back home. Your country is united, now more than in sixty *years*. I have none of that. I've lost my country. *I want it back.*"

"I'm sorry. It, um, it, you, you must be lonely."

"It's something no *uitlander* could understand."

"A foreigner, you mean?"

"There's no translation." Ilse yawned, although she didn't want to.

"I see you're tired," Jeffrey said. "I'm pretty bushed myself. Some sleep will help. We'll wake you in six hours. I'll post a schedule for the shower."

"How *military* of you."

Jeffrey blinked. He actually seemed hurt. "The submariner day is eighteen hours," Jeffrey said. "Three six-hour watches. One on, two off, usually."

"I'll get awful jet lag fitting into that."

"You can ask the corpsman for a sleeping pill."

"No."

"There's one other thing," Jeffrey said. "The captain asked me to bring this up with you. You'd mentioned you knew people in our navy."

"Just some guys I went out with in San Diego."

"Captain Wilson, he, uh, he wants to know. In South Africa, did you know people there?"

"You want to pick my brain, for intelligence?" Not *again*. Didn't I get enough of this in Washington?

"Something like that," Jeffrey said. "There's one guy, he was high-profile. Now he's in command of *Voortrekker*."

"Voortrekker?"

"That's their ceramic boat, commissioned a year before *Challenger*, built in Germany with help on the propulsion plant from Russia. It was supposed to be a *concession*, a gift from the German bankers, a legal bribe to get to make some lucrative loans to a Boer-controlled armaments conglomerate. The hull's a composite multilayered matrix, like tank armor, but much less dense than steel."

"I know," Ilse said, "Sessions told me. And the Germans have their *Deutschland* and the Brits have HMS *Dreadnought*. And the Japanese started the whole thing."

"Yeah, there was an arms race," Jeffrey said. "Anyway, we thought you might have met *Voortrekker*'s captain, Jan ter Horst."

Ilse stiffened.

"What's the matter?" Jeffrey said.

"I know him."

"Very well? If we could understand his mind-set, in case we go up against him, it would help."

"Yes, I know Jan ter Horst." Ilse said the name with bitterness.

"What's he like?"

"Arrogant. Innovative. He'll take shrewd risks, and he learns very quickly. Aggressive, a brilliant leader, religiously devout. One of the instigators of the Putsch."

"Sounds like a tough character."

"He's the best they have, and he knows it. If you ever do encounter him, be very, *very* careful."

"Sure you're not exaggerating?" Jeffrey said.

"I'd fear for my life if I were you. I really would. He's ruthless, more than you can possibly imagine."

"The problem is he did the Severodvinsk school, in Russia, not the British Perisher, then went to sea a lot on Russian SSNs, for the experience. Now our agents can't get his file in Moscow or anywhere else."

"I can help. But just so far. Be warned, for future reference. . . ."

"You have my attention."

"I won't be with you long, and I want you to survive this war. Jan ter Horst *enjoys* being unpredictable, and he loves to rub it in. He's very energetic, and he has a *wild* imagination." In spite of herself Ilse gave a secret smile. "He's also a terrific liar." Unlike you, Jeffrey Fuller. You're too easy to figure out. In some strange way you're even sweet. Predictable but sweet. Both could cost you.

"How come you know so much?" Jeffrey said.

"Up until the Putsch, for two years, Jan and I were lovers."

12 HOURS LATER (D DAY MINUS 4)

"Morning, sir."

"Morning, sir."

Jeffrey nodded back. The two enlisted men got coffee, then took off. Jeffrey turned back to the table, piled with lethal-looking gadgets.

Sitting in the booth in the enlisted mess was Lieutenant Shajo Clayton, now in his element. Ilse sat across from Clayton, but Jeffrey stood—it helped him think. Four SEALs sat at another booth, adjusting bulky cases that said DANGER HIGH VOLTAGE on the sides. Two of these men, Clayton said, were logistics and equipment guys not going on the raid; they were alternates, just in case.

The other four men in the augmented team were in the booth across from Jeffrey, all blindfolded, racing each other to field-strip and reassemble South African assault rifles. COB, off watch, was timekeeper, obviously enjoying himself. A pile of twenty-dollar bills sat on the table, almost lost amid the trigger groups and slide stops.

"How you guys making out?" Jeffrey said.

"Halfway there," COB said. "Winner's best of fifty."

"Best of *fifty*?" Jeffrey said.

"Hey," Clayton said, "endurance counts."

"I guess it does," Jeffrey said. "Okay, Shaj, what's next?"

Clayton tossed Jeffrey a combat helmet and gave one to Ilse too. Jeffrey put his on. Clayton asked one of the mess management crew, cleaning up from breakfast, to kill the lights.

"Flip down the helmet visor," Clayton said. Jeffrey did.

Twin oculars came down before his eyes, flat-screen displays. The stereoscopic image began to switch back and forth, between infrared and low-light-level television. Jeffrey looked around the room. The data coming at him blew his mind.

"Total tactical awareness," Clayton said. "Notice how the contrast's enhanced by the flickering positive-negative effect."

"I see it," Jeffrey said.

"That's great for your reaction time."

Jeffrey glanced at a bulkhead. On IR he could see

right through the wall, to the racks and sleeping figures in the accommodation space beyond.

"This is awesome," Ilse said. Jeffrey studied her through his visor, until she turned to look at him.

"They're like the X-ray goggles they advertise in comic books," Jeffrey said. He squelched the thought before it could go further.

"The helmet's ceramic," Clayton said. "Stops a thirty-cal at almost point-blank range. Neutral buoyancy too, though you have to watch out for trapped air. The battery's conformal. Feel that little switch inside, by your right ear? That controls the interval. You might try half a second on each mode for starts."

Jeffrey played with it, making the picture flash back and forth faster and then slower. "Antiblooming feature?"

"These have pixel gain control. Lets you look right past glaring headlights and see someone in the shadows, all in real time."

"What about a mushroom cloud?" Ilse said.

Clayton laughed. "Keep your fingers crossed," he said. "These don't have much EMP shielding. By then we should be done and out of there."

Jeffrey reached to his left ear and folded down the tiny built-in mike. "What about our comms?"

"Digitized voice, encrypted," Clayton said. "Using frequency-agile low-probability-of-intercept radar pulses."

"Not plain radio?" Jeffrey said.

"Nope. Too easy to detect or jam. These go through trees and bushes better. The signal bounces well through building clusters too, and windows, hallways, things like that. You get distortion from multipath, but it's workable."

"Super," Jeffrey said.

"Lights, please," Clayton called. The crewman hit the switch and the fluorescents came back on. "Speaking of which, the moon will be well up as we insert, two days past full, so there'll be plenty of light through the clouds to drive the image intensifiers. In a completely darkened room you'd stick to infrared."

"Right," Jeffrey said.

"Next," Clayton said. He gave Ilse and Jeffrey diving masks, with wires that ran to little chest packs.

"The mask fits under the helmet?" Jeffrey said.

Clayton nodded. "And the rig's compatible with mixed-gas Draegers."

"You still use those things?" Jeffrey said. He turned to Ilse. "They're closed-circuit scuba gear, rebreathers. The works fit across your chest so you can reach everything easily."

"I've heard of them," Ilse said.

"There've been improvements," Clayton said. "A U.S. contractor beefed up the endurance of the O_2 renewer, the carbon dioxide scrubber's more efficient, and they've got heliox for deeper depth. . . . They also added a mike to the mouthpiece, for clandestine digitized underwater telephone."

"You mean like gertrude?" Jeffrey said.

Clayton nodded. "Except now it's low probability of intercept and frequency agile, encrypted, just like our radio."

Ilse donned her diving mask and turned it on. "Wow! It's a head-up display!"

"See everything you get there?" Clayton said.

"Left side's time and depth, water pressure, and compass heading," Ilse said. "Plus other stuff. I'm not sure how to read it."

Jeffrey held his to his face and smiled. "It's a swim board."

"Yup," Clayton said. "Except it keeps your hands free, and it has inertial nav with programmable way points and a steering bug. Senses water temperature and currents too, and gives you swimmer speed over the bottom. And," Clayton added, holding up a palm-sized object, "watch *this*. Ultrasonic sonar simulator. Your skipper gave permission, it won't get through the hull." He switched on the handheld transducer. An indicator began to pulse on Jeffrey's mask display, showing the bearing to Clayton's hand.

"Jeez," Jeffrey said, "you've got built-in acoustic intercept!"

"Uh-huh," Clayton said. "The hydrophones react to any loud noise too. Figure of merit's pretty poor, the directivity could be better. But it does give back your sense of undersea direction."

"This could come in handy," Jeffrey said.

"Amen, bro," Clayton said. "Like if some patrol boat screw starts up, or someone's dropping antiswimmer charges, you need to know which way they are before they know where *you* are."

"What's this other stuff?" Ilse said. "The numbers on the right?"

"Diver data," Clayton said. "Monitors your physiology objectively—which is kinda hard to do yourself when someone's shooting at you. Pulse and respiration, remaining air supply, O_2 partial pressure and consumption rate."

"How does that part work?" Jeffrey said.

"You have to put the chest pack on. It picks up from your body, like a lie detector, and from the regulator valves."

"That's clever," Ilse said. She modeled the chest pack, which was broad and flat. "You forgot a lady's model," she said deadpan. The thing squashed her breasts. "It's heavy."

"Not when you're swimming," Clayton said. "Same density as seawater, won't affect your buoyancy, like the flak vests we'll wear over it, underneath the Draegers."

"Great," Ilse said.

"It also shows your rate of rise or dive," Clayton said. "It sets off an alarm—the transducers vibrate at your temples—if you go too deep or start coming up without exhaling, like if you're wounded or you just go stupid. That feature can be switched off in tactical situations. It's loud enough for your swim buddy to hear. I'll be yours, by the way."

"You really thought of everything," Ilse said.

"You bet," Clayton said. "Remember, when in doubt while going up or down, thirty feet per minute always works."

"Right," Ilse said. "I have a scuba Openwater Two certificate."

"I've kept at it myself," Jeffrey said. "I'm a qualified safety diver. Hull inspections mostly, for maintenance or damage, and for any sabotage when we leave port."

Clayton nodded. He held up a little keypad, also with a wire. "Dive computer, standard navy tables and the classified aggressive ones. This goes on your wrist, plugs into the pack. The output shows up on your mask. Keys are big enough for frozen fingers or some hard corner of your gear."

Ilse laughed, obviously impressed. Two more crewmen came into the mess, grabbed coffee and donuts, stared at the group with all their weapons, and left quickly.

"How long do these batteries last?" Jeffrey said.

"Long enough," Clayton said.

"What's the mean time between failures? I've a sneaky feeling these were rushed into production."

"Like so many other things." Clayton shrugged. "Long enough. As long as some still work, and we stick together, we're okay. We're taking backup gauges, analog mechanical, for the basic data."

Jeffrey nodded.

"We'll have practice sessions," Clayton said, "in a partly flooded lockout trunk. That's how we'll calibrate your weight belts. COB can provide warm seawater—you know it's icy at our present depth."

"Super," Jeffrey said. "I just wish we'd started this two months ago."

"You heard the briefing," Clayton said. "We don't got two months. . . . Don't worry, it'll come together."

Jeffrey looked at Ilse and she shrugged.

"Next," Clayton said. He unlocked a case and took out a pair of pistols.

Jeffrey lifted one by the butt, keeping his fingers well away from the trigger. A big orange safety plug rested inside the bottom of the butt, where the magazine would go. A thick sound suppressor formed an integral part of the barrel. Held to the muzzle by a short lanyard was a cap to keep out mud and water.

"These are handmade prototypes," Clayton said. "The first *truly* silenced autoloading pistol."

"Hey," Jeffrey said, "there's no ejector port."

"These have electric ignition, with caseless rounds. No firing pin, no receiver slide or cocking lever, and no ejector port."

"Hence no cycling noise in operation," Jeffrey said.

"Yup. Shoots as fast as you can squeeze the trigger. Subsonic rounds, of course."

"Caliber?" Jeffrey said.

"Fifty," Clayton said.

"Jesus."

"Stopping power."

"Praise the Lord and pass the ammunition," the SEAL chief in the next booth said. Jeffrey heard the steady slap and clicking as the SEALs continued their race. They were eager and competitive, all of them experienced operators, not one man under twenty-five.

"Pick yours up," Clayton said to Ilse. "It's not loaded."

"It's heavy," she said, hefting the weapon.

"Ever shoot before?"

"Just paper targets. Rimfire twenty-twos."

"Good," Clayton said. "We'll teach the proper stance. The thing is with a fifty, it really kicks."

"Um, I bet it does," Ilse said.

"We'll show you guys how to field-strip this and everything," Clayton said.

"We're only using pistols?" Ilse said.

"These are just for you two, as our mission specialists. The rest of us, the shooters, we have something similar but in thirty-cal full-auto, two-handed carbine style."

"I'm not happy going in without a live firing drill," Jeffrey said.

"Wouldn't think of it," Clayton said. "We brought a bullet trap and we've got soft-nosed training rounds. Captain Wilson gave permission, given what's at stake."

"If you say so," Jeffrey said. He wondered how *that* would look in his service jacket. Unusual accomplishments on XO tour: fired live rounds in the submarine.

"Just don't take them on the mission," Clayton said. "Dumdums are illegal. Geneva Convention says they can shoot you on the spot."

"Not if I shoot first," Jeffrey said.

"Good man, Commander."

"I'm awfully out of practice," Jeffrey said.

"Don't sweat it," Clayton said. "We've got a hundred hours for working up. You too, Ilse. We have conditioning and team integration all planned out, and you can read the manuals on this stuff in odd scraps of time."

"Okay," she said. "Um, how many rounds per clip?"

"Eighteen for the pistols. Two columns side by side." Clayton handed Ilse a dummy round, colored blue.

Jeffrey looked at it too. It was rectangular, with a pointed bullet sticking from one end. As Ilse passed it to him, their fingers brushed.

"What loads you packing?" Jeffrey said, making himself stay all business once again.

"We alternate," Clayton said. "Teflon-coated, and copper-jacket hollow point, both three hundred grains. A double-tap takes care of most contingencies, and you don't need to keep track of what's in the chamber." Jeffrey nodded, satisfied.

"If these guns are electric," Ilse said, "what if they short out? And seawater's corrosive."

"Good point," Clayton said. "And don't forget, blood's a good conductor too. We use waterproof equipment bags, made of Kevlar, till we come ashore. They have adjustable flotation bladders so they won't sink." He pointed to the weapon in her hand. "But per your question, these are made of special plastic and they're rated to ten meters with the clip in and the muzzle plug. Just in case."

"They won't go off by accident?"

Clayton smiled. "You need to practice safety like with any firearm."

"Wait a minute," Jeffrey said, studying his pistol. "These things have iron sights."

"With tritium dots for night work," Clayton said. "But that's all just for backup. Put your helmet on again, then plug this wire into the bottom of the pistol grip. Twist clockwise and it locks to double as a lanyard." He gave the gear to Jeffrey, then showed him how to activate the power on the weapon.

Once hooked up, Jeffrey saw a cross-hair reticle in his visor image. It moved when the pistol moved, aimed where the pistol aimed.

"Accelerometers and very-low-energy laser interferometers," Clayton said, "with each helmet tuned to a different wavelength so they won't clash. The visor always knows exactly where the weapon's pointing, even if you're off target and the bad guy's on the skyline."

"No more red dot on the target?"

"Nope. Too obvious, and with smoke or fog or dust that laser beam would lead right back to you. *This* way your kill won't know that you just drew a bead. Until, that is, he suddenly checks out."

"I like it," Jeffrey said. He glanced at Ilse. She looked doubtful.

Clayton touched her shoulder. "Killing's never easy for the good guys."

Jeffrey nodded as old memories returned. "We have four days for clicking in."

"What's *that* mean?" Ilse said.

"Altering our minds," Jeffrey said. "Bonding, and turning off the outside world. Forgetting who we are, becoming what we need to be, to get this done."

CHAPTER 11

D MINUS 3

As Jeffrey finished dressing, he heard dull thumps through the bulkhead from Ilse's cabin right next door. He wondered what she might be doing—some kind of exercises, probably. She did seem in great shape. Jeffrey bent to tie his shoelaces and Commodore Morse knocked and entered.

"Good day, Commander," Morse said brightly. He put a thick sheaf of files on the upper bunk, then began to strip down to his Skivvies.

"Good morning, sir," Jeffrey said.

"Thanks again for sharing your little sanctum with me."

"It's no problem, Commodore, that rack is meant for guests. I get to know some interesting people. Besides, it's nice to have the company." The thumping next door stopped.

Morse grabbed a towel and his toilet kit. "And it's nice to be on a real warship. Surface units make me nervous. . . . And *aeroplanes*? Forget it."

"They say the same about us, sir," Jeffrey said, and both men grinned.

"Good Lord," Morse said, "now she's singing."

Jeffrey heard Ilse through the bulkhead, but he couldn't make out the tune. She seemed to have a good voice, though. It struck him what a complicated person Ilse Reebeck was, moody and intense, sometimes so American in her speech and thinking and sometimes so unreachable.

A minute later someone knocked. "Come in," Jeffrey called. It was Ilse, rosy pink and wide-awake.

"Oh, excuse me, Commodore," she said, seeing Morse there in his underwear. She was wearing a denim jump suit, baggy in some places and a bit too snug in others, with a *Challenger* baseball cap in matching blue.

"I like to shower *before* I sleep," Morse said, slightly embarrassed.

"I'll remember that for next time, sir," Ilse said. "I just got up an hour ago."

Morse nodded, then went through the side door into the CO/XO shower. He turned on the water, then *he* started singing.

"I'm on watch in twenty minutes," Jeffrey said to Ilse. He checked himself one more time in the dressing mirror. "I need to scan the log and take some reports before then. What's up? Did you sleep well?"

"Fine, yes. These mattresses are very firm." Ilse looked at his, as if to see if it was different.

"Good back support," he said.

"I want to work with Lieutenant Sessions on the Agulhas Current," Ilse said. "We'll have to head right through it and I can help."

"That's good," Jeffrey said. "Talk to the navigator too."

"You give permission?"

"For sure," Jeffrey said, liking how she looked with that cap on. She'd bunched her hair up above the little plastic sizing strip at the back, making a kind of ponytail. "So far you've been a real help, Ilse. Your enhancements to our models made a difference when we fought those Axis diesel subs. It's like having a sailing master aboard, twenty-first-century style."

"You mean the guy who advised the captain in the old men-o'-war?"

"Yeah," Jeffrey said. "Currents, soundings, weather, tides, wooden ships and iron men."

Ilse smiled. "Was he part of the crew?"

"Warrant officer."

"What's that mean?"

"It's like being a noncommissioned officer, like a master chief, but you're more senior. Your pay and privileges are in line with a lieutenant maybe, even a lieutenant commander." Ilse seemed to like that.

"Can I follow you around while you get ready for your watch?"

"A little tour?" Jeffrey said.

Ilse nodded.

"Ready?" Jeffrey said.

"Yes."

"See," Jeffrey said, "the oncoming watch standers already took over, except for me."

"You always go last?" Ilse said.

"On this boat, yeah. The main thing's consistency."

"Now what?" Ilse said.

"I'll take reports, starting with the helm."

"Sir," LTJG Meltzer said, "fly-by-wire ship control is rigged for nap-of-seafloor cruising, top speed twenty-six knots, general course now two one five, following route laid down by the navigator."

"Sir," COB said, "our depth is five two four zero feet, material condition ZEBRA, patrol quiet in the boat."

"Thanks, COB, Meltzer," Jeffrey said, then turned to Ilse. "I make up a watch bill every month. I try to mix people around now and then so all the crew can work together. But I also like to have the battle stations roster on duty often so they stay sharp as a group, not just at general quarters."

"Like now," Ilse said. "They're your lead-off team."

"Yup, the most experienced guys." Jeffrey sat down next to the off-going OOD at the command workstation. Jeffrey quickly skimmed the newest entries in the handwritten logbook, then spent more time on Captain Wilson's most recent instructions.

"Running as before, sir," the OOD said as Jeffrey finished. He was a junior officer from Engineering. "No new equipment casualties, no threats, all scheduled drills complete and satisfactory."

"Good," Jeffrey said. "Captain told me he was turning in."

"Yes, sir. Night orders are to go to modified ultraquiet at oh three hundred Zulu."

"I saw that, very well. . . . Next to fill me in, Ilse, shall be the navigating department."

"Sir," the senior chief on duty said, "we're driving south-southwest between the Soudan Bank to starboard and Rodrigues Ridge to port. Our position is 18 degrees 46.1 south, 60 degrees 14.4 east. Central Madagascar is six hundred miles off our starboard beam."

"Very well, Assistant Navigator," Jeffrey said. "Ilse, in older boats he'd be called the quartermaster."

Jeffrey brought up several displays on the command console one by one. "Now I'm taking a good look at the big picture in the boat. Pumps and valves and tankage lineup first, including filtration desalinators. . . . Air quality—we have radiacs and mass spectrometers for that."

Ilse nodded.

"Next," Jeffrey said, "is reactor and steam plant lineup and key-point pressures and temperatures. Look away for a minute, Ilse, this stuff is classified. . . . Then come loads on the turbogenerators and hydraulics. . . . And weapons status. See how you read the weapons board?"

"Little symbols," Ilse said. "Um, torpedo tubes, and, and missile silos?"

"We call that the vertical launch system, VLS, for our Tomahawk cruise missiles."

"How come so much is red?"

"Either we're too deep or fast to launch, or the weapon presets and firing solutions aren't loaded. Or we haven't flooded and opened the outer doors. The big Xs through the port torpedo tubes remind us they're inoperable now."

"This is great—it gives you everything at once. It's, like, idiot-proof."

"That's the idea." Jeffrey used the intercom to review secondary machinery status with the engineering officer of the watch, the EOOW. Satisfied, he hung up the mike.

"*Challenger*'s a new ship," Jeffrey said. "The propulsion plant's still breaking in. Changes in key performance variables can give us hints of trouble. So far everything looks good."

Jeffrey stood and walked with Ilse the few paces to the sonar area. He peered at all the console screens.

"Morning, sir," Lieutenant Sessions said. "No nuclear detonations detected in this theater during the previous watch."

"A quiet night," Jeffrey said. "What's happening locally?"

"We have some neutral merchant shipping off our stern, sir. They'll be in our baffles soon but they're well distant and the range is opening fast. These submerged contacts here are biologic."

"Very well," Jeffrey said. "Sonar, I want you to get Ilse familiarized with our bottom nav and mapping capabilities. Pretend she's joined your division fresh from SUBSCHOL."

"Yes, sir," Sessions said.

Jeffrey glanced at a chronometer—it was 2326 Zulu. "Well," Jeffrey said, "now it's my turn."

Ilse thanked him and sat down next to Sessions. Jeffrey went back to the OOD. "I relieve you, sir."

"You have the conn," the OOD intoned, rising from the console.

"This is the XO," Jeffrey announced, "I have the conn."

"Aye aye, sir," the CACC watch standers said. The ex-OOD went aft.

Jeffrey sat down and made some entries in the log, then settled into the command chair, grateful for the familiar routine of conning the ship. He was glad that for the next six hours the total concentration would relieve his mind of other things, including thoughts of Ilse Reebeck that weren't related to work.

"This gravimetry display is unbelievable," Ilse said.

"It's the closest thing to magic *I've* ever seen," Sessions said.

"It doesn't use stored data?" Ilse said, her eyes glued to the screen.

"Nope. It's completely independent of any database *or* our previous course *or* even the need to be moving. You just turn it on and there it is."

Ilse saw a crisp rendering of the seafloor terrain around the boat, contours and perspective drawn in by computer—a synthetic view as if she were peering through a window in the bow. Her other screen showed the corresponding bird's-eye view, looking down at *Challenger*. Ilse ignored all the numbers to the sides, course and speed and everything, riveted to this raw live imagery of the world outside the hull.

"What's the image resolution?" Ilse said.

"At short range," Sessions said, "better than ten meters."

"And it's all derived from local gravity?"

"Uh-huh," Sessions said. "Several groups of gradiometers and accelerometers throughout the boat. They measure changes in mass concentrations from different bearings."

"And this is all continuous motion," Ilse said, "in real time?"

"Yeah, the same thing COB and Meltzer have right now. It's refreshed every ten seconds."

"It must use lots of processing power."

"It's worth it," Sessions said. "We've got a hundred times the original *Seawolf*-class computer capabilities. The basic gravimeter math's nonclassified, but ours has special stuff civilian geologists don't know about."

"How new is this?"

"They were testing one on USS *Memphis* back in the late nineties at DEVRON TWELVE, our squadron. That's what we do. We're operational SSNs and we also test technology and tactics, working with the Naval Underwater Systems Center in Rhode Island, and the various contractors."

Ilse stared at the terrain estimation display. "You can see right through things!"

"Sure," Sessions said. "Matter's transparent to gravity, right? One seamount shows up past another. Good thing too, else we couldn't go this fast so close to the bottom."

"You must use some kind of stored data as backup, don't you?"

"We do," Sessions said, "and to speed these calculations also. We have decent bottom charts, for gross verification and course plotting."

"You don't just feel your way?"

"Not usually. Hitting a basalt cliff head-on would be embarrassing."

"Yeah," Ilse said.

"The helm guys need to stay real sharp," Sessions

said. "At twenty-six knots we move one boat length every eight seconds. Watch this."

On-screen Ilse could see that the canyon they'd been following took a sharp turn to the left. As if on cue to her thoughts the boat banked to port. She watched as *Challenger* followed the canyon leftward, still hugging the deep ravine's right wall, several hundred feet up. The boat leveled off as it came out of the turn.

"You can see why we don't stream a towed array," Sessions said.

"Neat," Ilse said. "But how come we don't stay right on the bottom?"

"Stealth. It's too obvious. If we follow one wall partway up, we still get all the benefits of terrain masking."

"And I guess that makes it tougher for the enemy to lie in ambush or plant a mine."

"You got it, Ilse. It also gives us more lateral clearance, room for turning sideways just in case. Right down on the canyon floor we'd be boxed in."

"Can you use this under ice?" Ilse said. "For ice avoidance?"

"Maybe someday," Sessions said. "It's great to fix your posit under the ice cap, update your inertial nav, since you can't just pop up for a GPS fix then, even in peacetime. Instead we orienteer from the gravimeter, based on distinctive bottom features and our charts. For ice *avoidance* we have to use our sail-mounted high-frequency sonar, which radiates and has short range and can't see past a bummock or berg. The problem with the gravimeter is the density gradient's not strong enough—rock or sediment versus water's one thing, but *ice* versus water's something else."

"Then what about detecting other subs? Or surface ships?"

"Smart question," Sessions said. "No good, unfortunately, is the answer. Floating surface units and submarines displace a mass of water equal to their weight, right? So unless you're *really* close, there's not enough change in the gravity field."

"What if you *are* close?" Ilse said.

"There's another problem if they're moving," Sessions said. "It adds a centripetal gradient that's unknown to the algorithms, not like own-ship velocity. And if you *do* know target range and course and speed, who needs the gravimeter?"

"What about a nuclear sub, though, one that's motionless or on the bottom? The reactor compartment must be extra heavy. Wouldn't that show up, compared to spaces full of air, as a mass field discontinuity?"

"Now you're getting into classified stuff," Sessions said. "But it's no secret gravimetry can help you avoid something man-made that's real heavy, like an oil drilling platform, since it doesn't move."

Ilse went back to her screens. Watching *Challenger*'s swift progress through the benthic topography was fascinating. The boat followed an S-curve between underwater peaks, hard right and then hard left again. Ilse could see it coming, on the bird's-eye view, and she watched the other picture as they took the turns, like looking out the windshield of a car.

"I have another question," Ilse said, "if this isn't secret."

"Try me," Sessions said.

"I need to understand this to help you navigate. How come Jeffrey isn't giving orders?"

"You mean no helm commands?"

"Yeah. When we fought those diesel boats, Captain Wilson kept saying make your course this, make your depth that, hard right rudder. . . ."

"Nap-of-seafloor's different. That's one reason we have senior people at the helm. Commander Fuller can overrule them, even take control himself if need be from his console, but this is different from maneuvers near the surface. *Here* we follow the terrain."

"So our detailed course is a given," Ilse said. "Mother Nature calls the shots."

"Pretty much."

"Could you fight a battle this far down?"

"I suppose," Sessions said. "The enemy would have to find us first. Down here you get lost in the sonar grass, just like with radar, and even look-down acoustic Doppler, which tracks suspended particles, gets confused by multiple currents at different depths."

"So more depth means more protection?" Ilse said.

"Yeah," Sessions said. "It's not just that you get more thermal and salinity layers to hide behind—"

"Plus the deep scattering layer too," Ilse said, "as schools of biologics migrate up and down the water column every day."

"That's right," Sessions said. "Anyway, the point is, if the enemy is sort of overhead, the spherical attenuation model holds. The intensity of our self-noise as received by the other guy goes down with the *square* of range, so ten times deeper means just one percent the signal strength."

"I should bone up on this stuff," Ilse said.

"You *need* to," Jeffrey interrupted. "There's a series of tutorials you can run on the computer, with homework problems and everything."

Ilse realized he'd been listening in. There really *is* no privacy on a submarine, she told herself. "Yes, Commander," she responded, slightly irked. "I'll look at the tutorials once I'm done with the gravimeter." Jeffrey turned back to his console.

Ilse watched her screens again. She saw large boulders show up now and then. Probably from underwater landslides, from seismic activity she knew never really ceased. Sometimes she saw talus slopes, rubble built up over eons at the base of undersea escarpments.

"You can fiddle with the picture if you like," Sessions said. "Use your trackmarble to look ahead, or rotate the presentation and see things from a different angle." He showed her how.

"This is fun," Ilse said. "But I have another question. With nap-of-seafloor, we're not too exposed, you know, to enemy sensors planted on the bottom?"

"Yes and no," Jeffrey butted in again. "That's why we use broken terrain, where it's hard to place a trip-wire grid and seafloor current eddies make for lots of false alarms. We'd avoid a smooth, flat open-ocean basin at all costs, for just that reason."

"Oh, okay," Ilse said.

"Another thing," Sessions said, "with the exotic nonacoustic ASW methods, like surface-wake anomalies, is they need minutes or hours of supercomputer time to make sense of the raw data, by which point you're tens of miles away. That's why we always zigzag these days, even out in blue water, deny the enemy our base course and speed."

"Right," Ilse said. Boy, do these guys love their shop talk.

"And now," Sessions said, "please excuse me." He got up and started walking the line of sonar consoles, talking to his people. Ilse went back to her screens. *Challenger* plunged onward.

Up ahead, on the display, she noticed an interesting formation of big rocks on the bottom, where the canyon opened out. The rocks lay in a perfect triangle.

"What's that, Helm?" she heard Jeffrey say.

"More boulders, sir," Meltzer said. "We'll pass well clear."

"Very well, Helm," Jeffrey said.

As they got closer to the boulders, Jeffrey watched the gravimeter's resolution sharpen. "That middle one. COB, if you will, gimme a close-up."

The image changed as *Challenger* seemed to leap ahead.

Jeffrey stared. *"All stop!"* he shouted. "Hover on manual!"

"All stop, aye," Meltzer said.

"Rig for ultraquiet," Jeffrey said.

"Aye, sir," COB responded instantly. The CACC lights blinked urgently and Sessions dashed back to his seat. Phone talkers hurried to their positions as Jeffrey reached for the handset to call the captain.

"Captain's in the CACC," the messenger announced. Jeffrey turned to see Wilson right behind him, in boxer shorts and slippers.

"What is it?" Wilson said.

Jeffrey pointed. "Those three objects on the bottom there. Around the next bend, range about one thousand yards. They look too much like subs."

"I see them," Wilson said.

"The closest one," Jeffrey said, "beam-on to us—that mass gradient can't be natural. I think we're seeing reactor shielding, Captain, and a core."

"Awfully big reactor for a vessel of that size," Wilson said. "Each of them's barely a hundred feet from stem to stern."

"Who'd be down here?" Jeffrey said. "Japanese?"

"In the war zone?" Wilson said. "They'd love to know what's going on, but they're not crazy."

"Something new the Axis has?" Jeffrey said.

"It's possible," Wilson said. "The other two could be ceramic diesel/AIPs."

"Or a clandestine seafloor habitat?" Jeffrey said. "For intel gathering maybe?"

"Maybe," Wilson said.

"The way they're all just sitting there, sir," Jeffrey said, "like they've circled as a laager Boer style, I don't like it."

"I don't either," Wilson said. "XO, I have the conn. Chief of the Watch, sound quiet general quarters. Man battle stations antisubmarine."

Jeffrey slid over, but Wilson stayed in the aisle, studying the helm screens. More crewmen hurried into the CACC and powered up their consoles.

"Captain," Jeffrey said, "recommend we get in closer, get some visuals, and do a full sound profile on these contacts. We can't just sneak around them and leave unknowns in our rear."

"I concur," Wilson said. "Fire Control, prepare to launch a long-range mine reconnaissance system vehicle."

"Prepare to launch an LMRS, aye," Jeffrey said. "Recommend we skip autonomous mode to stay covert."

"Concur," Wilson said. "Belay acoustic uplink, use the fiber-optic tether."

"Recommend we warm up the Mark 88 in tube three," Jeffrey said.

"Warm up the nuclear torpedo in tube three," Wilson said.

"Messenger of the Watch," Jeffrey said, "bring the captain some black coffee and his bathrobe, please."

Jeffrey concentrated on the screen, his right hand glued to the trackmarble. "Proton magnetometer's getting something, Captain. Field lines are bunching up."

"What's the range?" Wilson said.

"From the nearest mass concentration to our probe, four hundred yards."

"Get closer. Make it three."

Jeffrey tapped some keys, increasing the image intensification gain to a factor of 10,000. Diffuse and point-source bioluminescence, blues and greens stirred up by the torpedo-shaped LMRS, gave him a fuzzy view for a few yards ahead of its nose-mounted charge-coupled eyes. Jeffrey gingerly piloted the probe up off the bottom, inching it closer to the enemy subs, using a dip in the ground for cover.

"Definitely ferrous hulls," he said a minute later, eyeing the magnetometer again.

"Take it to two hundred yards," Wilson said.

"Aye aye, sir," Jeffrey said. "I'll hang a left, see where that fissure goes."

"Sonar," Wilson almost whispered, "anything?"

"Slight flow noises from bottom currents, sir," Sessions said. "Nothing artificial."

"Okay," Wilson said, "they're meeting their hotel load off batteries or fuel cells, and cooling that reactor convectively or just letting it run hot."

Jeffrey listened to the conversation as he gently moved the probe. "Ready now," he said.

"Pop up and take a look," Wilson said.

Jeffrey increased the CCD image gain once more, to 50,000 times. As the probe rose slowly, he saw the lip of the fissure moving down the screen.

"Whoa!!" Jeffrey ducked the probe back down, his heart pounding in his throat.

"What was that?" Wilson said.

"A bow dome, sir. *Big*." Jeffrey ran the replay. "Should we flood tube three?"

"Sonar," Wilson said, "any reaction?"

"Negative, sir," Sessions said. "No sign they know we're here."

"Should we flood tube three?"

"Negative," Wilson snapped. "They'll hear it. We have to back off first to fire anyway."

"Captain," COB interrupted, "*that* sub's not showing on the gravimeter at *all*."

"Or the probe's not where it should be," Jeffrey said. He checked his screens and enunciators. "Negative on a guidance flaw. Position overlay matches with dead reckoning." Again he brought the probe up. "Captain, look at this . . . a gigantic crack in the fiberglass."

The probe rose over the top of the enemy sonar

dome. "It's just the cap," Jeffrey said. "There's nothing behind it."

Wilson sputtered. "We found a goddamn wreck."

"A fresh one, sir," Jeffrey said. "No growths yet, and hardly any sea snow."

"All right," Wilson said. "Check out that middle contact now."

"Aye aye, sir," Jeffrey said. "I'll be careful—a wreck's the perfect spot to hide an ambush."

"Sonar," Wilson said, "what's happening?"

"No change, Captain."

Jeffrey moved the probe. "Something here." The murky picture showed a twisted, fractured, splintered mass.

"That used to be the sail," Wilson said. "See? There's the mounting for the port-side fairwater plane. . . . What's left of it."

"I'll go around," Jeffrey said. Suddenly ahead of the probe there loomed another mass, a huge one. "The reactor compartment," he said.

"Get closer," Wilson said. "Switch to active line scan. Lowest emitter power."

The picture changed, no longer an eerie natural glow. Now it was much sharper, more detailed. Jeffrey could see tattered steel, wires, and cables waving in the current. He saw a small dogged hatch in the middle of a bulkhead, next to broken pipes.

"The forward accessway," he said, "into the reactor tunnel." He brought the probe in closer, already suspecting. He could see the writing now, fragments of the safety warnings posted near the access door. "It's one of ours, sir," Jeffrey said. "Early *Los Angeles* class. Unimproved 688, pre-751 hull number."

"One of the flight-one boats still in commission," Wilson said. "Make that past tense."

Jeffrey nodded. "It's not a lengthy list, Captain, who

she could be. . . . Sir, the crew may not have had time to destroy the crypto gear, and it probably wasn't all cremated by the atmosphere compression. Maybe we should try to find the stuff, before the enemy does."

"No, XO," Wilson said. He frowned. "We'll have to take the chance that this engagement was a double kill. We'll report it later. We don't have time *or* the right tools to do a proper inside search here."

For a while no one spoke. Jeffrey moved the probe along the side of the middle hull section, knowing this chunk would have been unoccupied.

"Radiation?" Wilson said.

"Just normal background," Jeffrey said, "when you account for the added seawater shielding. I'm getting a minor thermal plume, that's all."

"Good," Wilson said, "the reactor's stable. That core should be clean too. This boat would've been refueled recently."

"And no hull implosion," Jeffrey said. "It must have flooded first, before they went through crush depth."

"Switch back to passive," Wilson said. "Move to the next masscon contact, the one to starboard. Watch out for wreckage—there'll be a nasty debris field out there."

"Understood." Jeffrey worked the trackball and his keyboard, once more seeing through the LMRS's eyes by the faint glow of bioluminescence, strobed by natural flashes and sheet lightning. A fish darted past, then another, too quick to make out details. Jeffrey guided the probe around a shadowy pile of mangled metal.

"Auxiliary machinery?" Wilson said.

"I can't tell," Jeffrey said. "It made quite a crater."

"Keep going."

"I'm at the second contact now."

"Okay, switch back to active laser line scan."

"Looks like the forward hull," Jeffrey said. "Probe's over the accommodation spaces, sir."

For another long moment no one spoke.

"The hull's intact," Jeffrey finally said, to break the silence.

"Move back and forth," Wilson said. "I want to know what sank her."

"Oh boy," Jeffrey said when he found what he'd been looking for. "Here's the forward escape trunk, sir. Busted in completely."

"Not solely from blast shock," Wilson said. "The rim's too whole. That was water pressure, rupturing the weakened welds. Trunk gave out before the hull, catastrophic flooding. Again, no implosion."

Jeffrey saw more tortured pipes and cables down inside the trunk. "I'm moving on." Soon he reached the dead sub's bow.

"Smashed in," he said. "Looks like she hit nose-first."

"This part did anyway," Wilson said as the probe explored the chaotic flattened tangle. "She may have broken up on the way down, from the strain, tumbling at over a hundred knots terminal velocity."

"Yes," Jeffrey said. He studied the image-enhanced display. "Look at how the ballast tanks accordioned. . . . I see fragments of the sonar sphere."

"What's that thing off to the left?"

Jeffrey moved in closer. "It's a body, sir." Wormlike creatures swarmed around it.

"Christ," someone said.

"Easy, people," Jeffrey said. He took a breath. "There'll be more, inside or outside. We have to do this."

Wilson sighed. "XO, go to the engineering plant now."

Jeffrey piloted the probe, being careful not to snag the fiber-optic line. He stayed well off the bottom, afraid of what he'd see there. For a while the screen showed little, then the after portion of the hull came dimly into view.

"Here's what did it," Jeffrey said. "That crack, it runs

ten yards along the hull. . . . A near miss from something nuclear, Captain."

"The crack's right where the steam turbines would be," Wilson said.

"Hopeless flooding," Jeffrey whispered. "They'd lose propulsion quickly. There's no way they could save her after that."

"Let's try for a positive ID," Wilson said. "Something with a serial number, a logbook, a uniform with a name on the shirt, anything."

Jeffrey swallowed in spite of himself, then felt weak at his own show of emotion. We're intruders here, he told himself. This is hallowed ground . . . and a charnel house. He forced himself to shift the probe once more.

"The men back aft died fastest," COB said as he watched his screens. "If it had to happen, they were the lucky ones."

"No," Jeffrey said, "nobody was lucky on that boat. Crushed or burned or drowned, gouged by shrapnel, scalded by live steam, there's no good way to die in a submarine."

CHAPTER 12

D MINUS 2

"Come in, XO," Jeffrey heard Wilson call. Once more he wondered how the captain always knew when it was him. The way I knock? My footsteps? That sixth sense skippers have? Jeffrey entered the CO's state-room.

"You look like a fugitive from Hell Week Two," Wilson said.

"I feel that way, Captain." Jeffrey wore a white undershirt with the SEAL emblem in red, dark green swim trunks, and black battle booties. He was still sweating and breathing a little hard.

"Just morning PT, XO, or something special today?"

"Both, sir," Jeffrey said. "Climbing ladders against the clock, crawling through the bilges with full gear, dancing quietly around simulated bushes, hopping gingerly past simulated mines. . . . And the virtual-reality training aids are quite realistic, great for your reaction time, and to maintain depth perception."

"Good," Wilson said. "I like your moccasins."

"They're something new that Clayton brought, Kevlar-lined throughout."

"Laces *and* Velcro?"

"They won't get sucked off by swamp mud, sir. Our swim fins fit right over them. With these on we could run for miles on coral or broken glass." Jeffrey was grateful now for his daily workouts on the ship's treadmill, in the aft auxiliary machinery room.

Wilson chuckled. "You're happy with the plan."

"It's all based on sound military principles, Captain."

"And Clayton's leadership?"

"He's smart, sharp, his men all seem devoted. I just need to tag along and do what he tells me."

"No problems, XO, taking orders from a junior?"

"I trust his tactical judgment."

"And Miss Reebeck?"

Jeffrey smiled. "She's really getting into it, Captain. She's a natural shooter."

"Many Boers are. . . . Not that I like repeating ethnic stereotypes. How'd you judge her emotional state?"

"Pretty good, considering what she's been through, becoming a displaced person and everything else. Good enough for what we have to do."

"How's your leg holding up?"

Jeffrey glanced down at the old scars on his left thigh, the puckered entrance wound dead center, the overlapping crisscrossed lines of surgical incisions. "It's a little sore, Captain, but it hasn't stiffened any. The corpsman gave me ibuprofen."

"Monaghan working out okay as assistant XO?"

"Good practice for him, sir, and he's really helping with my normal work load. I'm sure he'll do fine the few hours I'm away."

"Good. Speaking of which, take a look through these." Wilson handed Jeffrey a folder and diskette.

"What's this, sir?"

"Partial maps of the Durban minefields and the Boer SOSUS grids."

"How'd we get this, sir? An inside source?"

"Nope, the hard way. One of the newer *Los Angeles*–class boats, *Springfield*, went in and waved her coattails, loud enough to draw off their patrols. During this nice diversion the second *Seawolf*, *Connecticut*, snuck by and eyeballed everything with her LMRS. . . . That's top secret."

"Super," Jeffrey said.

"Now, I see *you* have something for *me*."

"Here, sir," Jeffrey said, passing the message slip. "Our address and another letter group came in through the on-hull ELF antenna when we rose to bellringer depth."

Wilson read the slip. "The final go-ahead code," he said. "The mission's on, definitively."

"They're asking us to pop up again for one last intel download. Captain, request permission to trail the medium baud rate floating wire antenna."

"Negative."

"Sir?"

"We stay deep."

"But, sir, there could be important info. A weather update or opforce disposition changes."

"I know, XO, but it's my decision. If something crucial happened, we'd've been scrubbed altogether, and for us as the attacker nothing's more important than surprise."

"But we wouldn't radiate. We'd just receive."

"That's not a *just*, XO. We'd make a datum for the enemy."

"But, Captain—"

"No. Just because *we* don't have something that can spot a long, thin wire floating half a foot beneath the surface of the ocean doesn't mean *they* don't. Remember who invented cruise missiles and ICBMs."

"I hadn't thought of that, Captain. I see what you're getting at."

D MINUS 1

"So your regulations actually *require* an officer to be at every meal in the enlisted mess?" Ilse said.

"Not just *Challenger,*" Jeffrey said. "It's navy-wide. For morale and to check the food."

"And this morning it's your turn."

"Thanks for joining me."

Ilse smiled. "You're welcome, Commander Fuller." As they worked their way through each snug, cramped compartment, she watched how Jeffrey walked, relaxed yet energetic, twisting and turning smoothly to get past people or equipment. He might be slightly favoring that leg, but Ilse decided not to say anything. From what she'd seen of the exit wound at the back of Jeffrey's thigh, it must have been awful. Now it was all hidden by his khaki slacks, nicely snug at the rear. Not in Clayton's league, but then Clayton was somewhat younger.

Again Ilse watched Jeffrey walk. An honorable wound, she told herself. Whatever happened, he'd been hit facing the enemy. Jeffrey ran his fingers through his hair, and she realized now the gesture was a habit. A few strands were out of place. She was about to reach and fix them, but they'd arrived at the mess.

"It's busy now," she said.

"Zero five-thirty's the middle of the breakfast rush."

Jeffrey and Ilse traded greetings with the crewmen eating in the booths, and with the mess management staff doing the cooking and serving. The layout was American-cafeteria style and the mix of smells was delicious. Ilse was working up a big appetite the last few days, burning it off as she went.

Jeffrey ordered first. "Scrambled eggs, fried potatoes, double order breakfast sausage." Then he grabbed a large black coffee and some OJ.

Ilse decided to have the same, especially the coffee. Then she took a closer look and wrinkled her nose. "These eggs are powdered, aren't they?"

Jeffrey shrugged. "So's the OJ, but the bread's fresh-baked. Look on the bright side." He rocked on the balls of his feet, holding his tray and surveying the crowd. "There's an opening. Follow me." He led her to a partly empty booth and they sat with a pair of crewmen. Both had black eagles and other stuff on their sleeves. The men were obviously pleased by the company, Ilse's especially.

"We caught some glimpses of your training," one man said. His shirt pocket was stenciled KERR.

The other man, SCUTARO, shook his head theatrically, with a big smile on his face. "You wouldn't catch me doing stuff like that in a million years. Gimme a nice, safe submarine any day."

"What do you guys do exactly?" Ilse said.

"We're in the weapons department," Kerr said.

"We service the units," Scutaro said.

"And we check the presets and then stand by to fire on local control during general quarters."

"And now we do the manual loading too."

"Sorry about your mates," Ilse said.

"Thanks," both men said.

"They saved the ship," Kerr said, "getting those shores in place."

"Talk about courage," Scutaro said. "They *had* to know we'd never get that outer door shut in time."

"Hey," Kerr said, "leave us not mope about our departed comrades. They're in heaven now, right?"

"At least *they* don't haveta eat these lousy eggs," Scutaro joked. He swallowed another forkful.

"The eggs are just as bad in the wardroom," Jeffrey said, obviously proud of his men's high spirits.

"Let me ask you a weapons question," Ilse said, "if this isn't classified."

"Shoot," Kerr said, and Scutaro cracked up.

Ilse laughed too. "Very funny. I've been curious about why the nuclear warheads you're using are so small." She started buttering her toast.

"Small is relative, ma'am," Scutaro said. "Dot one KT's still a hundred tons of high explosive."

"But how come you don't use something really big?" Ilse said. "Like ten kilotons, or fifty?"

"Remember, Ilse," Jeffrey said, "these are *torpedo* warheads. By definition we can't be very far away when one goes off, not much more than the maximum range of the unit, which with an ADCAP is some thirty nautical miles. Most engagements are well inside that distance, since everyone's so quiet nowadays."

"If the bang's too big, *we'd* get blown up too," Kerr said.

"Or damaged, which is bad enough," Scutaro said.

"Past a certain point it wouldn't make much difference," Kerr said. "Any damage risks bad flooding. Except for those humongous Russian boomers, no sub can take a lot of flooding. You're just too heavy, go right to the bottom no matter what you do."

"At least nuclear power makes us more survivable," Kerr said, "compared to a diesel/AIP in a melee situation. We can skedaddle twice as fast as them if we need to, cut the enemy fish's closing speed substantially, and stay at ahead flank till its fuel runs dry."

"The rule of thumb," Scutaro said, "is a torpedo needs to be one and a half times as fast as the targeted sub to be sure of a kill. And by the way, our Improved ADCAPs are *very* fast."

"Even then we still need a good firing solution," Kerr said. "Otherwise our weapon could pass well ahead or astern, too far off to pick up the other guy in its passive search cone, or even active mode."

"And worst of all," Jeffrey said, "now he knows you're there, and he's *really pissed*."

Jeffrey and Ilse walked back to their state-rooms after breakfast.

"Time to change to sweats again," Jeffrey said. "Just one day to go." Ilse was quiet, so he added, "That's the problem with real combat. You train so hard you're exhausted going in."

"Um," Ilse said. "Would you come inside for a minute? I want to talk to you about something."

They went into her room. Jeffrey took the single chair, figuring Ilse would perch against her rack, but she stayed standing. Jeffrey realized she'd switched to one of her serious moods again.

"Did you ever kill someone?" she said.

"When I was a SEAL?"

"Yes."

"Yeah, I did."

"The same time you were wounded?"

"I can't talk about that mission."

"Can't, or won't?"

"It's secret."

"How did it feel?"

"I told you already, painful. The recovery was worse."

"No. I mean killing. How did it feel?"

"Cold. Empty. Scary. . . . Necessary. I try not to be introspective, Ilse, about certain things. Experience taught me that the hard way."

"Jan once said I think too much."

"Oh."

"If something goes wrong," Ilse said, "I want you to kill me."

"What?"

"Just what I said. If we're in danger of being captured. I know too much."

"Ilse, this is *not* the time for negative thinking."

"I'm not being negative, I'm being a realist. This whole thing's so rushed."

"Ilse, SEALs don't leave people behind. They certainly *don't* kill their own."

"I'm *not* your own. And think of what I've seen and overheard the last few days. I couldn't hold out forever under torture. They use drugs and electricity."

"Um," Jeffrey joshed, "can't you ask Clayton? After all, he's the man in charge."

"He's too young."

"Huh?"

"He still thinks he's immortal."

Jeffrey nodded. "You need to, secretly, to get the job done."

"He might . . . he might do it prematurely if we get in a fix, or, or wait too long."

"Couldn't you just shoot yourself?" Jeffrey said. "You know, in the head? I'll be glad to tell you when."

His attempt at humor failed miserably, as Ilse turned away, obviously hurt.

Jeffrey stood up and moved closer, not sure what to say. Then he remembered the video of her brother being hanged. He awkwardly put one hand on Ilse's shoulder. She turned and held him tight, looking up with tears in her eyes.

"Promise me, Jeffrey Fuller. Promise *now*."

CHAPTER 13

ABOARD *CHALLENGER*, NEARING DURBAN

The sonar speakers filled the hushed CACC with noise. Enemy steam turbines and gas turbines whined in the distance, prop screws churned, and water jets of fast patrol boats rushed and whooshed. Diesel engines throbbed and burbled. Helos plopped their dipping sensors under clattering rotor blades. From all directions Boer and German surface unit hulls and hydrofoils hissed and pounded in the constant roaring waves. And from all directions came their active pinging sounds, close or far away, high-pitched or rising sawtooth or bass.

Ilse and Sessions had shifted to sonar consoles at the fore-end of the row of seven, farther from the navigator but closer to Jeffrey at Fire Control. Ilse, along with Jeffrey, wore jet-black combat clothing, a Gortex-like whole-body stocking that also served as wet suit.

"There," Ilse heard Jeffrey say tightly, "another one. Move in. Move in with the LMRS."

"I've got it," COB said. "It's in disguise like the rest of 'em."

"Watch the turbulence," Jeffrey said.

"I've got it," COB said.

"Turn the LMRS sideways, unmask the synthetic-aperture array."

"Turning sideways, aye."

"Be careful," Jeffrey said. "Don't get too close."

"I've got it," COB said.

Ilse studied the live feed on one window of her screens. She could see an innocuous mound covered with sponges, anemone, starfish. Jeffrey had explained that modern bottom influence mines were equipped with odd projections, to speed colonization by sea life for camouflage. These mines were CAPTORs. They opened an outer casing to launch an ASW torpedo when their software felt a good contact was near.

"Confirmed," COB said. "It's a mine, a live one." Ilse could see the outline of its workings now, a kind of X ray in ultrasound.

"Tag it 32," Jeffrey said, speaking to the tactical plotting team whose stations lined the CACC's starboard bulkhead next to the relief pilot's position. Almost three dozen bottom mines on their track so far. Not one of them was a dummy.

Ilse saw the little symbol for the latest threat appear on the bottom chart on her screen, a "V" in red with a dot inside and the numeral 32. On her other display, picked up by the LMRS's image-intensified CCDs, she watched a siphonophore float past, long and thin, gelatinous, its body lined with stomach pouches, some digesting kills caught by its 10,000 little fingers. The LMRS loitered well ahead of *Challenger*, the unmanned undersea vehicle scouting at a safe distance.

"Helm, compensate," Captain Wilson snapped, breaking Ilse's reverie. "We're drifting again."

"Aye aye," Lieutenant Meltzer said, tense as he piloted *Challenger*, hugging the bottom, blending in, using the bow and stern auxiliary maneuvering unit thrusters constantly.

"A pattern's showing, Captain," Jeffrey said. "Rows parallel to the bottom current. This minefield's not so random as we're meant to think."

"You're right, XO," Wilson said.

Ilse superimposed the minefield map they'd been building onto the terrain contours from the bird's-eye-view gravimeter. She set up her own data in another window, bottom geology and local hydrographics. The Agulhas Current here ran several knots, south-southwest along the eastern coast of Africa. The Agulhas extended down this deep, five hundred fathoms, past the anoxic minimum, well into the zone that teemed with biologics.

"Commander," Ilse said, "if we continue on this course, we'll reach soft bottom, diatoms and foraminiferal ooze. Our hull will stand out on sonar."

"Very well, Oceanographer," Jeffrey said. "Captain, recommend we come to port, to stay stealthy and make more progress west toward our objective."

"We'll have to thread this row of mines first," Wilson said.

"The Boers are clever," Jeffrey said. "We'll be broadside to the current if we try to do it gingerly."

"We'd drift down over one for sure," Wilson said.

"Sir," Jeffrey said, "at point-blank range our synthesized magnetic field won't fool the CAPTORs. They'll figure out we really *are* a submarine, not some expendable minesweep probe in target emulation mode. They'll launch inside our antitorpedo arming run."

"I concur, XO," Wilson said. "It'd be tight enough getting through this barrier in still water. The mines are spaced a hundred yards apart, shorter than us from stem to stern."

Jeffrey had explained to Ilse that *Challenger* carried electric coils inside the hull for actively de-gaussing her machinery. Special onboard shielding, a Faraday cage, suppressed the fields from *Challenger*'s main propulsion motors. It was Jeffrey's idea to program the in-hull coils to create an intentionally flawed reproduction of USS *Seawolf*'s 3-D magnetic signature.

This was a double bluff, to make the CAPTORs think that *Challenger* was actually a minesweeping sled trying to detonate the mines in place. Since the smart mines were designed to be sweep resistant, they ought to stay inert. Ilse kept her fingers crossed.

"Captain," Jeffrey said a moment later, "COB's found some clearance past this line here with the LMRS. Recommend we slip through the barrier crabwise; our propulsion system's quiet enough. Then we can slow down, send the unmanned vehicle farther on to scout along the next leg of our course."

"Concur," Wilson said. "XO, since this was your idea, you take the conn."

"Aye aye," Jeffrey said. "This is the XO, I have the conn."

"Aye aye," the watch standers said.

"Helm," Jeffrey said, "listen up. We only get one chance with this. I want to put on a quick burst of speed and then drift between mines 31 and 32 at an angle of forty-five degrees to the current. As our pivot point crosses dead center between the mines, use our remaining steerageway to come to port to keep our stern from trouble. When we're completely through, turn to starboard. Face north-northeast, bow-on to the current, and hold us there."

"Understood, sir," Meltzer said.

"Okay," Jeffrey said. "Here we go. Helm, using auxiliary propulsors only, rotate the boat onto a three three five heading."

"Heading three three five, aye," Meltzer said.

"Now we're starting to be driven downstream," Jeffrey said. "On my mark, go to ahead two thirds smartly. We're deep enough the pump-jet won't cavitate."

"On your mark ahead two thirds smartly, aye."

"Ready . . . Ready . . . *Mark.*"

"Maneuvering acknowledges ahead two thirds smartly, sir."

"Very well," Jeffrey said. "Steady as you go. . . . Steady. . . . All right, we have enough momentum. Helm, all stop, stop the shaft, then feather the shaft to minimize our drag."

"All stop," Meltzer said, "stop the shaft, feather the shaft, aye. . . . Maneuvering acknowledges."

"Now let us drift without propulsion noise or wake," Jeffrey said. "This current turbulence should mask our lateral pressure wave at such slow speed. Helm, on my next mark use left standard rudder, make your course two nine zero. . . . *Mark.*"

"Left standard rudder, two nine zero, aye. . . . Steering two nine zero, sir."

"Steady," Jeffrey said, "steady. . . . Our stern's drifting too much, *hard left rudder*!"

"Hard left rudder, aye."

"Make your course two six zero."

"Make my course two six zero, aye," Meltzer said. "Steering two six zero, sir."

"Okay," Jeffrey said, "okay, that's better, we've shimmied through. Now take our way off, Helm. Back one third smartly. Right standard rudder, make your course zero two zero."

"Back one third smartly, aye, make my course zero two zero, aye. Maneuvering acknowledges back one third smartly. Steering zero two zero, sir."

"Very well, Helm," Jeffrey said. "All stop, hover on manual."

"Maneuvering acknowledges all stop, sir. Hovering on manual."

"Very well, Helm," Jeffrey said.

"Good job, XO," Wilson said.

Good job, Jeffrey Fuller, Ilse silently cheered.

Still in the game, Jeffrey told himself, as *Challenger* loitered past the line of mines, holding position all too near the next one. This close inshore they'd have conventional warheads, not nuclear. Directed energy probably. This far down, even with a foot-plus-thick ceramic hull, a big shaped charge meant certain death.

It made sense the minefield began out past the 3,000-foot curve—since maximum effective magnetic-anomaly detector range was some five hundred yards, this was the greatest depth at which surface and bottom sensors combined would offer perfect coverage.

"Master 14 aspect change," Lieutenant Sessions called. Jeffrey's TMA team confirmed that one of the enemy surface contacts had just altered course.

"Captain," Jeffrey said as he studied his plots, "on its present heading Master 14 will pass directly overhead."

"Turn off all fans and air scrubbers," Wilson said. "Turn off all freezer compressors." COB acknowledged. With twenty warm, sweaty, heavy-breathing bodies in such close confinement, the CACC quickly got stuffy.

"Sonar," Jeffrey said, "any blade rate difference on that contact? Could they have heard our fancy footwork just before?"

"No blade rate difference, Commander," Sessions said. "No sign they've detected us."

"Target classification?" Jeffrey said.

"We're getting clearer tonals now. She's German, sir, *Klasse* 103B destroyer." Sessions spoke briefly to one of his staff. "From our tapes she sounds like the *Rommel*."

"An aged ship, but deadly," Commodore Morse said. Jeffrey thought he seemed awfully relaxed, then remembered Morse had been through this before, against Argentina's *General Belgrano* and her escorts, in the Falklands War.

"Captain," Jeffrey said, "*Rommel* hasn't been pinging like the other patrols. Her slow speed suggests she's retrofitted with a towed array."

"She's still coming right for us," Sessions said.

"Sit tight, people," Wilson said. "We're boxed in by the mines."

Morse actually smiled. "There's naught to do but pray."

In a few minutes *Rommel* passed close by to starboard—obviously the mines were programmed to ignore Axis shipping.

"Captain," Jeffrey said, "we're getting scattered blue-green laser pulses, looks like a variable-depth LIDAR projector, trailing deep."

"Enough to paint our hull?" Wilson said.

"It's touch and go, sir," Jeffrey said. "If it was our own side's equipment, return signal strength would be right at the detection threshold."

"Any change in the destroyer's behavior?" Wilson said.

"*Mechanical transient!*" a sonarman shouted. "Range and bearing match Master 14!"

"What is it?" Jeffrey said. "And lower your voice."

"Object in the water," Sessions called. "Probable depth charge! . . . Confirmed, confirmed, *depth charge coming down*!"

"Phone Talker," Wilson said, "collision alarm. All hands rig for depth charge."

"Gimme a status update, Sonar," Jeffrey said. "What's the depth charge depth? How far off is it?"

"Passing through twelve hundred feet now, sir," Sessions said. "It's a noisy one, it's tumbling. . . . It's drifting right in our direction. . . . *Second* depth charge coming down!"

"COB," Wilson said, "can we get out of the way?"

"Not by much, sir," COB said, "not if you want to keep quiet and stay in one piece."

"Even if they miss," Jeffrey said, "we'll get sympathetic detonations from the CAPTORs all around us."

"First one's passing through two thousand feet!"

There was a *bang* outside the hull, then the smell of urine as a seaman peed his pants.

Sessions turned to Jeffrey and grinned boyishly. "That sounded like an empty spray can imploding."

Jeffrey snorted. "*Rommel* just threw out the garbage."

Jeffrey glanced at Ilse as she dared exhale. She looked on the verge of giggling in relief.

"All right, everybody," Jeffrey said, "back to work." He turned to the embarrassed seaman. "Go get cleaned up. I've done that in my time. It's a natural reflex, don't sweat it."

"Man," someone said, "I'm wide-awake *now*."

"Enough, people," Jeffrey said. "Sonar, what's Master 14 doing?"

"Steaming as before, sir. I think we're okay."

"Good," Jeffrey said.

Morse smiled at Jeffrey. "That wasn't so bad, was it?"

"The last thing the bad guys expect," Jeffrey said, "is an Allied sub deep in their minefield." He chuckled. "That's why we're here."

Ilse was really sweating now in the odorous CACC. Fifty mines so far on their route plus two more thread-the-needle sprints. They'd practiced some of this in simulations, but that was play-pretend with made-up data. Now *Challenger* was utterly committed and this was partly Ilse's idea. She looked at the large-scale terrain display once more.

There it was to the north, the bulge in the continental shelf, remnant of the 130-million-year-old geological stretching that split India from Africa. Beyond the huge plateau, in deeper water, lay three seamounts, extinct underwater volcanoes, labeled by the soundings at their peaks. Each projected high from off the ocean floor, almost 1,000 meters deep around their bases. Mount 183 rose dead ahead of *Challenger*, Mount 146 loomed ten miles to the north, and Mount 98, the tallest, sat on a small plateau of its own ten more miles east of 146.

Here, amid these seamounts, the bottom currents from the Agulhas Current were channeled, cornered, and forced to divide. Here fluid turbulence scoured the bottom, sweeping round the seamounts' flanks, then grew chaotic in their lee before resuming course. Here, Ilse had concluded, *Challenger* should lurk. At the base of Mount 183, amid the stones and shells and boulders, constant flow noise would conceal the vessel's presence, boundary separation round the terrain would scramble enemy Doppler, and the hull would go unnoticed.

The steady movement of the water would let the sub keep up three knots to cool her reactor, ram-scooping cold seawater through her main condenser. It would also help her maintain steerageway, all while hovering stationary over the ground with auxiliary thrusters.

The drift and mix of currents would disperse the vessel's thermal plume. Upwellings of ocean nutrients, lifted along the forward face of Mount 183, would feed vertebrates and phytoplankton near the surface, increasing turbidity and so decreasing LIDAR range. The seamount's massive bulk would shield the boat from enemy sensors, and the broken contours would help cloak *Challenger* with confused reverb and shifting horizontal water density gradients.

Ilse knew that these same conditions foiled the use of the Boer sound surveillance system, generically called SOSUS, which was why the seamount peaks and valleys were so heavily mined. To everything else was added acoustic interference from heavy industry along the South African coast, mechanical vibrations through the earth, more noise confusing hydrophones near the bottom. A more perfect hiding place, Ilse told herself, for an SSN crew with the nerve for it, could hardly be imagined. But *Rommel* made one thing clear: pinned down here among the CAPTORs, beneath the constant Axis ASW patrols, if once detected *Challenger* would surely be destroyed.

Ilse eyed her screens again. She checked and double-checked the boat's indicated position against the charts, the gravimeter, and the data she'd brought with her. Finally she cleared her throat.

"Commander Fuller, this is the spot."

"Very well, Oceanographer," Jeffrey said. "Helm, all stop. Hover on manual."

"Maneuvering acknowledges all stop," Meltzer said. "Hovering on manual."

"Captain," Jeffrey said, "with your permission we'll get rolling."

"Proceed, XO," Wilson said. "Godspeed, and I relieve you."

"You have the conn," Jeffrey said.

"This is the captain, I have the conn."

The watch standers acknowledged.

"COB," Wilson said, "we're safe enough for now, and the equipment and crew effectiveness require it. Reactivate the air-conditioning, please." COB acknowledged.

Jeffrey, Ilse, and Meltzer stood up. The navigator took over at Fire Control, and the relief pilot sat in as helmsman. Commodore Morse walked the departing threesome down the passageway toward the Ocean Interface Hull Module at the aft end of the accommodation spaces. On the way they stepped over supply crates, lashed to the deck and covered with floorboards. Then, there in front of them, ten paces before the beginning of the reactor compartment shielding, was a large sphere with a hatch in its side. The hatch was open, revealing a ladder.

Jeffrey stepped into the sphere, then looked up

through the massive hatch of the mating collar. Shajo Clayton grinned down at him.

"Checklists are almost completed," Clayton said.

"Best of luck," Morse said, shaking everyone's hand. "Remember that saying from somewhere or other: He who dares wins." He looked Ilse right in the eye. "And she who dares wins too."

Ilse smiled. "You're enjoying all this, aren't you, Commodore?"

"Busman's holiday," Morse said. "Old British custom, you know."

"Let's move," Clayton said. "We're behind schedule, we'll lose the tide."

Jeffrey let Ilse and Meltzer precede him up the ladder. He shook hands with Morse again.

"I want to hear all about it when you're back," Morse said.

"Wish us luck," Jeffrey said, then remembered that Morse just did that.

Jeffrey climbed the ladder and went through the hatch. Now he stood in another sphere, the hyperbaric lockout chamber within Lockheed Martin's sixty-five-foot-long, fifty-five-ton Advanced SEAL Delivery System minisub, the ASDS. Above his head was the minisub's roof hatch. One SEAL, the senior chief of Clayton's boat team, was in the little two-man control compartment forward. Meltzer joined the chief, taking the other position. Jeffrey and Ilse followed Clayton aft, into the transport compartment. Clayton's five shooters were all sitting there, dressed in black, pumped up and excited.

"We saved the two front seats for you," Clayton said.

"Terrific," Jeffrey said. "I *hate* bulkhead seats."

"If you get seasick," Clayton said, "just keep facing forward."

Jeffrey chuckled. Ilse made a face.

"Now," Clayton said, "let's think about this. I'm in tactical command of the mission, Meltzer's in charge of the ASDS, and you're senior officer present afloat, except we aren't afloat yet. Then there's Captain Wilson. So who gives whom permission to get under way?"

"We should go through proper channels," Jeffrey said.

"Um, yeah," Clayton said. "But from the top down, or vice versa?"

"Maybe we should form a committee," Ilse said from across the narrow aisle. "You know, to study the question." She made eye contact with Jeffrey, and he thought she looked very beautiful. The black hood she'd pulled up really did something for her.

"Is ten a quorum?" Jeffrey said. "You can be chairwoman, tie breaker." Easy, Jeffrey told himself. We could all be dead in an hour or two. That's no reason to flirt.

There was a dull thump from forward, another from aft. Then Meltzer's voice came over the intercom. "Hatch secured, swimmer delivery vehicles secured, SDV tow bridle in place. We have a window in the threat TMA, *Challenger* now popping up."

"I don't feel anything," Jeffrey said a little later. "Do you?"

"No," Clayton said. "You don't if everything works right."

Meltzer came back on. "We're at two hundred fifty feet. Ocean Interface conformal hangar is flooded and equalized, *Challenger*'s pressure-proof bay doors are open. ASDS ready to disembark."

Jeffrey picked up a mike. "We're all set back here."

"That was all so quiet," Ilse said.

"That's the idea," Jeffrey said. He fastened his seat belt and Ilse did the same.

"They should put pictures up or something," Ilse said. "It's like a subway without windows in here."

"Travel posters," Jeffrey said, smiling at her again.

The ASDS lurched, shimmied, rose, and moved forward.

"We're under way," Meltzer said. "*Challenger*'s dropping down."

"Any sign we've been spotted?" Jeffrey said into the mike.

After a pause Meltzer answered. "Negative. I'll turn on the data repeater, you can watch."

An LCD screen lit up: depth, course and speed, a nav chart, a sonar display. Jeffrey couldn't help but study the data. He reminded himself he should trust Meltzer—the kid was very well trained. So was the SEAL, in effect now chief of the boat.

But Jeffrey couldn't help it. "Pilot, can you give us the last tactical picture they downlinked from *Challenger*?"

"One sec, Commander," Meltzer said.

More info appeared on the screen, a slightly stale snapshot from *Challenger*'s powerful sensors. Jeffrey examined the picture: the seamounts, the plateau, the coast. Red diamonds were everywhere, surface ship contacts. Their speed vectors ran through his head. He tried to relax, just a passenger now, but he simply couldn't help it.

Another voice came on the intercom, the SEAL chief copilot. "We're rounding Mount 183. Commencing approach to the objective. We're starting a tape to put through our transducers. Do you want to hear it back there?"

Jeffrey palmed the mike again. "Yeah, play us some slow dancing." That might calm him down. A whale song filled the compartment.

"Briefing folders, everybody," Clayton said, handing them out. "Last chance for any questions, and your bright ideas."

The ASDS put on some up-bubble, heading toward

shallower depth. Nearer the surface the sub surged and heaved, too small to escape the wave action of the man-made hurricane topside.

"Hang on," the SEAL copilot said. "It's rough out there with the storm."

The ASDS pitched and rolled even harder. Jeffrey saw the depth gauge fluctuate as each wave propagated past, piling on pressure in turn, the wave height aggravated by conflict between the Antarctic swells from one direction and the high winds from the other. Abruptly the minisub aimed sharply upward, leveled off, and there was a loud fluting sound from the overhead.

"Compressed air venting," Meltzer's voice said as they dived back down. "We'll do that again in another few minutes. Real whales stay under awhile, Ilse said."

Jeffrey turned in his seat. "Can you tell from the recording, Ilse? Are we a boy whale or a girl whale?"

CHAPTER 14

"Commander Fuller," Meltzer's voice said a few minutes later. "Can you come forward, please? We may have a problem."

Jeffrey got up and went through the lockout chamber into the control compartment. He had to bend his head—the ASDS was only eight feet high on the *out*side. The mini-CACC was cramped, switch banks and monitors everywhere, dominated by the four 21-inch LCDs and big joy stick of the integrated control and display system.

"What's up?" Jeffrey said.

Meltzer pointed to the broadband sonar, the tonals, the TMA plot. "This new contact, Master 18. It's been acting like it's following us."

"Hmmm," Jeffrey said. He looked at the traces on the tactical picture, then examined the bottom chart. "We're paralleling the two-hundred-fathom curve now, the south edge of that big plateau. Could be he is too, part of his patrol routine."

"But he changed speed—he's closing the range. And on this course, two five five true, he's pooped constantly by the waves."

"No one would do that by choice," Jeffrey said. "What kind of ship?"

"A *Warrior*-class patrol craft, sir, just four hundred tons."

"They're not meant for ASW," Jeffrey said. "Last we knew they just had cannon, machine guns, and antiaircraft missiles. . . . But they *can* do thirty-five knots. They outmaneuver us even in this weather, even when we're well submerged. . . . So let's see what he's up to. I'll stay."

"Hello," the SEAL copilot said a little later. "More company. Designate this Master 19." A new line was descending his waterfall. The SEAL began running a new TMA.

Soon Jeffrey saw another red diamond pop onto the tactical screen. "Classification?" Jeffrey said.

"*Sachsen*-class destroyer," Meltzer said. "By Blohm *und* Voss, no more than two years old."

"*This* one's our worst nightmare," Jeffrey said, "with all the latest antisubmarine toys."

"Six thousand tons full-load displacement," Meltzer said.

"Yup," Jeffrey said. "Complete with active towed array, six torpedo tubes, state-of-the-art variable-frequency sonar, and depth-charge racks. *Plus* two Super Lynx helos with dipping sonar, sonobuoys, and MU-90 lightweight fish."

"And we're a lightweight submarine," the SEAL chief said.

Jeffrey nodded. "Just thought I'd tell you what we're up against."

"She's changing course," Meltzer said.

Jeffrey saw the lengthening dot stack veer off from the vertical. "Update the tracking solution," he said. "I can't call it the firing solution, the ASDS is unarmed."

"Here we go," Meltzer said. "Constant bearing, sir, and signal strength is increasing."

"She's on an intercept course," Jeffrey said.

"Speed's higher too, sir," Meltzer said. "Twenty-nine knots."

Jeffrey frowned. "That *Warrior* class called for help."

"What do we do?" Meltzer said.

"They may depth-charge us on general principle," Jeffrey said, "whale antics or no."

"Or just for sport if they're bored," the SEAL chief said.

"And if they find out what we really are," Jeffrey said, "from the wreckage, they'll know our mother sub is nearby too. . . . Get Ilse in here."

Ilse jumped when the intercom called. Jeffrey was forward a while, Meltzer's voice sounded worried, and now they needed *her* up front. She and Clayton traded nervous glances, then she went through the lockout vestibule.

In the little CACC she wedged herself into a corner, hip-to-hip with Jeffrey. Whatever else was going on, his closeness made her feel better. The top of her head just touched the overhead when she stood up straight. She noticed the copilot was juggling the trim—her shifting weight was enough to be felt. She looked at Jeffrey.

"They're suspicious," he said.

"The Boer patrols?"

"I want to do something to get them to leave, something whalelike that no sub would do."

Ilse read the displays. In spite of the tension she smiled. She was getting good at this: raw sonar data, then TMA, and finally the big tactical picture.

"How long since we last spouted?" she said.

"Eight minutes forty seconds," Meltzer said.

"One option's to run to deep water," Ilse said. "Sperm whales can do five thousand feet."

"I wish *we* could," Jeffrey said, "but we're small enough they might lose us anyway, and with our batteries we're dead quiet too. It's ten miles to reach the *two*-thousand-foot curve."

"How long would it take us to get there?" Ilse said.

"Top speed," Jeffrey said, "half an hour or so."

"That sounds like forever," Ilse said.

"Our SDVs couldn't take it either," Jeffrey said. "Even two thousand's way past *their* crush depth, and that ends the mission right there."

"No," Ilse said, "we have to keep heading inshore."

"Agreed," Jeffrey said, "and brazen it out in their faces."

"Helmsman," Ilse said, "let's keep up the cover. Weave back and forth while I think."

"Sir?" Meltzer said.

"Do it," Jeffrey said.

"Yes, ma'am," Meltzer said. "By how much?"

"Twenty degrees left and right."

"Yes, ma'am." Meltzer played with his joy stick. Ilse and Jeffrey swayed together, bracing themselves on each turn.

"This recording you're playing is just what we need," Ilse said. "It's a female calling to others, asking them where is the food."

"Good," Jeffrey said.

"Master 18's now off our port quarter," the SEAL chief said. "Master 19's converging from the north."

"They're boxing us in," Jeffrey said.

"What do you do when you breach?" Ilse said.

Meltzer twisted in his seat, straining his neck to make eye contact. "Shoot up, release compressed air, go down again."

"Do you break the surface?"

"No."

"And what color is the hull?"

"Jet black," Jeffrey said. "But one three-inch shell and we're finished."

"We have to come up again soon," Ilse said. "To breathe, whales uncover their blowhole. You usually see some of their back, a big glossy shape in the water. In storms they act a particular way, otherwise they could drown."

"So we hide in plain sight," Jeffrey said, "call the enemy's dare, push the mimicry far as we can. Sailors who serve in these waters would have seen whale behavior before."

"We need to do it like this," Ilse said. "Get under a wave, a big one. They come in sets, so we watch for the tallest. We speed up and go through its face, surging into the trough of the previous one. We blow when we're down in its lee."

"And give them a glimpse of our top," Jeffrey said, giving Ilse a devilish smile.

"Is there anything there to betray us?" she said. "A periscope, antenna, a sail?"

"No," Jeffrey said, "we don't have a sail, and the masts fold down hydraulically on the exterior overhead. Our little side thrusters retract into the hull, and our diveplanes and rudder would look like fins, I hope."

"Good," Ilse said. "And any small fittings, bumps and stuff, they'll look like barnacles or wounds."

"What's happening?" Clayton called on the intercom.

"We've got company," Jeffrey said. "Sit tight back there."

"That's easy for you," Clayton said. "*You're* a submariner these days."

"I've taken command," Jeffrey said. "Just till we're out of the woods."

"Yes, sir," Clayton said, clicking off.

"Raise the periscope, please," Ilse said.

"Just enough to be able to see," Jeffrey said.

Meltzer tapped a key.

"What's the wind?" Ilse said.

"Based on the strength of the wave action," Meltzer said, "given the tide and the current and incoming swells, it's a fresh gale from out of the west."

"About thirty-five knots," Jeffrey said. "Maybe forty or so in a ship's upper works."

"And it's pitch-dark outside?" Ilse said.

Jeffrey peered through the 'scope, then looked at the depth gauge once more, then back to the 'scope. "Turn up the picture gain," he said. The copilot reached for a knob. "Yup," Jeffrey said, "it's pitch-dark."

"On image intensification," Ilse said, "that destroyer will just see a blob. We're giving off warmth, aren't we?"

"Yes," Jeffrey said. "Electronics, crew comfort, titanium battery cans, and propulsion. We'll look normal enough on IR."

"Let's hope so," Ilse said.

She saw Jeffrey frown. "The SDVs on the tow bridle," he said.

"They flap around as we move?"

"On a ball joint," Jeffrey said.

"Do they make any noise?"

"Flow noise."

"Mechanical noise?" Ilse said. "Banging or thumping?"

"They're pretty well damped and cushioned."

"Then they'll seem like our tail," Ilse said. "Cetaceans don't always expose it. A full leaping breach takes some work."

Again Jeffrey frowned. "There'll be lightning up there, and what if they turn on a searchlight?"

The ping from the destroyer was deafening.

"What's our hull made of?" Ilse said.

"Nonmagnetic steel," Jeffrey said, "with a composite exostructure."

"Stealth coatings?"

"Something that acts like whale blubber."

Ilse glanced at the chart. "We should head a bit more to the south."

"How come?" Jeffrey said. "Avoid the destroyer?"

"Not exactly," Ilse said. "There's a salinity halocline right along here, freshwater output from the rivers. It'll help distort enemy sonar."

"Would a real whale do that?" Jeffrey said.

"Real whales don't like being pinged so hard."

"Very well, Oceanographer," Jeffrey said. He gave Meltzer the orders.

Ilse saw the copilot tapping his keys, adjusting the ballast for less-salty water.

"I need to look through the periscope," Ilse said. "I have to be able to see."

She and Jeffrey struggled to trade positions, rubbing each other up close. Her hand accidentally brushed his crotch. "Excuse me," they both said at once. Ilse tried not to blush, glad that the lighting was red. She leaned forward, one hand on the 'scope, and with the other she gripped Meltzer's headrest. The destroyer pinged them again.

"I've been watching the gauges," Ilse said, keeping her face to the eyepiece. "The next big wave should come by any second."

"We're in the leading trough of one now," Jeffrey said.

"Bring us up to ten feet," Ilse said.

"Sir?" Meltzer said.

"Do as she says," Jeffrey said.

"Ten feet, aye," Meltzer said. "Our depth is ten feet."

"Can you slow up a bit, to keep pace with the waves?"

"Make turns for twelve knots," Jeffrey said.

"Make turns for twelve knots, aye."

"Copilot," Ilse said. "Turn the gain up all the way."

"Yes, ma'am," the SEAL chief said.

"I'm just getting some glow now," Ilse said. "How do you aim this thing aft?"

"The handle," Jeffrey said. "Flick with your wrist."

"Okay," Ilse said, "I've got it. . . . Is there inertial navigation aboard?"

"Good stuff," Jeffrey said.

"Then, Helmsman, maintain level flight by your INS readings. Ignore what you see as our depth."

"Level flight, aye," Meltzer said.

"Let this wave overtake us," Ilse said.

"Make turns for ten knots," Jeffrey said.

"Making turns for ten knots, aye."

"Keep calling our psig," Ilse said.

"Five pounds per square inch gauge outside water pressure," Meltzer said. "Six psig . . . eight . . ."

"Okay," Ilse said, "the glow's fading now. That says the wave's coming."

"Ten psig," Meltzer said. "Twelve."

"Let it keep overtaking us," Ilse said.

"Fifteen psig."

"That's a twenty-foot wave," Jeffrey said.

"Eighteen psig," Meltzer said.

The destroyer pinged them again, from much closer. Ilse could hear its sounds now through the hull, the scream of gas turbines, the syncopated churning of twin five-blade props.

"Get ready to put on some speed," Ilse said.

"Twenty-two psig."

"Jesus," Jeffrey said, "a rogue wave. This one's at least thirty-five feet."

"Full speed ahead!" Ilse shouted. "Come up by ten feet!"

The acceleration threw her rump backward. Still glued to the 'scope, she said, "Stand by to spout."

"Stand by to spout, aye," Meltzer said.

"The glow's gotten much brighter," Ilse said.

"A searchlight," Jeffrey said. "Don't look right at it—they might see some glint."

"Come up two more feet," Ilse said. She flicked her wrist again, aiming the 'scope more toward the glow, the objective lens at a safe oblique angle.

They breached and she saw the destroyer, all 150 meters, all too clear through the bloom-control image, riding the trough with the ASDS. Big gun at the bow aimed right at her, missile launchers behind, a torpedo tube mount farther aft. The high bridge, the mast, tall air intakes, the smokestack. Low helo deck at the stern. The helos were gone—they must be up flying. But people were out next to drums in a rack.

The searchlight swept past in the rain, came back, and fixed on her.

"Spout!" she whispered as loud as she could. "Down 'scope now, now, *now*!"

The harsh fluting sounded, then the image grew dark as the mast folded back and they plunged through the preceding wave.

"Now go deep," Ilse said, "like we're feeding."

"How deep?" Jeffrey said.

"To six hundred feet if you can. As steeply as possible, quick."

"Pilot," Jeffrey said, "make your depth six hundred feet. Forty-five degrees down bubble smartly."

"Make my depth six hundred feet, aye," Meltzer said. "Forty-five degrees down bubble, aye."

The deck tilted forward and Ilse almost slipped. The 'scope handle banged on her head.

"Commander," the SEAL copilot said, "aspect change on Master 19. Blade rate is increasing too."

"What the hell's going on?" Clayton called, his voice low and clipped on the intercom.

Ilse watched the destroyer's TMA. A new dot appeared but off-center. Then came a second, a third.

She saw Jeffrey reach for the mike. "The destroyer is turning away."

Jeffrey stared at the display from the starboard side-mounted high-frequency sonar. On low-power tight-beam it swept back and forth, gradually building a picture. The old wreck loomed large, longer and higher than the ASDS with its tow.

"That's a nice chunk of non-degaussed metal out there," the copilot said. "Some merchie's misfortune, our gain."

"Mmph," Jeffrey said. "She must have foundered and then landed upright. I wonder if anyone drowned."

Ilse shrugged. "Five miles from shore, with this brisk a current . . . storms here brew up pretty fierce."

"Let me hear the wreck's flow noise," Jeffrey said. The SEAL punched some keys and a low rush and hiss filled the air.

"Any backwash or eddies?" Jeffrey said.

Meltzer took his hand off the joy stick and waited. Jeffrey watched the INS.

"Negative, sir," Meltzer said. "Not this close-in on its downstream side. ASDS holding position."

Jeffrey turned to Ilse. "Questions or comments?"

"No, it's just like we planned."

"Then let's get moving," Jeffrey said. "Lord knows who's watching us now."

Jeffrey went aft to the transport compartment. Ilse and the SEAL chief followed. The other SEALs looked up from checking their gear. "We've arrived," Jeffrey said. "Way Point Zulu. Aptly named I should think."

Clayton smiled. "King Shaka would be proud. . . . Let's get you and Ilse outfitted."

Clayton helped Jeffrey don all his swim apparatus and flak jacket, then assisted Ilse. Jeffrey strapped on the rest of the stuff he could wear in the water: survival knife on his left leg—really a tool, not a weapon—K-bar fighting knife on his right, titanium double-edge dive knife on his left arm above his keypad, and of course his inflatable buoyancy compensator, which doubled as a life vest. Last of all came his weight belt, so it could come off first just in case. He put on his mask, tugging the straps, and checked out its head-up display.

Everyone drew breaths through their enhanced Draegers, to verify the regulators and mixed-gas supply. The raiding party crammed into the lockout compartment, Jeffrey and Ilse and all seven SEALs with equipment. Someone dogged the transport compartment hatch.

Jeffrey turned to Meltzer, the stay-behind, who looked back from his pilot's position. "You know the drill," Jeffrey said. "Act like a whale, be here for the rendezvous."

"Aye aye, sir," Meltzer said.

"See if you can breach for long enough to copy the message traffic for *Challenger,* and scout around in case we're near a Boer ASW safety lane."

"Understood, Commander," Meltzer said.

"In fact," Jeffrey said, "when you have a chance, get in touch with *Challenger* by long-range secure acoustic link. Tell them I recommend deploying both the LMRSs, to scope out the minefield more while they're waiting for us. Be careful, but pop up your ESM mast now and then, to grab some electronic intel and help our mother ship triangulate on contacts."

Meltzer nodded. He closed the forward hatch and dogged it from the other side. "Beginning equalization," his intercom voice echoed inside the sphere. A hissing noise started as air was pumped in. Jeffrey and the others kept swallowing, squeezing their noses and blowing, to clear their sinuses and ears. The hissing went on and on—once or twice the chamber creaked.

Finally Meltzer came on again. "Chamber's equalized to one six five feet saltwater. You're now breathing six atmospheres absolute. You're cleared to open the bottom hatch. Good luck."

Clayton reached to the bottom hatch, spun the wheel, and let it slowly drop open. Beneath them, rippling slightly, was a pool, the pitch-black ocean.

"I want to see everyone's cyalume hoop," Clayton said. "Okay, check your buddies one last time, then check your regulators again. Start using them, get out of this nitrogen."

The regulators had built-in diaphragms open to the ambient environment. A series of springs, reducing valves, O-rings, and pistons fed each swimmer gas on demand at a pressure in exact harmony with whatever their depth. Jeffrey knew this had all better work right, else their lungs would collapse or explode.

Clayton checked Ilse, the SEAL chief checked Jeffrey, then Clayton and the chief checked each other. Jeffrey watched in silence while Clayton surveyed the rest of the team, buddied in a pair and a threesome. When all was in order, Clayton positioned his mask, put on his flippers, and dropped chest-deep into the hole.

Treading water casually, he looked up and pulled off his mouthpiece. He exhaled deeply, then took a breath. "We're ten feet from the bottom, remember. Be careful, don't leave any tracks in the sand." He redonned his mouthpiece and sank, and the chief followed quickly.

The chief reappeared in a minute. "We're ready. Watch out for nocturnal eels." He popped down again.

Jeffrey and Ilse went midway in the group. Jeffrey sat on the hatch coaming, fastened his big combat swim fins, held his mask and mouthpiece securely in place, and rolled forward.

The water was sixty-five degrees Fahrenheit, cool, comfortable in moderate doses with the protection of snug bodysuits. Finally the last SEAL was down.

"Grab the line, people." Clayton's voice, now quacky from high-pressure heliox, rang through transducers at Jeffrey's temples. Jeffrey reached up and groped with his hand. Good, got it, the rope that led back to the stern.

The big hatch swung closed, killing the red battle light. Jeffrey saw eight eerie cyalume glows, greenish, plus his own on his arm, but nothing more past his amber mask display. The water appeared fairly clear here, as Ilse had predicted.

"Take a minute, get acclimated," Clayton said.

Jeffrey steadied his breathing. He realized he was starting to sink, so compacted was he by the crush of the water—he let a smidgen of gas into his soft-pack redundant-bladder buoyancy compensator. He felt for the flat underbelly of the ASDS as a reference point, then floated horizontally.

Jeffrey brought his free hand to the flexible part of his mask, pinched his nose through the rubber, and swallowed. He unsealed his nostrils and exhaled into the mask. There, that's better. It took care of the Squeeze, helping his body adjust. It was years since he'd been down this far, outside an SSN hull.

"Comms check, status check, sound off," Clayton said.

"One, good to go," the first shooter said.

When Jeffrey's turn came, he said, "Four, good to go," distorted by the helium's high speed of sound, filling his mouthpiece and larynx. Ilse was Five, Clayton Six.

Finally the last SEAL said, "Nine, good to go." The digitized gertrude was working. Jeffrey wondered idly if it could somehow be programmed to compensate for the effect of the gas on their voices. But at least this way they avoided nitrogen narcosis, oxygen toxemia at depth, and too-strict limits on bottom dwell time from nitrogen infusing their tissues and blood. Rapture of the deep, oxygen seizure, decompression sickness—Jeffrey knew all were killers.

"Move aft and mount up," Clayton said.

CHAPTER 15

Ilse had swum with dolphins before, but it was something else to *be* one, riding inside the dolphin-shaped robotic swimmer delivery vehicle. She let her legs follow the motion, up and down again and again as her stealth SDV drove her forward. Its flukes and flippers gave tremendous momentum, far faster than the sustained one knot the best combat swimmer could do, far more efficient than the best man-made shafted rotary propulsor.

Ilse smiled to herself inside her mouthpiece, the Draeger now feeding pure oxygen as she maintained shallower depth. She rushed for the surface and sprinted and blew. She felt like a mermaid, a water nymph.

On her augmented dive mask display, plugged into the onboard computer, she could see the rest of the team arrayed in an arc, like a pod of natural cetaceans. They made twelve knots over the bottom, steering course three two five, but actually moving on course two nine five, because of the leeway of the current. The water was warmer now, near the surface, 72°F.

The active sonar in the SDV's head, just like a real dolphin's melon, gave off whistles and clicks, mapping the sea and its floor. Some emissions were ultrasonic, but Ilse could feel them nevertheless, slight tickling on her scalp and chin as she rested her forehead on sorbothane padding. The dolphin was equipped with glass eyes, optical-quality portholes. Each time she breached she watched lightning bolts shatter the sky.

"Form up more tightly on me," Clayton called. "We'll ride on a wave, conserve power."

Ilse flexed her elbows and worked the hand controls mounted on both sides of her head. She aimed a bit more to the right. As the mechanical dolphin edged into the turn, the stowed equipment bags pressed on her hips, not uncomfortably but enough to know they were there. She could hear the slight whirring of drive motors, and her eardrums felt each change in depth. The SDV was free-flooding, through blowhole and anus, quite anatomically correct—its jaws didn't open, its face was fixed in a grin. With a knob on the control grips she fine-tuned the air bladders, adjusting her buoyancy and trim.

"Go deep," Clayton ordered. "This roller is breaking." Ilse and the others obeyed. She could hear the roller crashing, feel the jumbling tug of its surge. She pitied a sailor adrift in such seas—each cubic meter of plummeting ocean weighed just over one metric ton.

"Patrol craft coming in," the SEAL chief's voice sounded.

"I see it," she heard Clayton say. She saw it too on her sonar, now that they were under the waves. It was off to port, undoubtedly laboring hard. It gradually drew in closer.

"Let's give the lookouts a show," Clayton said. "On my mark, when the range falls to two hundred yards, we'll close and then caper a bit off her bow."

"Watch out for the pounding and yawing," Ilse heard Jeffrey say, "and also watch out for her screws."

Now Ilse saw the coast on her sonar. Bearing three three zero relative were two rocky corners of land, slowly drawing closer as the robotic dolphins worked their way across the Agulhas Current. Between those two contacts lay the tidal estuary at the mouth of the Ohlanga River.

"Outer reef approaching," Clayton said. "Maintain twenty-five-foot depth. The surf here's terrific."

Ilse worked her handgrips, complying. She saw the reef in outline on her mask display, ten to twenty feet farther down, a hundred feet across, stretching as far north and south as her sonar would go. The sonar picked up biologics, looking like static or snow on her screen. Her dolphin was jostled by turbulent water, swells piling up to explode.

She'd dived these reefs in better days, in much better weather, for fun, and she'd tanned on the yellow sand beaches. She knew there were beautiful coral formations beneath her here, and tropical fish in breathtaking colors. Now all was blackness.

"Okay," Clayton said. "We're through. The sandbar's next. Form line ahead. Watch out for what's left of the shark nets."

The water was deeper again, some seventy feet, but suddenly shelving, the boulder-strewn inner surf zone coming up. Ilse shifted into position, the fifth in the column of dolphins of war.

"Now's the toughest part, people," Clayton said. "We're past high slack water because of delays. There are strong rips working against us, and even this close to spring tide it'll be very shallow."

Ilse saw on her mask that her pulse had gone over a hundred. This was the first time she really felt scared. She moved a bit closer to the dolphin in front of her, Jeffrey's.

"Six, Eight, I'm at bingo battery charge," she heard over the gertrude.

"Six, Four," Jeffrey called, "I'm close to it too. This storm is more work than the model predicted."

Ilse glanced at her own amp-hour levels. She was doing better, she weighed less.

"Keep going," Clayton said, and then something garbled.

"Six, Five," Ilse called. "Repeat, please."

Clayton's answer was unintelligible. The outgoing tide, the gale from the west unobstructed over the estuary, the Ohlanga's rain-bloated outflow, all made the swells pile up hard. The wave action on the inner bar was ruining sonar conditions, so thick was the air and sand being mixed with the water. Ilse's ears crackled constantly, though her range to the bottom was constant. They were all drifting now to the north, a strong longshore countercurrent inside the reef that was spoiling the dolphins' formation.

Suddenly reception came back for a moment. "*—fast,*" Clayton shouted. "This one's a rogue wave! Pull back, Three, pull *back*!"

"I'm out of control!" Three said. Three was the SEAL chief, Clayton's salty second-in-charge.

Ilse heard the roar of the plunging breakers getting louder, a crescendo in the darkness. There was a crashing concussion, a million tons of angry seawater falling mercilessly in on itself—the shock of it rattled her bones.

"Everyone circle between the reef and the bar," Clayton said. "Get down to four zero feet. That should be under the surge and the set."

Ilse turned tightly and dived. Her pulse read 128. Her respiration was 30, too fast. She switched back to heliox—if she kept hyperventilating, pure O_2 this deep would give her convulsions for sure.

"Three, Six," Clayton called. "Three, Six. . . ." Nothing. "Where's Three? Does anybody see Three?" No one answered.

"One, Six," Clayton said, "come in. Two, Six, come in."

Nothing.

"Six, Four," Jeffrey's voice said, "I was watching on sonar. I think One and Two made it through."

Then someone said, "Christ, I felt something snap."

"Give me a proper report," Clayton said.

"Six, Three, I'm damaged."

"Where are you, Three? Pulse on active."

Ilse saw him signaling off to her left, down near the bottom.

"I'm moving to help," Jeffrey said.

"Three," Clayton said, "watch your gas mix. Do you still have propulsion?"

A pause. "Yeah," the chief said, "but I'm blind. My head-up display's been knocked out."

"Keep pulsing," Jeffrey said. "I can talk you through if I know where you are. . . . Watch out, slow your rate of ascent."

"Three, Six, is your backup dive console working?"

"Uh, this is Three, uh, I've got magnetic compass and saltwater depth."

"Three, Six, don't forget to adjust for the freshwater river."

"Yeah, LT, I know the drill."

"Six, Four," Jeffrey said, "these rollers are just too powerful. We have to stay back in the troughs."

"Concur," Clayton said. "We might graze the bottom, but I'd much rather that than be pounded to pieces."

"I'm ready for another go," Three said.

"Form line abeam," Clayton said. "This is taking too long. We'll all chase the next twenty-footer. And watch out, people, don't get skewered by one of the sharpened-steel landing craft obstacles."

The last SEAL accelerated hard, then leaped the semi-submerged barbed-wire entanglement that protected the river and beaches. So, Jeffrey told himself, all we have to worry about now is getting shot at.

The dolphins avoided the mud flats, following a deeper channel near the south bank of the wide Ohlanga estuary mouth. On his sonar Jeffrey could see the bank and the channel—the north bank was lost in the clutter. When he broke the surface, Jeffrey could make out through his eyeholes, by the flicker of lightning, machine-gun posts overlooking the beach promenades. The sandbagged emplacements on top of the dunes looked like igloos. The nearer one's weapon tracked him and the other SDVs from almost point-blank range, till the team moved upriver past its arc of fire. Jeffrey was sure the MGs on the far bank were trained on them too—at four hundred yards they were in easy killing range for 12.7mm tripod-mounted crew-served fire, even in such adverse weather and lighting conditions. Jeffrey saw poles on the near bank that looked like aiming stakes. He wondered if the SDVs' path had been registered for mortars and artillery.

But the intel was correct. These were disciplined troops; they didn't waste ammo on wildlife. Ahead now Jeffrey's display picked up the pilings of the viaduct that carried the M4 national motorway over the Ohlanga. Two searchlights snapped on, one near each bank, catching the dolphins in enfilade. Right above them, as the column of raiders approached the bridge, Jeffrey saw soldiers lean over the rail.

"Maintain speed," Clayton said. "Don't hit one of the pylons."

"Four, Three, how am I doing?"

"You're fine, Chief," Jeffrey said. "Just hold this bearing." As the searchlights swept past, Jeffrey got a glimpse of SEAL Three. "Jesus, Chief, your whole dorsal fin snapped off."

"When that rogue wave hit, I got rolled over twice on the bar."

As Jeffrey got closer to the motorway bridge, the pilings spread farther apart on his mask display.

"Four, Six," Clayton called, "any pearls of wisdom for all of us combat virgins?"

"Yeah," Jeffrey said. "Some things you never get used to."

They were almost up to the bridge. Jeffrey's legs waved constantly inside the fake dolphin's flukes, making slow progress against the flood current which was strengthened by a venturi effect between the concrete abutments. He knew he was splashing, the SDV's equivalent of screw cavitation, but that couldn't be helped and it was sort of realistic. Real bottlenoses coming upstream to eat or play would make splashes too. Hopefully the sentries wouldn't notice or care that *these* dolphins were larger than any others they'd seen.

"A guard's going to throw something," Jeffrey heard Ilse hiss.

"Easy," Jeffrey said, "easy. These things are lined with Kevlar, and we've got flak jackets on underneath."

"It looks like some kind of grenade!"

"Don't panic, Ilse," Jeffrey said. The SEAL chief was safely under the roadway now, so Jeffrey slowed down. "I'm right here, Five, right next to you." It occurred to Jeffrey that if razor-sharp white-hot shrapnel did penetrate the high-modulus aramid fibers and hit human flesh, these dolphins would bleed just like real ones.

Jeffrey looked up through an eyehole. A soldier looked straight down at him and tossed something.

"Fuck!" Ilse said.

Then, in the searchlights, Jeffrey saw the object flutter away.

"Five, Four, we're okay," Jeffrey said. "It was just an empty cigarette pack."

"All right," Clayton said. "This is a good quiet spot. Hold put while the chief and I do a recon."

Ilse let her SDV idle at four feet of depth to the keel, its dorsal fin barely submerged.

Clayton came on again. "It's clear, and air quality is acceptable. All shooters dismount, upend your dolphins, blow ballast, and surface for unloading. Four, Five, you two stay under while we form a perimeter."

Again Ilse waited. Eventually she heard, "Four, Six. Five, Six. Mission specialists dismount, upend your dolphins, blow ballast, and surface for unloading."

Ilse undid her connections to the dolphin's electronics. By feel she opened the clips that held shut the SDV's belly. She dropped down under it, still breathing through her Draeger. She flipped the SDV over. This wasn't easy. Even submerged, hence neutrally buoyant, it massed almost three hundred pounds. She used one of its flippers for leverage. Finally she reached inside for the control grips and fully inflated the bladders. She held on and rode the thing up to the surface. She kicked with her swim fins, treading water. Driving rain pelted her head.

She felt some resistance against her fins, more than just the water. With the next lightning bolt she saw why. She was surrounded by tall reeds, the salt marsh of the Umhlanga Lagoon Nature Reserve. She waited, straining her ears against the constant noise of the wind.

Jeffrey and Clayton swam over as the sky flickered once more. Now out of their Draegers and masks, they wore battle helmets instead, with visors flipped down and switched on.

"Feeling better?" Jeffrey said.

"Yes," Ilse said. "Come on, we have work to do."

Silently they pulled her SDV into shallower water. Now she saw some of the other dolphins, floating inverted as if they were dead—she wondered if one of them was the cargo carrier slaved to SEAL Seven's control. There was no sign at all of the SEALs.

Ilse's feet touched the soft gooey bottom, stirring up bubbles of gas. It stank. She figured this was as good a time as any for a clandestine pee—diving had a diuretic effect on the body.

Jeffrey and Clayton helped her remove her equipment bags and change into her battle kit. She positioned the high-impact goggles that would protect her corneas from dust and smoke and worse. Then she switched on her helmet and lowered the imaging visor. Lastly she pulled off her flippers. She stowed them inside the dolphin with her other unneeded gear. Clayton and Jeffrey submerged the SDVs one by one, disappearing under the water to clip them shut, free diving, then surfacing again for air.

Ilse adjusted her helmet to sit more comfortably, then tightened the padded chin strap. Using hand signals, Clayton led her onto dry land near a mangrove tree. She got down on her haunches, looking around, the visor's green monochrome low-light-level TV and false-color IR alternating every half second. The raindrops scattered infrared, but even so, she could see about three times as far with the infrared photodetectors than she could with the multistage image intensifiers. Sight lines were broken by trees and dunes.

Ilse let the saltwater run off her body, then adjusted her vest. Its front was laden with gas mask, canteens, field dressings, half a dozen ammo clips, primary and backup radiation dosimeters, and four different kinds of grenade.

Ilse shifted her hip holster slightly and opened the strap that held her big pistol in place. She checked that the weapon was loaded, and switched on the power. She practiced quick drawing three times, to loosen up and make sure her aiming reticle worked. Satisfied, she looked at Clayton and Jeffrey.

She waited while Jeffrey dabbed her with waterproof

blackface, like shoe polish, from a small tin. She noticed Clayton was using some too, despite his ebony complexion.

"Keeps my sweaty skin from shining," he said, grinning at her in the dark. Jeffrey positioned her helmet mike.

The SEAL chief handed out bottled water. "Draeger air's very dry. Rehydrate."

"Thanks," Ilse whispered. Insects were starting to find them, and she put on odorless bug repellent. The air was humid and heavy, in spite of the low-pressure front of the dying hurricane.

"Comms check, status check, sound off," Clayton whispered. Soon everybody was ready. "Remember, watch out for bushbuck and wild boar. But think of them now as our friends, constant false alarms for enemy urea sniffers and infrared." Clayton turned to Jeffrey as an especially strong gust punished the reeds. "At least with this weather we don't have to worry about motion detectors."

"Or startling the birds," Jeffrey said.

Ilse nodded. "There are a lot of really nice species here." She'd seen a crested guinea fowl once, and an osprey nest full of young.

"I feel like we oughta say something," Jeffrey said. "As far as I know we're the first Allied troops to land in occupied southern Africa."

"Lafayette, we are here, or something," Clayton said.

"Anyway, Ilse," Jeffrey said, "for what it's worth, welcome home."

Ilse's breathing was steady and hard, and so was her perspiration. The grade averaged 10 percent as they worked their way inland, and her equipment weighed forty pounds. She couldn't complain, though—the men were all carrying twice that. They formed single file on a trail, one of the reserve's walking paths—this would mean fewer surprises. Sight lines were still short, from the rain and the plant life. If they moved through the sandy underbrush instead—normal tactics in bush—with the noise of the wind and flailing branches they could blunder into a patrol, triggering a chaotic encounter battle. A stand-up fire fight now would ruin everything.

In a few minutes they did hear a patrol coming, from the other direction, upwind. The men were talking in Afrikaans, not happy being out in the storm. Ilse and Jeffrey and the SEALs moved off the trail at a bend. They blended with the terrain, using dips in the ground and deadfall. Jeffrey found her a good spot behind a broad strelitzia tree, then he silently crawled away. Ilse pressed her cheek low, trying to meld with the dune. The smell of the mulch was intense. Heavy raindrops pattered her backside, falling through leaves overhead.

"A perfect L-shaped ambush site," she heard Jeffrey say, just audible on the circuit.

"I know," Clayton whispered inside her helmet. "It's a shame to just let them go by."

The patrol got closer and closer. Ilse tried not to breathe. One Boer said something vulgar, another snickered coarsely. Ilse was sure she'd be spotted, her heart was sending such hammerblows through the ground. An insect stung her neck, a burning that grew sharper as it fed. A snake slithered over her ankles. She waited to feel the kick of a boot, the prodding of a gun barrel, the jab of a bayonet. She waited for the stutter and flash of assault rifles, the full-auto spray of hard pointy bullets that would shred foliage and her flesh.

Soon the enemy squad was past, oblivious to their presence. The gale broke too many stalks and twigs, and the rain flushed the gravel-strewn trail—the SEAL team's spoor went unnoticed.

"Nine, Six, status," Clayton said when the soldiers could no longer be heard.

"Six, Nine, wait one." Then, "They're not sneaking back. Rear is secure."

"Be careful," Jeffrey said. "They might have been noisy on purpose. There may be another squad further on, hoping they've put us off guard."

"I concur," Clayton said. "You all heard the man, stay focused."

On Clayton's word they each drank an entire canteen so the water wouldn't slosh. They moved out again, cautiously, falling in line by the numbers. They headed west, paralleling the river. After a measured number of paces they turned south, into the Hawaan Nature Reserve. The way grew even steeper, the ground more soil than sand. Ilse's breathing came hard.

"Six, Four," Jeffrey said, "a helo's coming."

"Four, Six, I don't hear it yet."

"Six and Four, Five," Ilse said, "shouldn't we just ignore it?"

"Five, Four," Jeffrey said, "you're right. We'll look like a normal patrol, an extra because of the storm. I doubt they have the connectivity to validate us or not."

"Concur," Clayton said. "All numbers keep moving."

SEAL One, Ilse knew, had the point. He carried a small ground-penetrating radar, for detecting land mines and booby traps, buried or fastened to trees. It would also give some indication of metal weapons to the flanks or the front, and by changing modes One could scan for tunnels and foxholes.

So far they'd bypassed ten mines, all plastic, sweep-resistant types sized to maim, not kill. Each time SEAL One found a mine the person behind him would kneel by it to warn all the others. That person let everyone else go by, resting in the meantime—if you could call that resting. Then he took position in front of Nine, who constantly brought up the rear.

Jeffrey had just had mine guard duty again, so Ilse walked behind SEAL One. The next booby trap would be hers. The helo passed low overhead, hovered up there past the acacia tops, then tore away in the dark.

"Eight, Six," Ilse heard, "did you copy their traffic?"

"Six, Eight, negative. Everything's deeply encrypted."

"Pick up the pace," Clayton said.

The terrain was getting rocky, and Ilse's legs were very sore. She reminded herself the whole hike to the Sharks Board was barely three miles—it seemed like forever already. She passed some eucalyptuses, then erica, protea, heather. She finally broached the plateau. Suddenly Ilse saw One freeze. She paused and then moved toward him, since he didn't give her the danger sign. All she had to do now was crouch and point at the mine, as she'd done once before, but she still felt nervous as hell.

SEAL One hit the deck and crawled forward, his mine detector abandoned, his machine pistol gripped in both hands. "Contact, contact, contact," he whispered.

Ilse dropped to the ground. She knew he hadn't been spotted, since she didn't hear any shots. But then she remembered their weapons were silenced—could the Boers have silencers too?

"One, Six, report," Clayton said.

"Six, One, disregard, clear." Then One added, "Oh Christ."

Ilse crawled up and joined him behind a wild almond tree, lugging the mine detector, her pistol out in her hand. Through her visor she saw what One had spotted. Ahead was a clearing with benches, one of the arboretum's picnic areas. Near its center some mannequins twirled in the wind. Then she saw they weren't mannequins.

Each body hung a half meter or so from the ground. All of them were naked. Three were men, two were women, all Caucasian. Their hands were tied behind their backs. Nooses were tight round their necks, simple slipknots, nothing fancy, the ropes fastened to a stout oak tree branch. The heads were cocked inanely at different angles, one woman looking down with her chin near her chest, as if she were shy or had watched herself as she died.

Both women's hair had been braided, crudely, to keep it out of the way. Their legs were also bound snugly at knees and ankles, so they bent slightly. For some reason the men's legs weren't tied—they pointed straight down toward the ground, their now-useless genitals dangling between. From the way each corpse twisted and swung, Ilse could tell they were stiff, though the women's breasts jiggled strangely as their feet jostled each other, no rigor mortis in the fat underlying their nipples.

From the look of the bodies, their flat bellies, they all appeared fairly young, fit. Maybe they were troops who'd spoken out one time too often. Maybe the others in their unit had been made to watch in the clearing, or even to yank the benches out from under them. Did they hang them all at once, or one at a time so the remaining victims could watch and listen? Ilse knew it could take five or ten minutes before each stopped struggling completely, and then they'd hang limp, hips cocked slightly forward, buttocks and members relaxed.

As Clayton and SEALs One and Seven scouted, Ilse moved toward the corpses. Their faces were horribly swollen and dark, eyes bulging blindly, tongues sticking out, giving them from the neck up an odd uniformity, androgynous, sexless. Ilse looked farther down, fascinated in spite of herself. From the length of one woman's pubic hair, either she trimmed it frequently or she couldn't be more than sixteen—Ilse could make out the cleft of her crotch, as rainwater streaked down her thighs.

Ilse realized Jeffrey was standing next to her now, also staring. This had happened recently, probably the evening before—the bodies weren't bloated yet, and there wasn't much of a smell. If they'd lost control of their bowels and bladders while led to the gibbet or on it, the deluge had washed it away. If the men came hard like some did, there wasn't a trace of it now. But the associations were too strong for her. Ilse turned to Jeffrey and buried her head, helmet and all, in his chest.

"*Use* the anger," Jeffrey said, holding her, stroking her back. "Feel it stirring your blood."

DOWNTOWN DURBAN

Gunther Van Gelder ordered another straight gin. This wasn't recommended for people recovering from heatstroke, but he needed something to deaden his mind. The cabaret was noisy and crowded, full of tobacco smoke and wild people, and the raunchy floor show music blared. Given the late hour and very strict curfew, the customers were all military officers, high-powered politicos, and women they'd brought as their dates.

Several people had offered to buy Van Gelder a drink. His naval uniform with gold submarine badge did the trick. But each time he politely refused. He needed to be alone. Several whores who worked the bar had approached him aggressively too. Again he refused, not because he didn't like girls. He was just in the wrong sort of mood. He'd been at sea too long. The changes around him were shocking.

The war was going so well, everyone said. Axis strength was increasing, the Allies a mere empty shell, right thinking had total control. Was this, then, why the nightly news on the one TV station still working—government-owned—always opened with more executions? Was this why even right-thinking Boers averted their eyes from the sky, wearing dark sunglasses outdoors even at night, afraid of an infernal nuclear flash? Was this why children were starving, white children, and people were eating their dogs?

Careful, Gunther, he told himself. This is dangerous talk, even alone in your mind. Van Gelder laughed, chiding himself at the irony, that he'd come *here* of all places for solitude. But a submariner made his own privacy wherever he went, internally.

Duty, patriotism, glory, and honor. Disaffection, dissent, treason, and death. There was no middle ground anymore. Slavery, oppression, environmental destruction, all were common currency of this New Order that wanted to run half the world. It was becoming too much like the last New Order, the torchlight parades and the terror, the fearful or eager obedience, abdicating all moral standards, the marching bands and the slaughter. He could see it much too clearly now—how could everyone else be so blind?

Another woman approached him. She wasn't bad-looking, this one, nice clothes and subtle makeup—but then the resurgent Union of South Africa's brave fighting men deserved the best of the best. She fingered Van Gelder's qualification badge, the diesel boat over oak leaves and trident which he'd striven so hard to deserve. She couldn't possibly know what it stood for, the sacrifices, the risks. She offered to party for free.

Van Gelder told her to leave him alone, and looked at his watch. He was due back on *Voortrekker*, inside the bluff, in barely a couple of hours, and he knew he was getting intoxicated. He had a responsibility, to his captain and ship and his crew.

Van Gelder sighed. When push came to shove, there really *was* no escape. The navy was his life, his family, the underwater world was his home, the sea his most passionate mistress.

The hooker was very persistent. She told him he was

cute and snuggled against him. She said she'd do whatever he wanted, and reached for his crotch.

Very well, Number One, he told himself, then laughed at his own little joke. There were other distractions than drinking, other forms of release and denial. He asked the young woman her name.

CHAPTER 16

UMHLANGA ROCKS

To Jeffrey it seemed Ilse had gotten past some kind of hump, made some sort of decision. Her eyes and her jaw said no nonsense now, and her tone of voice backed it up. SEAL Two, their corpsman, treated the welt on her neck with an ointment.

After more mines, another helo, and another enemy patrol, the team egressed the Hawaan Nature Reserve. They skirted a commercial nursery, closed and looking abandoned. Apparently they'd made it through the main defensive crust along the water's edge. They moved south, paralleling the beach, through forests and fields bordering a residential development, exclusive homes on big tracts. The houses were quiet, bare, completely blacked out. Jeffrey thought them evacuated.

The raiding party changed course to the west, inland again, and climbed more. They crested the ridge above Umhlanga Rocks, crossing the skyline in a clump of trees down on their bellies. This side of the crest there were no structures, no local roads. The ground in front of them dropped off steeply, and it was tricky to balance with their gear. Fully exposed to the weather, face-on to the wind and the rain, their progress was slowed to a stagger.

Somewhere below them, Jeffrey knew, lay the N2 Freeway, the major multilane artery that paralleled the coast— it was ten miles straight to downtown Durban. Jeffrey thought he heard heavy truck engines going north from the city, either troop movements or a supply column. They were too distant to see anything, no hope to get useful intel. Three miles beyond the N2, the briefing maps had shown, was a major railroad line, but no sign right now of a train. Beyond that, Jeffrey also knew, were the Durban defense district's mobile reserves, including main battle tanks.

The group headed south again. They avoided a remotely operated antishipping/antiaircraft radar site ideally placed on the ridge. The team kept a safe distance from Autumn Drive, a dead-end road with a police station. Twice in natural clearings in the woods they found camouflaged heavy-machine-gun nests, stocked with lots of ammo and with perfect fields of fire—both emplacements were unoccupied, with no thermal signature, lying in wait for an Allied invasion.

They hauled ass farther on, paused to take five, and turned back toward the Indian Ocean, back over the ridge crest. Behind Jeffrey now, inland across the N2, was the sprawling Mount Edgecombe Country Club, presumably deserted this time of night. To Jeffrey's left, in the direction of the Ohlanga estuary from whence they'd come, was a ten-acre overgrown field.

Off to Jeffrey's right was a small airstrip, meant for microlights and gliders before the war. Past it lay more unused land, and in another mile came the tall concrete structures of the Tongaat-Hulett sugar refinery.

Now the local flying club was defunct, the short runway broken up, long steel rods driven in to skewer an airborne assault. The SEAL chief and two of his shooters found the place protected by several old men, retired cops or home guard militia. They died quickly, silently, to protect the rear, the bodies concealed where they'd later be blasted to pieces.

Jeffrey and Ilse and the SEALs were 3,500 yards south of the estuary, 1,400 yards in from the beach, at an elevation of four hundred feet. Before them, eastward, just down the hill on the way to the sea, were the empty outdoor amphitheater, caltrop-covered tourist parking lot, and two-story beige-brown concrete-and-masonry headquarters building of their target, the Natal Sharks Board.

Seeing the bodies hanged in the clearing had forced Ilse to make a decision. There was so much death all around, so many lives being snuffed, what difference was one more, her own? It was best to assume she would die so she could get on with her job. Fear was a useless distraction; concern for survival was dulling her edge. If the mission failed, her death was the least of anyone's worries.

Somehow—perversely, she knew—seeing it this way would help. It brought her a calm concentration, turned everything into a game—granted, a blood sport—an adventure with outcome unknowable, one she'd do her damnedest to win.

She gazed at their objective, vague shapes through her visor, strobed by frequent lightning. The heat signature of the installation told her the laboratory staff was going full bore. Inside that building, behind the blackout curtains, an abomination was taking shape, perverting fifty years of world-class research on marine biology and swimmer safety. By morning Ilse's life might be over, but tonight her task was direct: cauterize these people and what they were doing, send them straight to a hot man-made hell.

Jeffrey crouched amid the chilly runoff in the erosion gully on the south flank of the Sharks Board. He peered into the dripping viewer scope, seeing through the fiber-optic cable—the image was constantly streaked by the heavy downpour. SEAL One panned the cable's other end around. Jeffrey knew One was at the very edge of the semitropical underbrush, wearing a lightweight gillie suit he'd pulled out of his backpack. The gillie suit was designed as sniper camouflage, with an insulated silver lining to suppress the point man's infrared.

"One, Four," Jeffrey whispered. "No guard dogs?"

"Four, One, no," the point man said. "Just foot patrols."

"Pan right," Jeffrey said. "Show me the missile bunker." The image shifted as ordered. "Hold it." Jeffrey zoomed in as lightning flickered again. He studied the emplacement, its rounded corners jutting from the slope. Its bulk was nestled in dead ground inside the asphalt crescent formed by the main entrance's big U-shaped driveway. More thunder rumbled.

"The bunker's thermal signature's diffuse even this close," Jeffrey said. "Looks like they put a resistor grid under the reinforced concrete."

"Yeah," Clayton said as he lay to Jeffrey's right. "Just like with the lab in the basement."

"We can't tell if it's occupied."

"That's the idea."

Something out of focus blocked Jeffrey's view, then passed. He realized it was a soldier.

"One, Four, what are they carrying?"

"Different stuff, Commander," SEAL One whispered, sounding scratchy above the roar of the driving rain. "I see some H&Ks, some Uzis and Galils, and homegrown models."

"One, Six," Clayton said. "Are they using silencers?"

"Everyone I've seen so far, boss, yes. And night-vision goggles."

Jeffrey turned to Clayton. "It's like we thought," Jeffrey said. "Stealthy security. Nothing excessive or obvious. No hostage encampments nearby, to draw attention or make for witnesses."

"That must be why they put a missile bunker here," Clayton said. "An excuse for the fence and patrols."

"Six, Three," came over the circuit.

"Go ahead, Chief," Clayton said.

"Four sentries on the roof. They shift around a lot, trading off the corners."

"Chief," Jeffrey said, "what about inside?"

"IR shows a bunch of them in some kind of meeting on the second floor. In a conference room, I think, watching TV."

"That sounds like research staff," Jeffrey said.

"There are also two people in offices, on the downhill side of the structure, near the overhang by the entrance. They're sitting, haven't moved in a while."

"First floor?" Jeffrey said as sweat and rainwater dripped from his nose.

"Two soldiers inside the front door," the SEAL chief said, "two by the back exit, two by the stairs to the basement. Two more in the pantry area—one of 'em's making coffee, the other just lit up a smoke."

"Anyone else on one?" Jeffrey said.

"No roving patrols or staff."

"The audiovisual center?"

"The auditorium wing is empty."

"The boat workshop and garage?"

"Wait one, some heat sources in there. . . . Okay, that's just machinery. It's empty."

"The relief shift must bivouac down in the village," Jeffrey said, "by the disused hotels and shopping malls. . . . What's the total number of outside guards?"

"Twelve right now," the SEAL chief said.

"Three, Four, wait one," Jeffrey said. "Break break. One, Four, what's happening to the east?"

"Four, One, Umhlanga Rocks Drive is totally dead, no

sign of reinforcements. One vehicle in front, soft-skinned truck, light-duty Samil-20 four-by-four, engine's cold."

Jeffrey turned to Clayton. "That makes two dozen shooters, half a platoon, plus whatever they have in the bunker and basement."

"Unfair odds," Clayton said. "For them."

"Three and One, Four," Jeffrey said. "Can you tell which one is their officer?"

"Four, One, negative. No one's been acting in charge."

"Four, Three, no obvious sergeant either. If one of 'em's actually present, he's smart enough not to show."

Jeffrey turned to Clayton again. "So their HQ squad could be downhill, or here but somewhere hardened."

"Yeah," Clayton said.

"I want Ilse to take a look," Jeffrey said. Clayton got out of the way. Jeffrey slid sideways and watched Ilse crawl through the mud to the viewscope.

"It's just like it used to be," she said. "Except for the fence and the bunker . . . and the soldiers, of course."

"You sure?" Jeffrey said. "One, pan around again. Ilse, watch for anything strange, bumps in the ground, things sticking out of the building."

"Those video cameras," Ilse said. "The ones covering the lawn. That's new. This was a low-crime area."

"Okay," Jeffrey said.

"Six, Seven," another SEAL called.

"Go ahead, Seven," Clayton said.

"Ground-penetrating radar sweep is complete. Water and sewage go downhill, east, as expected. Gas comes in that way too. No PVC conduits or buried pipes on the other exposures."

"Seven, Four," Jeffrey said. "Are you sure? Have you confirmed all phone and power and data lines lead out above the ground?"

"Four, Seven, roger, Commander. Wires and high-baud optic lines go up the utility pole by the workshop."

"Six, Eight. Six, Eight."

"Eight, Six," Clayton said. "Go ahead, Eight."

"The box is in place," SEAL Eight said, "on the biggest palm tree that overlooks the outdoor amphitheater."

"Eight, Four," Jeffrey said, "is the main building roof covered?"

"Affirmative. There's a great line of sight from the box."

"Eight, Four, acknowledged," Jeffrey said.

"All numbers, Six," Clayton said. "Pull back and get behind solid terrain."

Jeffrey and Ilse and Clayton withdrew to the gully. SEAL One soon joined them there. They hugged the ground as water sloshed over their bodies and gear.

"All numbers, Six. Status check, comms check, sound off."

Everybody was ready.

"With your permission, Commander?" Clayton said.

"Let's do it," Jeffrey said. He gripped his pistol in both hands, keeping it out of the mud. The power diode glowed discreetly, green because the safety was on. The round-count said 18, a full clip. Jeffrey looked to his left. Ilse had her weapon out too.

"All numbers, Six. Safeties off, weapons tight."

Jeffrey worked the switch with his thumb. The diode changed to red.

"Eight, Six," Clayton called.

"Six, Eight, g'head."

"Eight, on my mark you'll be weapons free with the box. On the next lightning flash after that, fire the box. . . . *Mark*."

In seconds there was more lightning. It flickered

strangely this time, and there was an immediate *boom* as if the lightning was right overhead.

"Eight, Six, status?"

"Wait one, LT."

There was popping and whistling on the circuit now, and Jeffrey crossed his fingers that their little trick had worked. A flux compression generator just set off a non-nuclear electromagnetic pulse device.

It was over in microseconds. The gigantic current produced emissions across most of the spectrum, propagating horizontally. Power lines, antennas, radios, laptops, and phones, everything with unshielded circuits in line of sight was destroyed, even if it wasn't turned on. Within the short range of the box, protection required thick metal or concrete, with sealed surge protectors on all leads and feeds. The raiding party loitered outside the area covered. Inside the Sharks Board's perimeter only the basement lab and the missile bunker were safe.

"Confirmed detonation," Eight said. "The treetop is shattered and burning."

"Effect on the installation?" Jeffrey said.

"Looks like a winner, Commander. Power lines are down and took the fiber optics with them. The building's been blacked out and I see small fires inside. Call it a hard kill. People are reacting now, using CO_2 extinguishers. Jesus, that stuff's cold—it's blue on my visors."

"Four, Three," the chief called, "the guards are milling around. They're starting to gather near the tree. The ones on the roof are leaning over the parapet."

"Naturally, Chief," Jeffrey said. "How often do they get to see something struck by lightning?" Over the noise of the rain, Jeffrey heard shouting between the guards, since their radios were fried, but their voices sounded curious more than alarmed.

"All numbers, Six," Clayton said. "Status check, sound off quickly." No one had equipment damage, and radio reception was clearing. "All numbers, Six, prepare to commence the assault."

"Okay," the SEAL chief called, "they're starting to calm down, going their separate ways now. The rain's put out the fire in the tree, and one of the basement's backup diesel generators just came on-line."

Jeffrey looked at Clayton and smiled. "*Now* we get to have our perfect L-shaped ambush. Any return fire'll be backstopped by the ridge uphill or the buildings at the dead airstrip. May I do the honors, Lieutenant?"

"By all means, Commander Fuller. I see old habits die hard."

"Seven and Nine, Four," Jeffrey said. "On my mark, shoot your flash-bang grenades onto the roof. All numbers, choose your targets by azimuth zones like we practiced. You'll be weapons free when you see the explosions on top of the building." Jeffrey waited for another lightning bolt, then the rumble of thunder. "*Mark.*"

He didn't hear the rifle grenades being launched since the rifles were silenced. He did hear and see the grenades going off, like another direct hit from the storm.

The SEALs lying in the underbrush on both sides of Jeffrey and Ilse commenced firing. So did the rest of the team, uphill, from over the lip of the amphitheater. The guards began to stagger and drop, caught in a merciless cross fire. Jeffrey added his own contribution, aiming carefully with his reticle. Every time he fired while the imager was on infrared he could see the track of the bullet, made even hotter by friction with air. It was like watching tracer rounds. He could also see the effects as each round struck home, the spreading and spraying of blood coded red-hot on his visor, then cooling as the body instantly went into shock, and the kaleidoscope of colors on the face of his target from pain and awareness of death.

"This gives me the creeps," Jeffrey said.

"Huh?" Ilse said as she changed clips on her pistol.

"A full-auto fire fight," Jeffrey said, "but we can talk in normal tones and there isn't any hot brass."

"You know," Clayton said as he reloaded his rifle, "you're right."

Jeffrey picked off two more guards who came around the front of the building. The range was thirty-five yards, long for a pistol shot, but the 3-D visor hologram reticle was better than a sniperscope.

"These electric guns are weird," Jeffrey said.

"Ground-level troops are all dead," the SEAL chief called from the rear of the Sharks Board. "Roof guards are still reeling, and the inside ones are confused. The electrified fence is deenergized—the diesel must not be rated for it."

"Grenadiers hit the roof again," Jeffrey ordered. "Fence breachers move in."

SEAL Seven launched another flash-bang. SEAL One grabbed the mine probe. SEAL Two rose and rushed forward, wielding a compressed-air-powered bolt cutter. He quickly sliced a gash through the chain link and high-voltage wires. Jeffrey, Ilse, Clayton, and the three SEALs ran through the gap, then headed right.

"Climbing-rope team starting up," the chief reported from the uphill side. He sounded breathless.

"Okay, Ilse, good luck," Jeffrey said. He left her with Two and Seven, crouching at one corner of the main building near the entrance. Jeffrey and Clayton and SEAL One made for the side door of the missile bunker. SEAL One scanned for booby traps, then went down the poured-concrete steps.

"Door's locked," he said. "Shielding's too good, can't tell if anyone's in there." He pulled out a length of det-cord and a timer and fastened some in a circle around the electronic lock in the door. He ran back up the steps. "Fire in the hole," he said. The three of them hit the deck. There was a sharp *crack* and the stink of spent explosives. SEAL One was on his feet. He kicked in the door and threw in a flash-bang grenade while Jeffrey and Clayton covered him. SEAL One dashed inside.

Jeffrey saw One roll to the ground and start shooting. The bunker wasn't unoccupied. One kept firing, bright muzzle flashes, ricochets pinging and whining. Then he was hit, low down, under his flak jacket. Jeffrey lunged into the bunker. He saw a Boer soldier dead, another taking cover behind the missile, firing at it on purpose. The Boer saw Jeffrey and brought his rifle to bear. Jeffrey aimed at floor level, between the missile launcher struts, and shattered both the man's ankles. As the soldier collapsed, screaming, Jeffrey fired into his abdomen, his neck, his face.

SEAL One was moaning, clutching a bad pelvic wound.

"He got my spine," One said. "I can't feel my legs."

Clayton bent down to help him. The room was filled with smoke.

"The missile!" Jeffrey shouted. "Check out the missile!" Clayton approached it, carrying the detonator box and a heavy bag of equipment. Jeffrey pulled a field dressing from his load-bearing vest. He urged One not to move.

"Warhead's intact," Clayton said. "The bastard shot up the arming section, not that *we* care. . . . Rocket motor's a mess. Good thing it's solid fuel—the stuff landed all over the place. . . . Physics package gamma and neutron emission spectrum checks out."

"Confirmed it's not a dummy?" Jeffrey said. "We've got live U-235?"

Clayton nodded.

"All numbers, Three," Jeffrey heard. "Roof level secured. Four more enemy dead, no friendly losses."

"Three, Four," Jeffrey said, "SEAL One's hit, bad. Missile secured." Jeffrey turned to Clayton, who seemed distraught over his man.

"Leave me," One said. "I'll be okay."

"Do you want some morphine?" Clayton said.

"No," One said, "I have to hold down the bunker. Bandage the exit wound and give me a local. Hook up a plasma drip and give me back my weapon." The smell of blood was thick.

"Shaj," Jeffrey said, "takc carc of him. I'm going over to Ilse's team to lead the main attack. We have to keep up the pressure—we can't let the Boers regroup." Jeffrey grabbed a South African assault rifle and all the ammo he could find on both of the bodies. He noticed the one he'd killed was a lieutenant.

"I'll catch up with you in a minute," Clayton said. He held a spray can of antihemorrhage wound-fill foam.

Jeffrey saw Clayton's jaw and eyes set tight as he treated SEAL One with ruthless efficiency. Jeffrey knew that feeling all too well.

CHAPTER 17

Outside the bunker Jeffrey grabbed SEAL One's mine-detecting scanner. He ran through the rain for the front steps into the Sharks Board, then threw himself to the ground. There were no targets, no return fire.

"Three, Four, status?" Jeffrey called.

"We've breached the roof-level stairway bulkhead," the SEAL chief said. "We're starting down to the second deck."

"Three, Four, okay, Chief. We're assaulting the front entrance now."

Jeffrey got up and waved to Ilse and the two SEALs with her. The four of them charged up the tile-covered steps, between the aluminum handrails, firing at the glassed-in entryway. By their muzzle flashes Jeffrey glimpsed the stickers to the right of the doors. The admissions fee was ten rand for adults, six for kids and oldsters, and they took Visa and MasterCard. Then all the glass shattered and the team ran through, maintaining a volume of fire.

Two guards were visible inside, behind an armored see-through partition that was stopping Jeffrey's rounds. A transceiver sat on a table, its outer casing charred. The guards were heading for the back of the building, where Jeffrey could hear frag grenades and screaming from upstairs. The guards turned when Jeffrey's group came in by the front door. They fired instinctively, but their rifle bullets grazed the partition without going through.

"Blow it down!" Jeffrey shouted. He and Ilse took cover behind two big concrete planters in the lobby. SEALs Two and Seven placed a small satchel charge against the base of the partition, then joined Jeffrey and Ilse. Both guards fled to the rear after popping chemical smoke grenades that blocked IR. The satchel charge went off with a roar—the partition was in ruins. The foursome dashed straight through, tossing stun grenades into side rooms and following up with volleys from their weapons.

Jeffrey's South African R4 clicked empty. He reloaded on the run, another thirty-five-round clip, then fired right through the plasterboard interior walls. The air filled with white dust. His receiver parts clattered noisily, and spent shell casings clinked. He tossed another grenade, then sprayed more bullets after it—the pantry room, unoccupied.

They swept the first floor quickly. The guards had all taken cover inside a sandbagged and armored vestibule, protecting the stairs to the basement lab. SEAL Two was using the radar scanner. "This deck's been structurally reinforced. That's the only way down."

The Boer guards shot at SEAL Two through firing slits in their miniature fortress, and Two hit the deck.

"Four, Three, upper level clear, all occupants terminated. We're at the bottom of the staircase down to you. We'll give covering fire so you can breach the vestibule enclosure."

"Good," Jeffrey said. "Shoot from hip level into the slits. We'll crawl under your suppressing fire and put satchel charges in place."

SEALs Two and Seven each grabbed a pair of

satchels from their packs. Jeffrey dropped his rifle and grabbed a satchel too. He held his pistol in one hand.

"Chief," Jeffrey said, "open fire." The SEAL chief and the two men with him, Eight and Nine, hit the slits of the enclosure. Jeffrey crawled forward with Seven and Two, shooting on the way. They took cover at the base of the sandbags, which were leaking from all the bullet holes.

Two frag grenades came out of a firing slit and landed on the floor. Whoever threw them was hit—there was a scream inside the vestibule. Jeffrey turned. He couldn't reach the grenades. The SEAL chief saw them too. He ran from the stairwell and flung himself, landing just as they detonated. He was lifted off the deck by the concussions, then bounced back in a heap, helmetless and smoldering. Jeffrey knew he was dead, shards of steel through his heart. The other men in the stairwell kept firing at the slits.

"Arm the satchels!" Jeffrey shouted to Two and Seven. Then they pulled well back. "Fire in the hole!" Jeffrey screamed. SEALs Eight and Nine stopped shooting—they must have gone up the stairs.

There was a huge eruption, the loudest explosion so far, and Jeffrey's visor screens blanked out the glare. Jeffrey was deafened; he choked on the fumes and the sand. Rubble was burning and the museum displays were a mess. Pieces of shark skeleton were scattered all over the place. Every window on the first floor was blown out—Jeffrey could feel the breeze. It was helping clear the smoke.

The Boers' enclosure was wrecked. Two bloodied soldiers took cover behind fallen piles of sandbags, firing viciously, one of them now using a light machine gun on a bipod. Six other figures lay limp, some of them dismembered.

"Eight and Nine," Jeffrey said, "open fire again—make them keep their heads down." Just then Clayton arrived, crawling up beside Jeffrey. Both men winced as ricochets zipped by.

"One isn't going to make it," Clayton said.

"The chief bought it too," Jeffrey said.

"I saw," Clayton said. "Let's give them a taste of their own medicine." Clayton took two fragmentation grenades from his vest. More enemy slugs snapped overhead, pulverizing the walls. Clayton held a grenade in each hand and Jeffrey pulled the pins.

Clayton popped the spoons. "One, two, three," he counted. Then he yelled "Grenade!" and tossed them both at the Boers.

Jeffrey hugged the floor, his arms protecting his head. There was a stabbing flash and a sharp double *crack*, brief screaming and writhing, then stillness and silence, except for more painful ringing in Jeffrey's ears. He saw Eight and Nine rush the Boers, firing into their bodies, long past when they were dead.

Jeffrey turned to Ilse. "Get some fire extinguishers and put out whatever's burning!" Ilse nodded. "Don't forget the bodies!" Jeffrey shouted after her. "We don't want their ammo cooking off!"

Jeffrey and Clayton threw concussion grenades down the stairs, then clambered into the basement. They took a bend in the debris-strewn concrete hallway, then came to a door.

Clayton examined it carefully. "It's solid steel, no lock we can reach, the hinges are on the inside."

"Crap," Jeffrey said. "They'll be trying to signal for help."

Clayton turned to his men. "Get the thermite lances!"

SEALs Eight and Nine came down, carrying rods three feet long, and wearing asbestos gauntlets. They put on dark goggles, then donned their gas masks, then pulled out igniters for the rods. The rods began to burn, a hissing, brilliant white. Eight and Nine held the rods to the door, starting to burn their way through. Soon Nine said, "It looks like three-inch armor plate." He and Eight kept working. SEAL Two set up a battery-powered fan on the steps, for ventilation.

"Two and Seven," Clayton said. "Police up the bodies outside, dump them in the workshop. Establish perimeter security, the amphitheater, the road." The two men nodded and left.

"This'll go faster if we help," Jeffrey said, then he coughed from the fumes. He and Clayton put on their gas masks and lit two more lances. Above the thermite's eager, potent hiss Jeffrey heard Ilse working upstairs, the squirting sound of extinguishers.

They were all on their third set of lances, the last they had. They were almost done making a hole at the base of the door, big enough to run through at a crouch.

"This is the exciting part," Jeffrey said, sweating in the built-up heat. "We know the biosafety four containment's at the other end of this level. We don't know what else is down here or how many personnel."

"I'm worried they'll have school kids," Clayton said. "Experiment subjects, for hostages."

"This thing ain't over," Jeffrey said.

"We're just about finished," Nine said. A small lip in the middle of the top cut held the square chunk of door in place. SEALs Nine and Eight held the lances to the side. The thermite kept sparking and smoking, and the air stank from burned steel.

"We can fit the peeper through here," Eight said. "It's cool enough now, LT." He pointed to one spot where the jagged gap flared slightly.

Clayton went to the door. He bent the tip of the fiber-optic wand and pushed it through the cut. He looked through the viewer. "The lights are on inside, but I don't see people or weapons. The front walls and partitions are heated and insulated. They're opaque to IR. . . . I don't see any booby traps, but I can't be sure."

Jeffrey took Clayton's place at the viewer. He twirled the wand between thumb and forefinger, to make the lens pan around.

"You're right," Jeffrey said, "more shielding. Another layer of security, even in there." Jeffrey could see worktables covered with papers, different kinds of cabinets, big black binders on bookshelves, a few desktop PCs. Then he saw a TV monitor, hooked to a VCR.

Something was showing on the screen, but the angle was too oblique. Several chairs were grouped in front of the set, empty, one knocked over, as if people had been sitting and watching and then scattered with the attack. That meant they were still down here somewhere, farther in. Jeffrey saw a central corridor with doors off to both sides. The corridor ended in some kind of air lock with a porthole. Through the porthole he saw stainless steel. Above the air lock a red light was flashing.

Behind Jeffrey, Ilse came down the stairs. "The fires are out," she said. She smelled distinctly of smoke. She crouched on the concrete floor, her black wet suit snug around her thighs. She clutched her pistol in both hands, pointed toward the overhead. She looked incredibly sexy.

"What now?" Ilse said.

"Look through the viewer, get oriented," Jeffrey said. Ilse put one eye to the ocular. "Memorize what you see," he told her. "Visualize going in."

"Okay," Ilse said. "I'm ready."

Jeffrey let the two SEALs take a peek. "Everyone change to hollow point only," he ordered. "No armor-piercing rounds near the containment." He pulled from his vest an ammo clip color-coded green, with distinctive ribbing. He cleared his pistol and reloaded with the clip. Ilse and the others did the same.

"Finish the cut," Clayton said. "After we go through, fan out. Don't damage computers or notebooks. Shoot only when you have targets, kill everyone you see. If they have a child, he won't make much of a shield. Aim for the bad guy's eyes, like we trained. His fingers'll go slack instantly."

"What do we do with the hostage?" SEAL Nine said.

"We'll worry about that if it happens," Jeffrey said.

"Any second now," Eight said, working his torch.

"One, Six," Clayton called. "One, Six, how you making out?"

There was a pause. "Six, One, I'm cold, and thirsty."

"Pull up your wet-suit hood," Clayton said. "You'll feel warmer. And drink from your canteen. If you need more water, just call me." Clayton sounded choked up.

"One, Four," Jeffrey said. He had to clear his throat. "You did a great job going in there. We're on the next-to-last phase now. We'll be back to you soon. Hang tough."

"Yeah," One said, obviously in pain.

"Two and Seven, Six. Any outside activity?"

"Six, Two, negative."

"Six, Seven, no unusual radio traffic, nothing at all from the lab. . . . I think the rain might be stopping."

Ilse watched SEAL Nine give the metal slab a shove. It fell inward with a clank. Eight dashed in, Nine followed. Jeffrey went after Clayton, then Ilse duck-walked through.

Jeffrey held back, protecting Ilse now as the rest of the team moved forward. Ilse pulled empty equipment bags and two digital cameras from her pack and started rifling the desks. The SEALs advanced, covering each other methodically, shouting "Clear" as they checked each office in turn.

"*Shit,*" Ilse said, eyeballing several computers. "The backs are off. They took out the hard drives themselves."

"I don't see any floppies or CD-RWs either," Jeffrey said. He pointed to empty spaces on the desks, where disk holders had probably been. Bullets hit the door and Ilse and Jeffrey ducked.

"They've been destroying the evidence," she said, "the whole time we were breaking in."

"You're the expert, Ilse. What do we do?"

"I don't see any lab notebooks either." More bullets clanged off the door and the TV monitor imploded.

"Shaj," Jeffrey shouted—inside the lab his radio was jammed. "*Shaj!* We need to take a *prisoner*!"

"Look for an older bald guy!" Ilse yelled at the top of her lungs. "I have a feeling he'll be in charge!"

"Come on," Jeffrey said. He and Ilse dashed forward, pistols drawn. They passed two dead Boer soldiers, one with sergeant's stripes. They caught up with the SEALs.

"No one else in sight," Clayton said. "We searched all the offices, and this whole wall's shielded. . . . The encapsulated diesel generator's over there."

"Keep it running," Jeffrey said. "We need the power in the bunker."

Ilse peered around. "They've wrecked every PC and took the laptops with them. They must have gone through the containment air lock."

"Wouldn't they be killed?" Jeffrey said.

"No," Ilse said. "This outer lock's a precaution. Up to level three's a shirt-sleeve environment. You only need space suits in BL-4."

"How do we get this thing open?" Jeffrey said.

Ilse worked the air lock.

"Let's go," Jeffrey said. He yanked the handle of the

inner door and pushed. The door gave a fraction and stopped. He put his shoulder to it. Nothing. "It's barricaded," he said.

"The Halligan tools," Clayton said. SEAL Eight pulled two special crowbars from his pack. Eight and Clayton jammed the forked ends into the crack. Using all their strength, they forced the door open an inch, then lost their points of leverage.

"Jaws," Clayton said. SEAL Nine handed him the tool. Nine worked the hydraulic foot pump while Clayton held the expanding tips to the jamb of the door. Jeffrey covered the opening from above Clayton's head while he worked, using Nine's weapon. Eight covered the opening from floor level, aiming between Clayton's legs. When there was enough clearance, Clayton dashed through. Again Ilse went last.

A floor-to-ceiling freezer rested against the door. It was unplugged, but her visor told her everything inside was still frozen. The team was in an area of marble-topped lab benches, centrifuges, polymerase-chain-reaction machines. They double-checked under the tables—the area was clear. "Keep going!" Ilse shouted.

The wall in front of them was shielded. They went through another door, with no barricade this time. Two men in white lab coats turned to face them, unarmed. Four others fed diskettes and papers into fires blazing in the exhaust hoods of biosafety three. SEALs Eight and Nine made them move aside.

"Save whatever you can," Jeffrey said. Eight and Nine closed the hoods to smother the fires.

In the middle of one wall was another air lock, much heavier and with a different mechanism. A big red 4 was painted on the hatch. Jeffrey looked through the porthole. "Someone's in there," Jeffrey said. "He's putting on a suit."

"He'll try to lock himself in," Ilse said, "then wait until we leave. Let me get this thing open." She peeked through the porthole, then worked the door mechanism and yanked the handle. Suction fans began to roar.

The bald man took hold of the inner door. "Get back or I'll open it."

"You can't," Ilse said, "not while this one's ajar. The interlocking won't let you."

The Boer turned. *"You,"* he said, staring at her. He held the space-suit hood under one arm.

"Otto," Ilse said, covering him with her gun. "I somehow *knew* you'd be behind all this."

The man grabbed a ring hung by a chain from the ceiling and pulled. Nothing happened.

"Come on, Otto," Ilse said, "use your head. The alkali hot bath won't work now either. . . . Or do you use liquid nitrogen?"

"How did you get here?" Otto snapped. "Who did you come with, the Special Air Service? A parachute drop on the airstrip?"

"No," Ilse said as Jeffrey and Clayton came up behind her. "U.S. Navy SEALs."

"I should have known," Otto said, dripping venom. "You always *were* too close to American culture."

"Come out of the air lock," Ilse said.

"No," Otto said. "You'll have to kill me first."

"You'd like that, wouldn't you?" Ilse said. "Another martyr for the cause, and all your secrets die with you. . . . *Not a chance.*"

Jeffrey and Clayton went past Ilse and grabbed Otto by the arms. He struggled, but Nine moved in and gave him a shot of morphine in the neck.

"You filthy sons of bitches," Otto cursed. "You racially polluted scum!" He looked right at Ilse. "You miscegenating *whore*! I'll tell you *nothing*!" His voice was already slurred, his eyelids drooping.

"No, Otto," Ilse said, patting him on the shoulder as he slumped to the floor. She gave him a great big smile.

"You don't know U.S. Naval Intelligence. They have ways to make men talk."

"Commander, Ilse, check this out," SEAL Eight said. He was still covering the other prisoners with his machine pistol. Jeffrey and Ilse came over. Eight pointed to another TV monitor and VCR.

"It's a kid," Jeffrey said. "He's having convulsions."

"The archaea," Ilse said. "This must be what they were watching."

"Get the tape," Jeffrey said. "At least we'll have it as data."

"Wait a minute," Ilse said. "It's on record, not play. This is live feed we're seeing."

"It's happening *now*?" Jeffrey said.

Ilse turned to the air lock. "Somewhere in *there*."

SEAL Eight handed Ilse a partly burned research diary, then did a radar scan through the wall. "Yeah," Eight said, "in there. No one else, he's alone."

Ilse eyed the pages, the binding scorched and still warm through her flameproof gloves. Base gene sequencing homology, initiation codons GUG, UUG, CUG, and so on. Grams dry weight per mol-hour culture growth rates, and substrate uptake kinetics.

"Isn't there something we can *do*?" Clayton said, staring at the monitor.

"Nothing that would save him," Ilse said. "See the way his face looks melted, how his limbs flop? He's lost all muscle tone. The infection's far advanced."

"Can't we . . . ," Jeffrey said. He had to clear his throat. "Can't we go in and *help him*? You know, a morphine overdose, *anything*?"

"The procedures to get in there safely," Ilse said, "the decontamination afterward . . ."

The child was shivering and writhing, more like a rubber dummy than a human. Pink foam oozed from his mouth, and his chest heaved erratically. He made animal grunting sounds that came over the speakers in stereo.

"Christ," Jeffrey said, "his eyeballs keep jerking in different directions. They aren't even in sync."

"He's in some kind of inner chamber," Ilse said. "Look."

The child was strapped to a bare metal gurney, under robotic grapnels hung from the ceiling. He soiled himself once more and the upper-intestinal effluent dripped to the floor. There was a sump in the white tile floor, in one corner next to autopsy tools—hoses, saws and knives, retractors. Beside them were the mechanical hands and thick viewport of a glove box.

"It makes sense," Ilse said, "a higher biosafety zone past BL-4. Biosafety level *five*."

"We just have to *watch this*?" Jeffrey said.

"What do you want me to do?" Ilse snapped. "Suit up and go through the air lock, move the stretcher to the waldoes with the grapnels, then reach in and grab a scalpel and *cut his throat*? He can't last long now anyway."

Electrodes were taped to the boy's forehead and over his heart. Ilse ransacked the level three work area near the monitor, trying to find the readouts. She gasped when she saw his EEG traces—his brain waves were wild, chaotic and jagged.

As Ilse flipped through more research papers, Clayton turned to the prisoners. "Did you do this to him?"

No one answered.

"Did you do this to him?" Clayton screamed.

"*He* told us to," one Boer said, pointing to Otto asleep on the floor. "The whole *project* was his idea."

"They threatened our families," another pleaded.

"Did they?" Ilse said. She'd seen enough in the notebooks. "I don't believe you, any of you. You all look too well fed, too pleased with yourselves. You were burning the records too eagerly." The way their posture slumped showed she was right. "You're all guilty of war crimes."

None of the Boers spoke.

"What do we do with them now?" Clayton said.

There was a gurgling scream from the monitor. The child had chewed through his tongue. Blood spurted from his mouth—he was drowning in it, and his skin was gray, not brown. His eyebrows and jaw worked violently and his lips and nostrils flared and spasmed, a caricature of someone making silly faces. He couldn't be more than ten.

"Commander Fuller," Ilse said. "These notes clearly document systematic efforts to genetically engineer a lethal strain of archaea. *Successful* efforts. Are you satisfied by what you see? Have the rules of engagement been met?"

"Yes," Jeffrey said quietly.

An electronic tone sounded. Ilse looked at the monitor. The child lay totally still. Ilse glanced at the life signs equipment. His electrocardiogram was flat.

Ilse turned to the enemy scientists. "This is for him and my brother." She opened fire at the Boers, shooting each of them twice in the head.

CHAPTER 18

INSIDE THE MISSILE BUNKER

Jeffrey watched as Clayton studied the South African nuclear physics package. Clayton used a handheld fluoroscope and an ultrasound probe, leaning over the access hatch near the front end of the missile. SEAL Eight took pictures with a digital camera and took notes for Clayton. Clayton's instruments were hooked up to a laptop they'd brought with them, kept a safe distance from the fluoroscope emitter. Imagery flickered on the laptop screen.

"This the first enemy warhead you've ever seen?" Jeffrey said. He had to bend his head down while he stood, because of the low bare concrete overhead in the bunker.

"This is the first one *anybody's* seen," Clayton said, "so far as I know. Okay, here we go. . . . One sophisticated design. Compact, lightweight, uses very little fissile material. Eight, write this down in case the laptop's damaged later."

Jeffrey saw Clayton glance again at SEAL One, being ministered to by SEAL Two and Ilse at the other end of the bunker. "Commander," Clayton said, "you pay close attention also. In case I don't make it back."

"Understood," Jeffrey said.

Clayton cleared his throat. "The active ingredient,

the fissile material, is a seven-centimeter hollow sphere of uranium 235." He ran some calculations. "That would weigh five kilograms."

"That's *all*?" Jeffrey said.

"This design achieves critical mass by density compression."

"What's the fuel enrichment?" Jeffrey said.

Clayton eyed a special radiac. "Ninety-three percent."

"That's high," Jeffrey said.

"Higher's more efficient."

"Did we guess right, three KT?"

"I'll tell you in a minute," Clayton said.

Jeffrey glanced at the laptop screen. He saw the different warhead layers: initiator at the very core, tamper, shock buffers, neutron reflector. "What's this shading here, around the edges of the image?"

"The next layer out," Clayton said, "a coating of boron. That's to stop stray neutrons on the atomic battlefield, prevent a fizzle from predetonation."

"Okay," Jeffrey said, "which is one problem you don't have underwater. H_2O blocks neutrons." Jeffrey eyed the sonogram. "Now comes the firing system, outside the boron."

"Yup. . . . Again, ultrasophisticated. The inner portion's a fast-detonating high explosive, surrounded by slower-detonating hollow cones, with foil slappers at the apex of each cone, wired to the krytrons."

"The krytrons are what give perfect simultaneous ignition at all the apexes," Jeffrey said.

"Correct. The firing current vaporizes the metal foil, like when a house fuse blows. Each slapper functions as a tiny rifle."

"The explosion wave moves down the cones," Jeffrey said, "the wave fronts turn convex, and you have a broad base of ignition for the secondary charge."

"You got it, Commander," Clayton said. "That gives

you a nice implosion wave. . . . This baby should yield four kilotons."

"That'll do the job quite well," Jeffrey said. It occurred to him it would also really do the job on an Allied amphibious ready group and its thousands of marines.

Ilse came over and looked at the bomb. She had blood on her gloves.

"The whole thing sounds too elegant," Jeffrey said.

"It is," Clayton said. "This is how our own new A-bombs work. From what we can tell here the Axis isn't lagging any. And remember, a fission weapon can yield up to a megaton, using multiple critical masses."

"You're kidding," Ilse said.

"Our boomer fleet's own H-bombs only yield some three hundred kilotons," Jeffrey said.

"Okay, folks," Clayton said, "intel briefing's over. Time to cut the wires into the krytrons."

"How many krytrons are there?" Ilse said.

"Ninety-two."

SEAL Two glanced up from tending his mortally wounded comrade. "Commander, hand me another plasma pack. This one's empty and we need to get his BP higher." Jeffrey fiddled in his bag and pulled out the blood extender.

He handed it to Two, then crouched next to SEAL One. "How you feeling?" Jeffrey said.

SEAL One took the oxygen mask from his face. "Hurts like hell at the base of my spine, can't feel a damn thing lower down." He was pale and sweaty.

"You still cold? Want another jacket?"

"No. Thanks. This gillie suit's good for treating shock. . . . But it's awful stuffy in here, and I'm choking from the stink."

Jeffrey turned up the bunker's ventilation.

"And get this bald asshole away from me," SEAL One said. "Sleeping Beauty here." He made a face at Otto, still out cold. Jeffrey dragged the prisoner to the far corner, none too gently, and left him by the two dead Boer soldiers. Otto started snoring.

Jeffrey went back to SEAL One, then made eye contact with Two, saying quietly, "You're *sure* there's no way we can take One back with us?"

Two shook his head. "Moving him's out of the question. The dolphin ride would flex his pelvis constantly. You saw the fluoroscope: he's got secondary projectiles all through his lower GI tract. He'd bleed out in no time."

"What if we just towed his SDV?" Jeffrey said.

"We still have four klicks on foot through the rough to get back to the river . . . *if* we don't hit more patrols and helos."

"Then how about this?" Jeffrey said. "New egress plan." Clayton turned to listen, a wiring crimper and dental mirror in his hands. "We change to Boer uniforms and use that truck out front," Jeffrey said. "We go right down the main drag through Umhlanga Rocks like we own the place. We ditch the truck inside the nature reserve."

SEAL Two shook his head again. "The surf and wave action would be fatal, not to mention going on a Draeger in his condition. Commander, the underwater pressure would send blood clots to his lungs, his heart, his brain. . . ."

"Leaving the truck in the reserve would give them a clue," Clayton said. "And if we were stopped along the way, it would all be over."

"They'll have roadblocks," Ilse said. "And they *invented* paranoia."

"You're right," Jeffrey said. "It's not about any of us escaping safely. The key is the enemy can't know we were ever here, so they'll believe this thing was internal sabotage."

"Guys," One said. "Cut it out. I'm dying, okay? I can deal with that. It comes with the job sometimes."

"We never leave a man behind," Jeffrey said. "Never."

"It'll be a cremation," SEAL One said. "Yeah, a cremation in place, a nuclear cremation."

Jeffrey looked at One, so young to die and yet so chipper. Tears came to Jeffrey's eyes. This static phase of the mission was turning into one big mood crash for him, hiding out and working on the bomb. Ilse seemed to use her rage, barely slaked, to deal with it. That, and the immediacy of helping treat SEAL One, seemed to keep her from the depression Jeffrey felt come on.

"I can do something useful," One said. "I can guard the bomb after you leave."

"That's true," Jeffrey said. He took One's hand. "It could make the difference. . . . Hey, Shaj, can you rig up some kind of switch? You know, to set off the bomb right away, in case of enemy interference?"

"Not a problem," Clayton said.

"How much time you figure I got left?" One asked Two.

"You'll be alert for long enough."

"Just try not to sneeze or something," Jeffrey said, "and hit the switch by accident before we're out of range."

One laughed, despite the pain. "Bring the chief's body in here. He deserves decent burial too, and I don't want to die alone."

"Six, Nine," Ilse heard in her helmet. She knew SEAL Nine was the downhill perimeter security guard.

"Nine, g'head," Clayton said.

"Trouble, boss. We got company."

"What is it?" Clayton said. Ilse reached for the butt of her pistol. The weapon was cooler than before.

"A runner," SEAL Nine said, "some kind of messenger.

Must have been sent up 'cause they lost contact in the village."

"Nine, Four," Jeffrey said, "does he have a radio?"

"Affirmative. I can hear it. He's turned it up to monitor the traffic."

Clayton turned to Jeffrey. "We better take him out."

"Let's hope he isn't wearing a life signs monitor alarm," Jeffrey said.

"Yeah," Clayton said. "None of the other soldiers were."

"Nine, Four," Jeffrey said, "take out the runner."

"Four, Nine, understood."

There was silence on the circuit, then Ilse heard Nine say "Shit." There was heavy breathing on her headphones, grunting in two different voices, and the sounds of snapping branches.

"Crap," Jeffrey said. He took off out of the bunker with his fighting dagger in his hand and a frightening expression on his face—*eagerness.*

As Jeffrey topped the steps, Ilse heard a meaty thud over the radio, more grunting, then a gurgling moan.

"Nine, Six," Clayton hissed. "Nine, Six, come in."

No response.

"Nine, Six. Nine, Six."

Then Ilse heard a shuffling sound on the radio, more thuds and thumps and grunting, a tearing noise, then a drawn-out exhalation that ended in a rattling sigh.

"Four, Six," Clayton called. "Four, Six." Nothing. Ilse sat up anxiously.

"Six, Four," Jeffrey called. Jeffrey sounded winded. Ilse relaxed a little—he was okay.

"Four, Six, g'head," Clayton said.

"Six, Four, runner's been neutralized."

"What about Nine?" Clayton said.

"Nine bought it," Ilse heard Jeffrey say. "The runner slit his throat before I could get to him."

"Did the runner get off a warning?" Clayton said.

"No," Jeffrey said. "We'd have heard it through Nine's open mike."

"We need a plan," Clayton said.

"I'm bringing the runner's radio and paybook," Jeffrey said.

"Eight," Clayton said. "Help Commander Fuller bring in Nine's body and hide the runner, then you take downhill guard."

"What about the bomb?" Eight said. "It's a two-person job to rig it to the flux compression generator, to fire the krytrons."

"I know," Clayton said. "We're running low on manpower here."

"Could I help?" Ilse said.

Clayton looked at her. "I think you need to."

SEAL One started coughing uncontrollably, grimacing, then reached up for SEAL Two. "More local. Please. Gimme another shot."

Ilse peered through the hatch at the foot-wide physics package sitting in the missile. By her own count, from the initiator at the very core to the wires attached to the krytrons, it had a dozen layers. She knew it wasn't really dangerous now, giving off sporadic alpha particles and weak neutrons and soft gamma rays from spontaneous fission—whatever got past the reflector and dense high explosive would be stopped by clothes and skin or was virtually harmless in short doses. Still, just looking at the thing gave her the creeps.

"It's essential we get each connection perfect," Clayton said. "If just one krytron misfires or goes off too soon or late, the implosion wave's distorted. We just scatter U-235 around the bunker, or worse, we crack open the archaea lab without the heat to sterilize it properly."

"What do you want me to do?" Ilse said.

"Watch this little oscilloscope screen. Make sure the peak of the curve hits right at the tick mark here, and its full wave form comes up above this threshold line. That'll mean we have a good solid connection."

"That's so all the signals get there at the same time?"

"Yeah," Clayton said. "And keep your eyes glued to this display window. We're looking for an inductance of one hundred nanohenries and a capacitance no more than one hundred microfarads total. We need a nice square firing pulse, with a rise time under two microseconds. If something's off, you tell me. I'll compensate at my end in the arming gear. That's what this little keyboard's for."

"We have to do this with ninety-two different krytrons?" Ilse said.

"SEAL Eight and I already did a few, but yeah. . . . It'll go faster once we get in rhythm. Don't rush it, Ilse, please. A slipup here would be bad."

Jeffrey came back to the missile bunker after hiding the runner's body. He'd already cleaned his K-bar and now he wiped blood off the Boer walkie-talkie. "Somebody who speaks Afrikaans needs to monitor this. Here's the dead guy's paybook—you'll know his name and unit."

SEAL Two looked up. "I can do that, sir. Ilse and Lieutenant Clayton are kinda busy now."

"The radio has built-in encryption," Jeffrey said. "That's good—it garbles voices. Also, the atmospherics'll still be bad up here from the EMP box we set off. You pretend to be the runner. Don't rush your answers. Whisper a translation to me, I'll tell you what to say."

SEAL Two flipped through the paybook. "Okay. I'll let you know as soon as I hear them call this guy. Meantime, I want you to do something for *us*. SEAL One's BP keeps dropping and he's slightly cyanotic. He needs whole blood. You're the only one here with his type, B positive."

"You want me to stand right here?" Jeffrey said.

"Yeah," the SEAL corpsman said. "Gravity feed should do it. I got two empty one-pint bottles I want to fill from you. Roll up your sleeve."

"These bottles aren't sterile," Jeffrey said.

"Like that really matters," SEAL One said.

"You hungry?" Jeffrey said, bending down to One. "Wanna candy bar?"

"Last meal?" SEAL One said. "Yeah. And more water."

Jeffrey rolled down his sleeve just as the runner's unit called in from the village. SEAL Two translated.

Jeffrey put his lips to SEAL Two's ear. "Tell them you're at the Sharks Board and there was some kind of voltage surge. Say they thought they were struck by lightning but that wasn't it. Tell them the missile's fine, everything's fine, and they're cleaning up the mess."

SEAL Two passed that on. A different voice came from the walkie-talkie speaker. SEAL Two whispered, "It's the senior corporal. He says he'll report it to the power company, and they'll probably send a repair crew from Durban in the morning. He says missile control keeps bugging him that we dropped off the line. He wants to talk to the sergeant."

Jeffrey made the facial expression for "yikes," trying to think on his feet. He felt groggy from the blood donation. "Okay," he whispered, "tell him the sergeant's in the head, I mean the latrine, having a long slow one."

SEAL Two relayed, and Jeffrey heard the corporal laugh. Then the corporal asked for the lieutenant.

"Tell him to wait one," Jeffrey said. "Then *don't* hit talk." Jeffrey ran his hand over his face. He stared at the overhead but his mind was blank. Then he glanced at Ilse and got an idea. Jeffrey used his helmet mike. "Seven, Four . . . Seven, Four."

"G'head, Four."

"Seven, when you cleared the upper level, were there any female staffers?"

"Yeah, a couple."

"Good-looking or ugly?"

"One of each."

"Okay, thanks." Jeffrey turned to Two. "Tell the corporal the lieutenant's otherwise engaged, out in the truck with a lab technician."

Again the corporal laughed. Then he said more in Afrikaans. "He wants me back down there," SEAL Two said.

"Tell him they want you to stay put here, to help beef up the guard, because of the alert, with the voltage surge and everything."

SEAL Two passed that into the walkie-talkie, in fluent Afrikaans of his own. The corporal's answer was long.

"Big problem," Two whispered. "He says that's a good point, strengthening security, something bad could happen between now and dawn. He's rousing the rest of the platoon. They'll come on duty now instead of at daybreak."

"Um, uh," Jeffrey said, "ask him when they'll get here." Jeffrey felt like he was shitting a brick while he waited for the answer. Just like the alleged sergeant, ha ha.

"They have to shave and eat," Two said, "then walk up for the exercise. Just about an hour, probably."

"Tell him understood."

SEAL Two said something else in Afrikaans and put down the walkie-talkie. "Done."

"Did he sound suspicious?" Jeffrey said.

"Not that I could tell," Two said, "but then, if he was smart, he wouldn't have let on, would he?"

Jeffrey turned to Clayton. "You hear all that, Shaj?"

"Unfortunately."

"We got a deadline," Jeffrey said. "Start the timer now and set it for fifty, repeat five zero, minutes. Then we need to finish up and get out of here."

Clayton's eyes widened. "There's no way we'll be back in the minisub by then."

"I know," Jeffrey said. "Work fast. I have to run up to the roof of the Sharks Board, get precise wind speed and direction for the ROEs."

"What, you can't just stick a wet finger outside the bunker?"

Jeffrey shook his head. He pulled a handheld anemometer from his pack, then peeled a couple of chocolate bars and wolfed them down. He drank a whole canteen. *My* last meal? he wondered.

The rain had almost stopped. The air outside the bunker was so fresh, Jeffrey realized now how much it stank in there. He trotted up the front steps of the Sharks Board. The place was a shambles.

His Kevlar moccasins crunched on the broken glass in the entrance lobby. Farther in was a mix of nasty smells. Tattered blackout curtains flapped and fluttered in the wind, but otherwise there was an eerie silence. The walls were peppered, no, shredded, with holes from bullets and grenade shrapnel and from the blast of satchel charges. Broken ceiling tiles, shattered fluorescent light bulbs, twisted aluminum struts lay everywhere. The concrete facing of structural columns was badly pocked, deep .50-caliber armor-piercing hits, shallow ones from hollow point, and smaller nicks from Boer 7.62 and 5.56 mm full-metal-jacket rounds. Jeffrey stepped on expended brass and stepped around discarded ammo clips.

His feet stuck to the drying blood where the SEAL team's chief had died. Inside the shattered strongpoint leading to the basement stairs, the enemy soldiers' broken bodies were growing cold. What surprised Jeffrey was how much paper was scattered there: orders and records blown from packs and pockets, torn photos and singed scraps of letters from loved ones back home.

Through his IR imagers Jeffrey saw warm spots in the debris. A flare-up now would be a disastrous attention-getter, embers fanned into a conflagration by the strong breeze coming through. Jeffrey decided to give the smoldering wreckage a quick once-over. Three big CO_2 extinguishers sat on the floor where Ilse had left them neatly in a line, but all were empty. Nearby lay a fire ax, its wooden handle splintered near the tip, probably by a bullet. Jeffrey found another extinguisher with some charge still in it, and he did a hasty overhaul.

He mounted the staircase to the second deck, itself badly pockmarked. Sprawled across the steps near the upper landing lay a body in a lab coat. The whole top of its head was gone. The deck two stairwell door was off its hinges. Jeffrey glanced away as he passed the landing. He'd experienced enough carnage tonight, enough to last a lifetime. He continued toward the roof.

Jeffrey reviewed the ROE standards in his head one final time. The setting was in fact ideal. The rising ground behind the Sharks Board would shield people inland from the flash pulse and the blast wave, while strengthening the effects in the immediate area of the lab. With a surface burst there'd be no Mach stem, that terrible shock front when an airburst merged with its own ground reflection. The Indian community of Phoenix and the black townships of Greater Inanda should be safe except for broken windows, and intel said almost everyone had taped theirs up to keep down flying glass—after all, there *was* a war on.

The biosafety level five containment was in the part of the basement closest to the missile bunker, and a quick radar scan had verified the intervening ground was soil, not bedrock. There were indeed no hostage encampments protecting the site, and as near as Jeffrey could tell from the team's approach march, SEAL Eight's scouting down the hill, and direction-finding of the signal traffic, Umhlanga Rocks itself was part of the militarized coast defense zone.

Jeffrey's one concern was flash blindness, which could happen even miles from ground zero. The general impairment of vision lasted only seconds or minutes. The insidious problem was focusing of thermal energy on the retina, for anyone looking directly at the early fireball. The image of the mushroom cloud was burned forever into one spot on the victim's field of view. Worse, the retina would be fused to the underlying sclera, creating mechanical stress in the eye. Over months or years the retina could tear and hemorrhage, needing invasive surgery to counter permanent total blindness.

Then there were the cataracts. More reason, Jeffrey told himself, to end this damn war soon—minority populations weren't getting adequate health care under New Apartheid. At least with the storm and the strict curfew few civilians would be exposed.

Jeffrey walked through one more shattered doorway and surveyed the roof. The feeder horns and pre-amp cans of the microwave dishes were scorched, and the coaxial leads of the whip antennas were melted. The four dead soldiers were gone—Jeffrey saw their blood trails on the steps. The SEAL abseil-rope-climbing group had dragged them to the second floor, out of view from the air. Jeffrey felt glad not to see them; he was weary of the endless death and suffering. He pulled himself together.

A South African heavy machine gun on a tripod sat under a canvas tarp on the roof, overlooking the main entrance and the missile bunker. The SEAL chief had wisely left it there, held in reserve. Devastating to troops in the open, it was an extremely long and heavy weapon, stupefyingly noisy, and its cigar-sized rounds could go for miles. It must have been winched up to the parapet recently—it wasn't in any satphotos in the briefing notes. Jeffrey gave prayerful thanks it had stayed under wraps for the boat team's initial assault. The SEALs were almost out of ammo as it was, and against this monster the raiders would've been decimated.

Jeffrey walked to the other end of the roof. He held up his anemometer. The wind was slowing, definitely. It was high time to set off the bomb.

CHAPTER 19

"Come on, let's go, let's go!" Clayton said.

"We got the Boer arming circuits and the guidance package," SEAL Eight said.

"I have the captured walkie-talkie," SEAL Two said.

"Someone take a sample of the missile fuel," Jeffrey said. "Just grab a chunk."

"I'm all set with the remnants of the lab notes," Ilse said. "And the videocassette."

"Let's get Ilse's friend onto the litter," Jeffrey said. "Put in an airway so he can't choke on his tongue, and hold it in with surgical tape. That'll double as a gag if he comes to."

Two and Eight hefted Otto onto the collapsible stretcher. "Cripes," SEAL Eight said, "this guy needs a low-fat diet bad."

"Who *is* he?" Jeffrey said. "Tell everybody, Ilse. We might have more casualties, we still got a long way to go."

Ilse cleared her throat. "Herr Doktor Professor Baron Otto von Schleiffer und Schaffhausen, late of the Kaiser Wilhelm Institute for Applied Neurobiology. Racist fanatic, sexist pig, Putsch insider. He was close to the South African oceanographic community. He and I didn't get along."

"We should leave the spare bomb detonator and EMP box here," Jeffrey said. "Lighten our load, we'll move faster. With SEAL One as bomb guard we don't have to worry about the stuff being spotted by Boers. It'll all be totally vaporized."

"You're right," Clayton said. "Everybody dump stuff you won't need." The team made a pile of odds and ends, forced-entry tools and voltmeters, climbing ropes and welding gauntlets.

"You're okay with the switch?" Jeffrey said to One.

SEAL One shifted slightly and bit down a grunt of pain. "I hear anybody coming, I flip up the plastic cover and push the big red button twice."

Jeffrey nodded. "That'll fire the flux compression generator that puts the voltage through the krytrons. Don't worry, you won't feel anything. . . . And just in case, the whole setup has an antitamper mechanism. Some joker tries to monkey with it, *boom*."

"And *don't* worry about us," Clayton said. "You think you hear someone coming, blow the bomb."

"Hey, look," One said. "When you get back, I want some kind of memorial at Arlington. Maybe some of my atoms'll drift down there from the mushroom cloud and everything. Promise me."

"I promise," Jeffrey said, knowing that it wouldn't really happen. A 4-KT-sized warhead, especially one with characteristics of an underground explosion, created tropospheric fallout—it didn't rise into the stratosphere and hence did not get worldwide distribution. That didn't preclude a memorial stone, of course. Jeffrey put a hand on SEAL One's shoulder. "Is there anybody you want us to take a message to?"

"No."

"No parents, fiancée, anything?"

"Nope."

"Commander," Clayton said, "every one of us was

picked because we don't have attachments. No kids, no spouses, or ex-spouses even, and we're all estranged from our families one way or another."

"You didn't tell me that," Jeffrey said.

"The powers-that-be put our chance of making it back at one in four."

"I'm frankly glad you didn't tell me *that* part," Jeffrey said. "Let's prove them wrong. . . . Speaking of which, I want to crank open the bunker's armored door, the launch port."

"How come?" Clayton whispered. He'd started gazing down at One and was almost too choked up to talk.

"I want the gamma rays unhindered heading out to sea. That'll give a good strong EMP in this whole sector, give the ships and aircraft other things to worry about than us."

Clayton helped Jeffrey work the mechanism, and the heavy door came up. Jeffrey saw the grooves on which the launcher would roll out, after which the jet blast shield deployed. This one was a so-called zero-length rail launcher system. In an emergency it could be fired from right in the bunker, but tonight this missile wasn't going anywhere.

"Come on, LT," SEAL One said as Clayton bent to kiss his forehead. "I hate good-byes, get outta here already."

Jeffrey looked at the timer. "Thirty-eight minutes to go. Shaj, you take the point with the land mine sensor—they might have planted new ones. I'll bring up the rear, Ilse goes in front of me. Eight, Two, you guys grab the stretcher and we'll pick up Seven on the way. Same route we came in—not recommended practice, but for just that reason it might work. Now, at the gallop, *move it*!"

• • •

DURBAN

Gunther Van Gelder walked south along Prince Road, a block in from the beach, heading for the end of Addington Point. He heard the constant pounding of the surf, smelled it in the air, even felt it through the ground. He could see his way in the dark by the flashes of lightning and by the subdued blue glow from the covered headlights of occasional cars and trucks—the military blackout was very thorough. The curbs at each corner were painted Day-Glo white, to help prevent skinned knees and broken ankles.

He glanced over his right shoulder, just as a distant lightning bolt backlit the clouds from over the horizon. Now that the weather was clearing, he could see well up the coast, even make out the silhouette of the darkened lighthouse at Umhlanga Rocks. He smiled to himself about his thrusting, panting labors of the past hour, then resumed course.

Another sentry stopped him to check his papers. The soldier told him gruffly to put on his flash protectors. Van Gelder had a pair, a parting gift from the woman he'd just been with. She'd explained she could get a new pair in the morning—they were sold on the street by unemployed coloreds who made them by hand. The irony struck Van Gelder: if anthropologists were right about mankind evolving in Africa, then the native blacks, so-called Bantus, apartheid's lowest untouchables, had the only true pure blood in the world and everyone *else* was colored. The elation of his rutting, the savored sights and smells, the teasing and the giggles, the warm wet furry gripping, and his explosive flooding gift and release, all popped like a bubble.

Van Gelder sighed. He donned the protectors, a crude cardboard frame with Mylar lenses, like the things school kids used to watch a solar eclipse. The sentry said they weren't a joke; there was a stiff fine for civilians caught not wearing them. They were assembled with cheap glue, but the rain at last had stopped. Now with the damn things on his face, with their scratchy pinching earpieces, Van Gelder was almost blind. He had to brace them by hand—the wind was still doing a brisk Beaufort 6, some twenty-five knots, backing slightly now from out of the west to out of the west-southwest. Van Gelder made slow progress by looking down past the lenses at the sidewalk near his feet, and once in a while he'd cheat to see where he was.

He passed a small tank farm and then a heavily guarded prison. Rumor had it the jail was filled with interned American businessmen, with a separate cellblock facing downtown for senior VPs and up. Van Gelder finally reached the tip of the point. At the tug jetty he picked up the ferry across the harbor mouth.

The ride was short but rough—the incoming swell beyond the breakwater was nasty. The cross chop of the outgoing tide tossed the little launch, as big Natal Bay drained through the narrow entrance channel. By the time he stepped onto Bluff Quay, on the north side of the jutting Cape Natal peninsula, Van Gelder's uniform was damp from windblown spray.

The long quay paralleling the foot of the bluff was busy and loud, the air filled with machinery growling and clanking. Dock workers wearing night-vision goggles used forklifts to unload railroad cars, and there was steady traffic through the blast doors into the bluff. As lightning flashed yet again, Van Gelder spotted the prefabs of hostage camps along the seventy-five-meter-high summit of the bluff, alternating with big radomes, tall antenna masts, and hardened bunkers for missiles. Somewhere up there he thought he heard a baby cry.

He lifted his glasses a moment. At ground level a kilometer away, toward the foot of the peninsula, loomed more tank farms and storage silos, huge grain bins and coaling slips. Van Gelder could see the superstructures of bulk cargo vessels and tankers. In the foreground was Salisbury Island, part of the naval installation, really a Y-shaped appendage jutting from the cape. Tied up in berths 10 and 12 were two of the new Spanish-built *Sitron*-class strike corvettes, strengthening local antiaircraft defenses while they refueled. The wind carried a ceaseless cacophony from that part of the harbor, a throbbing of engines and pumps, a moaning and screeching of gears and hydraulics.

Van Gelder stepped aside as an Eland armored car rolled past, its 90mm high-velocity gun aimed straight ahead, its big tires splashing the puddles. He smelled its diesel exhaust, mixed with the odors of fuel oil and dead fish, pumped bilges and raw sewage and rotting trash. To him these were reassuring, his home port's waterfront at work, and the extra hubbub of the war effort lifted his mood.

Van Gelder had a few minutes before reporting. He decided to prolong his stroll, just to the beginning of Island-View Channel and back.

UMHLANGA ROCKS

The egress march was a mad dash of panting and peering, a downhill slalom speed record past a dozen-plus enemy mines, desperately scanning for Boer patrols the whole time. Twice Jeffrey and the others had to hit the deck and roll into the bushes, letting more soldiers go by, then it was back on their feet on the double. Loading the SDVs became a frenzy of silent activity, but finally everything was set. Otto was safely taped up in the KIA'ed chief's dolphin, the eyeholes shuttered, his Draeger set on heliox and his arms strapped to his sides, a mask on with no readouts and no sound.

SEAL One's empty dolphin was slaved to Two's. Clayton controlled Otto's, Seven the cargo SDV, and SEAL Eight guided the other empty, Nine's. They went with the river this time, not against it, and in a wild charge of flailing mechanical flukes they were past the bridge, the pillboxes on the beach, even the barbed-wire entanglement. They rode the rip through the surf, using the outgoing tide, and after thunderous pounding and buffeting all ten SDVs were clear. Jeffrey had to keep swallowing; his punished eardrums hurt bad.

Jeffrey read his chronometer. Any second now.

"All numbers go deep," Clayton ordered. "The seawater's good shielding."

"Don't get too close to the bottom," Jeffrey warned. He twisted his handgrips and dived. On his head-up display he saw the blips of the other dolphins.

There was a brilliant blue-green flash through Jeffrey's eyeholes, enough to light up the reef. There was a quick sharp bruising *thump-thump*, the ground- and airborne shock waves hitting the water. As the sparkling blue-green glow persisted, Jeffrey saw the bottom muck stir up, threatening to engulf him. There was another flash, more local, diffuse and flickering. Then *things* began to come down. His SDV was pelted. Jeffrey swore he saw a tail rotor go by. Five blades—an SA.330 Puma?

Jeffrey felt his dolphin back and surge.

"The seiche!" he heard Ilse shout, the terrible seismic sloshing. There must have been an underwater landslide. The outbound tsunami hit, tumbling him over and over and over.

DURBAN

A demonic purple-white flash lit the sky, 10,000 times brighter than lightning. Van Gelder hit the deck as he felt an unnatural warmth. The eerie sensation continued and he knew he was too exposed. Holding his cheap goggles flat to his face, he rolled behind a cargo crate. He heard auto brakes squealing and then a very hard crash. He saw dock workers scramble for cover, pulling others too blinded or stunned. Sirens began to go off amid shouting and screaming.

He looked up at the bluff. Its whole face stood out starkly in the unforgiving light. He saw people dash through the blast doors as the outer barriers closed. By a reflection in the side window of a staff car he saw something else in the distance, something that took his breath away, the most beautiful golden-yellow incandescence blooming into the air. He screwed his eyes shut and waited for the overpressure to kill him, but it didn't come. He heard a whimpering yell and a splash as a forklift ran off the quay.

As ship horns hooted alarms, Van Gelder glanced again at the car window. A mushroom cloud rose over Umhlanga Rocks. By its harsh illumination he noticed the lighthouse there was gone. On the slimy ground by his feet he saw two rats running in circles. One of them, sightless and panicked, hit a gantry crane head-on. He felt a tremor through the ground, but *still* the airborne shock wave hadn't come. He remembered to cover his ears.

Van Gelder watched the swirling, pulsing mushroom cloud shoot higher, frighteningly silent, red now near its base and capped by a giant smoke ring. The underside of the overcast glowed pink, and tendrils of ethereal blue now interlaced the fireball. Then a deafening *crack* sounded and the staff car windows were smashed. A sledgehammer punched Van Gelder's gut as the thundering roar went on. The negative pressure pulse hit, trying to tear out his lungs. The blast wind struck, moaning and screaming inhumanly, toppling unsecured cargo, enshrouding Van Gelder in sea spray and dust.

CHAPTER 20

Ilse floated helplessly. She had no diver data, no gertrude or sonar, and no propulsion or depth control. She knew that sensing up and down underwater in the dark was always hard. It wouldn't work to blow bubbles and follow them to the surface, the standard trick, wrapped up as she was within the dolphin. Besides, right now the surface was the last place she would ever want to be.

The pressure in Ilse's ears told her she was slowly rising, confirmed by her backup wrist-mounted mechanical pressure gauge. She thought she saw a slight glow through her eyeholes. If so, the SDV was upside down. She tried her hand controls again, but nothing happened. She tried to move her legs, to propel the vehicle the hard way, but it was useless.

"Any unit, Four, come in," she called into her mouthpiece mike. There was no answer. She double-checked that the fiber-optic link between her mask and the dolphin's electronics was firmly in the jack. The mask remained completely dark.

"Any unit, Four. . . . Any unit, Four." Nothing.

"Mayday, mayday, mayday, this is Four." Still nothing.

• • •

Jeffrey's tumbling dolphin went into a corkscrewing gyration, then he felt a bump. His sonar told him he was on the bottom, depth ninety-seven feet. He brought his SDV back up to ninety and strobed his secure acoustic IFF, Identification-Friend-or-Foe. Only eight other units responded—Ilse had dropped off the screen.

Jeffrey pulsed on active sonar. Now there were *ten* contacts. One of the two new ones was moving and one was not. The one that moved was big, too big, much bigger than the SDVs. It also moved too fast.

"All units," Jeffrey heard Clayton call, "sound off for a status check."

"Two," the SEAL team corpsman said.

Then there was a pause.

"Five, this is Four," Jeffrey called. No response. "Ilse, come in, please."

Eventually Clayton said, "Six."

"Six, Four," Jeffrey said, "I think Ilse's damaged."

"Acknowledged," Clayton said. "All numbers keep sounding off."

There was another lengthy silence.

"Seven, this is Six," Clayton called. "Eight, this is Six, come in."

Neither answered.

"Six, Four," Jeffrey said, "I have them both on IFF, immobile on the bottom."

"I see them," Clayton said. "Their slaved units are in shutdown mode. They must have all had system failures."

Jeffrey pulsed on active again. Ilse's SDV was barely moving, and the tenth contact was converging on her. The bogey weaved erratically beneath the surface.

"Six, Four, Ilse's in trouble. I think it's a shark. My sonar's holding her at shallow depth. I'm moving in."

Jeffrey's acoustic intercept showed Clayton pulse on active too. "I'll be your wingman," Clayton said.

"Negative," Jeffrey ordered. "Otto's priceless. You and Two guard him and the cripples. Form a defensive mulberry on the bottom, a spinning circle, with the units you control."

"Acknowledged," Clayton said.

"Activate your SharkPODs," Jeffrey said. He powered up his own, then saw the irony—the protective oceanic devices were invented by the Natal Sharks Board.

"I do not concur," Clayton said. "SharkPODs put electric fields into the seawater. Moving through a conductive medium creates a magnetic anomaly."

"Shaj," Jeffrey said, "we just set off an A-bomb up there. The last thing we need to worry about is our MAD signature."

After hesitating Clayton said, "Concur." Then he added, "Good luck, sir."

Jeffrey aimed toward Ilse and the shark.

Ilse felt a sudden turbulence, as if something had rushed right past her through the water. Then it returned and there was a sharp *thwack* against her legs. She was nearer to the surface now. Above her was burning fuel. She caught a glimpse of her assailant in silhouette. Ilse's blood ran cold. It was the largest great white she had ever seen, almost eight meters long. It had to weigh two metric tons, ten times her weight and her SDV combined.

She caught another glimpse. It was coming back.

Jeffrey drove his SDV between Ilse and the shark, hoping to repel it with his electric field. It had no visible effect. He switched the SharkPOD off and on again, then checked the status readout. It was functional, but the shark was too maddened by the A-bomb blast to notice or to care.

Through an eyehole Jeffrey saw the shark bite off one of Ilse's bowplane flippers, then spit it out.

Ilse felt a tug and heard a snap. It thinks I'm a dead dolphin, she realized. It's begun to feed. It won't be satisfied with just a fin or fluke. Its teeth are sharp enough to get through Kevlar.

Jeffrey told himself to think like Ilse would, think like a dolphin and a shark. From some long-forgotten nature show his brain screamed that bottlenoses sometimes fought great whites and drove them off, to protect their young, for example. *How, dammit?* They rammed them with their snouts.

Jeffrey turned as tightly as he could, built up momentum, and aimed for the shark. It easily avoided him, then returned to its main meal.

Jeffrey tried again while the shark was distracted, and butted it violently in the side. The shark turned and lashed at him. Through the murky light provided by the flaming avgas Jeffrey saw its mouth gape open. He twisted sideways just in time. He went for separation and altitude, going dangerously near the radioactive surface. He vented ballast and dived at the great white at top speed. He crashed into its midriff and then he fell away, badly stunned. The shark batted him with its tail and once again went for its prey, Ilse.

This isn't working, Jeffrey told himself. One good chomp and he'll crush her bones, rupture her internal organs, and wreck her Draeger. Then he'll taste her blood. There's only one thing left to do.

Jeffrey glanced at his depth gauge. Thirty or forty feet, fluctuating wildly with the surf. Too deep. He set his SDV to hover. He reached for his equipment bag. He unclipped the belly of the dolphin and bailed out.

He set the SDV to bottom and watched it sink. God knows what's drifting down around me, he told himself. Good thing I'm in a scuba, with mask and wet suit. At least the radioactive iodine and cesium will tend to float.

Jeffrey swam toward the surface with the equipment bag, close enough for the shark to notice. He flailed intentionally. Come on, you hungry bastard, come for *me*. The war's conditioned you that big explosions mean raw meat? That battles mean good eating, tasty human flesh? *Then come and get it*.

The shark seemed to read Jeffrey's mind. It went right for him, swimming closer toward the surface. Jeffrey pulled the pistol from his bag.

I can't fire submerged. Water in the barrel will make it blow up in my hand.

But the barrel plug is in. Jeffrey glanced at his dive data. Twenty feet, more or less. His pulse had topped 160. He switched his pistol off of safe to fire. The red diode glowed. The round-count readout said he had an armor-piercing bullet in the chamber. He prayed he wouldn't have a misfire—the only way to clear it was to first eject the clip.

The shark started its attack, turning sideways to lunge for Jeffrey with its jaws wide open. At the last possible moment Jeffrey pushed the pistol into the shark's left eye, barrel plug and all, levered his torso away from its mouth, and squeezed the trigger.

Ilse was desperate to know what was happening. She twisted her body to try to turn the dolphin but that didn't help. Then she watched something approach her from above—the shark, going wild. It disappeared from view and she saw something else through her eyehole. A human hand. The fuel above her was still flickering, and it looked like there were clouds of blood in the water.

Something knocked on the SDV. Ilse screeched inside her mouthpiece. Then she realized it was Jeffrey. They worked the clips to release her from the dolphin. They were close enough to speak directly through the water, shouting inside their mouthpieces. Jeffrey told her he was okay, then made sure she was all right too. He reached inside her SDV with his titanium dive knife. He pierced the ballast bladders and the vehicle started to sink. Jeffrey and Ilse held onto it together, riding toward the bottom, their cyalume hoops glowing side by side.

Jeffrey used his dive computer INS to navigate an expanding-square bottom search, and they soon retrieved his dolphin. "Six, Four," Jeffrey called once he'd plugged back in. "Six, Four."

"Four, Six, g'head."

"Shaj, Ilse and I are okay, but there'll be more sharks coming—they'll smell the blood. We have to get away from here."

"Half our vehicles have mobility kills already," Clayton said, "and it's five miles to the rendezvous."

Ilse tapped Jeffrey's shoulder. They traded mouthpieces so she could speak, each with a hand on the other's hip, floating close. "Six, Five," Ilse said, "some of us could ride outside the dolphins. We could hold on to the dorsal fins of the ones that still are working."

Jeffrey took his mouthpiece back. "No," he said. "We can't leave the broken ones behind as evidence, and buddy tows would slow us down too much. Our battery charges are almost empty as it is. We have to call the ASDS to come and pick us up."

"But there's no place to hide here," Clayton said. "That wreck inshore by the Ohlanga mouth is much too small for the minisub."

"The ASDS doesn't have to hide," Jeffrey said.

"There'll be lots of reverb from our demolition for a while, and settling from the landslide."

"It's not part of the plan," Clayton said.

"We have to *change* the plan," Jeffrey said. "I'll make the call." He turned up the power of his clandestine gertrude. "Whale One, this is Dolphin Four. Whale One, this is Dolphin Four."

"This is Whale One," Meltzer's voice came back immediately, scratchy and echoing from the range and the frequency-agile encryption. "Give me the recognition sign."

Jeffrey spoke slowly and crisply. "Recognition sign is beta sigma fy-uv niner. Give me the countersign."

"Countersign is copper purple granite apple."

"Confirmed," Jeffrey said. "Whale One, cancel Point Zulu rendezvous. Instead home on my IFF, retrieve dolphin team at my location now."

ABOARD THE ASDS

Jeffrey saw Lieutenant Meltzer peering in as the ASDS forward pressure chamber hatch swung open after equalizing. "Where's everybody else?" Meltzer said. He held a Geiger counter.

"We had three KIAs," Jeffrey said.

The team all cleared their weapons and put the firearms in a gold-lined box, to shield the tritium nightsights. Once the box was closed, the sensitive Geiger counter didn't click too much—a thorough seawater rinse was excellent decontamination.

Meltzer looked at Otto. "Who's this guy?"

"An EPW," Jeffrey said.

"A prisoner?" Meltzer said. "I picked up the explosion on passive sonar. Did you fulfill the objectives?"

"Yeah," Jeffrey said. "All except the last one, making a clean getaway from the hostile coast." Jeffrey turned to Clayton. "You guys catch a breather in the transport compartment. I'm taking command as pilot of the mini-sub."

Clayton nodded and undogged the rearward hatch of the lock-in/lockout hyperbaric sphere. Jeffrey and Clayton dragged Otto into the back and strapped him into a seat. Otto was coming round, so SEAL Two checked his vital signs and gave him another morphine shot. They returned to the pressure chamber and helped Ilse stow the critical equipment bags, the ones with lab records and missile parts and the captured walkie-talkie. Jeffrey went into the forward compartment. Ilse followed.

Jeffrey took the left seat and began reviewing screens and readouts.

"Sir," Meltzer said, "there's been another change of plan. You were right about a Boer safety corridor." He handed Jeffrey a message slip.

ASDS DATA PLUS ENEMY AIRCRAFT OVERFLIGHT
PATTERNS AND INSHORE MINEFIELD ANALYSIS
CONFIRM IDENTIFICATION TODAYS SUBMARINE SAFE
PASSAGE CORRIDOR X WELL DONE X CHALLENGER
WILL MEET/RECOVER ASDS DOWNSTREAM SIDE
BOTTOM HUMMOCK POSIT REL POINT ZULU RANGE
FIVE DOT NINE NM BEARING ONE FOUR SEVEN
DEPTH TWELVE HUNDRED REPEAT 1200 FEET X
ASDS SIGNAL CHALLENGER SOONEST WHEN TEAM
PICKUP COMPLETED X WILSON SENDS XX

"Great," Jeffrey said. "This way we'll make the docking two hours sooner."

"Yes, sir," Meltzer said.

"Twelve hundred feet, huh," Jeffrey said. "I guess the SDVs are expendable now." He turned to Ilse. "If their innards start to pop, enemy SOSUS'll just think that's Ms. Sperm Whale eating breakfast."

"Concur, Commander," Ilse said.

"Very well . . . *Oceanographer.*" Jeffrey smiled, then turned back to Meltzer. "Let's call home and then get moving."

Clayton came into the forward compartment and stood next to Ilse. "I can't sit still," he said. "I came to watch."

"Post-action heebie-jeebies?" Jeffrey asked. His hand was firmly on the joy stick, his course following an underwater cable he could see on the low-frequency synthetic-aperture bottom-penetrating sonar.

"Yeah," Clayton said. "The adrenaline's worn off."

Jeffrey nodded. He understood. At least driving the ASDS gave him something to do. It would all catch up with him later, Jeffrey was sure. He thought of coming back sometime to tap this cable.

"I feel pretty spaced-out myself," Ilse said.

"We can all relax once we get back aboard," Jeffrey said. "Have a good shot of medicinal brandy, take a snooze, we'll be good as new."

"I guess," Clayton said. "I wish I could say that for all my guys."

"I know what you mean," Jeffrey said. "How you makin' out right now?"

"You know," Clayton said, "it's strange. I thought I'd be real down but I got over that part fast. I feel much older suddenly. I feel, I guess, I don't know, kind of *seasoned*. It's not entirely a bad feeling."

"It's like they used to say in another war," Jeffrey said. "You've seen the elephant and changed forever."

"Did this happen to you, Commander?" Clayton said. "Back in the Persian Gulf?"

"I wish. By the time they cut down the drugs enough for me to have coherent thoughts, I was in the orthopedic ward at Bethesda."

"Did you lose anybody on that mission?" Clayton said.

"No." Then Jeffrey reminded himself: *I* did—my fiancée. "One guy was paralyzed, though. From the waist down. Too much damage for any nerve reconstruction."

"That's a shame," Clayton said.

"Not entirely," Jeffrey said. "He's won three gold medals in Special Olympics, the international ones, the big time. He's a high school principal now and also runs a Boy Scout troop."

"Watch out for an ex-SEAL in a wheelchair," Clayton said. He smiled, but Jeffrey sensed his pain.

"Look," Jeffrey said. "Command is never easy, Shaj. In war you tell people to do things, they get hurt, they die. It sucks but life goes on."

"I guess you're right," Clayton said.

"You brought six people back, out of nine," Jeffrey said. "For a mission they gave odds of one in four, that's real good work."

"There're just so many things I'd have done differently, if I'd only known."

"*Don't* second-guess yourself," Jeffrey said. "Combat's total chaos. It doesn't pay to overanalyze it afterward, ever. Trust me on that."

Clayton hesitated. "Thanks, Commander." He took a deep breath. "I'm gonna go in back and be with my people. Maybe we'll say a little prayer for the ones that didn't make it."

"Let's all do that right now," Jeffrey said. "It just seemed too creepy while SEAL One was still alive." Jeffrey flicked on the intercom into the transport compartment. "Just a brief devotion, guys, to give us closure." SEALs Seven and Eight came to stand in the control compartment hatchway.

Jeffrey cleared his throat. "Uh . . . Our Creator, we commend to You the souls of our departed comrades.

Watch over us as we harness the forces of nature in Thy bidding, and guide us on the path to a just peace."

Everybody said Amen.

OUTSIDE THE BLUFF AT DURBAN

Gunther Van Gelder practically screamed into the intercom. *"What do you mean you can't open the outer door?"*

"We're under attack," a metallic voice answered, sounding young and very scared.

"Christ, man," Van Gelder shouted, "that's why the interlocking has two sets of barriers! You open the outer blast door and let people in, then close it and open the inner one! That's how the goddamn thing's supposed to work!"

"I don't know, sir, it halves the protection."

"Look, you," Van Gelder said. "It's been more than half an hour and there was just that one explosion, a low-yield groundburst fifteen klicks away. It could simply be an accident, for all we know. If this was a real attack, there'd have been more missiles, they'd try to saturate our defenses. I haven't seen one AA battery open fire—*there aren't any targets for them!*"

"How, how do I know you're telling the truth?"

"You don't," Van Gelder said. He coughed and cleared his mouth of grit and dust. "But you know I'm still alive and breathing, right? So you have a choice. You can keep the blast door closed and hope Durban gets nuked so I get blown to ashes. If you fail to open this door immediately and Durban does *not* get nuked, I will personally blow *your* ass off once the all-clear sounds. The other choice is opening the door, in which case I'll be far more interested in rejoining my ship than putting you on report for stupidity and cowardice. Which I *will* do if you don't *open this bloody door*!"

The hydraulic mechanism began to whine, and the massive slab swung toward Van Gelder.

ABOARD *CHALLENGER*

"Docking solid," Jeffrey said into the ASDS intercom.

"Roger," COB's voice answered, "*Challenger* confirms a solid dock. Ocean Interface conformal doors are closing now."

"Acknowledged," Jeffrey said. He watched the little status presentation on the LCD as the pressure doors swung closed over the ASDS icon.

"Doors closed," COB said two minutes later. "Hangar bay still wet, hangar internal pressure relieved."

"Confirmed," Jeffrey said. "ASDS seawater gauges read as on the surface. Decompression sequence for repetitive group F dive table is completed, ASDS internal air pressure reads as on the surface."

"Commander," Meltzer said, "our radiacs and dosimeters all show inside normal tolerances."

"Very well, Copilot," Jeffrey said. "*Challenger,* radiology is satisfactory, no measurable on-board contamination, no personnel exposures of concern at this time."

"Acknowledged," COB said. "ASDS, you are cleared to open your lower hatch."

"Very well, *Challenger,*" Jeffrey said, "we are opening our lower hatch." Jeffrey flicked some switches, then unbuckled and stood up. He stretched, as much as was possible for his tall figure in the cramped confines. He and Ilse and Meltzer went into the central air-lock chamber, and Clayton and the SEALs joined them there. Jeffrey knelt and spun the wheel. He let the door drop open.

There was a small crowd waiting at the base of the ladder, including *Challenger*'s senior medical corpsman and several ASDS maintenance specialists. Jeffrey saw Commodore Morse's bearded face look up at him.

"Scratch one bioweapons lab," Jeffrey said. "Three SEALs KIA, and we took a prisoner."

CHAPTER 21

Half an hour later Jeffrey and Ilse walked together toward the CACC.

"It's amazing what a shower and a change of clothes can do for your perspective," Ilse said.

Jeffrey laughed. "That plus a swig of Wild Turkey and a strong cuppa coffee works every time."

"Thanks again for saving my life," Ilse said.

"Aw, shucks, it was nothing."

"I'll share a second-stage regulator with you anytime, Mr. Fuller."

Just then they reached the control room. Captain Wilson turned. "Welcome back," he said. Jeffrey quickly took reports from Monaghan and Sessions, then reclaimed his role as fire control coordinator. Lieutenant Monaghan returned to being navigator, and Ilse took a seat next to Sessions at a sonar workstation. Meltzer relieved the relief pilot.

Jeffrey scanned the navigation plots and tactical displays while Wilson conned the ship. Enemy surface units and airplanes and helos swarmed everywhere, in spite of loss and damage from the local blast and EMP. There were more than two dozen hostile contacts all around.

That count included submarines on ASW duty

beneath the fallout plume, Jeffrey noticed. The pounding surf was an ideal backdrop for ambient sonar and hole-in-ocean spotting of the quiet diesel boats, but was also one more reason *Challenger* hugged the ocean floor—plenty of all-revealing wave-action sound energy was coming through the thermocline.

Jeffrey eyeballed the minefield map and gravimeter screens that COB and Meltzer used. Meltzer, back at the helm, seemed remarkably wide-awake and chipper. Jeffrey smiled. Ah, to be that young again.

Jeffrey was impressed. Not only did Wilson come to meet the ASDS right inshore, but now *Challenger* was heading south-southwest along the coast within the safety lane. They were barely 20,000 yards out from Durban, but assuming that it *was* a safety lane and the boat stayed in its limits, they were immune to enemy fire: South African and German forces had to treat all submerged contacts in the lane as friendly.

This was standard wartime procedure to avoid blue-on-blue engagements, or, Jeffrey told himself, in this case red-on-red. Antisubmarine forces avoided the corridor intentionally—otherwise navigation error or an accidental weapons release could lead to tragedy. The Axis navy took great pains to disguise their daily safety lanes—but lurking in their midst for several hours, *Challenger,* with two LMRS probes and the ASDS as off-board recon platforms, had scoped the corridors out like Jeffrey recommended.

Jeffrey glanced at the conning screens again. *Challenger* made turns for four knots, moving more like seven because of the current, at a depth right now of 570 feet, up on the continental shelf. Her slow speed through the water cut down the subtle pressure waves thrown off by her passage, further enhancing her stealth. She still needed Jeffrey's magnetic-signature cloaking gambit to fool the mines, which made for some tense moments, since mines lay everywhere, but at least if noticed at this point, *Challenger* wouldn't be subject to depth charges and torpedoes from *Rommel* and that *Sachsen*-class destroyer and their cronies.

Jeffrey suspected the mines within the safety-corridor-of-the-day were switched off by acoustic remote control, to protect Axis submarines from faulty fuzing. If so, they'd be reactivated later, when the safety corridor changed—too bad there was no survivable way to check out Jeffrey's theory.

Jeffrey saw that the lane plotted on the nav chart took a bend to port.

"Helm," Wilson said, "left standard rudder. Make your course one four three."

"Left standard rudder, aye," Meltzer said. "Make my course one four three, aye."

Wilson turned to Jeffrey. "It's clever how they arrange it, XO. Inbound traffic comes down from the north, drifting with the current. Outbound vessels sneak off south, also using the flow."

"That's just what I'd do, Captain," Jeffrey said. "It lets the diesels save their batteries and helps their SSNs to make less noise. With the tighter vertical contours down the coast, it gives 'em a free ride out to the thousand-fathom curve."

"Take a look at this, XO," Wilson said. "Radio room just decoded it."

Jeffrey took the message slip. The news was four days old.

> SAS VOORTREKKER SIGHTED 67 SOUTH 09 EAST X
> DAMAGED BY Q-SHIP THEN SUNK BY MULTIPLE
> NUCLEAR DEPTH BOMBS X PASS GOOD NEWS TO
> ALL YOUR PEOPLE X VOOR IDENT AS SSN HIT USS
> RANGER X MAY RANGERS CREW NOW RIP AVENGED
> X CNO SENDS XX

"Well, that's a relief, sir," Jeffrey said. "Maybe the tide's starting to turn our way now." He went back to his screens.

Jeffrey noted that the exact layout of the safety route got vague ahead, as *Challenger* drew ever farther from the hummock where she'd waited for the minisub and deployed the probes. This was because the distance covered since retrieving the ASDS was starting to rival the effective range of the LMRS autonomous-mode acoustic links, especially in these noisy current-strewn and halocline-ridden waters.

"Sir," Jeffrey said, "recommend we deploy an LMRS again on a wire. We can send it on in front to scout our track while we keep moving. Have it scan the bottom for us, and use it to help triangulate the enemy patrol craft and helos. We ought to be clear of the coastal defenses before its battery runs down."

"I concur," Wilson said. "We'll get much better clues on where the safety corridor is or isn't. Chief of the Watch, deploy an LMRS with a fiber-optic wire. Make its course one four three true, run it out to five thousand yards ahead of *Challenger*. Then maintain that range to own ship and maintain the zero zero zero relative bearing when you can."

"Aye aye, sir," COB replied.

Jeffrey used a window on one of his screens to study the data from the probe. Visibility was poor, the water turbidity high from bottom muck still settling after the A-bomb shock and the heavy silting by rainstorm runoff all along the KwaZulu/Natal coast.

"COB," Jeffrey said, "get a close-up of that mine." Jeffrey looked at the UHF mine classification sonar image. "Captain," Jeffrey said, "this is interesting. This one's a regular bottom influence device, not a CAPTOR. Must be the Boers are worried a torpedo cutting loose so close to base might run erratic and home on the wrong side's vessel."

"You're probably right, XO."

Jeffrey told COB to check a few more mines along their course. None of them were CAPTORs either.

"Sir," Jeffrey said, "we're coming to another bend in the corridor. It turns to starboard here, to avoid the old ammunition dumping ground, and at this point it must lead right into the bluff. Recommend we push the LMRS further away from us, to explore the outbound safety track in detail. This near to Durban I suspect the whole area's forbidden to ASW."

"That's risky, Fire Control."

"Captain, it'll give us a clearer view of what lies ahead, increase our options in case we have an equipment casualty or something. It'll also widen our base line for triangulation, since we lost our thin-line towed array and the older fat line's less useful in the littorals."

"Very well, XO. I concur." Wilson gave COB the orders, then had Meltzer turn the boat to starboard on course two four zero.

"Captain," Jeffrey said a little later, "I'm wondering if while we're here we shouldn't drop some mines of our own. Who knows what we might sink."

"XO," Wilson said, "that *is* too risky. We'd make mechanical transients loading and sending them out, plus their own propulsion noise might be picked up, and launching them creates dead-certain proof that we were here."

"Understood, Captain," Jeffrey said. He almost blushed. The exhilaration of sneaking in this close to the heart of darkness was making him impetuous. I better cut that out, he told himself.

Commodore Morse came into the CACC. "I spent some time with the SEALs," Morse said. "Sounds like you all did a terrific job."

"Thank you, sir," Jeffrey said.

"You too, Ilse," Morse said.

Ilse turned and smiled. "Think there'll be women commandos someday, Commodore?"

"Maybe there are now," Morse said, "and they aren't telling." He winked.

Morse turned back to Jeffrey. "If I were you, I'd help Clayton write up the SEAL chief for a Medal of Honor. As a lieutenant commander and not part of his unit, your word as witness would add a lot of clout."

"That's a great idea," Jeffrey said.

"If I may," Morse said, "let me offer another suggestion."

Jeffrey noticed Captain Wilson didn't mind the input—the two senior men had gotten close since leaving Diego Garcia. "Go ahead, sir," Jeffrey said.

"One thing we learned in the Falklands," Morse said, "from all our surface ship losses, is the absolutely crucial importance of aggressive damage control. The SEALs are busy cleaning their gear and drafting their after-action reports, but that's mostly make-work."

"That's sort of true, sir," Jeffrey said. "It doesn't take *that* long to clean a rifle and rinse a regulator valve."

Morse nodded. "I think you ought to add them to your repair party roster. Good upper-body strength, terrific endurance, mental calm under pressure, and let's say they're very used to working in the face of death hip-deep or more in freezing seawater with salt spray in their eyes."

Jeffrey turned to Wilson. "Captain?"

"XO, manning questions are your call."

"I agree, then," Jeffrey said. "Thanks, Commodore. . . . Messenger of the Watch, once we secure from full ultraquiet, report to the engineer. Ask him to assign Clayton and his people to a damage control party somewhere forward."

"Assign the SEALs to damage control, aye, sir," the messenger said. He jotted in his notebook.

Jeffrey got up to stretch. His left leg was starting to ache terribly.

"Problem, XO?" Wilson said.

"Just my old wound, Captain. Overexertion, probably, or delayed reaction to the stress."

"How you feeling otherwise?"

"Tip-top, sir," Jeffrey said. Surprisingly that was true—the miracle of adrenaline.

"Phone Talker," Wilson said, "call the corpsman to the CACC."

"Sir, that's really not necessary," Jeffrey said.

"XO, here on Hans's doorstep I need you at a hundred ten percent. Let the corpsman give you an aspirin."

As Jeffrey walked around, his leg suddenly buckled. Morse caught him and helped him to sit down. The corpsman came. He started checking Jeffrey very carefully, testing his reflexes and listening to his chest.

"Will I live, Chief?" Jeffrey said.

"Sir," the corpsman said, "you may be having decompression sickness."

"That's ridiculous," Jeffrey said. "We followed procedure exactly."

"Commander, you know as well as I do decompression's a stochastic process. There're always people who show random hits not predicted by the data. The problem *you've* got is all the scarring in that leg. It doesn't fit well with any of the tissue compartment models that crank out the navy diving tables."

"So now what?" Jeffrey said. He reminded himself that two deep dives in a short period was especially risky.

"I'm giving you this painkiller. I'll check with you in half an hour. If the leg still hurts, you go into your rack and go on oxygen. Any twitching or slurred speech, dizziness or discoordination, you go into the hyperbaric chamber."

"Just what I need right now," Jeffrey said, swallowing the pill. He washed it down with coffee.

The corpsman looked Jeffrey in the eye. "Don't take chances with your health, Commander." He left the CACC.

Jeffrey went back to studying the LMRS downlinks. All of a sudden the bioluminescent glow flared up, much brighter than its background level. Then a big shadow seemed to cross the field of view.

"What the hell was that?" Jeffrey said. "COB, catch up to it, bring the LMRS closer."

"Bring the LMRS closer, aye." COB worked his joy stick. "I'm getting buffeting," he said. "The contact's not just drifting, there's wake turbulence."

"Sonar," Jeffrey said, "what's ambient Doppler show? Vortices from fins and flukes? Ilse, can you help?"

"Look at this," Ilse said. She relayed Jeffrey a false-color picture of the turbulence. It had a circular cross section.

"Pancake eddies," Jeffrey said. "*Enemy sub!* Designate the contact Master 26! TMA team start a plot!"

"She must be leaving on patrol," Wilson said.

"More likely a quick sortie to get her arse away from the next incoming A-bomb," Morse said.

"It's a diesel boat on batteries," Sessions said. "It's too quiet to be nuclear."

"COB," Jeffrey said, "don't lose it. Put the LMRS in trail, right in her baffles!" Jeffrey grinned, forgetting the pain in his leg. "Captain, we can follow Master 26 right out to sea."

ABOARD *VOORTREKKER*, LEAVING THE BLUFF SUBMERGED

The air in the control room still smelled very foul, even after three days of round-the-clock repair work and a jury-rigged new forward fan room installation.

"Synchrolift rolled out against the detents," Van Gelder said. "Outer subsurface blast doors closed behind us. Captain, we're ready to blow negative and get under way."

"Very well," Jan ter Horst said. "Bring us up ten meters smartly."

Van Gelder passed the orders, in his role as diving officer when leaving port. He watched *Voortrekker*'s depth decrease and hold. The pressure gauge declined by one bar exactly. The Agulhas Current caught the ship at once.

"Slow ahead," ter Horst said, "make revs for seven knots."

Again Van Gelder passed the orders and the helmsman acknowledged.

"That's fast enough to not waste any time," ter Horst said, "in case the Allies try to hit the bluff again. Not that ground-penetrator gun bombs would get through all the layered armor under the hostage camps, but we better hope the next one doesn't go off underwater."

"It seems less and less likely there'll be another blast, Captain," Van Gelder said.

Ter Horst harrumphed sarcastically. "Either that or they know they missed and they want to get us lulled before the next one! Seven knots lets us stay quiet and at this depth avoids a surface wake—no need to draw attention to ourselves. It also gives that *Daphne*-class pig boat a chance to draw ahead."

"Er, I concur, sir," Van Gelder said, abashed.

"Port ten degrees rudder," ter Horst said, "steer two zero five."

"Aye aye," Van Gelder said. "Steering two zero five, Captain."

"Very well," ter Horst said. "Stand by for the Umlazi halocline."

• • •

ABOARD *CHALLENGER*

"Helm," Wilson said, "left standard rudder, make your course two zero five."

"Left standard rudder, make my course two zero five, aye," Meltzer said. In a few moments Jeffrey heard, "Steering two zero five, sir."

"Very well, Helm," Wilson said.

"Commander," Ilse said, "we should be coming to another halocline. Salt content will decrease about two parts per thousand seawater."

"Very well, Oceanographer," Jeffrey said. "Helm, can you compensate for decreased buoyancy with up-angle on the sternplane functions?"

"Not the way she's been handling, sir," Meltzer said, "not at this speed without the bowplanes. We'll have to run the low-rpm variable ballast pumps."

"Very well," Jeffrey said. "COB, at your discretion."

"Adjusting buoyancy with quiet centrifugal variable ballast pumps, aye," COB said. "Ilse, you can't imagine how much it helps to know a halocline's coming. Sometimes when we hit one, it's like being in an elevator and the cable broke."

"It's quieter this way too," Jeffrey said. "We can do the pumping gradually."

"You're welcome," Ilse said.

Jeffrey watched *Challenger*'s depth decrease and her nose come up slightly. Then she dropped back down to proper depth and trim as she entered the less salty water bow-first.

"You're an artist, COB," Jeffrey said.

"This boat's a work of art," COB said.

At $3.7 billion, the most expensive SSN in history, she better be, Jeffrey told himself. *Challenger*'s construction drew on quality control standards so demanding Admiral Rickover himself would've been jealous. Defense analysts in the know had called the new ceramic fast-attack boats an RMA, a revolution in military affairs, one of the most important advances in undersea warfare since the advent of nuclear propulsion and deterrent strategic missile subs. Jeffrey knew the pressure was on to prove his vessel's worth, or there might never be another in the U.S. Navy, even if the good guys won this war.

"Captain," Jeffrey said a minute later, "something's been preying on my mind."

"What's that, Fire Control?"

"The ISLMMs, sir, the improved sub-launched mobile mines," Jeffrey said. "With respect, I want to recommend again that we deploy a few."

"XO, I agree with you completely that it'd be great to sink some Axis shipping, since we've paid the price of admission to the bastion. But our top priority *must* be an undetected egress."

"But that's the point, sir," Jeffrey said. "If you think about the mission overall, it's not specifically an *undetected* egress that we want. What's required is the enemy not draw some connection between our presence and the Umhlanga Rocks event."

"Go on," Wilson said. Looking around, Jeffrey realized he had Commodore Morse's full attention too.

"It's a gamble to assume we'll get away without being detected," Jeffrey said.

"Granted," Wilson said.

"Submarining's a *business* of calculated gambles," Morse broke in. "If you don't feel your gut twisting, you're probably not doing your job."

"Then consider *this* calculation," Jeffrey said. "We're using a safety lane to escape. We might be spotted doing it. We may have been spotted already, for all we know. We have no way to tell since they'd ignore us. *But*, records of the detection would be made, even if unwittingly, in submarine deck logs and surface-unit Combat Information Center data, and sonar tapes and so on."

"Concur with that part," Wilson said.

"That means the opposition could eventually reconstruct that there was an extra submarine, *us*—that we were present and we weren't one of theirs."

"Oh dear," Morse said. "I think I see where you're going with this."

"The point is," Jeffrey said, "if we plant some mines, we're offering the Boers a red herring, an excuse or reason for us to have come by. That way when they investigate the nuclear explosion, their paranoia can still run wild. The board of inquiry can find it credible that we were in the area by coincidence, and then they start the purge we're hoping for."

Wilson actually smiled. "Very finely reasoned, Mr. Fuller. You're saying it's actually the *lesser* of two risks to launch some mines, in the bigger picture."

"Exactly, Captain. The fact we did plant mines suggests we *weren't* trying to hide completely, we *weren't* responsible for Umhlanga Rocks."

"You're not afraid that we'll make noise and draw too much attention just a little *too* soon?" Wilson said.

"Sir, the LMRSs haven't found a single SOSUS hydrophone this close inshore, and ones looking back at us from deeper water will be impaired by lots of reverb off the bottom's upslope. It'd take them hours of computer time to eke out and confirm our signature."

"That's true," Morse said. "It makes us tactically invisible."

"Yes, sir," Jeffrey said, glancing at his displays again. "If Master 7 and Master 23 here don't change course, in a couple of minutes we'll have a good window to launch from outside their detection envelopes."

"Very well, Fire Control," Wilson said. "Prepare to launch two ISLMMs. Make the runs be short, place the warheads at your discretion."

"Prepare to launch two ISLMMs, aye," Jeffrey said.

"Before we do I want to check our baffles," Wilson said. "Master 26 still holding course?"

Jeffrey eyed his screens once more, then double-checked with COB, still piloting the LMRS in the diesel's wake. Jeffrey turned back to the captain. "Affirmative, sir, the contact's dead ahead, steering two zero five on batteries, range from us eleven thousand yards, no towed array. Sir, we're getting two side-by-side opposing swirls in the turbulence. I think Master 26 has twin screws."

"That would make her a *Daphne* class," Morse said. "They're forty years old. . . . Or maybe one of the Russian *Tango*s they bought used. *Foxtrot*s have *three* shafts."

"Very well," Wilson said. "Our side's forced to use some reconditioned obsolescent hardware too. . . . Helm, on my mark all stop, then right full rudder and turn sixty degrees to starboard, then use auxiliary propulsors to cancel our remaining way. We'll drift with the current and listen with the wide-aperture arrays, while Fire Control prepares to launch the mines."

"Understood," Meltzer said.

"Mark," Wilson said.

"All stop, right full rudder, aye," Meltzer said. "Maneuvering acknowledges all stop. . . . Steering two six five, Captain. . . . We're holding inside the corridor, sir."

"Very well, Helm," Wilson said.

Jeffrey went to work. Deciding exactly where to put the total of four conventional bottom influence warheads was a nontrivial exercise, especially on short notice. Of course part of his mind had been planning for it all along. He'd lay a line across the current, not parallel to it, so one sinking vessel wouldn't drift downstream and set them all off each in turn. He decided a spacing of two hundred yards would be tight but not too close, spread across the safety lane. If no good targets used this particular lane today, eventually they would.

"Captain," Jeffrey said, "I'm setting the mine software to wait twelve hours before arming, to give us a good chance to escape."

"Concur," Wilson said.

"I'll program them to detonate for submerged nuclear-powered contacts only. At our present depth, four hundred ninety feet, we're too far down for surface targets anyway. I'm giving them the acoustic signature of the *Rubis*-class SSNs the Axis captured from France. I'm also downloading Russian machine noise characteristics, since we know the Axis bought some compact mobile reactor plants and other main components. I'm entering our best guess at the German modifications."

"Concur," Wilson said.

Jeffrey finished entering the presets on his console. He relayed the information to the weapons officer, Lieutenant Bell, Lieutenant Jackson Jefferson Bell—third-generation navy, first-generation commissioned officer, two battle Es on his ribbons.

"Close the outer door, tube seven," Wilson said. "Drain tube seven and remove the Mark 88—we can't really use it at short range anyway. Load the first ISLMM into tube seven. We'll launch the second one from there as well."

Jeffrey passed the orders, then watched the changes in the weapons status window on his console. Tube seven's door icon switched closed and the tube icon changed from green to red. The indicators changed from FLOODED and EQUALIZED to NOT FLOODED. Then the inner door emblem popped open, and the nuclear torpedo icon vanished.

The screen told Jeffrey what he already knew. Tube one was busy with the LMRS, tube three was loaded with the other LMRS and flooded, and tube five—also flooded—held a Mark 48 conventional ADCAP whose gyros were spun up. All the port-side even-numbered tubes were unavailable from battle damage. The hydraulic autoloading gear on all tubes was unavailable; the operating mode was shown as MANUAL.

"Captain," Jeffrey said, "recommend we place a third ISLMM in tube seven once we fire the first two, as a backup in case of any failures. The units were pretty beat up by the weapons compartment flooding, even if they check out okay now."

"Concur, Fire Control," Wilson said.

"Captain, once we're through the bastion, should we engage Master 26?"

"Let's talk about that," Wilson said. "Leaving a silent calling card, the mines, to support our cover story's one thing. A flaming datum while we're here is something else. We *have* to get our prisoner back to base for interrogation. Since they destroyed so much of the lab notes, us putting the written records through a scanner, downloading their diskettes, and sending off a microburst once we get out to blue water like we originally planned just isn't an option. If we're prevented from reaching the Cape Verdes physically ourselves, our side loses all the intel, which was half our cause for coming here."

"And if we're sunk too near this coast," Morse said, "not only are we a treasure trove for the *other* people, but when they explore the wreck, they'll find Otto's body."

"Mine too, sirs, respectfully," Ilse said. To Jeffrey she looked slightly pale at the thought, even in the reddish light. "If the fish find us before they do, they'll still have dental charts."

Jeffrey shivered. "That would ruin everything."

"Cheer up, XO," Wilson said. "That's also part of the job sometimes, passing up a lesser target in favor of a greater one."

"Yes, sir," Jeffrey said.

"Commander," Sessions called, "no new sonar contacts."

"Very well," Jeffrey said. "Captain, our baffles are clear."

"Very well," Wilson said. "Helm, make your course two zero five, ahead one third, make turns for four knots."

Meltzer acknowledged.

Jeffrey fidgeted. It seemed forever before the torpedomen could get the first ISLMM cranked into the tube.

CHAPTER 22

ABOARD *VOORTREKKER*

"Sir," Van Gelder said, "Sonar has detected a mechanical transient dead ahead, close to the bottom."

"Range?" ter Horst said.

"Difficult to say. The signal strength was weak."

"Educated guess?"

"It could be distant, or it could be close but with an unfavorable contact aspect angle."

"What did it sound like?"

"A *clunk,* sir. A torpedo being loaded, maybe."

"Probably some kind of sound short on that *Daphne,*" ter Horst said. "Those boats are ancient, and even with the prewar modernization refit by our German friends, their crew training standards aren't up to yours and mine."

Van Gelder nodded. "We're close enough to home it doesn't matter. Still, they ought to be more careful."

ABOARD *CHALLENGER*

"Make tube seven ready in all respects," Wilson said. "Tube seven, firing point procedures, improved sub-launched mobile mine."

"Solution ready," Jeffrey said. "Ship ready. Weapon ready."

"Very well," Wilson said. "Open the outer door tube seven, and shoot."

"Unit from tube seven fired electrically," Jeffrey said. "Unit swimming out."

"Unit is running normally," Sessions said.

ABOARD *VOORTREKKER*

"Hydrophone effects!" Van Gelder shouted.

"*What?*" ter Horst said.

"Torpedo in the water bearing zero zero four! Torpedo is drawing left to right, range increasing!"

"Torpedo type?" ter Horst snapped.

Van Gelder turned to the sonar chief.

"Open-cycle axial piston engine," the chief called out. "Harmonics of sixty hertz plus strong lines at 750 and 1725."

"Captain," Van Gelder said, "it's a modified American Mark 48, one of their piggyback mine-deploying weapons."

"*Here?*"

"Yes, sir," Van Gelder said.

"Any contact on the sub? Acoustics, wake turbulence, anything?"

"Not since that mechanical transient," Van Gelder said. "*Seawolf*s and *Virginia*s are very quiet, sir, and pump-jets don't leave much wake."

"I know. That transient must have been them loading the torpedo tube."

"Torpedo bearing rate and speed guesstimate put its launch point five thousand yards from us," Van Gelder said.

"We'll use that for the sub," ter Horst said. "Begin a target-motion plot. I'll bet it's a *Seawolf* on a mining mission. They make bigger targets than *Virginia*s, but they have a bigger weapons load-out too."

"Torpedo changing course," Van Gelder said. "Constant bearing now, signal strength increasing. *It's aimed right at us!*"

"Not at *us*, Gunther," ter Horst said. "At the bottom somewhere on our course. Somewhere in the safety lane."

"Concur, sir," Van Gelder said, slightly embarrassed.

"Time to sidestep," ter Horst said. "Helm, port thirty rudder, steer zero nine zero."

"Aye aye, sir," the helmsman acknowledged smartly.

"Good thing it's not an ADCAP," Van Gelder said. "We're badly boxed in by the coastline and the sloping continental shelf and by the limits of the safety corridor."

"I know," ter Horst said. "It would be hard for us to run. . . . But the same thing holds for them, only more so, though I'd rather not find out for sure if the active mines outside the corridor ignore us."

"They won't ignore the *Seawolf*," Van Gelder said.

Ter Horst smiled. "We know they're there, but they don't know *we're* here."

"We have the advantage acoustically, sir, at least for now."

"That's right, with both of us so near the bottom. They're downhill from *Voortrekker*, so in looking at each other they have the upslope in their face while we have a clean field of view. They're in the sweet spot of our bow sphere while we know they haven't deployed a towed array—we'd hear it dragging intermittently."

"We have the weather gauge, so to speak," Van Gelder said.

"Leave the clever puns to me, Number One."

"Yes, Captain."

"I bet they're distracted by that *Daphne*."

"The Americans may plan to take her out once they reach deeper water," Van Gelder said.

"We'll just see about *that*," ter Horst said. "Rig for ultraquiet, rig for depth charge. Go to action stations and close up for attack."

"Recommend we use conventional warheads," Van Gelder said, "given our location."

"Concur," ter Horst said. "Warm up the weapons, tubes one through four. We'll start with one of our slower-running stealthy fish, set to home on wake and flow noise once we have a better TMA. We'll go active with it only if we miss and need a reattack."

"Sir, that warhead's fairly small."

"It's a trade-off, Gunther. I'd rather have the first shot be a total surprise. It'll do real damage, and then we finish them off with something bigger. Who knows, maybe they'll be forced to the bottom from flooding or have a mobility kill. We could capture all their crypto gear, even take some crewmen alive for a thorough interrogation." Ter Horst smiled sadistically.

"Er, concur, Captain," Van Gelder said.

"Sir," the sonar chief said, "torpedo has gone past our baffles, receding off the port quarter now."

"Very well, Sonar," Van Gelder said.

"Helm, steady as you go," ter Horst said. "That ISLMM may have another way point up its sleeve."

"My head is zero nine zero, sir," the helmsman said.

"Captain," Van Gelder said, "we should preset a range limit on our unit, to protect the *Daphne*."

"Yes, do it, and program the unit to detonate under target's hull. Warm up the decoys in tubes five and six as well. No point in being foolhardy—our friends out there have eight big tubes themselves."

"Captain," Van Gelder said, "enemy torpedo has changed course again, zero nine zero true. Doppler shows it still receding. . . . Torpedo engine noise has ceased. Both mines must have been planted."

"Helm," ter Horst said, "starboard thirty rudder. Steer two six five, put us back on track. . . . Number One, mark the mines' position, then deploy a message buoy with a warning smartly, Flash Double Zed priority."

"Aye aye, sir," Van Gelder said, "radio room is working. . . . *Second* torpedo in the water!"

"Shit," ter Horst said. "Starboard thirty rudder, steer three zero zero."

"Sir," Van Gelder said, "it's another mobile mine. It's drawing right to left this time."

"Ah, not a problem, then. . . . It's going to turn back soon."

"You're right, Captain. Here it comes."

"The Americans are so predictable." Ter Horst laughed. "Helm, return us to dead center in the outbound safety lane. Port thirty rudder, steer two zero five."

"Port thirty rudder, aye aye, sir. Steer two zero five, aye aye."

"Number One, prepare to launch an unmanned undersea vehicle probe. Use tube eight. I'm going to play doctor with that *Seawolf*."

"Captain?"

"The UUV's my proctoscope."

Van Gelder worked his panel. "UUV away."

"Now, Gunther," ter Horst said, "once our probe visually identifies the target, what do you think about shooting while we're all still in the safety lane?"

CHALLENGER

"Sir," COB said, "I've lost contact with that *Daphne* class, Master 26."

"What happened?" Jeffrey said.

"They just topped an outcropping south of the Umkomaas River outflow gully and the broken terrain beyond is making too much current turbulence."

"Very well, Chief of the Watch," Jeffrey said. "Start a snake pattern with the LMRS, try to recover the trail. . . . Captain, in the meantime we can probably find the rest of the no-fire corridor by avoiding any CAPTORs."

"Concur, Fire Control," Wilson said. "Helm, steady as you go."

"My course is two zero five, sir," Meltzer said.

"Sir," COB said, "still no sign of Master 26."

"Very well," Jeffrey said. "Make the LMRS follow a balloon track instead, take a good look at the minefield to our front."

For a few minutes no one spoke.

"Commander," COB said, "I'm getting *two* possible routes for the safety lane based on CAPTOR locations versus fixed-emplacement bottom mines."

"I see what you mean," Jeffrey said, studying the data. "One of the routes may be a cul-de-sac, a trap."

"But which is which?" Wilson said. "Do we take the straight path or the turn to port?"

"If I were an Axis coastal defense commander," Commodore Morse said, "I'd do the opposite of what I thought the Allies would expect me to do."

"Yes?" Wilson said. "Or would you? Mightn't you also take account of *that*, and then do what the Allies *do* expect you to do, to psych them out?"

"We could flip a coin," Jeffrey said. "That's probably what they did."

"Still no sign of Master 26," COB said.

"Very well," Wilson said. "Helm, all stop, hover on manual."

"All stop, aye, sir," Meltzer said. "Maneuvering acknowledges."

"Now," Wilson said, "one thing the Axis *will* do is try to rush our thinking. Instead we'll just sit tight while Lieutenant Monaghan and I study the bottom charts. . . . Helm, rotate sixty degrees to starboard on auxiliary propulsors. It's time to check our baffles again.

I don't want us rear-ended by the next enemy boat that passes through. If one does sortie soon, we'll get in trail and follow *them*. . . . XO, take the deck and the conn."

"This is the XO," Jeffrey said. "I have the deck and the conn."

"Aye aye," the watch standers said.

Jeffrey kept his eyes moving between the different screens. Wilson walked back to confer with Monaghan at the navigation table. Morse sat down next to Jeffrey at the command console, got comfortable, and opened his mouth to say something.

"Hydrophone effects!" Sessions shouted. "Coming from our baffles!"

"Range and classification?" Jeffrey said, calling up the starboard wide-aperture array displays.

"Torpedo in the water!" Sessions screamed. "Sub-launched, not a CAPTOR! Wide-field effects, *it's right on top of us*!"

The ocean roared and *Challenger* bucked upward hard. The shock blurred Jeffrey's vision as his seat pounded his buttocks—only the seat belt kept him from flying. Nearby mine warheads detonated sympathetically, sharp rumbling *blams* that forced the boat to port and then to starboard. The accelerometers built into the wide arrays showed the whole hull flexing nightmarishly, *Challenger*'s bow and stern ends whipping up and down.

Jeffrey turned aft quickly. Monaghan and Wilson were lying in a heap. Monaghan's neck looked broken and Wilson was unconscious. There was blood on the flameproof linoleum under Wilson's head.

"Helm," Jeffrey shouted, "ahead flank smartly!"

"Ahead flank smartly, aye!"

"Fire Control is firing noisemakers and jammers!" Jeffrey punched his console keys to launch the countermeasures.

"Maneuvering acknowledges ahead flank smartly!"

"Hard left rudder," Jeffrey said, "make a knuckle, make your course one zero five. We'll assume the jog to port's the safety lane and not a trap and make a run for deeper water."

"Hard left rudder, aye," Meltzer said. "Make my course one zero five, aye."

"Sonar," Jeffrey said, "designate our attacker Master 27. Gimme a bearing for a snap shot."

"Negative!" Sessions said. "No data on torpedo's inbound course!"

"Sir," COB said, watching his nav display, "the LMRS only works so fast. We'll run too near a mine soon, trip a CAPTOR for sure."

Jeffrey reached for a spare sound-powered phone. "Weapons, Control, this is the XO."

"Control, Weapons Officer," Lieutenant Bell's voice said.

"Arm all antitorpedo rockets."

"Arm all AT rockets, aye."

"Engineering, Control," Jeffrey said. "Gimme a damage control report."

"Control, wait one, Lieutenant Willey broke a leg."

Jeffrey eyed his screens impatiently. *Challenger*'s speed was mounting, and so far she was holding depth and trim. Damage data popped onto his status board—minor fires under control and leaky fittings quickly patched or isolated.

Jeffrey glanced at the small crowd gathered round the fallen men. A first-aid tech was giving CPR to Monaghan while trying to hold his head straight. Commodore Morse looked up from tending Wilson, who moved slightly and groaned. Morse made eye contact with Jeffrey. "I think he's got a fractured skull."

Jeffrey started toward them.

"Forget him!" Morse shouted. "She's yours now, *fight the ship*!"

Jeffrey turned in a circle, torn between two duties.

He limped back to his console. "Weps, warm up the units in tubes three and five. Once we fire, reload both tubes with ADCAPs, secure from ultraquiet if it helps speed up the work."

"Understood," Bell said.

"Helm," Jeffrey ordered, "follow the bottom, minimum clearance, modified nap-of-seafloor mode."

"Modified nap-of-seafloor, aye," Meltzer said.

"COB, trail three hundred feet of the fat-line towed array. We've *got* to have some baffles coverage."

"Trail three hundred feet of the TB-16, aye."

Jeffrey read the nav plot. *Challenger* was topping thirty knots. They were overtaking the LMRS fast, coming up on mines there wasn't time to classify.

"Sonar, stand by on the sail- and chin-mounted active HF mine-avoidance systems."

"Acknowledged," Sessions said. He cleared his throat.

Jeffrey launched more noisemakers and jammers, then glanced aft. "*What's taking him so long?* Phone Talker, call the senior corpsman to the CACC stat."

"Sir," COB said, "you need to—"

"*Yes,*" Jeffrey said. "Phone Talker, pass to all compartments. Captain's down, XO's in command of *Challenger*."

CHAPTER 23

"A direct hit, Captain," Van Gelder said, "and three secondary explosions from mines in target proximity."

"Good," ter Horst said, "that should break her back quite nicely."

"Sir," Van Gelder shouted, "reactor check valve transients, the *Seawolf*'s running at flank speed! She's altered course, near one zero zero true!"

"That's straight into the active minefield," ter Horst said. "Hah! She must be flooding, trying to plane up to the surface. Any ballast blowing sounds?"

"None detected, Captain."

"Good. Her hydraulics may be down, no valve control or steering."

"Sir," Van Gelder said, "we might have missed the EMBT blow with the explosions. They have an emergency system like ours that's independent of power."

"What's target depth?"

"Near the bottom, Captain. Her sink rate now just equals how the floor drops off."

"If they did a blow, it isn't working. . . . Any return fire?"

"Negative, Captain," Van Gelder said.

Ter Horst smiled. "Stealth fish, Gunther, works every time. They're clueless where we are."

"They may catch echoes off our hull with all this bubble noise and reverb, sir, more than we can cancel with our out-of-phase emissions. Or they may just take a snap shot up the corridor."

"Too true," ter Horst said, "so we'll use the bubbles for concealment. Helm, starboard thirty rudder, then port thirty rudder, then steady as you go. Take us to the inshore edge of the safety lane and keep the dispersing blast area between us and the target."

The helmsman acknowledged and the boat banked steeply to starboard, then to port, then leveled off. "My head is two zero five, sir."

"We'll turn to port where they did, Gunther," ter Horst said, "and follow them in trail. That way we'll be out of line of a snap shot and we can use them as a minesweeper. Arm the antitorpedo rockets just in case."

"Arm the antitorpedo rockets, aye," Van Gelder said.

"Target speed?" ter Horst said.

"Tonals show her still accelerating," Van Gelder said. "TMA team working now." Known range and course and bearing rate gave the unknown variable. "Captain, she's topping thirty-five knots."

"Let's see how long *that* lasts. Number One, retrieve the UUV."

"No contact with the UUV," Van Gelder said. "Assess the vehicle destroyed."

"Not surprising," ter Horst said. "Very well, reload tube eight with a nuclear torpedo. Helm, ahead full, do not cavitate."

"Ahead full, do not cavitate, aye aye," the helmsman said. "Turbine room answers steam throttles moving to ahead full, sir."

"Sonar confirms no cavitation," Van Gelder said.

"We can't let the *Seawolf* draw too far ahead," ter Horst said. "If we give them any separation, they may go for a nuclear snap shot."

"They might regardless, Captain," Van Gelder said.

"If they know they're doomed, they've nothing to lose. They'll try to take us with them."

"I wish you hadn't said that, Gunther. Very well, prepare to fire tube two. We'll use one of our Russian 65-series conventional heavyweights this time. The target's close, preset attack speed fifty knots. I know, that'll drag it out a bit—I want to make them shit their pants."

Van Gelder blinked. "Tube two, aye, preset attack speed fifty knots."

Ter Horst smirked. "Nine hundred kilograms of good German high explosives ought to finish them off. That's three times the wallop of their puny ADCAPs."

"Make tube five ready in all respects," Jeffrey said, "including valve lineup for punch-out with a water slug." The tube five door was already open. "Firing point procedures, tube five, snap shot on own ship's course. *Shoot*."

"Set," Lieutenant Bell said over the sound-powered phone. "Stand by. *Fire*. . . . Tube five fired electrically."

"Unit is running normally," Sessions said.

"Weps," Jeffrey said, one eye on the tactical display, "what height off the floor gives us the best area effect on bottom mines?"

"You mean like with an airburst from an A-bomb, sir?"

"Yeah."

"I'd need to run a calculation."

"Decide right now."

"Um, uh, try one five zero feet, sir."

"Pass control of the unit to me," Jeffrey said. He worked his joy stick. He steered the ADCAP over a mine and commanded the warhead to blow. *Challenger* shook from the string of sympathetic blasts, then shimmied as she passed through churning water.

"Make tube three ready in all respects including a water slug," Jeffrey said. "Helm, thirty degrees down angle as we cross the continental shelf. When we're well below the crest, turn hard to port. We need to get away from the fiber-optic line to the LMRS or we'll lose it for sure with the next explosion."

"Multiple detonations on target bearing!" Van Gelder said, raising his voice above the noise.

"The first one sounded different," ter Horst said.

Van Gelder studied the sonar screens. "Confirmed! Captain, initial blast had power spectrum of a Mark 48. Others were our CAPTORs, no arming runs."

"Did the Americans fire at the *Daphne* and have a premature?"

"Sir," Van Gelder said, "they may be trying to blow a pathway through the mines."

"Cheeky," ter Horst said. "It's a shame their CO has to die. Do we know which boat it is?"

"Propulsion tonals extremely faint," Van Gelder said, "cannot determine hull number."

"We'll find out soon enough, during the salvage operation."

"Target depression angle rate is positive, sir," Van Gelder said. "They're past the continental shelf, their depth increasing fast."

"Flooding noise?"

"Impossible to tell."

"Hull-popping sounds?"

"Nothing, Captain," Van Gelder said.

"Interesting," ter Horst said. "*Los Angeles*–class boats and the *Virginias* start popping at three hundred meters. *Seawolf* hulls have stronger steel, thick HY 100, but they'll reach their crush depth soon if this keeps up."

"Sir," Van Gelder said, "we're coming to the shelf escarpment now."

"Helm," ter Horst said, "thirty degrees down angle as we near the cliff. Take us to the deeper bottom smartly."

"Thirty degrees down angle, aye aye, sir," the helmsman said.

Van Gelder braced himself as *Voortrekker* nosed over. "Captain, we lost the contact. They may have made a knuckle while masked from us by the shelf edge."

"Very well," ter Horst said, "time to launch another 65. Number One, make tube two ready in all respects including opening outer door. Tube two, firing point procedures, generated bearings on the *Seawolf*."

"Torpedo room is ready," Van Gelder said.

"Enable active search three thousand meters from target," ter Horst said. *"Shoot."*

"Torpedo in the water!" Sessions shouted. "Bearing two two zero relative!"

"Sir," COB said, "we're about to hit live mines."

Jeffrey hesitated, for just a moment. "Maintain course and speed! Tube three open the outer door! Firing point procedures on tube three, snap shot own ship's course!"

"Sir," Sessions said, "if we keep ignoring Master 27, they'll continue firing at us."

"We can't afford to turn and fight them now," Jeffrey said, "much as I would like to. Our rate of fire's too low." *Challenger*'s damaged weapons compartment was down to World War II reloading technology, and as good as Kerr and Scutaro were, they weren't the first team—the boat's best torpedomen were on eternal patrol in the meat locker.

"Tube three shoot!" Jeffrey ordered.

"Set," Bell reported over the sound-powered phone. "Stand by. *Fire*. . . . Tube three fired electrically."

"Unit is running normally," Sessions said. "Sir, incoming torpedo has gone active!"

"Range and range rate?" Jeffrey said as he launched more countermeasures.

"Twelve hundred yards and gaining on us ten yards every second!"

"Classification?" Jeffrey said.

"Strong 1420 tonal," Sessions said, "gas turbine powered. . . . It's a German-licensed Russian *series*-65!"

"Weps," Jeffrey said, "on the AT rocket battery, target incoming torpedo. At one-second intervals, fire a salvo of three."

"Antitorpedo rocket noises!" Van Gelder said, watching the sonar screens and the live feed from the torpedo's fiber-optic wire. "Unit from two tube has been destroyed!" The blast wave struck, deafening through the hull and sonar speakers. *Voortrekker* seemed to stagger for a moment on her course.

"Torpedo in the water!" the sonar chief shouted. "Closed-cycle Rankine steam turbine, a Mark 48 Improved ADCAP, range from us increasing." Another blast, followed by a series of crackling explosions.

"What a waste of mines," ter Horst said. "Very well, prepare to fire tube one, another 65. This time use maximum attack speed."

"Tube one, aye aye," Van Gelder said, "maximum attack speed."

"Make tube seven ready in all respects including a water slug," Jeffrey said. "Open the outer door. Ignore ISLMM way-point presets, pass weapon control to me."

"Aye aye," Lieutenant Bell said.

"Firing point procedures on tube seven, snap shot own ship's course, *shoot*."

"Set," Bell said. "Stand by. *Fire*. . . . Tube seven fired electrically."

"Unit is running normally," Sessions said.

Jeffrey watched the tactical display. The ISLMM moved forward slowly, its speed at first—even with the water slug—barely more than *Challenger's*. Then it accelerated away. Jeffrey brought the unit to 400 feet from the bottom. He programmed the first mine to detonate ten seconds after jettison, then commanded the ISLMM to drop the warhead. It should go off at about 150 feet. He brought the ISLMM itself down to 150. It was moving even faster now with the weight of just one warhead. On his ten count Jeffrey fired the second warhead. The resulting concussions once more jarred his bones.

"Loud explosions bearing zero nine zero!" Sessions said. "Both ISLMM warheads and seven enemy bottom mines!"

"Very well, Sonar," Jeffrey said.

"Torpedo in the water!" Sessions said. "In our baffles, another 65!"

"Weps," Jeffrey said, "stand by on the AT rockets."

"Second torpedo in the water!" Sessions shouted. "Relative bearing two six five. Otto fuel closed-cycle engine, wide-field hydrophone effects—*a CAPTOR's after us!*"

"Keep your voice down, Sonar," Jeffrey said, "you'll get hoarse. . . . Weps, take out the CAPTOR."

There was a roaring sound, diminishing quickly, then a dreadful double *crack*.

"Incoming CAPTOR-fish destroyed," Sessions said.

"Good shooting, Weps," Jeffrey said, but the AT rocket supply was running low. "Helm, hard right rudder, make your course zero nine zero."

"Hard right rudder, make my course zero nine zero, aye," Meltzer said. The boat banked into the turn.

"Sir," COB said, "more live mines are dead ahead."

Jeffrey glanced at his weapons board—all tubes were empty.

"Weps, how much longer to reload an ADCAP?"

Bell paused. "Thirty seconds, sir."

Too damn long. "COB and Sonar," Jeffrey said, "the LMRS probe—we're catching up with it now. Any sign of Master 26?"

"Nothing, Commander," Sessions said.

"Negative contact," COB said. "If she's smart, that diesel's clearing datum fast."

"Sonar," Jeffrey said, "get the LMRS specs from Weps. We'll try to use its active sonar as transducers, send a signal through the fiber-optic wire and put out a signature like *Seawolf*."

"Aye aye, sir," Sessions said. "Second 65 still gaining on us fast."

Jeffrey fired more noisemakers as *Challenger* rushed past its own probe. "COB, put the LMRS on a reciprocal course, make noises like a *Seawolf—now*."

"Unit from tube one has passive lock on target," Van Gelder said, "depth six hundred meters. . . . Sonar reports target reversing course!"

"So he's turned to fight at last," ter Horst said, "or he's hoping to bottom in shallower water. Tube two status?"

"Tube two reloaded with another high-explosive series-65."

"Tube two, target the *Seawolf*. Program maximum attack speed and fire on generated bearings."

"Torpedo room is ready," Van Gelder said.

"Shoot," ter Horst said.

"Target is reversing course again!"

"Hah!" ter Horst said. "We've got them on the run. Her captain's lost it, Gunther. It's almost over now."

• • •

"Helm," Jeffrey said, "all stop."

"All stop, aye," Meltzer said. "Maneuvering acknowledges all stop."

"Another torpedo in the water!" Sessions said. "*Another* 65 incoming in our baffles!"

Challenger began to coast. Jeffrey fired more noisemakers—he had few left, he needed to parcel them more carefully, and this deep they didn't work well from the pressure.

"COB," Jeffrey said, "bring the LMRS back to us and then lead it around to port and out in front."

"Understood," COB said.

"Sonar," Jeffrey said, "increase probe's active signal intensity by three decibels *now*."

"Doubling signal intensity, aye," Sessions said.

"Status of incoming torpedoes?"

"Sir, the first one's tracking the LMRS—it's got passive lock. The second one's in passive search, coming in our direction."

"COB," Jeffrey said, "the 65s are biggies. Put the LMRS three hundred yards off the bow, hold it there at *two* five zero feet up from the bottom."

"Understood."

"First incoming torpedo passing down our port side now," Sessions said. "Torpedo speed is seventy-five knots."

Jeffrey heard its awful scream first swell and then diminish, the whining of the gas turbine and counterrotating screw props.

"Weps," Jeffrey said, "stand by on the AT rockets. Target the second torpedo."

"On the AT battery," Bell responded, "target the second torpedo, aye."

A huge eruption shook the boat. Mines went off like strings of firecrackers—in front of *Challenger,* then to the sides, even back behind her.

"First 65 has detonated!" Sessions yelled. "LMRS destroyed!"

Jeffrey smiled. *"Helm, ahead flank smartly."*

"Unit from tube one has detonated on target," Van Gelder shouted. "Impact on the *Seawolf* at a depth of eight hundred meters!" There was a noise like rolling thunder, and endless concussions pounded the hull. "Multiple secondary explosions from bottom mines as well!"

"Finally," ter Horst said. "No one could live through *that*."

"Concur," Van Gelder said as surface reflections echoed and *Voortrekker* rocked. He glanced at his tactical displays. "Captain, recommend we command-detonate the unit from tube two, to avoid endangering the *Daphne* and nearby surface craft."

"Concur. Self-destruct the weapon."

Van Gelder passed the order to the torpedo room. In moments the fiber-optic feed showed DETONATED and the other data ceased. The noise and buffeting hit, then more shivering bubble pulses and echoes from the surface.

"Sir," Van Gelder shouted as he gripped his handrests, "we're picking up target propulsion transients!"

"That's impossible!" ter Horst said.

"Captain, our sonar algorithms confirm the target *not* destroyed! Intermittent ambient sonar contact on her hull!"

"Target depth?"

"Now well past one thousand meters! . . . Passive sonar contact lost, course unknown, no bulkhead ruptures or implosion sounds."

"Are you *sure*?"

"Sir," Van Gelder said, "the explosive rebound *psheew* of a steel sub past its crush depth is impossible to miss!"

"Challenger," ter Horst gasped. "We've found her, Gunther, *yes*! Warm up the nuclear-tipped 65s in tubes seven and eight."

• • •

"Sir," Sessions said, "high-frequency mine-avoidance sonar indicates we're now clear of the minefield. Second incoming torpedo has detonated prematurely."

"Very well," Jeffrey said. "Probably a self-destruct before they lost the wire from all the turbulence out there. How's our bow cap doing?"

"Real banged-up now, sir. Self-noise from boundary-layer flow is up by four more decibels."

"Helm," Jeffrey said, "slow to ahead two thirds, make turns for twenty-six knots."

"Ahead two thirds, make turns for twenty-six knots, aye," Meltzer said. "Maneuvering acknowledges ahead two thirds, making turns for twenty-six knots, sir."

"I want to put some bearing separation between our attacker and the stirred-up water, throw Master 27 off our trail and let them think we're dead from progressive flooding. Helm, make your course one three seven. That'll also unmask our starboard wide-aperture array."

"Make my course one three seven, aye," Meltzer said.

"At this point," Jeffrey said, "the best strategy's to head for deeper water at top quiet speed, dive beneath whatever limit Axis fish can handle. This course'll take us to the thousand-fathom curve a little faster, then we use full nap-of-seafloor cruising mode."

"Our depth is three eight zero zero feet now, sir," COB said.

"Very well, Chief of the Watch," Jeffrey said. "If intel's right, we're more or less safe now, at least from nonnuclear devices, and A-bombs probably won't catch us so long as we don't give Hans another datum once we're well offshore of the latest one. At twenty-six knots and with the stormy seas up there we can outrun any surface ships they have, and conditions aren't good for airborne dipping sonars either."

"*Captain*," Sessions said, using Jeffrey's formal acting title, "intermittent passive sonar contact bearing two eight four on Master 27, reflections off her sail and bow sphere using reverb from the last torpedo detonation."

"Range?" Jeffrey said, turning to face Sessions, who was busy eyeing data from his staff. Jeffrey almost started when he saw Ilse sitting there—somehow he'd forgotten all about her.

Jeffrey glanced aft. Captain Wilson and Morse were gone and the senior corpsman was working hard on Monaghan, now wearing a neck brace with his head taped to a backboard. The corpsman paused from giving artificial respiration to put a defibrillator to the navigator's chest.

"Clear!" he said, his forehead damp with sweat. Jeffrey realized he'd already done this several times—he smelled burned skin and hair. Tunnel vision, Jeffrey told himself. I got so fixated on the battle I forgot about my crew. I can't afford to do that.

"Captain," Sessions said, "contact bearing too far sternward to triangulate or range-gate by wide-aperture array, and no surface bounce range possible. Ambient sonar signal strength puts distance to Master 27 at roughly fifteen thousand yards. Cannot classify the contact based on ambient signature alone."

"Very well," Jeffrey said.

"Sir," Sessions said, "recommend another turn to starboard for a better wide-array incidence angle, a tighter estimate of contact range and possible capture of tonals."

"Negative," Jeffrey said. "That would bring the contact's bearing closer to our beam, make *us* a bigger apparent target and also expose the starboard maximum in our radial self-noise profile."

"Understood, sir," Sessions said.

Jeffrey read his TMA display. The latest datum showed Master 27's course unchanged, still zero nine zero true.

"They haven't turned to follow," Jeffrey said. "I think they've lost us, Sonar, and we're both too close to other

Axis forces for them to go for area effect with an atomic warhead."

"Concur, sir," Sessions said. "Doppler indicates the range is opening. No sign of weapon launch or loading transients on Master 27's bearing."

Commodore Morse came back to the CACC. "It looks like Captain Wilson doesn't have a broken skull, just a bad concussion. They say he's completely out of action for at least two days."

"Understood," Jeffrey said, then he glanced at Monaghan again.

"They put him in your rack," Morse continued. "They're stitching up his scalp now."

"Why not the CO's state-room?" Jeffrey said distractedly.

"You need the data repeaters in his cabin, when you turn in for some rest. . . . You know you're acting captain now."

"I got a heartbeat," the corpsman called.

"Can you keep him going?" Jeffrey said. Then he tried to stand. He could barely put weight on his leg now.

"I don't know," the corpsman said. He inserted a plastic airway down the navigator's throat and started squeezing rhythmically on a breather bag. "It's a nasty translation injury, like you'd expect from a torpedo hit. Neck vertebrae are crushed, his spinal cord's been damaged, maybe severed altogether. He needs to be on a life support respirator and we don't have one aboard."

"Come on, Chief," Jeffrey said. "We've got a boatload of fancy pumps and spark-proof motors, a lifetime supply of pure O_2, and some of the best engineers in the world. We'll *make* a respirator."

"Sir," the corpsman said, pressing down on Monaghan's chest to get him to exhale, "that could take us hours."

"Then we give him artificial respiration for hours. . . . Phone Talker," Jeffrey ordered, "SEAL medic to the

CACC stat. . . . They'll go in the hyperbaric chamber in the ASDS together, on oxygen, and the SEAL'll breathe for Monaghan, however long it takes. When the respirator's done, we lock it into the chamber with them."

Jeffrey eyed his weapons screen. Tubes one and three were loaded now with ADCAPs. Turn and rise and fire on Master 27? Get set to use one of the precious Mark 88s, a deep-capable nuclear torpedo, since *Challenger*'s ADCAPs were conventional?

Jeffrey turned to Sessions. "Sonar, can you tell me Master 27's depth?"

"Sir, passive contact lost as reverb dwindled. Doppler showed her moving but less fast than us." Sessions worked his keyboard and conferred with Ilse. She worked her keyboard too. Sessions looked up. "Sir, last elevation angle datum applied to local ray trace path shows Master 27 passing through three thousand feet."

"Are you *sure*?"

"Sir, the calculations check."

"Any sounds of hull distress? A bad equipment casualty, maybe, or hit by friendly CAPTOR fire?"

Jeffrey waited as Sessions scanned his tapes.

"No inrushing water or hatches popping, sir, no escaping bubbles or collapsing frames. . . . No high-speed dive flow noise or groaning steel . . . and no impact with the bottom."

Jeffrey made eye contact with Ilse.

"It's Jan's boat," Ilse said. "This far down it has to be."

"Yeah," Jeffrey said. "The Axis doesn't use titanium hulls."

"*Deutschland*'s in the North Atlantic," Morse said, "busy devastating the convoys from America."

Jeffrey looked around the crowded CACC, silently cursing the typically overoptimistic battle damage assessment. "*Voortrekker* survived, people, and now she's after *us*. Our battle isn't over, it's just begun."

CHAPTER 24

"Number One," ter Horst said, "launch another message buoy, Flash Double Zed priority again. Message reads: Am in contact with USS *Challenger*. Am best platform to prosecute, all units stand clear my chase, ter Horst sends. . . . Add our position, depth and course and speed, and get it off immediately."

"Aye aye, sir," Van Gelder said.

"Load tube six with a nuclear 65. Prepare to fire a salvo of three."

"Sir, this close to shore?"

"I'm not going to detonate them *here,* Gunther. I'll run them twenty thousand meters further out, use a nice wide spread, since we don't have the target localized. That'll put the bursts a comfy forty klicks from land."

"Sonar," Van Gelder said, "what's the wind?"

"Still backing, sir," the sonar chief said, "from west around to south. Wind's coming out of roughly two four zero now. I'd say speed's down to maybe twenty knots."

"The dangerous semicircle must have passed," ter Horst said, "and the storm's recurving northward, but the wind's still blowing nicely out to sea."

"Yield setting on the warheads, Captain?" Van Gelder said.

"Maximum yield. Twenty thousand meters is a touch

more distance than Wilson could have covered running at top quiet speed. So wherever he actually is, *Challenger* should be inside lethal range of one of the blasts."

Van Gelder read his tactical display. "Sir, there are friendly units on the arc you plan to sanitize."

"We just warned them," ter Horst said, "with that message buoy. . . . Don't use active search—our fish might just pick up a wreck."

"Captain," Van Gelder said, "with respect, messages take time to relay, ships need time to clear the area, and these two *Navors*-class coastal minesweepers are much too small to stand the shock and tsunami."

Ter Horst eyed the screen. "Gunther, Gunther, Gunther. You know as well as I do all target-motion analysis is notional. This just shows who we think perhaps *might* be at these positions, approximately speaking, based on estimates and projections, subject to judgmental guesses and any sensor error. This data isn't *real*. Those minesweepers might well be somewhere else, or they might not be there at all."

"Captain . . ."

"For all we know," ter Horst said, "there could be other *hostile* units we might eliminate, support for *Challenger* we haven't yet detected. So it's a wash, as far as I'm concerned."

"Very well, sir," Van Gelder said reluctantly. He worked his weapons menu screen. "Tubes six, seven, and eight now loaded, all nuclear torpedo gyros spooling up to speed."

Ter Horst eyed him piercingly. "Your compassion is misplaced. This is war."

"Helm," Jeffrey said, "all stop."

"All stop, aye," Meltzer said. "Maneuvering acknowledges all stop."

"Ilse," Jeffrey said. "You know Jan ter Horst. What's he gonna do next?"

"Kill us all," Ilse said. "Any way he can, the sooner the better."

"You think he'll launch nuclear torpedoes this close to shore?"

"Yes."

"This close to friendly units?"

"He'll convince himself it's his duty. They'd be martyrs. Friendly losses definitely won't stop him."

"And if we fire a weapon now ourselves, it'll let him and half the Axis navy get us localized," Jeffrey said. A nearby searching surface unit pinged again as if for emphasis.

"What's the bottom here?" Jeffrey said.

"Hard sand," Ilse said.

"Very well, Oceanographer," Jeffrey said. "Chief of the Watch, bottom the boat."

"Put her on the bottom, aye." COB did the evolution so smoothly Jeffrey hardly felt or heard a thing. The only indication was a minor down-angle, three degrees.

"At least this way we won't be smashed against the seafloor," Jeffrey said, "we'll be sitting there already, and the sand just might help cushion the concussion." Jeffrey turned to Commodore Morse. "He'll probably fire onto zero nine zero true. That's presumably his last known course for us, and it's also the mean bearing away from land."

"Makes sense," Morse said. "Let me give you some advice, though, while we're waiting to find out."

"Sure," Jeffrey said, now bracing himself for a criticism.

"You're trying to do too much. Get Lieutenant Bell up here as acting executive officer."

Jeffrey grabbed his phone-set mike. "Weps, come up to the CACC, assume the right seat at the command console. Have the senior weapons chief relieve you at the special weapons console."

Bell acknowledged.

"And take off that sound-powered phone," Morse said. "That's what the phone talker's for. Your job's to delegate."

"Direct hit, Commodore," Jeffrey said. He removed the bulky unit. He took a deep breath. "Phone Talker, repeat to all hands. Rig for depth charge, prepare for a close-in nuclear detonation."

"Set all three units for straight runs," ter Horst said. "Gyro angles thirty right, zero, and thirty left."

"Straight runs, thirty-degree triple fan spread, aye," Van Gelder said. "Torpedo room acknowledges gyro angles set."

"Set detonation depth one thousand meters."

"One thousand meters, aye. Torpedo room acknowledges one thousand meters set."

"Detonation yield one kiloton."

"One kiloton, aye. Torpedo room acknowledges one kiloton."

"Program all fish for maximum attack speed after a quiet runout of four kilometers on nonconflicting random starting doglegs," ter Horst said, "to disguise our own location."

"Twenty knots four thousand meters random doglegs, aye," Van Gelder said, "then seventy-five knots thereafter, aye."

"That just might make Wilson panic," ter Horst said, "when he hears one of those 65s come at him like a freight train. If he gives us a datum, we'll control the units through the fiber-optic wires, send all three in his direction."

"Understood," Van Gelder said. "Sir, for that matter

why not shoot the weapons one by one? When they hear the first go off atomic, if they're still alive, waiting for the second and the third would be slow torture."

"I like your thinking, Gunther, but two problems. Wilson's not the type to buckle from slow torture."

"You know him, sir?"

"Not well, but we've met, at a Naval Submarine League banquet in Washington once. Didn't hit it off. Lack of chemistry, as the Americans would put it. From what I saw I wouldn't want to face him in a waiting game. Sudden shock, that's the thing, though slim chance enough that that would work. But more importantly, the first warhead would ruin sonar in this sector for a while, and would help *Challenger* guess what range from launch we're detonating at, so it's best to flush them everywhere at once."

"Understood, sir," Van Gelder said. He glanced ruefully at the TMA plot.

"Turn your key now, Number One."

Van Gelder took out his enabler, pushed it into the slot, and twisted. This is murder, he told himself. Those minesweepers have wooden hulls, each crew has forty men.

"Captain is enabling," ter Horst said. He turned his key.

"Torpedo room is ready," Van Gelder said. "Tubes six, seven, and eight prepared to shoot."

"Fire six," ter Horst said.

"Tube six fired," Van Gelder said.

"Fire seven."

"Tube seven fired."

"Fire eight."

"Tube eight fired."

"All units operating properly," the sonar chief said.

"Time to detonations?" ter Horst said.

"Nine minutes, Captain," Van Gelder said, "unless the weapons find the target sooner."

• • •

"Torpedo in the water," Sessions said. "Another 65, Captain, bearing three four five, range about twelve thousand yards."

"Torpedo course?" Jeffrey said.

"Zero six zero," Sessions said.

"Well away from us," Jeffrey said.

"*Second* torpedo in the water! *Also* a series-65. . . . Torpedo course is zero nine zero, sir."

"A spread?" Jeffrey said. "He's using conventional warheads then, fanning them out with a passive sonar search."

"We'll see," Morse said. "If I were him, I'd make them go active at ten thousand yards."

"*Third* torpedo in the water," Sessions said. "This one's heading one two zero!"

"Coming toward us," Jeffrey said. "Phone Talker, relay to all hands. Repeat for emphasis, incoming torpedo, rig for ultraquiet, rig for depth charge."

"Aye aye, sir," the phone talker said.

"Sir," Sessions said, "most hostile contacts on our tactical plot appear to be changing course and heading out to sea."

Jeffrey glanced at the TMA. "Good," he said, "we have them foxed. They must think we're further offshore than we really are."

"Time to detonations?" ter Horst said.

"Four minutes, sir," Van Gelder said.

"Signs of our quarry?"

"Nothing, Captain."

"Wilson isn't stupid. If he runs or launches countermeasures *too* soon, he'll just draw more fire and make our own job easier."

"Yes, sir," Van Gelder said. He looked again at the tactical display. Every surface unit was fleeing for open water, heading away from the area where all the mines and torpedoes had been going off. Obviously someone in higher headquarters who knew ter Horst took his "Stand Clear" very literally. But even at their maximum speed of sixteen knots, the little minesweepers were doomed.

"Watch carefully for a hole-in-ocean contact just before the sonar whiteout hits," ter Horst said.

"Acknowledged, Captain," Van Gelder said. He spoke with the sonar chief.

"If we localize *Challenger* as we destroy her," ter Horst said, "it'll speed up the salvage operations. Crypto gear and other good intel are time sensitive, you know."

"Yes, Captain," Van Gelder said.

"While we're waiting," ter Horst said, "reload tubes six through eight with nuclear torpedoes. Use deep-capable units now."

"Third torpedo closing," Sessions said. "This one will pass us close to port."

"Torpedo status?" Jeffrey said.

"Still in passive search mode, sir, still straight running."

"Lying doggo was a good idea," Morse said, almost whispering. "They might not go active till they're past us."

"Good," Jeffrey said. "On this sandy bottom we'd stand out like a billboard at close range, our sail and control surfaces especially, our active out-of-phase masking notwithstanding. We're deep enough the pressure's squashed our anechoic tiles to the point of uselessness."

"Torpedo at closest point of approach now," Sessions said. "Range nine hundred yards."

• • •

"One minute to detonations," Van Gelder said. "Still no fresh datum on *Challenger*."

"Very well, Number One," ter Horst said.

"They've run for over fifteen thousand yards already," Jeffrey said. "What are they waiting for?"

"They may have overestimated how much ground we'd cover at top quiet speed," Morse said. "That's bad. It suggests *Voortrekker*'s faster."

"The torpedoes might be programmed for circular searches," Jeffrey said. "They'd loop back this way on active after a dash ahead to cut us off."

"We'll see," Morse said. "If so, we'll be right in the search cone of the fish on one two zero."

Jeffrey nodded. "I—"

A dreadful concussion jarred the boat and a doomsday cacophony washed over *Challenger*.

"First torpedo had a nuclear warhead!" Sessions shouted as the deep bass roar went on and on.

The bubble pulses caught the sail, tilting *Challenger* to starboard. She stayed that way against the sand, listing six degrees.

A second volcanic *boom* went off, much closer, shaking Jeffrey to his bones. He tasted copper in his mouth—the gum at one capped tooth had started bleeding. More hard blows struck the ship, dwindling as the fireball throbbed and plummeted for the surface. *Challenger* listed ten degrees to starboard now.

"Both of those were one-KT explosions!" Sessions yelled.

"Third time's lucky," Morse said.

"I told you," Ilse said.

The third torpedo blew, pounding Jeffrey's core. *Challenger* slammed sideways, grinding across the bottom. All the nerves in Jeffrey's teeth felt on fire, and his left leg twisted painfully. Relentless reverb banged and banged, the ship listing more and more—fifteen degrees, twenty degrees, thirty degrees and rising. Jeffrey's eardrums hurt again, like at Umhlanga Rocks but worse, his tortured hearing assaulted by endless unearthly rumbling.

"Third torpedo has detonated!" Sessions shouted, sticking to procedure when it was barely possible to speak again. "The range from us was seven thousand yards!"

Jeffrey shook his head to clear his brain. He noticed Ilse and the crewmen in the CACC did the same, looking at each other wide-eyed, amazed to be alive. Jeffrey studied the automated damage control reports. Minor problems only. "Hah! This boat's incredible!"

"There's a reason we named ours *Dreadnought*," Morse yelled in Jeffrey's ear.

"You always use that for your first of types," Jeffrey shouted, smiling, pitching his voice above the constant roaring from outside.

"At least *we're* consistent!" Morse yelled back.

"Chief of the Watch," Jeffrey said as the decibel level and ugly vibrations diminished, "lift us off the bottom." Jeffrey turned to Lieutenant Bell. "XO, have the engineer blow water through the sea pipes, clear out any sand we just picked up. And tell him not to worry about the noise."

"Aye aye, Captain," Bell said. He spoke to the phone talker, relaying Jeffrey's instructions.

"Sonar," Jeffrey said, "how's our bow cap?"

"Still there, Captain," Sessions said.

"Wide-aperture arrays?"

"Minor dropouts in the complex, sir."

"Can you compensate?"

"Affirmative, no substantial degradation, but our chin-mounted HF system is destroyed."

"Projector and receiver both wiped off?" Jeffrey said. "Not surprising. Chief of the Watch and Helmsman, how's the boat handling?"

"Normal in all respects," COB said, studying his screens.

"Concur," Meltzer said, testing his control wheel.

"That's the spirit," Morse said to Jeffrey. "You're their CO now in every way that matters. Let the crew just do their jobs."

"Helm," Jeffrey said, "make your course one zero zero. Ahead two thirds, make turns for twenty-six knots."

"Make my course one zero zero, aye," Meltzer said. "Ahead two thirds, make turns for twenty-six knots, aye. . . . Maneuvering acknowledges turns for twenty-six knots, sir."

"Time for us to do a disappearing act," Jeffrey said, "and sneak out past the Boer SOSUS." He listened to the ocean's rumbling, burbling whoosh. "We'll head right through the blast area, cloak ourselves in the aftermath of all the steam and bubbles. Chief of the Watch, keep your eyes glued to our buoyancy and trim, and shut unneeded sea valves."

"Aye aye," COB acknowledged.

"Assistant Navigator," Jeffrey said to the chief now filling in for Monaghan, "set the secure fathometer to maximum power, and *you* keep your eyes glued to the reported depth below the keel. This is gonna be one heck of a ride."

"All units detonated," Van Gelder said, sticking to procedure. A bit redundant saying it aloud, he thought, his ears still aching.

"Any sign of *Challenger*?" ter Horst said.

"Negative, sir," Van Gelder said. "No hole-in-ocean or ambient sonar contact, and it's impossible to detect any breaking-up noise now."

"Very well," ter Horst said. "Helm, steer one two zero. Make your depth twelve hundred meters smartly, then follow the bottom."

"Steer one two zero, aye aye, sir," the helmsman said. "Make my depth twelve hundred meters smartly, then follow the bottom, aye aye."

"We'll sweep from south to north," ter Horst said, "and do a salvage search. We'll go active with our chin-mounted HF sonar when we reach ground zero of the last torpedo."

"The bottom's sand or mud," Van Gelder said.

"Exactly," ter Horst said. "Even with bad acoustic conditions we should find some wreckage easily. Their reactor vessel's a third of a meter of manganese-molybdenum carbon steel on every side. Parts of *that* thing would survive a direct hit from an H-bomb."

CHAPTER 25

Challenger finally seemed back on an even keel. Ilse was ready for another shower—after that roller-coaster ride through the atomic blast zone her body was damp with sweat. She'd gone beyond exhaustion now, long past feeling tired. Anaerobic respiration, she told herself, my second wind. Toxins are building up throughout my body. I just can't feel them yet.

"Good job, COB and Meltzer," she heard Jeffrey say.

"I can see the new gray hairs already," COB said.

Jeffrey chuckled. "New London ought to add this problem to the simulator training. Assistant Navigator, make a note in the deck log. Egress through the sonar whiteout seems a natural tactic, regardless of a boat's depth capabilities. . . . You do need a strong stomach, though."

"Aye aye, sir," the assistant navigator said.

Ilse studied the local bottom charts, trying to make herself useful. Through the CACC speakers she could hear the constant gurgling, hissing roar outside the hull, the noise level dropping only slowly with the range because the three ground zeros formed an extended linear source—she'd been doing her homework on sonar. Interlaced with the lingering explosion effects was maddened pinging by surface units in the distance.

"Oceanographer," Jeffrey said.

Ilse turned to face him.

"What would Jan ter Horst be thinking *now*?"

Ilse gave Jeffrey a funny look. "I didn't know him in a professional capacity, Commander." She immediately regretted the choice of words. She saw Jeffrey blush.

"Extrapolate," he said. "Anything's better than nothing. He'll be doing the same with us."

"He'll try to make sure we're dead."

"He won't just take it for granted, after that atomic ruckus?"

"No," Ilse said. "Jan takes nothing for granted." She made a face.

"What do you mean, exactly?" Jeffrey said.

"Rumor had it, when he was at sea he had people checking up on me."

"The jealous sort, you mean?"

"Very."

"Was he married?"

"*Commander,*" Ilse said, giving him a dirty look.

"Sorry," Jeffrey said, "I'm not too good at this."

"That's all right. No, I used to tease him he was a bigamist, married to his career and to his ego."

"Very funny," Jeffrey said, obviously not meaning it.

"He'll want to gloat over the carcass now," Ilse said, "*Challenger*'s remains. . . . And he *won't* want to share credit for locating the kill with another captain."

"So he'll come looking for the wreckage right away."

"Yes, I think so," Ilse said. "And he won't find any, will he?"

Jeffrey frowned. "XO, take the conn."

"Aye aye, sir," Bell said. "This is the acting XO, I have the conn."

"Aye aye," the watch standers said.

"Ilse, Commodore," Jeffrey said, "join me at the navigation plotting table, please." Jeffrey hobbled over. Ilse rose and followed him.

She and Morse and Jeffrey conferred with the assistant navigator. The local nautical chart was already up on the main horizontal flat screen. The assistant navigator brought a copy onto the smaller working screen.

"Overlay the locations of the nuclear blasts," Jeffrey said, bending over the table, using it to help support his weight. The assistant navigator worked the keyboard and three red Xs popped onto the working screen.

"Okay, Chief," Jeffrey said, "now add the torpedo tracks." Three lines appeared, leading back from the Xs toward an area nearer the shore.

"Hmm," Jeffrey said. "If I were ter Horst, I'd search the arc along the Xs, on the inner edge of the sonar whiteout zone. Use my HF gear to look for *Challenger*'s debris."

"Makes sense," Morse said.

"Whichever end he starts at," Jeffrey said, "north or south, he'll have to go slow. Sonar conditions are still pretty awful. There'll be high attenuation loss from bubbles and stirred-up particles. Right, Ilse?"

"Absolutely."

"And high-frequency sound sheds its energy the fastest," Jeffrey said, "so his search will cover fairly narrow swaths."

Morse smiled. "Are you thinking what I'm thinking . . . *Captain*?"

Ilse looked up. "You're going to shoot at him."

"Does that bother you?" Jeffrey said. "If you're emotionally involved, I need to know it now."

Damn you, Jeffrey Fuller, Ilse thought. After everything we've been through together on this mission. "My whole family's dead or disappeared because of him."

"Sorry," Jeffrey said. He sounded like he meant it. "Here's my plan," he said. "We have four Mark 88s left. It's time to use one. We'll program it to run along the arc through all the Xs, starting near our end, the south. We preset it to move just over the bottom, using slow speed, twenty knots, until it locks on *Voortrekker*."

Morse nodded. "That'll give it plenty of cruising range to turn back and try again if needed."

"Affirmative," Jeffrey said. "We'll make the unit ping on active at low intensity so it won't be blind, and at the same time *Voortrekker* won't hear it coming till too late."

"They may think its pings are their own garbled side-scan echoes," Morse said, "or stray signals from a friendly. Doppler will be chaotic out there now."

"All the better," Jeffrey said. "We'll preset the frequency to forty-five kilohertz, since some of their frigates use that for mine avoidance. We'll have the weapon do a wigwag search, to help disguise its base approach course. We'll preset the warhead for maximum yield."

"Decimal one KT?" Morse said.

"Best we can do," Jeffrey said. "Ilse, you know these waters. Am I missing something?"

"No," she said. "We have to strike back quickly. But why not use two fish? Send one to search down from the north end of the arc."

"We're awful low on ammo," Jeffrey said quietly, "and awfully far from home. The Mark 88s are the only weapons we can operate at depth. ADCAPs and ISLMMs will fail much past three thousand feet, and that's on a good day. And to launch our Tomahawks we'd have to be much shallower than that."

"Okay," Ilse said. "I was just curious." She noticed Jeffrey's eyes were strangely hooded for a moment. Is he concerned I challenged his authority, or is this some personal quirk? I noticed it when we first met, he's the sensitive type outside of purely military circles. . . . Could it be he has trouble making shop talk with a woman . . . or that he *likes* it? Still single at his age, and so damned good-looking too, I wonder what's the deal.

"Fire Control," Jeffrey said, "I aver that ROEs apply

for hot pursuit in enemy territory, authorizing use of tactical nuclear weapons undersea."

"I concur," Bell said.

"Assistant Navigator, make a record," Jeffrey said. "Fire Control, get a nuclear Mark 88 loaded and enabled in tube seven."

"Aye aye," Bell said. "Tube seven, load an 88."

"Also prep the other three Mark 88s," Jeffrey said. "Use tubes one, three, and five. I've a feeling we may need them in a hurry."

"Make tube seven ready in all respects," Jeffrey said, "including opening outer door. Firing point procedures on tube seven, programmed area search."

"Solution ready," Bell said. "Ship ready. Weapon ready."

"Match generated bearings and *shoot,*" Jeffrey said.

"Tube seven fired electrically," Bell said. "Unit swimming out."

"Unit is running normally," Sessions said.

"Time to make some tracks," Jeffrey said, "and here comes the really dangerous part. Chief of the Watch, disengage shallow water valves and pumping hardware, line up abyssal suite."

"Line up abyssal pump and valve suite, aye," COB said.

"Helm, all stop," Jeffrey ordered. Meltzer acknowledged.

"Phone Talker," Jeffrey said, "relay to all hands. Now transiting the deep sound channel under combat conditions. Rig for superquiet." Jeffrey knew the deep sound channel was formed by sound wave bending, in the region where seawater stopped getting colder with depth and then hovered just above freezing. The deep sound channel acted like an acoustic superconductor, and the slightest noise would propagate for countless miles.

Morse raised an eyebrow at Jeffrey. "Superquiet?"

"Aye, sir," Jeffrey said, abashed. "I'm making a lot of this up as we go along. . . . Chief of the Watch, give us five tons negative buoyancy and let us drift on down."

"Five tons of negative buoyancy, aye," COB said.

"The thing that makes me really nervous," Jeffrey whispered, "is that the upslope toward the continental margin will tend to focus sound energy right at their SOSUS nets."

"Too true," Morse whispered back. "With all the pinging going on up there, someone may get an echo despite your active masking."

Jeffrey glanced apprehensively at a depth gauge—passing through 6,000 feet. "With the beating *Challenger*'s taken, the hull might start popping shallower than normal."

"They'll sound like shotgun blasts on enemy passive sonar," Morse said quietly. "Let's hope nobody's trailing a hydrophone down here."

"Keep your fingers crossed," Jeffrey mouthed.

"Still no sign of anything," Van Gelder said.

"We've got lots more ground to cover," ter Horst said.

"Sir, I've been thinking."

"That can be dangerous in today's world, Gunther."

Van Gelder hesitated. "Understood, Captain. But hear me out, sir, with respect. I'm looking at what that Q-ship did to us in the Antarctic. If you adjust for warhead yield and range, I'm not sure how badly we hurt *Challenger*."

"Go on."

"She may have used the same tactic we did when those British planes came after us, staying well inside the limiting circle of possible egress distance covered."

"You mean you think we missed?"

"Sir!" the sonar chief called out. "New passive sonar contact on starboard wide-aperture array. Sounds like a mine-avoidance sonar but it's at our depth. . . . *Incoming torpedo bearing one zero zero!* Range three thousand meters, approach speed twenty knots!"

"*Verdammt,*" ter Horst snapped. "Helm, ahead flank maximum revs!"

"Ahead flank maximum revs, aye aye," the helmsman said. "Turbine room answers steam throttles are wide open, sir."

"Range-gating active lock," the sonar chief said, "too close to cancel it, *torpedo accelerating to end-game speed*!"

"What type is it, Number One?" ter Horst said.

"Closed-cycle liquid-metal fuel," Van Gelder said, "geared turbine and pump-jet propulsor. An American Mark 88, Captain."

"Torpedo gaining on us!" the chief shouted.

"Firing jammers and noisemakers now," Van Gelder said.

"No time to launch a decoy," ter Horst said, "and the things don't always work. Prepare to fire tube seven, deep-capable nuclear torpedo. Tube seven snap shot on course one zero zero, minimum yield, our depth."

Van Gelder reached for his special weapons key at the same time ter Horst pulled his own out. "Weapon enabled!" Van Gelder shouted.

"Open the door and *shoot*!"

"Tube seven fired!" Van Gelder said. "I have control of the weapon."

"Helm," ter Horst said, "port thirty rudder smartly, make a knuckle, minimize our profile."

"Port thirty rudder smartly, aye aye, no course specified, sir."

"Get that incoming torpedo, Number One," ter Horst said between clenched teeth. "Intercept and smash it."

Van Gelder read his screens, then checked the trigonometry. "Detonation in three seconds."

He flipped up the plastic cover and pressed ARM. The light went green. He held his breath and then pressed FIRE. The status screen said DETONATED.

Jeffrey, Ilse, Morse, and the assistant navigator were still gathered round the digital nav display. *Challenger* was right over the bottom at 7,800 feet, and Jeffrey considered it okay to talk in normal tones again. Apparently they'd made the trip down through the deep sound channel safely, given the lack of enemy fire. The hardest part right now was restoring neutral buoyancy, since COB had to pump those five tons from the negative tank against the outside pressure, plus an extra gallon of water for each ten feet of depth they'd added simply to adjust for hull compression—and he had to do it quietly.

There was a sudden roar in the distance, building into an ear-splitting crescendo that died off slowly, seeming to spasm as surface and bottom reflections hit.

"What was that, XO?" Jeffrey said.

"Captain," Bell said, "unit from tube seven has detonated."

"Weapon effect?" Jeffrey said.

"Impossible to tell."

A half second after the signal came back through the fiber-optic wire, a gigantic *kaboom* kicked *Voortrekker* in the stern, jarring Van Gelder forcefully against his seat back, rolling the boat to port, and surrounding him in sound that was more felt than heard, a physical sensation of ungodly Armageddon that made him want to curl up in a ball.

Instead Van Gelder gripped his console with both hands, watching the damage control enunciators, dreading what he'd see. The blast was simply too powerful—the enemy warhead must have gone off an instant before the weapon did, subjecting the boat to both A-bombs at once.

"Very well, Fire Control," Jeffrey said. "Assistant Navigator, give me the 30-by-30-degree square centered at 40 south, 25 east."

The senior chief brought the large-scale chart onto the screen.

"At this point," Jeffrey said, "I think discretion is the better part of valor. If we try a battle damage assessment on *Voortrekker* and they're still alive, they'll pull the same trick we just used."

"I concur, sir," Bell said. "Conditions are poor now for a reattack. We're low on ammo and there's too much ground for us to cover. The priority should be our egress."

Jeffrey nodded. "Now we've disengaged from enemy forces, it's time to make our getaway."

"I agree," Morse said. "Remember our objectives. At this stage survival equals mission success, a strategic win for us."

"We have this whole area to get through, people," Jeffrey said, gesturing at the map, "this whole area for hide-and-seek inside Axis territory."

"Where do you want to aim for?" Morse said.

"Hmm," Jeffrey said, studying the chart. "Our best bet is to insert somewhere in the Mid-Ocean Ridge. I'm guessing that's what Captain Wilson and Monaghan planned. Hundreds of miles of rifts and faults on both sides of the endless central spreading valley. No one would ever find us till we wanted to be found."

"That's what I'd do too," Morse said.

"So just how do we get there?" Jeffrey said.

"Hmmmm. . . . We need to bypass areas that are too deep for us. We'd stand out much too well against the bottom. Assistant Navigator, shade in red everything below our crush depth."

"Which estimate of our crush depth do you want to use, sir?"

"NAVSEA's latest work's the most refined I know about," Jeffrey said. "Based on their tests and calculations, let's go with fifteen thousand feet."

The assistant navigator hit some keys. Large areas of the map turned red.

"Okay," Jeffrey said. "We also need to stay down low, not just for stealthy nap-of-seafloor routing away from the shallows but also to avoid the deep sound channel. It's our glass ceiling, folks—we break it we get cut. Assistant Navigator, shade everything less than seven thousand feet in blue."

The assistant navigator hit more keys.

"What we see is what we get," Jeffrey said. "We need to avoid the continental shelf off Cape Town and Port Elizabeth, and the huge Agulhas Basin south of that is way too deep, well over twenty thousand feet."

"Northeast of us," Ilse said, "we'd hit the Mozambique Plateau and then the Almirante Leite Bank, also too constricted and too shallow."

Jeffrey stared at the map. "That leaves southeast, this neck of less-deep ground between the south edge of the Mozambique Basin and the northeast edge of the Agulhas Basin, a kind of hump where the bottom's at our crush depth. That route would take us straight to the Prince Edward Fracture, the closest point of insertion to the ideal topography along the spreading ridges. The final approach has lots of seamounts too, good hiding places that cut off long-range sonars."

"The seamount flanks are moonscapes," Ilse said. "There's no erosion underwater."

Jeffrey nodded. "The deep bowls of the basins on either side of this hump-neck make me really nervous, though. They're too wide open and we'd be too far off the bottom. Enemy ships could easily drop temporary ambient-look-up SOSUS grids, then make short work of us with twenty-KT depth bombs."

"And what about the Axis air groups based on the Prince Edward Islands?" Morse said. "They'll be right in our face as we get to the fracture."

"If we stay deep and run quiet," Jeffrey said, "we give them a huge area to search under adverse terrain and acoustic conditions, except for right at the choke point at the hump between the basins. It's also the route they may think we'd be least likely to follow for exactly that reason, Commodore, their heavy air support."

"Go where we hope they don't expect us?" Morse said.

"That's basic doctrine, sir," Jeffrey said.

"I'm not disagreeing," Morse said.

"Ilse," Jeffrey said, "what kind of bottom would we find along this hump?"

"Well," Ilse said, "it's part of a divergent boundary between lithospheric plates. The hump itself is caused by molten rock upwellings deep within the mantle, called diapirs, that lead to magma chambers."

"What's that mean in English?" Jeffrey said. He smiled.

"Sorry," Ilse said. "It means the bottom is bare rock and uneven. There are some shield volcanoes, the low-lying multiterraced kind."

"We're trained to usually avoid such areas," Jeffrey said. "How live are these volcanoes?"

"Sometimes very," Ilse said. "The hump-neck at the Prince Edward choke point does have active hydrothermal vents."

"Okay," Jeffrey said. "One more reason they won't think to look for us right there."

"There's another item we need to cover," Morse interjected. "What will *Voortrekker* do if they're still alive?"

"Aye," Jeffrey said, "that's the puzzlement."

"No it's not," Ilse said. "They'll try again to sink us."

"Concur with *that*," Jeffrey said. "Hmmmm. . . . Well. . . . I think if I were them I'd think this through the same way we just did, and aim for the same place. The choke point's like a gateway to the Fracture Zone. It's only forty nautical miles from side to side, eighty thousand yards, very easy for one SSN to set up a barrier patrol."

"Sure you don't want to use a different route, then," Morse asked, "on further consideration?"

"No," Jeffrey said. "I'd rather take on ter Horst there, on sort-of-equal terms, deep down and one-on-one, even if his boat *is* faster and quieter than us, as it appears to be. We lose contact with *Voortrekker* at this point, God knows how many ships and lives will be destroyed. My every instinct, banged up as we are, is to get this damn thing over with *now*."

"Good," Morse said. "That was a trick question. I was testing you."

"Jan will feel exactly the same way," Ilse said. "Get this damned thing over with. . . . *If* he's still alive."

"Very well," Jeffrey said. "Helm and Chief of the Watch, make your base course one six five, commence nap-of-seafloor cruising mode. Ahead two thirds, make turns for twenty-six knots."

Meltzer and COB acknowledged.

"We'll try to stay above twelve thousand feet when possible," Jeffrey said. "Less strain on the hull and sea pipes."

"Understood," COB and Meltzer said.

"Fire Control and Sonar," Jeffrey said, "we'll stop occasionally to keep our ears peeled, especially in our baffles."

"Understood," Bell and Sessions said.

"Good plan," Morse said. "Ter Horst could be waiting out there anywhere. . . . The pressing question is, how do we find *him* before he finds *us*?"

"I don't know," Jeffrey said, "and we don't have very long to think about it. The quiet transit to the choke point should take just about a day."

Van Gelder watched his screens in disbelief. Was *this* true death, entering a fantasy where life went on impossibly? Was this the hell he'd earned?

Someone farted, probably from fear. Van Gelder had to bite his cheek to keep from giggling madly. That detail wasn't fake—he was alive.

Van Gelder read his data. The incoming torpedo had gone off barely outside lethal range. Maybe it mistook *Voortrekker*'s weapon, rushing to make the intercept, for *Voortrekker* herself.

Some boxes on Van Gelder's damage control panel showed yellow and others red, but nothing that couldn't be dealt with, nothing that would slow the vessel or hurt her battleworthiness. Yet this punishment must have taken years off the hull's service life—dry-dock tests would show.

"Son of a *blery kaffir,*" ter Horst said, his cursing another reminder that Van Gelder was alive. "They actually got a shot off at us!"

"Yes, sir," Van Gelder said.

"What does it take to kill these bloody people?"

Jeffrey got up from the command workstation and stretched. He craved sleep very badly, but that was out of the question for now. He glanced around the control room for the umpteenth time in the last half hour. Imagery flickered on all the consoles, watched intently by *Challenger*'s crew. *His* crew, he reminded himself, at least till they were out of immediate danger, or captured or dead.

This was supposed to be every XO's dream: his first independent command. Why did it have to come in the form of such a nightmare?

Jeffrey sighed. Ilse heard him and turned and made eye contact. She smiled, and this helped him feel better.

"Ilse," he said, "you've done so much already, do you want to grab some rack time maybe?"

"No," she said, "I better stay here in the CACC. You might need me."

"Good, thanks," Jeffrey said, stifling a yawn. "Sorry, it's the hour, not the company."

"That's okay," Ilse said. "How's your leg doing?"

"I can hardly bend it now, hurts like hell, but I feel fine otherwise. I think I bruised the kneecap when that first torpedo hit, back in the minefield."

"Call the corpsman?" Ilse said.

"He has more important things to do," Jeffrey said. "That's why we can't just sit still near the bottom for a month and wait for the Boers to forget about us and go away. We need to get the badly injured to hospitals ASAP, Monaghan and the others."

"Sure you don't have any symptoms of the bends yourself?" Ilse said, standing and looking at Jeffrey from up close. "Brain stroke, lungs exploding, incoherent drooling?"

"Very funny," Jeffrey said. He saw two crewmen glance at him and Ilse, then give each other meaningful looks.

"I'm heading aft for a sec," Ilse said. "Let me at least get you some Advil or something."

"Okay," Jeffrey said. "And, Messenger of the Watch, put up a fresh pot of coffee, please. Ask the mess management chief to send around some sandwiches and hot oatmeal. We'll do crew breakfast at modified condition

ZEBRA. I don't know about you, Ilse, but suddenly I'm starving."

Ter Horst looked up from the navigation plotting table and sighed. "Much as it pains me to admit it, Gunther, we can't be everywhere."

"Concur, sir," Van Gelder said. "If I were the Americans, I think I'd head for the Prince Edward Fracture."

"Indeed. Why?"

"Whatever their primary mission, they know we're now at maximum alert. They may have local stealthiness, but their presence has been made known. They've lost the initiative, and sooner or later they have to try to escape from our home waters. It seems to me the best way is to get to the tectonic spreading seam as fast as they can, avoid our ASW forces as much as possible. But from what we've seen so far, sir, *Challenger* is clever and aggressive. The Prince Edward Islands won't deter them. If anything, they'd head there as a double bluff."

"I said to leave the puns to me, Number One. But I concur. I just wanted to hear you say it all out loud."

"Yes, sir," Van Gelder said.

"Very well," ter Horst said, "prepare another radio buoy, Flash Double Zed priority once more."

Van Gelder took a message pad and pen. He'd tidy up the wording and then supervise encryption in the radio room.

Ter Horst cleared his throat. "Message reads, 'Continuing pursuit USS *Challenger*. *Voortrekker* will transit to choke point at north end Prince Edward Fracture. Prince Edward Island forces stand by in support but do not, repeat do not, engage submerged contacts unless requested specifically this vessel. Ter Horst sends' . . . Got all that, Number One?"

"Yes, Captain."

"Pretoria can hardly disagree with us—they've no good way to communicate. They'd be foolish if they tried, and more the fools if they ignore me."

"Concur strongly, Captain."

"Very well. We'll do an end-around past *Challenger*, try to cut her off. Helm, steer one six five."

"Steer one six five, aye aye, sir," the helmsman said.

"Make your depth twenty-two hundred meters."

"Make my depth twenty-two hundred meters, aye aye, sir."

"Engage terrain-following cruise mode."

"Engage terrain-following cruise mode, aye aye, sir."

"We'll head south at top quiet speed," ter Horst said. "Helm, half ahead, thirty knots."

"Half ahead, thirty knots, aye aye, sir. . . . Turbine room answers steam throttles set for half ahead, making revs for thirty knots, sir."

"Number One," ter Horst said, "once you see that message buoy off, you take the conn. I want to do a walk-around inspection of our running repairs, speak to the crew in small groups as well. Then I plan to take a nap. . . . Have me awakened in four hours and I'll relieve you. Then you get some rest yourself. Gunther, you look tired."

CHAPTER 26

12 HOURS LATER

Jeffrey's head jerked upright and he realized he'd been dozing at his console, after hours of poring through the on-line sonar technical manuals. It all came down to who would have the better first-detection range, *Challenger* or *Voortrekker*. He'd hoped for inspiration somewhere in the circuit diagrams, but Jeffrey's muse had most cruelly abandoned him.

He noticed that Commodore Morse was standing in the aisle—that must have been what woke him.

Jeffrey rubbed his eyes and looked at Bell, who had the conn. "Any contacts?"

"Nothing, sir," Bell said. "We thought it best to let you sleep."

Jeffrey glanced at a chronometer. He'd been out for forty minutes. "Boy, do I need to take a leak."

"So do I," Morse said. The two men headed aft. "I just finished visiting the wounded," Morse said.

Jeffrey chided himself. "One more thing I didn't think of."

Morse waved dismissively. "The men all understand. You're working very shorthanded."

"How's the captain?"

"The corpsman let me talk to him for just a minute. I told him you're doing a great job. He said he wasn't surprised."

"I should stop in," Jeffrey said as they entered the empty CO state-room.

"Don't," Morse said. "He's out again. His brain's swollen, you know. That's what a bad concussion is—tissue abraded against the inner skull ridges. Needs time for all his neurons to get back to normal. Total rest, so let him be."

Jeffrey noticed that Wilson's family pictures were gone from his desk, presumably moved next door to be with him. Jeffrey deferred to Morse, who used the head first. When it was Jeffrey's turn, he glanced at himself in the mirror. He needed a shave and his cheeks looked pale and jowly. He wondered if that was fatigue, or middle age coming on early. He tried to imagine how he might look with a moustache. *Where did that come from?* he asked himself.

When he'd done his business, he and Morse lingered in the captain's quarters.

"How's Monaghan doing?" Jeffrey said.

Morse sighed. "As well as can be expected, they told me. He regained consciousness for a little while, was actually communicating by Morse code using his eyelashes, since they have the respirator hooked up through his trachea."

"That's clever," Jeffrey said. "Who thought of Morse code?"

"Monaghan did. Took the SEAL a minute to catch on. But then he went into a coma. His blood gases don't look very good. We need to get him proper care and quickly."

"I know," Jeffrey said. "He has four kids."

"The engineering staff used spare parts to jury-rig a shock gimbal for his litter, so at least he's protected from further mechanical stress."

"Good," Jeffrey said. "Lieutenant Willey's initiative always has impressed me."

"You'll be glad to learn Ilse's friend Otto is well cared for too. COB made the arrangements, in his role as your master-at-arms. Our fiendish EPW is under guard by at least two people at all times, one officer and one enlisted."

"Just like an atom bomb," Jeffrey said.

"He's trussed up nice and snug so he can't harm himself."

"Where are they keeping him?" Jeffrey said.

"A storage compartment next to the goat locker," Morse said. Jeffrey knew that meant the chiefs' office and berthing area. "For a while," Morse said, "they had him on display in the enlisted mess."

"You're kidding," Jeffrey said. He laughed.

"No. The lads took to rubbing his head for luck. Seemed like he was going to have a stroke, though, so they had to put a stop to that."

"Morale's all right, then?" Jeffrey said.

"Clayton and his boys told everybody about you and that shark. Plus whatever else they could talk about. Seems your stock is high among the crew now, Mr. Fuller."

"It's hard to believe all that was only yesterday," Jeffrey said. He and Morse started back to the CACC.

"I also took a little walking tour," Morse said, "into the spaces I'm allowed. Told people what it was like back in my last war, the olden days in Her Majesty's Submarine *Conqueror*. Seemed to help relieve some of the tension."

"Thanks, Commodore," Jeffrey said. "I don't know what I'd do without your help."

"I'm sure you'd manage," Morse said, "just with considerably greater difficulty." He chuckled. "I told your men about the time we almost hit an uncharted seamount south of the Falklands because our charts went back to 1777, and how our trailing wire antenna once got tangled in the screw. How we had to surface and send divers over the side while rather vengeful Argie fliers might have found us any moment."

"Puts current things in perspective, doesn't it?" Jeffrey said.

They'd arrived back at the command console. Jeffrey sat again, eyeballing the navigation and gravimeter displays. The boat was at 11,750 feet, making twenty-six knots on base course 192, well masked by the rugged terrain.

"Anything yet?" Jeffrey said.

"Still no hostile contacts near our depth, sir," Bell said. "We're threading a series of repeatedly branching fissure canyons now, using a path through the whole complex I picked at random. It was Miss Reebeck's idea. Makes it very hard for someone else to guess which way we'd come."

"Terrific," Jeffrey said.

"Recommend we stop and drift again in another fifteen nautical miles," Bell said, "to listen when we reach this ridge." He pointed to a bunching-up of topographic contours on the bottom chart.

"Concur," Jeffrey said, bending over to read the screen. "If we cruise in a slow circle when we get there, we'll be able to scan in all directions using the bow sphere and both wide-aperture arrays, get the best sensitivity possible on all bearings and frequencies. Our crinkled bow cap's interfering flow noise stops whenever *Challenger* does."

"Understood," Bell said. "We're still at a real disadvantage, sir, when we approach the choke point. To get away we have to move. *Voortrekker* can just sit there."

"I know," Jeffrey said.

Jeffrey turned to look at Ilse. She was dozing at her station, a wrapped towel forming a kind of pillow to cushion her head against her shoulder. She was snoring softly, as were several others in the CACC.

"I think she's rather cute while she's asleep," Morse said.

"Foxy too," Bell said, giving Jeffrey a suggestive look.

"Cut it out, guys," Jeffrey said.

"No," Morse said. "You're not getting any younger, Jeffrey."

"Come on," Jeffrey said, "we're in the middle of a battle, in the middle of a war." He glanced at Ilse again, his eyes staying on her longer this time. Her features seemed softer than when they'd first met, and in sleep she wore a peaceful smile.

Jeffrey went back to his screens, once more studying the terrain that lay ahead around the choke point, trying to imagine where Jan ter Horst would hide, where he would pounce. Jeffrey wracked his brain over how *Challenger* could possibly get in the first detection, on *Voortrekker* rather than a salvo of her nuclear torpedoes inbound at high speed on the last part of a dogleg.

Sonar superiority, Jeffrey told himself. How can we possibly achieve sonar superiority?

4 HOURS LATER

Ilse was studying the terrain around the choke point. Beside her Jeffrey and Sessions were going over sonar hardware specs and signal processing algorithms. Neither man looked very happy. Suddenly there was a distant rumble.

"Transient's classification?" Lieutenant Bell called from the command console.

Sessions quickly reconfigured his displays. "Nuclear explosion, sir. Bearing three three seven, wide-aperture array gives range approximately fifty-five nautical miles." Then another one went off. "Ten miles further away from us, sir," Sessions said, "on bearing three two nine."

Ilse heard a third sharp rumble, mixing with the dying echoes from the other two. "That one was much closer," she said.

"Affirmative," Sessions said. "Range thirty-five nautical miles, relative bearing three three four."

Jeffrey stood. "Off the port bow," he said, "between us and the choke-point hump. Sonar, what was warhead yield?"

"Working on that, sir," Sessions said. Ilse watched as he conferred with his staff. "Estimate each at about one kiloton, Captain."

"Very well," Jeffrey said. "Fire Control, your thoughts."

"One KT sounds small for depth bombs, sir," Bell said.

"Concur," Jeffrey said. "That's more the size of an Axis torpedo warhead. . . . Sonar, can you tell the detonation depth?"

Ilse worked quickly with Sessions on a refined estimate.

"Depth in each case was about twelve thousand feet," Sessions said.

"It's Jan, isn't it?" Ilse said.

"Yeah," Jeffrey said. "He's not trying to create a cordon. The warheads were set off too far apart, and they don't lie on a straight line or an arc."

"They aren't on a single bearing from any particular firing position either," Bell said, "so he didn't shoot a spread at a suspected contact with uncertain range."

"Concur," Jeffrey said, "and he wasn't working from one good TMA, leading a moving target. He'd've had to launch those weapons half an hour apart to put the furthest torpedo that far out and then have simultaneous blasts."

"Concur, sir," Bell said.

"*Voortrekker*'s expended an awful lot of nuclear torpedoes since making contact with us," Sessions said.

"At least half a dozen to our one," Jeffrey said. "We only have three left now, so you'd think they'd start to run low too, even fresh from reprovisioning at the bluff."

"That's the whole point," Ilse said. "Jan's making sure we know he's there, somewhere in front of us, and taunting us by visibly wasting ammo. He's messing with our minds."

2 HOURS LATER

Ilse and Jeffrey were grabbing a quick bite in the enlisted mess, visiting with the crew, released from general quarters a few at a time so they'd be in top form later. Bell had the conn again and knew where Jeffrey was.

One man finished eating, then lit a cigarette. Ilse bummed one off him—she didn't smoke but really needed one right now. She took a deep draft and then the both of them exhaled, blowing toward the overhead.

She saw Jeffrey give her and the crewman a funny look.

"Sorry, sir," the crewman said, "I'll put it out."

"What?" Jeffrey said. "Oh, no, no, that's okay. It's just that, um, uh, you two gave me an idea." Jeffrey seemed to stare off into space. "Yeah," he said, "this just might work."

"*What* just might work?" Ilse said.

"It'll take a lot of careful effort," Jeffrey said, "and luck. Heavy-duty calculations, Ilse, using every bit of data that you've got. Conditions have to be perfect, and the whole thing might backfire. . . . Hmmm. . . . We might not have the vertical directivity to filter out the noise, and there might be too much Doppler distortion along the line of bearing."

"What are you talking about?" Ilse said, trying to stifle her annoyance, reminding herself Jeffrey *was* acting captain of the ship.

Jeffrey looked at her and grinned like a little boy. "I'll explain it on the way." He stood up. "To the sonar consoles!"

"You said there were hydrothermal vents around the choke point," Jeffrey said as they rushed down the narrow, bending companionway and past some enlisted berthing spaces.

"That's right," Ilse said.

"Active ones?"

"Yes."

"They give off heat, right?" Jeffrey said.

"Of course."

"And they spew dissolved minerals."

"That's what makes black smokers smoke," Ilse said. "Sulfides and sulfates precipitating when the superheated water meets the ice-cold ambient ocean."

"The precipitation builds up to make the chimneys," Jeffrey said.

"And it feeds the archaea and the tube worms," Ilse said.

"But it doesn't all precipitate out, right? Some stays dissolved?"

"Sure," Ilse said as they went up a steep ladder. "You can detect trace chemicals miles away sometimes, like helium 3."

"So the water isn't only hotter," Jeffrey said, "it has greater mineral content, like having higher salinity."

"Yeah. *So?*"

"Don't you see?" Jeffrey said. "Horizontal and vertical thermoclines and haloclines, in the megaplume above a vent!"

"Oh," Ilse said. "I, I do see what you're getting at. . . . *Acoustic lensing*."

"Right," Jeffrey said. "Sound refracts away from water with higher speed and toward water with lower speed, and higher temperature and more dissolved minerals both mean higher speed. Each vent plume acts like a concave lens. It makes sound rays diverge."

"Um . . . I concur."

"And they occur in fields," Jeffrey said, "the vents do."

"Sometimes," Ilse said.

"If you have *two* vents *near* each other, the place *between* them acts like a *convex* lens, like in a magnifying glass."

"I guess that's true," Ilse said as they reached the CACC.

"Sonar superiority," Jeffrey said. "With lenses we can make a telescope."

CHAPTER 27

1 HOUR LATER

Jeffrey checked the gravimeter again. *Challenger* was following the side of a long escarpment on the east edge of a caldera, a huge bowl of volcanic origin.

"Torpedo in the water at our depth!" Sessions hissed. "Bearing three five nine, drawing left to right and closing, an inbound spiral course of unknown origin!"

"Range?" Jeffrey said, his heart pounding now.

"Bow sphere contact only! Signal strength implies about ten thousand yards, approach speed seventy knots!"

"Right in our face," Jeffrey said. "No data for a snap shot at *Voortrekker*, and if we turn away, we just make a better sonar target for that fish."

"Concur, sir," Bell said.

"Countermeasures and AT rockets are useless this far down," Jeffrey said. "Their exhausts are strangled by the pressure."

"Decoys and UUVs won't function either, sir," Bell said. "They'd implode right in the tubes the minute we equalize."

"Phone Talker," Jeffrey said, "quiet collision alarm."

"Quiet collision alarm, aye, sir."

"Helm," Jeffrey said, "all stop." He didn't wait for Meltzer's answer. "Fire Control, make tube three ready in all respects including opening outer door. Set lowest yield, dot zero one KT. Ter Horst might not know our range, so swim the unit out."

"Dot zero one KT," Bell said, "and swim the unit out."

"Tube three," Jeffrey said, "firing point procedures on the incoming torpedo. Intercept and detonate the unit through the wire. Match sonar bearings and *shoot.*"

"Set!" Bell said. "Stand by. . . . *Fire!* Tube three fired electrically."

"Unit is running normally," Sessions said.

"Chief of the Watch," Jeffrey said, "stationary dive, rate of descent five hundred feet per minute."

"Stationary dive, aye," COB said, "five hundred feet per minute, aye. No maximum depth specified."

"Time to weapon intercept?" Jeffrey said.

"Two minutes," Bell said.

"How did he find us?" Jeffrey said.

"I don't know, Captain," Bell said.

Jeffrey eyed the displays. Do a one-eighty at the base of the escarpment and run back into God knows what? *Voortrekker* could easily have another torpedo lurking there. Turn to starboard instead, course 270, into the caldera that went far down past *Challenger*'s crush depth? Rise and head to port and wind up naked against the escarpment crest, a dead setup for another shot? Ter Horst chose his ambush well. *How did he find us?*

"Helm," Jeffrey said, "the moment our unit detonates go to ahead full smartly, then use hard right rudder."

"Upon detonation go to ahead full smartly hard right rudder, aye."

"Course, Captain?" Bell said.

"Two seven zero and follow the bottom." The caldera.

"Sir," COB said.

"Yes," Jeffrey said, "but it's the last thing he'll expect and he'll lose us in the reverb from these slopes."

• • •

Jeffrey saw Bell punch the button to fire the warhead.

The cataclysmic shock broke fluorescent light bulbs everywhere. Something threw *Challenger* backward and pressed her down.

"That explosion was too strong," Jeffrey said. "They must have detonated the torpedo as our own weapon came up to it."

"Confirmed!" Bell shouted. "Our unit did not detonate!"

"Clever bastards," Jeffrey said.

"Maneuvering acknowledges ahead full smartly!" Meltzer said. "My rudder is hard right!"

Challenger banked to starboard.

A reverberating shock wave hit and the starboard list grew sharper. The boat put on a nasty forward trim.

"Sir," COB shouted, "our depth is fifteen thousand feet!"

"Sir," Meltzer yelled, "we're in a snap roll from that reverb catching the sail! Without bowplanes I do not have control of the boat!"

"Helm," Jeffrey said, "disengage fly-by-wire and work manually on hydraulic backup. Try to get us out of this uncoordinated turn."

"Understood," Meltzer said.

"Sir," COB said as he helped Meltzer, "our hull's so compressed we're losing buoyancy. I'm having trouble compensating even with the pumps lined up in series."

Before Jeffrey could answer there was a crackling crunch from all around, then a nonstructural weld in the port-side CACC bulkhead snapped.

"We're squashing inward," Jeffrey said. The depth gauge showed 15,200 feet. The pressure gauge showed 450 atmospheres. "If we do an EMBT hydrazine blow now, it'll take forever to work and we'll be helpless once it does, a sitting duck."

"Sir," the phone talker said, "torpedo room reports heavy misting round the tube eight door repairs." At this depth, Jeffrey knew, the bilge pumps couldn't possibly keep up with a major leak, and at this depth *any* leak was major.

"Captain," Ilse shouted. "Look at the gravimeter!"

Jeffrey saw the image on his screen, the wall of the escarpment. It was shimmering, starting to give way.

"It's an underwater landslide!" Ilse said.

"Helm," Jeffrey said. "Ahead flank smartly, full rise on the diveplane functions." The forward trim amounted to a twenty-five-degree down-bubble.

"Ahead flank smartly, aye," Meltzer said. "Full rise on the diveplane functions, aye." He flicked the engine-order dial with one hand while he pulled back on his control wheel with the other and then turned it, his face grimacing in concentration. "Maneuvering acknowledges ahead flank smartly."

The depth gauge showed 15,400 feet. The gravimeter showed a gap in the escarpment, growing into a vicious gouge—it couldn't track the moving boulders, it just showed their effect.

"Sir," COB said, "soundings are eighteen thousand feet!"

"Acknowledged," Jeffrey said. Deep enough to die.

"A seismic sea wave's coming any second from the avalanche!" Ilse yelled.

The depth gauge showed 15,600 feet. The hull groaned again and the ESM room bulkhead started warping against the overhead. Dust from crumpled insulation fell on Ilse and the sonar people.

A terrible roaring shove struck the ship and the inclinometer went to forty-two degrees starboard list. Fifteen thousand *eight* hundred feet.

"Sounds like we buried them alive," Van Gelder said, "before *Challenger*'s torpedo could intercept our unit."

"Mmph," ter Horst said. "I wouldn't entirely count on

that. Serves me right for trying to not be *too* profligate with our weapons expenditure. . . . Sonar, any contact on the target?"

"Negative, sir," the sonar chief said. "Conditions are impossible."

"Very well," ter Horst said. "Number One, detonate the other nuclear torpedo."

"Detonate the unit from tube two, aye aye," Van Gelder said.

Ter Horst waited till they heard the distant blast, dulled by the intervening escarpment wall. "Now then," he said, "if we can't hear them, they certainly can't hear *us*. Helm, set maximum revolutions, steer one six zero."

"Set maximum revolutions, aye aye, sir," the helmsman said, "steer one six zero, aye aye. . . . Turbine room answers steam throttles are wide open, sir."

"We'll head directly to the choke point now," ter Horst said. "It should take us three hours. We'll wait for Wilson there, after we string the last of our deployable hydrophone line beyond the bases of the seamounts on both flanks of the hump."

"Understood," Van Gelder said.

"Eventually," ter Horst said, "if we don't make contact, we'll come back here and use our bottom-penetrating sonar to locate their reactor compartment under all that rock. One way or another the verge of the Prince Edward Fracture will be *Challenger*'s final hunting ground."

Another atomic detonation went off harshly somewhere past *Challenger*'s starboard quarter. The force of it was amplified and drawn out by the backstop of the escarpment wall, and the gravimeter showed another huge section starting to give way. Above it all Jeffrey heard a *snap*, and water sprayed into the passageway forward of the ship control station.

"It's just freshwater," COB said, bypassing the rupture while he tried to do three other things at once. There was computer hardware near that pipe but nothing shorted out.

"It couldn't stand the flexing and the shock," Jeffrey said. "Our sea pipes are much stronger but something's gotta give." The huge main steam condenser cooling loops—vital to the propulsion system's thermodynamic cycle—were made of a different ceramic composite than the hull, designed to withstand intense pressure from *within*—shear instead of strain—but only up to a point. *Challenger's* hull openings were her weak spots, like in any submarine.

The gravimeter showed a giant avalanche now, and another seismic sea wave caught the ship.

"Sir," Meltzer said, "we're at *sixteen thousand feet*! I cannot get a positive angle of attack!" More moaning crunching sounded and the deck began to warp.

"Very well, Helm," Jeffrey said. "Planing out of the dive just isn't working fast enough. All stop, stop the shaft."

"All stop, aye!" Meltzer said. "Maneuvering acknowledges all stop! Stop the shaft, aye! Maneuvering acknowledges stop the shaft!"

"If we need bowplanes," Jeffrey said, "we'll move in reverse. The sternplanes will become our bowplanes—they're much bigger and they'll have even more bite from the propulsor wash when going backward."

"Understood," Meltzer said.

"Back full smartly," Jeffrey said.

"Back full smartly, aye! . . . Maneuvering acknowledges back full smartly!"

"Be real careful," Jeffrey said, "this evolution makes us very unstable. One more seismic sea wave will be the end of us."

"Acknowledged!" Meltzer said.

Jeffrey eyed the gravimeter, praying hard against more landslides. "And try to get us on an even keel before we crash into that cliff."

1 HOUR LATER

"That's just what I was afraid of, Ilse," Jeffrey said, looking at the imagery off one of her CD-RW disks, the outflow from a hydrothermal vent she'd once studied in detail.

Sessions nodded. "There'll be massive Doppler distortion along the line of sight, sir, and constant rippling of the acoustic image in the perpendicular plane."

The three of them stared at the picture on Sessions' sonar console.

"Here's a thought," Ilse said. "We could do what astronomers do to deal with atmospheric turbulence. Active adaptive optics, except electronically. It's really the same problem."

"But we need a known bright reference star for that," Jeffrey said, "or the equivalent, and this all has to work continuously in real time."

"That's what I mean," Ilse said. "What if we emit an active sonar beam, one that's directionally very tight, at minimum power? Wave it back and forth and grab the micro-echoes off the precipitation particles? That would give a picture of water motion in the megaplume."

"Sounds great in theory," Jeffrey said.

"We'd have to work the wide-aperture system as a phased-array antenna," Sessions said, "then digest all that raw data and reassemble everything for a sharply focused picture. . . . And *that's* just to use this telescope thing on *one line of bearing*." Sessions turned to Jeffrey. "I don't know, sir."

"We'll use finite elements for approximation," Jeffrey said. "The processes are chaotic but they're spatially continuous."

"That's true," Ilse said. "The functions would be differentiable, mathematically."

"We can do a narrowband search to simplify things," Jeffrey said. "Even if *Voortrekker* auto-hovers so their reactor pumps and the rest of the propulsion plant are quiet, they need a bunch of megawatts to run all their computers and their listening gear, and to keep their bow sphere warmed up for active melee ranging once the engagement starts. We'll listen for five-hundred-hertz tonals from their turbogenerators, and fifty-hertz sympathetic line hum. That'll help us filter out irrelevant noise impinging on our hydrophones."

"I concur," Sessions said. "The problem isn't writing the code to do all that, Captain. The systems administrator and his staff have been on it for a while already. They're boilerplating and building from tool kits with the commercial off-the-shelf software we have on board. The problem is running everything fast enough for the lens effect to work."

"We'll have to make as much space as we can inside our processors," Jeffrey said, "dump or switch off everything we don't need on the LAN, other programs, irrelevant data, pieces of the operating system even."

"Can you do that?" Ilse said.

"We have off-line double backups," Sessions said. "It'll be a ton of work to reinstall everything later."

"If we don't do this," Jeffrey said, "or it doesn't work, there might not *be* a later."

"Deployable hydrophone lines are both in place," Van Gelder said. "Ship is in auto-hover. Tubes one through eight are loaded with deep-capable nuclear torpedoes, all warhead yields preset to one kiloton."

"I want to take us closer to the bottom," ter Horst said. "Around here sound rays trend upward, since sound speed increases with depth. That'll put us in a shadow zone against another terrain-hugging boat."

"I concur," Van Gelder said. "It's one benefit of being so deep in the isothermal layer." He eyed a depth gauge. "Recommend we drop to forty-seven hundred and fifty meters, Captain."

"Helm," ter Horst said, "on auto-hover, stationary

dive, make your depth forty-seven hundred fifty meters."

The helmsman acknowledged.

"All deployable hydrophones are nominal, Captain," Van Gelder said, watching his sonar repeaters. "Our search plan focuses on sixty hertz and four hundred hertz, the base-line and high-frequency tonals of the American's dual-source AC electrical supply."

"Excellent, Number One," ter Horst said. "Now we wait, and listen."

Jeffrey and Ilse watched the live imagery from the ice-avoidance low-light-level TV mounted on the sail. The plumes in the vent field to *Challenger*'s front gave off faint luminescence, from the life-forms they fed and from chemical processes. The scalding water sprayed up from the chimneys, roiling black, spreading and mixing as it rose, the turbulence gradually subsiding with distance and elevation.

The sound of the large vent field came over the sonar speakers, rumbling and roaring like so many volcanoes or atomic bombs. Sessions filtered out the worst of the noise, which originated beneath the ocean floor or at the chimney mouths themselves. Commodore Morse looked on, kibitzing and offering moral support.

"My map of this field may be stale," Ilse said. "Sometimes a new smoker opens or an older vent dies off."

"From what we can see, your plot's accurate," Jeffrey said. "These two big plumes further in should give us a good objective lens."

"You'll be able to scan in azimuth by moving the whole ship," Morse said.

Jeffrey nodded.

"We've set our signal processors to isolate the fifty-hertz line and its harmonics," Sessions said.

"Good," Jeffrey said.

"The Mark 88s in tubes one and five are nominal," Bell said. "Just give us a target, Captain."

Jeffrey glanced at his weapons status screen. Tubes three and seven, the other working tubes, were empty. "Load tubes three and seven with ADCAPs," Jeffrey said.

"They're useless this far down, sir," Bell said. "And they only have conventional warheads."

"I know," Jeffrey said. "Just as a last resort."

Van Gelder stared at the gravimeter screens. Two huge seamounts loomed to port and starboard some 10,000 yards ahead, back toward Durban. The hydrophone lines covered the extinct volcanoes' off-side flanks, out to past the 5,000-meter curve. If *Challenger* came down either side, she'd have to cross a group of hydrophones at point-blank range. *Voortrekker* was in perfect position for an intercept. If *Challenger* came down the middle, she'd be ideally backlit by the noise source in the distance: the scattered hydrothermal fields, each the size of several soccer stadiums, that straddled the narrowest part of the choke point.

Van Gelder turned to look over the sonar chief's shoulder. They both watched the narrowband waterfalls for several minutes, scanning one bearing after another.

"Still nothing, Captain," Van Gelder said.

"Very well," ter Horst said. "They're out there. They're coming. I can feel it in my balls."

"Still nothing, Captain," Sessions said.

"We'll have to bring the boat up higher," Jeffrey said. "They must be further away than I expected, masked by ground shadowing."

"Either that," Bell said, "or this telescope isn't working."

"Helm," Jeffrey said, "on auto-hover, stationary rise, make your depth twelve thousand feet."

"Sir," Bell said, "we'll be awfully exposed like that, three thousand feet off the bottom. The pumps will be very noisy getting us up there, and the hull will pop."

"Those are chances we'll have to take," Jeffrey said.

"Make my depth twelve thousand feet, aye," Meltzer said.

"We also need to sneak our Mark 88s out there now," Jeffrey said, "so we can hit *Voortrekker* by surprise once we have a range and bearing. They'll be waiting somewhere between the hydrothermal field and those two 4,000-foot-high seamounts up ahead, staying within weapons range of the black smoker megaplumes."

"Sir," Bell said, "I don't want to seem a naysayer, but our units have limited cruising endurance even on low speed. We'd be gambling we make a contact before their fuel runs out."

"Understood," Jeffrey said. "But the ranges here are very large and sonar contact may be intermittent. If we use conventional tactics, a high-speed torpedo attack once we have a target, *Voortrekker* will hear and immediately get off a snap shot salvo. Once that happens, we can't count on hitting her with one 88 and stopping all incoming fire with the other."

"Understood," Bell said. "The best we could hope for then would be a double kill, both ships sunk."

"That's why we have to get our units out there now," Jeffrey said.

"At slow speed they'll orbit a couple of hours," Morse said.

"Understood," Bell said.

"Very well, Fire Control," Jeffrey said, "and keep asking the tough questions. . . . Now, make tubes one and five ready in all respects, including opening outer doors. Preset the weapons for twenty knots running speed. We'll control through the wire and circle one off each flank of the hump. Run them in nap-of-seafloor mode, with tracks five hundred feet off the bottom for terrain- and sound-shadow masking. Disable active pinging, reenable only on my command."

"Aye aye, sir," Bell said.

"Once we launch, be real careful not to lose the wires," Jeffrey said. "Run them out with room to spare around these hot vents."

"Understood," Bell said.

"Very well," Jeffrey said, "here we go. Firing point procedures, tubes one and five. Manual control of the weapons."

"Both units ready," Bell said.

"Tube one shoot," Jeffrey said.

"Set," Bell said. "Stand by. *Fire*. Tube one fired electrically. Unit is swimming out."

"Unit is running normally," Sessions said.

"Tube five shoot," Jeffrey said.

"Set," Bell said. "Stand by. *Fire*. Tube five fired electrically. Unit is swimming out."

"Unit is running normally," Sessions said.

"Very well," Jeffrey said. "The clock is ticking, and the weapon fuel is burning."

"Still nothing, Captain," Van Gelder said. "It's taking *Challenger* longer to get here than we thought."

"Patience, Gunther, patience," ter Horst said.

"Captain," Sessions said, "we're getting something now! Definite fifty-hertz tonals. I designate the contact Sierra 1. But we have a difficulty, sir. The indicated range is ninety thousand yards."

"Forty-five nautical miles," Jeffrey said. "The other side of the seamounts, well beyond the maximum range of our Mark 88s."

"Concur, sir," Sessions said. "This telescope works so well we're actually getting fifty-hertz bounces off both seamounts' inner flanks, letting us double-check the distance. Definitely ninety thousand yards."

"Sir," Bell said, "our units are committed. We are unable to shut down or retrieve torpedoes—they're not like our LMRS probes."

"I know," Jeffrey said. "I didn't think ter Horst would wait for us that far back. . . . Hmmm. The running ranges of our nuclear torpedoes are supposedly about the same as theirs, and at *Voortrekker*'s current position both seamounts could block their shots. . . . *Unless* . . . I'm starting to think they must carry some kind of deployable weapon, deep-capable CAPTOR mines or some sort of expendable SOSUS gear."

"You'll just have to make them come forward, then," Morse said.

"Concur, sir," Bell said. "But how?"

"We'll move forward briefly ourselves," Jeffrey said, "and give them something to shoot at—*us*."

Bell opened his mouth to object, but Jeffrey held up a hand. "Get ready to drop a wrench in the torpedo room, just to be sure."

"Hydrophone line contact!" *Voortrekker*'s sonar chief shouted. "Now passive contact on the bow sphere as well! Direct path, relative bearing zero zero two."

"At last," ter Horst said.

"Contact classification?" Van Gelder said.

"Mechanical transient, sir. Some kind of machinery noise. Might have been a casualty in torpedo room equipment."

"Indeed," ter Horst said. "So they've had some battle damage, or the crew's been worked past their endurance. Or both. What's contact range?"

"Sir," Van Gelder said, "distortion from the hot vents

is impairing our ability to triangulate using the deployed arrays."

"Give me your best guess of depth and distance," ter Horst snapped.

"Extreme range, sir," Van Gelder said, "about sixty-five kilometers. . . . For us to hear at all given ground masking effects, *Challenger* has to be above thirty-eight hundred meters. Conjecture that's her crush depth."

"Or it's as far down as they want to push their luck today," ter Horst said. "Interesting. . . . Well, we'll just have to move in closer."

"Sir," Van Gelder said, "that's risky and we'll lose the wires to the deployable hydrophones."

"We must strike while we have the enemy localized, Number One. At nearly five thousand meters depth ourselves, if we simply wait here for much longer, the hydrophones might fail anyway."

"Understood," Van Gelder said.

"Don't worry, Gunther," ter Horst said. "As we get closer, we'll pick up *Challenger* on hole-in-ocean, long before they see us on their ambient sonar. Closing the range before we fire will cut the running time of our torpedoes, improve the odds of a kill even if the units get in a high-speed stern chase against the target."

"Concur, Captain," Van Gelder said.

"Zero zero two relative is three two three true," ter Horst said. "Helm, steer three two three. Slow ahead, twelve knots."

"Aye aye. . . . Turbine room answers slow ahead, making revs for twelve knots, sir."

"Warm up the weapons, tubes one through eight," ter Horst said.

"Warm up the weapons, tubes one through eight, aye aye," Van Gelder said.

"Preset all weapons for maximum yield."

"Maximum yield, aye aye."

"Flood the tubes, equalize the pressure, and open the outer doors tubes one through eight."

"Sierra 1 signal strength is increasing slightly," Sessions said.

"That might just be from reduced particulate attenuation," Ilse said, "along our line of sight."

"Or ter Horst might be coming closer," Jeffrey said. "We have to be sure. . . . We need to triangulate, try to get cross bearings from another hot vent eyepiece."

"That one eight hundred yards north of us might work," Ilse said.

Jeffrey studied the vent field map. "Concur. Helm, ahead one third, make turns for four knots."

"Mechanical transients!" Sessions broke in.

"Classification?" Jeffrey said.

"Many torpedo tube doors being opened."

"How many is many?" Jeffrey said.

"Eight, I think," Sessions said.

"All of them," Jeffrey said.

1 HOUR LATER

"Still no new contact on the target," Van Gelder said.

"What's range to their last known position?" ter Horst said.

"Now forty-five kilometers, Captain. Query going active for a precise range and bearing."

"No," ter Horst said, "I think it's premature. They'd have a snap shot in the water before we even heard our ping come back."

"Good," Morse said. "You've picked up Sierra 1 again. I'd suggest you shuttle back and forth, to keep updating the triangulated range and start a TMA. Now you've calibrated both eyepieces, the data reduction ought to go much faster."

"I concur," Jeffrey said. "Helm, back one third, make turns for four knots. Return us to that other eyepiece vent location."

"Back one third, make turns for four knots, aye," Meltzer said. "Maneuvering acknowledges back one third, making turns for four knots, sir."

"Very well, Helm," Jeffrey said. "Now, people, listen up, we need to caucus. . . . We have a problem. Our lure to bring *Voortrekker* toward our weapons seems to have worked, but now that she's in motion, she'll be harder for us to track, and she's been alerted."

"But presumably they won't know about the hot vent lensing," Bell said.

"So we hope," Jeffrey said.

"Jan isn't likely to think of it," Ilse said. "He's not exactly in tune with the environment."

"He has a crew, remember," Morse cautioned, "an XO and sonar experts and so on."

Ilse frowned and nodded.

"As long as they don't go active," Jeffrey said, "we *may* be able to fool them about our actual range."

"Yes," Morse said. "When they hear the Mark 88s doing end-game runs without prior active searches, they'll guess at our range based on what they know of *Challenger*'s sonar sensitivity, and underestimate. They'll probably launch a snap shot spread, a nuclear shotgun blast—they've done that twice already since making contact at Durban—but it ought to all fall safely short of us."

"Concur," Jeffrey said. "So let's hope ter Horst doesn't go active. It would be a toss-up for him, revenge versus self-preservation, offensive accuracy versus his ping helping our own fish home in."

"Oooh," Ilse said, "I wouldn't want to count on anything there, knowing Jan."

"Mmph," Jeffrey said.

"Sir," Bell said, "we have an improved range estimate to Sierra 1 now, still too far to engage. Target speed appears to be ten or fifteen knots. I am repositioning the units from tubes one and five to intercept based on the latest 3-D TMA."

"What's target depth?" Jeffrey said.

"Fifteen thousand feet, sir," Sessions said. "The acoustic shadowing along the bottom is more than offset by ray path focusing at the intersection of the two big vent plumes, our main telescope lens."

"Good," Jeffrey said, "just as we predicted."

"But we still have a serious problem," Morse said.

Jeffrey nodded. "We were counting on using our Mark 88s for a slow-speed stealth attack against a more or less stationary target. Since *Voortrekker*'s moving, they'll be much harder to hit, and our TMA will be rather crude with this lensing effect."

"Plus there's the sonar reception time delay," Ilse said. "At thirty miles, say, until our torpedoes pick him up themselves and we can target directly through the fiber-optic wires, there'll be a half-minute lag between *Challenger*'s latest raw data and where Jan actually is."

"Correct," Jeffrey said. "So now the weapons will need to ping and make their end-game runs at high speed, from ten thousand yards away or more, and ter Horst will hear them coming. Against ceramic-composite hulls at this depth, Mark 88 warheads have a lethal range of only a nautical mile or so, *two* thousand yards. The enemy'll be able to counterfire low-yield warheads to intercept our incoming fish, and he'll spoil the whole attack."

"Still nothing, sir," Van Gelder said. "Again, query going active. *Challenger* may fear we were alerted by their mechanical transient. They may have withdrawn to widen the range."

"Don't go active yet, Gunther," ter Horst said. "Let's get just a little closer, try to spot them on ambient or hole-in-ocean first. I also want to get the far side of the vent field further in range of our weapons, in case, as you say, Wilson did decide to run."

"Understood, Captain," Van Gelder said.

"De-enable weapon active pinging, so the units don't waste fuel by driving heavily loaded turbogenerators or give themselves away prematurely. We'll rely on passive search instead, narrowband tonals only, with guiding through the fiber-optic wires."

"De-enable weapon active pinging, aye," Van Gelder said. "Presets completed, Captain, and we have a second full salvo prepositioned on the holding racks."

"Excellent," ter Horst said. "Now, begin varying our course and speed at random, say twenty-five percent more or fewer shaft revolutions and twenty-degree port and starboard rudder applications. I want to throw off *Challenger*'s TMA."

"Sir," Bell said, "latest data put Sierra 1 in extreme range of our weapons. Sierra 1 is zigzagging and fuel in both our units is running low."

Morse stood up straight and looked Jeffrey in the eye. "It's now or never, Captain Fuller."

"I don't like this setup," Jeffrey said. "The best that's gonna happen is a draw—we escape their fire 'cause they don't know our range, and they escape ours using nukes as AT rockets. A draw's a loss for us. They'd still be straddling our homeward track."

"We can't clear datum and start over again," Morse said. "No more good ammo."

"We *could* try to lure *Voortrekker* to shallower depth and then engage with ADCAPs," Bell said.

Jeffrey shook his head. "The crashing waves up there

give a perfect white noise backdrop. We'd only make ourselves a better target."

"Sorry, sir," Bell said. "I was just trying to help."

Ilse saw Jeffrey get that faraway look again. "I think you did, Fire Control, I think you actually did."

"Sir," Bell said, obviously confused, "target is now passing point of closest approach to our units. Recommend engaging promptly."

"Very well," Jeffrey said. "We only get one chance. Fire Control, bring the units up to ten thousand feet and maintain them at that depth. Keep them equidistant from Sierra 1 on opposite sides of her track best as you can. Commence high-speed run-in when both weapons are ten thousand yards from target. Give me continual unit and target location on my tactical screen, and prepare to detonate both weapons on my mark."

"But sir," Bell said, "they'll hear the units for sure that way, and why so shallow?"

"Enable active search on end-game run," Jeffrey said, "and use the data coming through the wire to enhance the TMA, but retain manual control of unit depth and course."

"Torpedo in the water!" the sonar chief shouted. "*Incoming torpedo bearing zero one five!*"

"Curious," ter Horst said. "That's dead abeam to starboard."

"*Second incoming torpedo bearing one nine five!*"

"Dead abeam to port. What's their range, Number One?"

Van Gelder read his screens. "Just inside nine thousand meters, sir. Approach speed of both is . . . sixty-five knots!"

"Ahead flank maximum revs!" ter Horst roared. "Maintain present course or we'll just end up closer to one of them!"

"Aye aye," the helmsman said smartly.

"Sir," Van Gelder said, "both torpedoes have started active search." The sonar chief put it on the speakers. A high-pitched bell-like *ting-ting* sounded, two-tone, Van Gelder realized, because each fish used a different frequency to avoid false echoes from the other. Beneath the *tings* there was a steady whine, the torpedo propulsion systems, and a nasty hiss, *Voortrekker*'s flank-speed flow noise.

"Number One," ter Horst ordered, "tubes one and two, snap shots on incoming torpedo bearings, minimum yield, *shoot*."

"Tube one fired," Van Gelder said. "Tube two fired."

"Both weapons are operating properly," the sonar chief said.

The propulsion noise got louder, with four torpedoes in the water now, but above it all Van Gelder heard the sweet *ting-ting* again, like a bellhop paging someone in a hotel lobby. "Sonar," he said, "what's incoming torpedo depth?"

"Both steady at three thousand meters, sir."

"Fifteen hundred shallower than us," ter Horst said, "which gives us extra separation. Good. Wilson must be afraid they might malfunction lower down. Incoming torpedo range?"

"Both now seventy-seven hundred meters, Captain," Van Gelder said. "Our units are climbing to meet them, time to intercept two minutes." Both American torpedoes pinged again.

"We'll smack them easily," ter Horst said. "Number One, snap shot tubes three through eight, aimed at *Challenger*'s last known bearing. Use maximum warhead yield. Detonate the weapons at staggered ranges, every ten thousand meters starting at twenty thousand meters, so their lethal circles will just overlap. Program in the detonation points in case we lose the wires, especially the ones that have to penetrate that vent field. Delay the detonations of the ones closest to us, to avoid warhead shock wave fratricide."

"Understood," Van Gelder said. "Sir, recommend we let the last fish go till end of run. It'll blow then automatically and might lock on a target sooner."

"Concur, a very good idea, and preset it to go active if it makes a passive contact but then loses it. What's time to interception of the incoming torpedoes?"

"Ninety seconds, Captain," Van Gelder said. He worked his console. "All weapons ready."

"Very well," ter Horst said. "Tubes three through eight, *shoot*."

"Tube three fired," Van Gelder said. "Tube four fired. Tube five. Tube six. Tube seven. Tube eight fired. Reloading all tubes now with nuclear torpedoes."

Again the *ting-ting* sounded.

"There'll be a lot of shadow masking at our depth," ter Horst said, "and I wouldn't want to go any shallower now, but since *Challenger*'s obviously found us, let's try for a proper firing solution on *her*. Sonar, using maximum power on the bow sphere, *ping*."

"Torpedoes in the water!" Sessions shouted. "Six, seven, *eight torpedoes in the water*!"

"This has to be a record," Morse said.

"Two are on divergent bearings," Sessions said. "Assess as countershots against our units. Six more on *constant* bearings, signal strength increasing—assess as snap shots aimed at *Challenger*. Sir, we're inside their effective range."

"Steady," Jeffrey said, "steady. Fire Control, pass control of the units to me and keep updating the TMA. I'll work one weapon with my joy stick and the other with my trackmarble."

"Sir," Bell said, "urgently recommend we move away. At this depth a one-KT warhead has a lethal radius of at least five thousand yards, and *Voortrekker*'s close enough to get us through the vent field."

"Sir," Sessions shouted, "datum on acoustic intercept! *Voortrekker* just pinged, *strong enough to get an echo off us*!"

"So now they'll know exactly where we are," Jeffrey said, "but it's too soon to pull back. We might lose the weapon wires."

"No target returns yet off our ping," Van Gelder said. "In thirty seconds we should get some kind of echo off the vent field plumes."

"What's depth of the incoming torpedoes?" ter Horst said.

"Unchanged," Van Gelder said, "both still three thousand meters. Range declining to six thousand meters now. Intercept by our units in one minute."

Again both incoming weapons pinged, the silvery bell tones coming faster as they range-gated on *Voortrekker*'s hull. Suddenly the pinging ceased and both torpedoes' propulsor whine got slightly sharper.

Van Gelder stared at his displays, the attack geometry. He did a hasty calculation on his console—since height-to-range was one to four, at this distance an aggregate delta-T of 40°C would—*Oh my God*. "Captain," Van Gelder shouted, "*plane up*! Recommend emergency blow while we still can!"

"*What?*"

"Sir, incoming torpedo *depth*! They've *fooled* us. We won't be able to intercept in time! If we boost our units' yield, they'll just take us with *them* instead!"

"What the hell are you talking about?" ter Horst said. "Have you lost your *mind*?"

"Don't you see, Captain?" Van Gelder said. "The Americans, they're going for undersea nuclear Mach stems, like an airburst, only much worse! A hammer and anvil strike, *two* shock waves hitting us simultaneously from opposite sides, after they both *redouble* when each *merges through the heated water with its own bottom bounce!"*

Ter Horst's face went white. *"Plane up, do an EMBT blow!"*

Voortrekker's nose bucked and hydrazine began to roar. Then both U.S. torpedoes detonated.

"Units from tubes one and five have detonated!" Bell shouted. It would be precious seconds till Jeffrey knew what effect they'd had on *Voortrekker*, if any.

"Six torpedoes still incoming at high speed," Sessions said.

"And this deep they'll all camouflet," Jeffrey said. "The fireballs won't break the surface."

"Concur, sir," Sessions said.

"It's high time to get our backsides out of here," Jeffrey said. "Helm, ahead flank smartly. Hard left rudder, make a knuckle, make your course two nine zero, back toward Durban."

"Ahead flank smartly, aye," Meltzer said. "Hard left rudder, aye."

"That'll take us off the track of those torpedoes," Jeffrey said, "and help make sure we outrun their fuel supplies." He glanced at a depth gauge to double-check: still 12,000 feet. "Helm, fifteen degrees down bubble smartly. Chief of the Watch, don't compensate till we reach fifteen thousand. Let us dive with negative buoyancy to pick up extra speed."

"Fifteen degrees down bubble smartly, aye," Meltzer said. He pushed on his control wheel—the deck nosed downward quickly.

"Transient bearing one two zero!" Sessions shouted. "Sierra 1 is doing a main ballast blow!"

"They figured out my trick," Jeffrey said.

"Sir?" Bell said.

"Mach stems from opposite directions dead abeam," Jeffrey said.

"Clever lad," Morse said. "A nutcracker suite, and with the seawater preventing neutron warhead fratricide."

"Sonar," Jeffrey said, "shut down your equipment before the enemy torpedoes start to detonate. I don't want to take a chance our gear's overloaded when the blast fronts get here through the lensing."

"Understood," Sessions said. "Our own units' shock waves will reach us momentarily."

The rumbling and shaking weren't as bad as Jeffrey expected, but *those* detonations had been tens of kiloyards away.

"All six enemy torpedoes still incoming, sir," Sessions said.

"Will we be able to outrun?" Jeffrey said.

"If we stay at flank speed," Bell said, "and don't have a propulsion casualty, it's still touch and go, sir."

Jeffrey picked up the mike for the 7MC. "Maneuvering, this is the captain. Push the reactor to one hundred ten percent." *Challenger* began to vibrate like a subway car.

Five atomic blasts went off at progressively shorter distances from *Challenger*, the last of them on the nearer side of the vent field.

"Sonar," Jeffrey said, "reactivate your hydrophones. We need the data to evade that final fish."

"Acknowledged," Sessions said.

"Last incoming torpedo still narrowing the range," Bell said. "Twenty thousand yards now, sir."

"What's its overtaking speed?" Jeffrey said.

"Twenty-five knots."

"What's its depth?"

"Fifteen thousand feet."

"Same as us," Jeffrey said, "and that's as deep as I want to push it." The hydraulic-ram main compensating pumps felt asthmatic as it was.

"Captain," Bell said, "should we head up toward the surface where our countermeasures work?"

"They didn't work against that 212's fish at Diego Garcia," Jeffrey said.

"There aren't any terrain features we can hide behind either," Ilse said. "We're over the Agulhas Basin at this point, nineteen thousand feet."

"Uh-oh," Jeffrey said, "I'm not thinking. Helm, right full rudder, make your course zero zero zero."

"Sir?" Bell said. "That fish will cut the corner on us."

"Yes," Jeffrey said, "it's a gamble. But we *have* to reach shallower ground."

"What's incoming torpedo's depth now?" Jeffrey said.

"Thirteen thousand five hundred feet," Bell said.

"Good," Jeffrey said, "and we're still at fifteen thousand, hugging the bottom. Looks like that fish is set to track five hundred meters above the floor but not below its crush depth, about what I suspected. . . . Fire Control, the range?"

"Ten thousand yards," Bell said, "and on an interception course."

"But we got its height-to-distance down to one to twenty," Jeffrey said, "so it's too close to the bottom for an effective Mach stem."

"Concur," Bell said. "That was smart, sir, veering north."

"It can still kill us the old-fashioned way very nicely," Jeffrey said.

"If it was a high-explosives warhead," Morse said, "it would impact in twelve minutes. One KT's in lethal range in half that time."

"It's obviously got passive lock on all our noise,"

Jeffrey said, "but if we slow down any, we just help it more, and making knuckles slows us down."

"It may be programmed to go active if it loses passive lock," Morse said. "I doubt then that we'd fool it with a knuckle."

"No," Jeffrey said, "but it might be using a passive-only proximity fuze. If we can somehow make it think it's overtaken and it's passing us, it may blow prematurely. . . . Helm, hard right rudder!"

"Hard right rudder, aye," Meltzer said. The boat banked hard to starboard.

"Helm, hard left rudder!"

The boat banked hard to port.

"A pair of knuckles just might do it," Jeffrey said, "make our self-noise seem to fade."

"Sir," Sessions said, "incoming torpedo has started pinging, ultrasonic at thirty-two kilohertz."

"That's cute," Jeffrey said. "Rudder amidships."

"Rudder amidships, aye," Meltzer said. *Challenger* steadied up on zero three five true.

"Torpedo is course-correcting," Sessions said, "once more on a constant bearing off our stern."

"It didn't work," Jeffrey said. He glanced at a chronometer. "That torpedo should have exhausted all its fuel already, even *with* not pinging till just now. The Axis must have an improved mod in the field. Useful intel if we live to share it."

"What's range to the torpedo?" Jeffrey said.

"Eight thousand yards," Bell said.

"Sonar," Jeffrey said, "put your broadband on the speakers."

A harsh screaming filled the CACC, gradually getting louder, the last incoming torpedo. Mad hissing and rumbling filled the background, the warheads that had already gone off. There was a steady sharp hiss also,

Challenger's own flow noise. The Axis fish's pinging was too high-pitched for the human ear.

"Sonar," Jeffrey said, "can you clean that up and say what else is happening out there?"

Sessions tapped his keyboard and spoke to his senior chief. "Sir, we're getting intermittent passive contact on something on the surface, assess it as Sierra 1. Best guess it's all their bilge and fire-fighting pumps."

"Sounds like we really hurt them, Captain," Bell said.

"But we didn't sink them," Jeffrey said. "Is Sierra 1 in motion?"

"Hard to be sure with all the reverb," Sessions said, "but we have enough slant separation over the camoufletted blast zones to drive a TMA."

"Good," Jeffrey said. "Fire Control, what's the dot stack tell you?"

"Sierra 1 is stationary, Captain," Bell said.

"Well *done*!" Morse said. "A mobility kill and fire and flooding damage too."

"Let's just see how *we* make out," Jeffrey said as he glanced at a sonar speaker, then tried to ignore the constant swelling screaming from outside. "What's torpedo range?"

"Seven thousand yards," Bell said.

"It's almost surely set for active-sonar proximity fuzing," Jeffrey said. "We can't suppress our echo signature this close, our back end's too complex a profile."

"If I were them, Captain," Bell said, "I'd program it to blow four thousand meters from us. Forty-four hundred yards."

Jeffrey nodded. "If it doesn't drain its fuel tanks soon, we've had it." He grabbed the 7MC. "Maneuvering, *more speed*. Push it to a hundred twelve percent."

"Range *six* thousand yards!" Bell said. *"It's turning into our baffles!"*

"Helm," Jeffrey said, "left standard rudder, no course specified."

"Left standard rudder, no course specified, aye," Meltzer said.

"At least this way we'll take a glancing blow off our port quarter," Jeffrey said.

"The floor drops off in that direction," Ilse said.

"Good," Jeffrey said. "Helm, ten degrees down bubble smartly, head for sixteen thousand feet. We'll get more counterpressure against the warhead and more speed as our hull compresses."

"Ten degrees down bubble smartly, sixteen thousand feet, aye."

"Range still closing," Bell shouted. *"Any second now!"*

"Phone Talker," Jeffrey said, "collision alarm and rig for depth charge. Sonar, deactivate the hydrophones again."

The CACC grew quieter but the torpedo could be heard outside the hull. Its screaming stopped.

The weapon detonated with a stupendous *crack* and several console screens went dead. *Challenger*'s stern dipped as COB and Meltzer struggled for control. Newly replaced fluorescent light bulbs shattered and the fixture covers failed, scattering broken glass. Insulation fell from the overhead and another freshwater pipe exploded. Smoke came out of one of the sonar workstations, flames crackled in the forward passageway, and high-voltage circuits arced and popped. The air took on a stinking bite as fire fighters struggled with CO_2 and foam.

Jeffrey tried to read his damage control display, but the vibrations were so bad he couldn't focus. He realized he'd been deafened—there was a painful throbbing in his head amid an eerie silence. The black smoke made him cough; it wasn't clearing. The CACC crew began to don their emergency breathing masks, plugging the tubes into the air lines in the overhead.

The insane shaking died down enough for Jeffrey to make out his screens, but incoming reports were fragmentary. *Challenger*'s reactor had done an autoscram from the shock. It would take a couple of minutes for Willey's people to safely restart, assuming there wasn't other, fatal damage. Meanwhile the boat was drifting, getting by on batteries. COB had to try maintaining depth by pumping variable ballast alone, an excruciatingly slow process against a head of 16,000 feet of water.

Jeffrey's hearing came back gradually. "Fire Control," he shouted, "status of the torpedo room?"

"More misting round the tube eight door," Bell said. "Tubes three and seven appear to be operational."

"Reload tubes one and five with Mark 48s!" Jeffrey said. "Navigating, get our gyros reset! Sonar, reactivate the hydrophone arrays!"

Morse put his hand on Jeffrey's shoulder. *"Don't,"* Morse yelled. "You don't know what shape *Voortrekker*'s in, how many nuclear torpedoes she has left."

"We'll have four ADCAPs in the tubes," Jeffrey said.

Morse ducked to keep his head below the thickening smoke. "Unless we scored a firepower kill, we'll be defenseless against more A-bombs once we show ourselves."

"She's dead in the water up there," Jeffrey yelled.

"So are we right now."

"We'll do a stationary rise and get in range on emergency diesel if we have to."

Morse shook his head firmly. "If their AT rockets are still functional, the chance of our success isn't worth a damn. It isn't worth the risk to *this* ship and her crew and intel payload!"

"Sir," Sessions shouted, "Sierra 1 has started active pinging!"

"Any torpedoes in the water?" Jeffrey said.

"Impossible to tell yet."

"And remember Axis air support from the Prince

Edward Islands," Ilse said, pointing to Meltzer's nav display for emphasis.

"Enemy Mach 2 nuclear-capable fighter-bombers are only minutes away," Bell said.

"Captain," Sessions yelled, "I'm getting acoustic coupling through the air/ocean interface, *sonic booms*. Assess many inbound aircraft bearing one three zero true!"

"You mean just let him *go*?" Jeffrey said.

"*Captain* Fuller," Morse said, "don't get emotionally involved *now*. We've more than accomplished what we came for, Umhlanga Rocks and everything else."

"Sir," the phone talker said, "Lieutenant Willey reports pump-jet turned over well on the battery, full propulsion restart in one minute."

Way to go, Engineering.

"Sir," Bell said, "you turned a standoff here from a loss into a *win*. You cleared the pathway home."

Jeffrey glanced at Ilse. She nodded ruefully.

"But . . . ," Jeffrey said.

"Jeffrey," Morse said. "To lay *Voortrekker* up for even a *month* or two at this point in the war is a vital achievement for the Allied cause."

Jeffrey sighed. He ran his hand over his face and looked at Ilse again. Again she nodded, giving him a crooked smile.

"There'll be other chances," Ilse said. "Jan will wait."

"Remember Jutland was a draw, Captain," Bell said, "but a strategic victory for the Allies in World War I."

Jeffrey hesitated. "Very well, Commodore. Very well, XO." He glanced down at his console screens. Power had come back already and *Challenger*'s speed was building. The smoke began to dissipate.

Jeffrey cleared his throat. "Helm, maintain flank speed. Left full rudder, make your course one five three. We'll turn around, jink randomly, and use the extended sonar whiteout to disappear inside the Fracture Zone."

• • •

Van Gelder and ter Horst glanced up at the sky. Waves slapped and sloshed against the hull. Friendly aircraft flew overhead in escort as *Voortrekker* chugged along on her emergency diesel. Occasionally other aircraft dropped more parachute-retarded nuclear depth bombs at a safe distance, all camouflets in the abyss, hoping to hit *Challenger*. But it was obvious they were shooting blind, just as *Voortrekker* had been when she fired another salvo at the enemy sub once stabilized on the surface. That last torpedo in the first bunch had been the clue, blowing when its fuel would've run out but on a divergent course, as if chasing a sonar contact that got away. A bottom search would tell for sure—they knew exactly where to look for wreckage—but ter Horst said he wasn't optimistic.

"Things are falling into place now, Gunther," ter Horst said.

"Captain?" Van Gelder said.

"You were right, you see, about there being just the one blast at Durban. It's all too neat. It wasn't a coincidence."

"I don't quite follow you, sir."

"*Challenger,*" ter Horst said, "and an A-bomb. . . . The bomb was designed to get our boats to sortie in a hurry, and it worked. *That's* why *Challenger* was laying mines just there and then. They found a way past all the armor in the bluff, and a way around our hostage strategy, by clever indirection."

"Except their timing was off, sir," Van Gelder said. "The explosion came a bit too soon, or *Challenger* too late."

"Yes. . . . And you say it went off at Umhlanga Rocks?"

"I thought so, Captain, right at the peak of the headland. It would be easy enough to find out, from the crater."

Ter Horst nodded. "I believe there was a secret installation on that hill. I *know* there was a missile bunker there."

"You think they're all connected somehow, Captain?"

"I do, Gunther, I do. The bomb may have been sabotage from within, coordinated with the so-called Allies. The fallout mix will tell. . . . And how else could they have known precisely where the daily safety corridor lay?"

"It doesn't seem possible," Van Gelder said. "We have such tight security everywhere."

"Treason," ter Horst said. "There'll have to be a formal investigation of it all. . . . *Voortrekker* will be laid up for a while—I'll use my influence to get to chair the board personally."

"While we're in dry dock, Captain, in the bluff?"

"Yes," ter Horst said. "And when I find out who among our people were responsible, I'll put the nooses round their necks myself!"

Two ex-French Mach 2 interceptors roared by low off the bow, like arrowheads with their canard winglets under the canopies—under the winglets the aircraft now wore Iron Crosses. They vanished over the horizon, then a messenger popped his head out of *Voortrekker*'s bridge hatch—Van Gelder resolved some minor matters quickly.

"Saved by a bunch of fly-boys, Gunther," ter Horst said a minute later. "Who'd have ever thought?"

"We did our best, sir," Van Gelder said. "The important thing is that we live to fight another day."

Ter Horst sighed. "This engagement was like in their Civil War, the battle between the world's first ironclads, *Monitor* and *Merrimack*. They fought each other to a standstill, then withdrew, and not for lack of courage on either side."

"Virginia, sir, not *Merrimack,"* Van Gelder said. "The South renamed her when she was rebuilt."

Ter Horst stared into space, then set his jaw. "I underestimated the Americans. I took much too much for granted, and I fell for their clever tricks. So be it, but I swear to you, no longer. Next time we meet *Challenger,* she and her crew will die."

EPILOGUE

MINDELO, SÃO VICENTE ISLAND, REPUBLIC OF CAPE VERDE, 10 DAYS LATER

The music blaring off the crowded patio was a kind of reggae with an African beat. The rhythm stirred Jeffrey's blood as he gazed across the narrow strait to Santo Antão, the next island in the volcanic chain, the 6,500-foot-high peak of Tope de Coroa bristling with antennas and missile sites. He glanced at his watch and his heart started pounding—thirteen hundred local, *finally*. Jeffrey turned back toward the hotel. Ilse was coming.

"Hi," she said. "I got your message." She wiped some loose strands of hair from her forehead. "I ate already, but . . ."

Jeffrey smiled. "So how were your first two days of so-called R&R?"

"More like an interrogation than a debriefing," Ilse said.

"Mine too," Jeffrey said. "Let's find some quiet." They walked together closer to the edge of the sheer cliff. The trade wind blew steadily from the northeast, as it always did. The weather was sunny and warm, as usual in Cape Verde. The slopes around were covered with sparse desertlike scrub. There were grains of sand beneath Jeffrey's feet, blown all the way from the Sahara, from four hundred miles east across the equatorial Atlantic.

"I'm sort of surprised they didn't fly you out immediately," Jeffrey said. He checked over his shoulder, then whispered, "You know, so you could work on the archaea."

"Others are at least as qualified as me, and *they're* U.S. citizens. They told me I have such a low travel priority it might be a couple of weeks before there's an open seat."

"Strange," Jeffrey said. "Clayton's gang's supposed to be on the next flight out today."

Ilse shrugged. "They gave me chits to use at the hotel. I don't even have any money. . . . I guess they need to drain Otto dry first, before I'd have much to do."

"Makes sense," Jeffrey said. Then he just looked at Ilse.

"They're playing Christmas music," she said.

"The words sound like some kind of Creole," Jeffrey said.

"It's called Crioulo, actually," Ilse said, "made from Portuguese and some African languages. There're bits of Portuguese in Afrikaans too. I can make out words here and there."

Jeffrey hesitated. "So what are your plans now, Ilse?"

"Sleep for about three days," she said.

"That's when I have to go," Jeffrey said.

"You mean with the ship?"

"Yeah," Jeffrey said. "We're being sent to dry dock on the East Coast. I'm not sure where yet, which yard or base. Repairs, upgrades. . . ."

"How's Captain Wilson?" Ilse said.

"Better," Jeffrey said. "I visited him this morning in his hotel room. They won't let him off the premises till we sail. Mandatory rest. He still gets terrible headaches."

"And your navigator?" Ilse said.

"They can do amazing things now with electrode implants and mechanical assists, they told me."

"Good luck to him," Ilse said. "Where's your submarine now?"

Jeffrey turned to the sea. At the base of the cliff the strong surf pounded and creamed. "Out there, somewhere," he said. "Deep and safe. We submerged as soon as we'd reammunitioned, and epoxied the bow sphere."

"You know where she is?" Ilse said.

"I do, but if I told you I'd have to shoot you."

Ilse giggled. "And you're commuting in the ASDS?"

"Yeah," Jeffrey said. "It's like our gig or something. Wasn't designed for that, but it comes in handy."

Ilse looked across the water, azure blue like the sky.

"Listen," Jeffrey said, "I'm totally buried in maintenance and paperwork, but I was, uh, I was wondering, I could carve out a few hours tonight, if you wanted to have dinner, just the two of us."

Before Ilse could respond, Jeffrey noticed someone approaching from the patio. He cursed under his breath.

The woman wore a Royal Navy officer's uniform, like everyone else here lacking insignia and badges, for security. "Excuse me," she said. "Are you Commander Jeffrey Fuller?"

"Uh, yeah," Jeffrey said.

"I'm Lieutenant Kathy Milgrom." She reached out her hand and Jeffrey shook it. Since Jeffrey was uncovered—hatless—they didn't salute. "Here are my orders, sir," Kathy said.

Jeffrey held the papers against his chest in case some satellite might be watching, and he read. Immediately he said, "Oh God. You're one of *them*."

Kathy nodded brightly. Jeffrey kept reading. It seemed that after eighteen months helping see HMS *Dreadnought* through the final construction and operational readiness phases, and upon the recommendation of Commodore Richard Morse, RN, Lieutenant Kathy Janet Milgrom was being seconded to USS *Challenger*. With the concurrence of higher authority in the United

States Navy, she would serve in a capacity to be determined by *Challenger*'s executive officer at his discretion. It was noted Ms. Milgrom was expert in sonar.

Jeffrey did a double take, then saw Kathy read his face.

"Yes, sir," Kathy said. "Commodore Morse and my father served together, in *Conqueror* during the Falklands crisis."

"Well," Jeffrey said, "I suppose now I should say Welcome aboard."

Ilse broke in, "I didn't know they had any women crew on nuclear submarines."

"It's supposed to be an *experiment*," Kathy said. "It's *very* controversial." Jeffrey caught her giving Ilse a wink. Ilse seemed highly unamused.

"You've talked to Captain Wilson?" Jeffrey said.

"Yes, sir," Kathy said. "For just a moment. He told me your ship's had a bit of experience with temporary mixed-gender manning, pardon my pun. He didn't give me details."

"Plenty of time for that later on, I suppose," Jeffrey said.

"I'm sorry to interrupt," Kathy said to Ilse. She turned back to Jeffrey. "I just wanted to quickly introduce myself, sir, before I went down to the ASDS in the harbor and caught the taxi, so to speak."

"I'm glad you did," Jeffrey said distractedly. "We'll get you started on settling in later this afternoon."

"Good-bye," Kathy said to Ilse. Kathy left.

"Um," Jeffrey said. "Sorry, Ilse, I, I, I sort of lost my whole train of thought there."

"I don't know, Jeffrey. I'm still so, so confused about how I feel, about what I did back there, that bad place we both went to."

Jeffrey nodded reluctantly, remembering the lab, those scientists, the A-bomb. "War makes good people have to do terrible things sometimes. That doesn't make you a bad person, Ilse. You helped stop something evil."

Ilse opened her mouth to reply, but a messenger from *Challenger* dashed up, escorted by an armed guard Jeffrey had never seen before.

"Sir," the messenger said. "*This.*" He handed Jeffrey the slip and Jeffrey read it to himself, first looking over his shoulder again. A *Virginia*-class fast-attack boat had been badly damaged in an engagement with two Axis-crewed *Rubis*-class SSNs near the Azores. Both ex-French boats were assessed destroyed, but the American sub had been forced to bottom on a seamount barely higher than her crush depth. The engineering spaces were flooded and the surviving crew were sheltering forward, without much power or air, and more German subs were closing in. *Challenger* was ordered to put to sea at once and render all possible assistance to the stricken American boat, including an attempt to rescue the crew using the ASDS, something never tried before in combat.

"What about Captain Wilson?" Jeffrey said to the messenger.

"The neurologist wouldn't allow him out of his room, sir," the messenger said. "He called the Shore Patrol and used his medical authority."

Jeffrey looked at Ilse. He knew she could see it in his eyes. "I have to go," he said. "Now."

Ilse simply stood there. Tears began to stream down her face.

"I, uh . . ." Jeffrey trailed off, his chest aching from how beautiful she looked.

"Sir, *come on,*" the messenger said, tugging Jeffrey's sleeve. "A car's waiting."

Not knowing what else to do, Jeffrey reached and took Ilse's hand. She just held his limply, her lip trembling.

"I'll try to find you," Jeffrey said. "Somehow."

Ilse tried to speak but couldn't. She pressed his hand and then turned her back. Jeffrey tore himself away and started for the patio, chiding himself that even after all these years good-byes were still so hard.

Another messenger dashed over breathlessly. Jeffrey held out his hand, but the youngster said he needed Miss Reebeck. Jeffrey grabbed the slip and skimmed it as both messengers kept eyeing their wristwatches. Jeffrey brought the slip to Ilse.

"Let's *go*," he told her insistently. "You've been assigned to my boat."

ACKNOWLEDGMENTS

First I must thank my formal manuscript readers: Commander Jonathan Powis, Royal Navy, who was sonar officer on the nuclear submarine HMS *Conqueror* during the Falklands crisis; Commander Peter D. Shay, USNR (Ret.), helo pilot who flew in combat with the SEALs in Vietnam; Lieutenant Commander Jules Steinhauer, USNR (Ret.), World War II diesel boat veteran, and carrier battle group submarine liaison in the early Cold War; retired senior chief Bill Begin, veteran of many SSBN "boomer" strategic missile deterrent patrols; and Peter Petersen, who served in the German Navy's *U-518* in World War II.

A number of other navy people gave valuable guidance: George Graveson, Jim Hay, and Ray Woolrich, all retired U.S. Navy captains, former submarine skippers, and active in the Naval Submarine League; Ralph Slane, Vice President of the New York Council of the Navy League of the United States, and docent of the *Intrepid* Museum; Melville Lyman, former CO of several SSBNs, and now Director for Special Weapons Safety and Surety at the Johns Hopkins Applied Physics Laboratory; Ann Hassinger, research librarian at the U.S. Naval Institute; and Richard Rosenblatt, M.D., formerly a medical consultant to the U.S. Navy.

Other submariners and military contractors deserve acknowledgment as well. They are too many to name here, but standing out in my mind are pivotal conversations with Commander Mike Connor, at the time CO of USS *Seawolf*, and with Captain Ned Beach, USN (Ret.), brilliant author and one of the greatest submariners of all time. I also want to thank, for the tours of their fine vessels, the officers and men of USS *Alexandria*, USS *Connecticut*, USS *Dallas*, USS *Memphis*, USS *Springfield*, the modern German diesel submarine *U-15*, and additionally the instructors at the New London Submarine School. I owe "deep" appreciation to everyone aboard the USS *Miami*, SSN 755, for four wonderful days on and under the sea.

Foremost among the publishing professionals who influenced my work is my wife, Sheila Buff, a nonfiction author with more than two dozen titles in bird-watching and nature, wellness and nutrition. My literary agent, John Talbot, who had the foresight to represent me based on some writing workshop exercises and a single nonfiction credit in *The Submarine Review*. My editor at Bantam Dell, Katie Hall, so accessible and responsive, who always insists on the highest standards and shows me how to meet them. Thanks also to Terry Bisson, award-winning writer, for being such a good teacher, and to John Ordover, seasoned editor, for being so demanding. To Louise Weiss, travel writer, for fact-checking me. To the late Grace Darling, formerly of the Council on Foreign Relations, one of the most wonderful people I have ever known. And finally, to personal friends Roy and Linda DeMeo, Susan Farenci, Marty and Carol Goldstein, Betty and Larry Steel, Gil Nachmani, and Linda Karr and Bernie Scutaro.

GLOSSARY

Acoustic intercept A passive (listening only) sonar specifically designed to give warning when the submarine is pinged by an enemy active sonar. The latest version is the WLY-1.

Active out-of-phase emissions A way to weaken the echo that an enemy sonar receives from a submarine's hull, by actively emitting sound waves of the same frequency as the ping but exactly out of phase. The out-of-phase sound waves mix with and cancel those of the echoing ping.

ADCAP Mark 48 Advanced Capability torpedo. A heavyweight, wire-guided, long-range torpedo used by American nuclear submarines. The Improved ADCAP has even longer range, and an enhanced (and extremely capable) target-homing sonar and software logic package.

AIP Air-independent propulsion. Refers to modern diesel submarines that have an additional power source besides the standard diesel engines and electric storage batteries. The AIP system allows quiet and long-endurance submerged cruising, without the need to snorkel for air, because oxygen and fuel are carried aboard the vessel in special tanks. For example, the German *Klasse* 212 design uses *fuel cells* (see below) for air-independent propulsion.

Alumina casing An extremely strong hull material which is less dense than steel, declassified by the U.S. Navy after the Cold War. A multilayered composite foam matrix made from ceramic and metallic ingredients.

Ambient sonar A form of active sonar that uses, instead of a submarine's pinging, the ambient noise of the surrounding ocean to catch reflections off a target. Noise sources can include surface wave-action sounds, the propulsion plants of other vessels (such as passing neutral merchant shipping), or biologics (sea life). Ambient sonar gives the advantages of actively pinging but without betraying a submarine's own presence. Advanced signal processing algorithms and powerful onboard computers are needed to exploit ambient sonar effectively.

ARCI Acoustic Rapid COTS Insertion. The latest software system designed for *Virginia-class* (see below) fast-attack submarines. (COTS stands for "commercial off-the-shelf.") The ARCI system manages sonar, target tracking, weapons, and other data, through an on-board fiber-optic local area network (LAN). The ARCI replaces the older AN/BSY-1 systems of *Los Angeles*–class submarines, and the AN/BSY-2 of the newer *Seawolf*-class fast-attack subs.

ASDS Advanced SEAL Delivery System. A new battery-powered minisubmarine for the transport of *SEALs* (see below) from a parent nuclear submarine to the forward operational area and back, within a warm and dry shirtsleeves environment. This permits the SEALs to go into action well rested and free from hypothermia, real problems when the SEALs must swim great distances or ride on older free-flooding *SDVs* (see below).

ASW Antisubmarine warfare. The complex task of detecting, localizing, identifying, and tracking enemy submarines, to observe and protect against them in peacetime, and to avoid or destroy them in wartime.

Auxiliary maneuvering units Small propulsors at the bow and stern of a nuclear submarine, used to greatly enhance the vessel's maneuverability. First ordered for the USS *Jimmy Carter,* the third and last of the *Seawolf*-class SSNs (nuclear fast-attack submarines) to be constructed.

Bipolar sonar A form of active sonar in which one vessel emits the ping while one or more other vessels listen for target echoes. This helps disguise the total number and location of friendly vessels present.

CACC Command and Control Center. The modern name for a submarine's control room.

CAPTOR A type of naval mine, placed on or moored to the seabed. Contains an encapsulated torpedo, which is released to home on the target.

CCD Charge-coupled device. The electronic "eye" used by low-light-level television, night-vision goggles, etc.

CERTSUB A certain hostile submarine contact.

COB Chief of the boat. (Pronounced like "cob.") The most senior enlisted man on a submarine, usually a master chief. Responsible for crew discipline and for proper control of ship buoyancy and trim, among many other duties.

Deep sound channel A thick layer within the deep ocean in which sound travels great distances with little signal loss. The core (axis) of this layer is formed where seawater stops getting colder with increasing depth (the bottom of the *thermocline;* see below) and water temperature then remains at a constant just above freezing (the bottom *isothermal* zone; see below). Because of how sound waves diffract (bend) due to the effects of temperature and pressure, noises in the deep sound channel are concentrated there and propagate for many miles without loss to surface scattering or seafloor absorption. Typically the deep sound channel is strongest between depths of about 3,000 and 7,000 feet.

ELF Extremely low frequency. A form of radio that is capable of penetrating several hundred feet of seawater, used to communicate (one-way only) from a huge shore transmitter installation to submerged submarines.

EMBT blow Emergency main ballast tank blow. A procedure to quickly introduce large amounts of compressed air (or fumes from burning hydrazine) into the ballast tanks, in order to bring a submerged submarine to the surface as rapidly as possible. If the submarine still has propulsion power, it will also try to drive up to the surface using its control planes (called "planing up").

EMCON Emissions control. Radio silence, except also applies to radar, sonar, laser, or other emissions that could give away a vessel's presence.

EMP Electromagnetic pulse. A sudden, strong electrical current induced by a nuclear explosion. This will destroy unshielded electrical and electronic equipment and ruin radio reception. There are two forms of EMP, one caused by very-high-altitude nuclear explosions, the other by ones close to the ground. (Midaltitude bursts do not create an EMP.) Nonnuclear EMP devices, a form of modern nonlethal weapon, produce a similar effect locally by vaporizing clusters of tungsten filaments using a high-voltage firing charge. This generates a burst of hard X rays, which are focused by a depleted-uranium reflector to strip electrons from atoms in the targeted area, creating the destructive EMP current.

ESGN Electrostatically suspended gyroscopic navigation. The latest submarine inertial navigation system (see *INS* below). Replaces the older SINS (ship's inertial navigation system).

Fathom A measure of water depth equal to six feet. For instance, 100 fathoms equals 600 feet.

Frequency-agile A means of avoiding enemy interception and jamming, by very rapidly varying the frequency used by a transmitter and receiver. May apply to radio, or to underwater acoustic communications (see *gertrude* below).

Frigate A type of oceangoing warship smaller than a destroyer.

Fuel cell A system for quietly producing electricity, for example to drive a submarine's main propulsion motors while submerged. Hydrogen and oxygen are combined in a reaction chamber as the "fuels." The by-products, besides electricity, are water and heat.

Gertrude Underwater telephone. Original systems simply transmitted voice directly with the aid of transducers, and were notorious for their short range and poor intelligibility. Modern undersea acoustic communications systems translate the message into digital high-frequency active sonar pulses, which can be frequency-agile for security. Data rates well over 1,000 bits per second, over ranges up to thirty nautical miles, can be achieved routinely.

Halocline An area of the ocean where salt concentration changes, either horizontally or vertically. Has important effects on sonar propagation and on a submarine's buoyancy.

Hertz (or Hz) Cycles per second. Applies to sound frequency, radio frequency, or alternating electrical current (AC).

Hole-in-ocean sonar A form of passive (listening only) sonar that detects a target by how it blocks ambient ocean sounds from farther off. In effect, hole-in-ocean sonar uses an enemy submarine's own quieting against it.

HUD Head-up display. Laser holography is used to project tactical information onto a transparent plate within the user's field of view.

IFF Identification-Friend-or-Foe. A radar or sonar system for identifying one's own aircraft or vessel to friendly units, for tactical coordination and to help avoid friendly fire. Encrypted pulses are transmitted when the IFF system is "interrogated" by properly coded pulses from another friendly IFF. Of course, the IFF can be switched off when at *EMCON* (see above).

INS Inertial navigation system. A system for accurately estimating one's position, based on accelerometers that determine from moment to moment in what direction one has traveled and at what speed.

Instant range-gating A capability of the new *wide-aperture array* sonar systems (see below). Because each wide-aperture array is mounted rigidly along one side of the submarine's hull, sophisticated signal processing can be performed to "focus" the hydrophones at different ranges from the ship. By focusing at four ranges at once and comparing target signal strengths, it is possible to instantly derive a good estimate of target range. The target needs to lie somewhere on the beam of the ship (i.e., to either side) for this to work well.

IR Infrared. Refers to systems to see in the dark or detect enemy targets by the heat that objects give off or reflect.

ISLMM Improved submarine-launched mobile mine. A new type of mine weapon for American submarines, based on modified Mark 48 torpedoes and launched through a torpedo tube. Each ISLMM carries two mine warheads that can be dropped separately. The ISLMM's course can be programmed with way points (course changes) so that complex coastal terrain can be navigated by the weapon and/or a minefield can be created by several ISLMMs with optimum layout of the warheads.

Isothermal A layer of ocean in which the temperature is very constant with depth. One example is the bottom isothermal zone, where water temperature is just above freezing, usually beginning a few thousand feet down. Other examples are (1) a surface layer in the tropics after a storm, when wave action has mixed the water to a constant warm temperature, and (2) a surface layer near the Arctic or Antarctic in the winter, when cold air and floating ice have chilled the sea to near the freezing point.

Krytrons Extremely fast-acting electrical switches used to detonate all of the implosion lens components in a nuclear warhead at exactly the same time.

KT Kiloton. A measure of power for tactical nuclear weapons. One kiloton equals the explosive force of 1,000 tons of TNT.

LIDAR Light direction and ranging. Like radar, but uses laser beams instead of radio waves. Undersea LIDAR uses blue-green lasers, because that color penetrates seawater to the greatest distance.

Littoral A shallow or near-shore area of the ocean. Littoral areas present complex sonar conditions because of bottom and side terrain reflections and the high level of noise from coastal shipping, oil drilling platforms, land-based heavy industry, etc.

LMRS Long-term mine reconnaissance system. A remote-controlled self-propelled probe vehicle, launched from a torpedo tube and operated by the parent submarine. The LMRS is designed to detect and map enemy minefields or other undersea obstructions. The LMRS is equipped with forward- and side-scanning sonars and other sensors. Each LMRS is retrievable and reusable.

Mach stem A phenomenon resulting from a nuclear explosion at an optimum height in the air. The Mach stem produces an extremely destructive shock wave moving along the ground. It results when the blast's initial shock wave bounces off the ground and then moves quickly through the now-heated air to catch up with and merge with the original shock front still moving outward from the airburst itself. This merging multiplies the overpressure greatly and is an important factor in the effectiveness of tactical nuclear weapons.

MAD Magnetic-anomaly detector. A means for detecting an enemy submarine by observing its effect on the always-present magnetic field of the earth. Iron anywhere within the submarine (even if its hull is nonferrous or degaussed) will distort local magnetic field lines, and this can be picked up by sensitive magnetometers in the MAD equipment. Effective only at fairly short ranges, often used by low-flying ASW patrol aircraft. Some naval mine detonators also use a form of MAD, by waiting to sense the magnetic field of a passing ship or submarine.

Naval Submarine League (NSL) A professional association for submariners and submarine supporters. See www.navalsubleague.com or call (703) 256-0891.

NOAA National Oceanic and Atmospheric Administration. Part of the Department of Commerce, responsible for studying oceanography and weather phenomena.

OBA Oxygen breathing apparatus. A self-contained respirator pack used on submarines to move around freely during emergencies such as fires. (Crew members are also supplied with breather masks that plug into nozzles in special air lines, for use while manning their stations or lying in their racks.)

Ocean Interface Hull Module Part of a submarine's hull that includes large internal "hangar space" for weapons and off-board vehicles, to avoid size limits forced by torpedo tube diameter. (To carry large objects such as an ASDS minisub externally creates serious hydrodynamic drag, reducing a submarine's speed and increasing its flow noise.) The first Ocean Interface has been ordered as part of the design of the USS *Jimmy Carter*, the last of the three *Seawolf*-class SSNs (nuclear fast-attack submarines) to be constructed.

PAL Permissive action link. Procedures and devices used to prevent the unauthorized use of nuclear weapons.

Photonics mast The modern replacement for the traditional optical periscope. The first will be installed in the USS *Virginia* (see *Virginia class* below). The photonics mast uses electronic imaging sensors, sends the data via thin electrical or fiber-optic cables, and displays the output on large high-definition TV screens in the control room. The photonics mast is "non-hull-penetrating," an important advantage over older 'scopes with their long, straight, thick tubes which must be able to move up and down and rotate.

Piezo rubber A hull coating that uses rubber embedded with materials that expand and contract in response to varying electrical currents. This permits piezo-rubber tiles to be used to help suppress both a submarine's self-noise and echoes from enemy active sonar (see *active out-of-phase emissions* above).

PROBSUB A probable (but not certain) enemy submarine contact.

Pump-jet A main propulsor for nuclear submarines that replaces the traditional screw propeller. A pump-jet is a system of stator and rotor turbine blades within a cowling. (The rotors are turned by the main propulsion shaft, the same way the screw propeller's shaft would be turned.) Good pump-jet designs are quieter and more efficient than screw propellers, producing less cavitation noise and less wake turbulence.

Q-ship An antisubmarine vessel disguised as an unarmed merchant ship to lure an enemy submarine into a trap. First used by the Royal Navy in World War I, in actions against German U-boats.

Radiac Radiation indications and computation. A device for measuring radioactivity, such as a Geiger counter.

There are several kinds of radiac, depending on whether alpha, beta, or gamma radiation, or a combination, is being measured.

ROE Rules of engagement. Formal procedures and conditions for determining exactly when weapons may be fired at an enemy.

SDV Swimmer delivery vehicle. A battery-powered underwater "scooter" used by SEALs, wearing scuba gear, to approach and depart from their objective.

SEAL Sea Air Land. U.S. Navy Special Warfare commandos. (The equivalent in the Royal Navy is the SBS, Special Boat Squadron.)

7MC A dedicated intercom line to the Maneuvering Department, where a nuclear submarine's speed is controlled by a combination of reactor control rod and main steam throttle settings.

SOSUS Sound surveillance system. The network of undersea hydrophone complexes installed by the U.S. Navy and used during the Cold War to monitor Soviet submarine movements (among other things). Now SOSUS refers generically to fixed-installation hydrophone lines used to monitor activities on and under the sea. The advanced deployable system (ADS) is one example: disposable modularized listening gear designed for rapid emplacement in a forward operating area.

Synchrolift A kind of gigantic forklift or elevator used to move an entire submarine at a shore base or a shipyard.

Thermocline The region of the sea in which temperature gradually declines with depth. Typically the thermocline begins at a few hundred feet and extends down to a few thousand feet, where the bottom *isothermal* zone (see above) is reached.

TMA Target-motion analysis. The use of data on an enemy vessel's position over time relative to one's own ship, in order to derive a complete firing solution (i.e., the enemy's range, course, and speed, and depth or altitude if applicable). The TMA mathematics depends on what data about the enemy are actually available. TMA by passive sonar, using only relative bearings to the target over time, is very important in undersea warfare.

***Virginia* class** The latest class of nuclear-propelled fast-attack submarines (SSNs) being constructed for the U.S. Navy, to follow the *Seawolf* class. The first of four currently on order, the USS *Virginia*, is due to be commissioned in 2004. (Post-Cold War, some SSNs have been named for states, since construction of *Ohio*-class Trident missile "boomers" has been halted.)

Wide-aperture array A sonar system introduced with the USS *Seawolf* in the mid-1990s, distinct from and in addition to the bow sphere, towed arrays, and forward hull array of the Cold War's *Los Angeles*–class SSNs. Each submarine so equipped actually has two wide-aperture arrays, one along each side of the hull. Each array consists of three separate rectangular hydrophone complexes. Powerful signal processing algorithms allow sophisticated analysis of incoming passive sonar data. This includes *instant range-gating* (see above).

BIBLIOGRAPHY

BAKER, A. D., III. *Combat Fleets of the World 1998–1999*. Naval Institute Press, Annapolis, 1998.

BEACH, CAPTAIN EDWARD L. *Salt and Steel: Reflections of a Submariner*. Naval Institute Press, Annapolis, 1999.

BLANK, LIEUTENANT COMMANDER DAVID A., PROFESSOR EMERITUS ARTHUR E. BOCK, AND LIEUTENANT DAVID J. RICHARDSON. *Introduction to Naval Engineering*. Naval Institute Press, Annapolis, 1985.

BODANSKY, DAVID. *Nuclear Energy: Principles, Practices, and Prospects*. AIP Press, Woodbury, NY, 1996.

BROAD, WILLIAM J. *The Universe Below*. Simon & Schuster, New York, 1997.

BURCHER, ROY, AND LOUIS RYDILL. *Concepts in Submarine Design*. Cambridge University Press, New York, 1995.

CLANCY, TOM. *Submarine: A Guided Tour Inside a Nuclear Submarine*. Berkley Books, New York, 1993.

COMMITTEE FOR THE COMPILATION OF MATERIALS ON DAMAGE CAUSED BY THE ATOMIC BOMBS IN HIROSHIMA AND NAGASAKI. *Hiroshima and Nagasaki: The Physical, Medical, and Social Effects of the Atomic Bombings*. Translated by Eisei Ishikawa and David L. Swain. Basic Books, New York, 1981.

CRENSHAW, CAPTAIN R. S., JR. *Naval Shiphandling*. Naval Institute Press, Annapolis, 1975.

DANIEL, DONALD C. *Anti-Submarine Warfare and Superpower Strategic Stability*. University of Illinois Press, Urbana, 1986.

DUNCAN, FRANCIS. *Rickover and the Nuclear Navy: The Discipline of Technology*. Naval Institute Press, Annapolis, 1990.

ERICKSON, JON. *Marine Geology: Undersea Landforms and Life Forms*. Facts on File, New York, 1996.

FLUCKEY, REAR ADMIRAL EUGENE B. *Thunder Below!* University of Illinois Press, Urbana, 1997.

FRIEDEN, LIEUTENANT COMMANDER DAVID R., ED. *Principles of Naval Weapons Systems*. Naval Institute Press, Annapolis, 1985.

FRIEDMAN, NORMAN. *U.S. Submarines Since 1945: An Illustrated Design History*. Naval Institute Press, Annapolis, 1994.

HEINE, JOHN N. *Advanced Diving: Technology and Techniques*. Mosby Lifeline, St. Louis, 1995.

HERVEY, REAR ADMIRAL JOHN B. *Submarines*. Brassey's, London, 1994.

HUGHES, CAPTAIN WAYNE P., JR. *Fleet Tactics: Theory and Practice*. Naval Institute Press, Annapolis, 1986.

KEEGAN, JOHN. *The Price of Admiralty: The Evolution of Naval Warfare*. Penguin Books, New York, 1988.

KEMP, PAUL. *Underwater Warriors*. Naval Institute Press, Annapolis, 1996.

KOTSCH, REAR ADMIRAL WILLIAM J. *Weather for the Mariner*. Naval Institute Press, Annapolis, 1983.

MACK, VICE ADMIRAL WILLIAM P., AND COMMANDER ALBERT H. KONETZNI, JR. *Command at Sea*. Naval Institute Press, Annapolis, 1982.

MEDVEDEV, ZHORES A. *The Legacy of Chernobyl*. W. W. Norton & Company, New York, 1992.

O'KANE, REAR ADMIRAL RICHARD H. *Clear the Bridge!* Presidio Press, Novato, CA, 1997.

RHODES, RICHARD. *The Making of the Atomic Bomb*. Simon & Schuster, New York, 1988.

———. *Dark Sun: The Making of the Hydrogen Bomb*. Simon & Schuster, New York, 1996.

Sontag, Sherry, and Christopher Drew, with Annette Lawrence Drew. *Blind Man's Bluff: The Untold Story of American Submarine Espionage*. Public Affairs, New York, 1998.

Stubblefield, Gary, with Hans Halberstadt. *Inside the US Navy SEALs*. Motorbooks International, Osceola, WI, 1995.

Urick, Robert J. *Principles of Underwater Sound*. Peninsula Publishing, Los Altos, CA, 1983.

Watch Officer's Guide: A Handbook for All Deck Watch Officers. Revised by Commander James Stavridis. Naval Institute Press, Annapolis, 1992.

Woodward, Admiral Sandy, with Patrick Robinson. *One Hundred Days: The Memoirs of the Falklands Battle Group Commander*. Naval Institute Press, Annapolis, 1997.

The following periodicals were also consulted extensively:

Naval War College Review. Naval War College, Newport, RI.

Sea Power. Navy League of the United States, Arlington, VA.

The Submarine Review. Naval Submarine League, Annandale, VA.

Undersea Warfare. Superintendent of Documents, Pittsburgh, PA.

U.S. Naval Institute Proceedings. U.S. Naval Institute, Annapolis, MD.

ABOUT THE AUTHOR

JOE BUFF lives in Dutchess County, New York, with his wife. *Deep Sound Channel* is his first novel.

If you liked Joe Buff's
DEEP SOUND CHANNEL,
turn the page to get a glimpse at his next undersea adventure,
THUNDER IN THE DEEP,
coming to
bookstores on July 31, 2001.

PROLOGUE

In mid-2001, Boer-led reactionaries seized control in South Africa, and restored Apartheid. In response to a U.N. trade embargo, they began sinking U.S. and British merchant ships. NATO forces mobilized, with only Germany holding back. Troops and tanks drained from the rest of Europe and North America, and a joint task force set sail for Africa—into a giant trap.

There was another coup—in Berlin. Kaiser Wilhelm's closest heir was crowned, the Hohenzollern throne restored after almost a century; a secret conspiracy planned for years. Germany would have her "place in the sun" at last. Coercion won over citizens not swayed by patriotism or the onrush of events.

Covertly, this Berlin-Boer Axis had built tactical atomic bombs. They ambushed the Allied naval task force underway, then destroyed Warsaw and Tripoli. France capitulated at once, continental Europe was overrun, and Germany established a strong beachhead in northern Africa. Germany captured nuclear subs from the French, and advanced diesel submarines from other countries. A financially supine Russia, supposedly neutral, sold weapons to the Axis for hard cash. Most of the rest of the world stayed out of the fight, from fear or greed or both.

Now, American supply convoys to Great Britain are suffering in another terrible Battle of the Atlantic. If the U.K.

should fall, the modern U-boat threat will prove that America's overseas trade routes are untenable. The U.S. will have to sue for an armistice: an Axis victory. America and Great Britain both own ceramic-hulled fast attack subs—such as the USS Challenger, *capable of tremendous depths—but, Germany and South Africa own such vessels, too. Now, as harsh winter approaches in Europe, the British Isles starve, the U.S. is on the defensive, and democracy has never been more threatened. . . .*

TWENTY YEARS AFTER DESERT STORM, IN A DIFFERENT SORT OF WAR

IN THE MID-ATLANTIC OCEAN, NEAR THE AZORES

Captain Taylor told himself it must have been that convoy battle raging in the distance. The shock wave and noise from yet another tactical nuclear detonation rocked his ship, the USS *Texas*—a steel-hulled *Virginia*-class fast-attack sub, Taylor's home, his mistress at sea, his relentless yoke of command responsibility. Taylor know from the feel of the shock that it was an Axis underwater blast, meant to shatter the Allied freighters' bottoms, now that their Royal Navy escorts were mostly neutralized. This far off, Taylor's sonar people wouldn't hear the breaking-up sounds or the screams. But by sheer chance the echoes from those A-bombs had given *Texas* away, mocking the quieting of her machinery, making useless the stealth coatings on her hull.

Robert Taylor, a beefy guy, was normally upbeat and jocular, but now he bitterly cursed his luck. The latest under sea blast-front bouncing off *Texas* would betray his depth and course and speed to the pair of Axis nuclear subs, which had him in pincers—they'd never have spotted *Texas* without that endless searing thunder off to starboard, from the east. Taylor and his crew, and his Special Warfare passengers, had far more important things to do than tangle with them now. His orders even forbade his helping the U.K.-bound food convoy.

Taylor's executive officer said he was ready to open fire. The small atomic warheads on the Advanced Capability (ADCAP) torpedoes were all enabled, the outer tube doors open. The silent stalking was over with. Inside Taylor's head, twenty long years of Navy experience and training—and of constant physical risk and separation from his loved ones—all became sharply focused on the next few seconds and minutes of mortal combat.

"Firing point procedures," Taylor ordered, "tubes one and two. Target Master One, match sonar bearings, and *shoot.*"

"Tubes one and two fired electrically!" the XO called out.

A heartbeat later the sonar officer reported four enemy torpedoes in the water, two each incoming from the port and starboard beams.

The *Texas* had six tubes in all. Taylor quickly launched another pair of his nuclear ADCAPs, targeting the other ex-French *Rubis*-class boat, Master Two. He decided to save the last pair for anti-torpedo fire, to try to smash the inbound weapons using area bursts. Anticipating this, inevitably, the wire-guided Axis fish began to spread out. Each *Rubis* had four tubes. Taylor was outgunned.

Suddenly there were *eight* incoming torpedoes in the water, *four* on either beam.

Taylor badly wanted flank speed, but the Advanced SEAL Delivery System (ASDS) minisub that *Texas* carried on her back created hydrodynamic drag. The SEAL team leader volunteered to man the little vessel to release it from its host, and a lieutenant (j.g.) wearing gold dolphins offered to serve as copilot. Taylor reluctantly gave assent. Another distant rumbling rocked the ship, reminding them all what was in store for *Texas*. The sonar officer put his passive broadband on the speakers.

The nerve-ripping whine of a dozen torpedo propulsion systems filled the Command and Control Center air, in 3-D quadraphonic. Taylor could almost feel those eight eager Axis A-bombs drawing closer by the second, ready to unleash new underwater suns. Their top speed was twice that of *Texas,* and the range was short enough to make survival touch and go. Taylor fought down his fear: Emotions like that had to wait. Repression and denial were survival tools.

The ASDS was ready. It was set loose.

Taylor snapped more orders. His tense helmsman made a knuckle in the water, then dialed up flank speed. *Flank speed,* everything *Texas* had. The normally mild-mannered XO, now frowning and sweating, kept launching noisemakers and acoustic jammer pods.

Taylor's eyes roved constantly, between the crewmen crowded around him and the color-coded data on his command workstation. Briefly he watched the plot of the newest contact, the battery-powered ASDS, as it tried to sneak away. It was by far the slowest thing out there, and without it their whole mission would fail, before it had even begun. Silently Taylor beseeched his God, not for himself nor even for his crew and their dependents, but for the entire Allied cause. Ever since the Double Putsch in Berlin and Johannesburg some six months back, this war had not gone well, not for the good guys.

It was almost time for Taylor to launch his two available nuclear countershots—tubes one through four were still busy being reloaded. For the humans involved, Taylor told himself sardonically, time may have seemed to slow down, but the torpedo room loading equipment ran its oblivious pace.

Grimly Taylor forced himself to *use* every moment and think. The longer he waited, the more those incoming fish would bunch up, and he stood a better chance of wrecking several with each precious ADCAP. But the longer he waited, too, the smaller grew that narrow margin of distance between *Texas* and the hostile warheads' kill zones. Underwater, a mere one kiloton would be immensely destructive.

Taylor studied the geometries on his screen, watching

the dozen torpedoes, projecting their tracks, asking himself what the enemy captains' next move would be. His judgment had to be perfect. *Now.* He gave the order to fire.

"Tubes five and six fired electrically!" the XO's voice shouted back.

The cacophony outside the ship increased once more—*fourteen* torpedoes in the water going one way or another, above the constant nasty hiss of *Texas*'s own flow noise, plus the unending ungodly roar of antiship A-bombs from that separate convoy versus U-boat battle in the distance. "Both units running normally!" a sonarman called.

Then came a deafening hammer blow, bad enough to shake the control room consoles in their shock-absorbing mounts. Plastic mugs flew from cup holders, splashing coffee on the deck. Taylor held on hard to an overhead fitting. He would've grabbed for a periscope shaft had there been one, but in the *Virginia*-class all outside imaging was done electronically.

"Whose weapon was that?" he demanded, as the turbulent shaking began to subside and his console began to reboot.

"Master One's!" the XO said. "One Axis fish went for our noisemakers!"

"How many torpedoes still running?"

"We need to wait for the reverb to clear!"

"What about our own units?"

"All six still functioning, sir. Good contact through the wires."

Taylor glanced at a depth gauge, then ordered his submarine shallower. This had always been standard doctrine in tactical nuclear war at sea, to benefit from surface cut-off effect, the venting of fireball energy into the air. The Cold War might be long over, the enemy different now, but the underlying physics hadn't changed.

Taylor went back to his screen. It was time to trigger those last two ADCAPs. Commands were relayed; the water around *Texas* heaved. The resounding cracks, so close, were much sharper this time, punishing Taylor's ears. The vibrations were much sharper, too. An overhead light fixture shattered, and nearby crewmen protected their eyes.

A phone talker, young and already scared, pressed his hands to his bulky headset, listened intently, and raised his voice. "Flooding in the engine room, lower level port side!"

Too many things were going on at once. Taylor ordered the XO aft, to oversee repairs. The weapons officer deftly stepped in as Fire Control Coordinator. The tactical plot was refreshed. The nearest threat icons showed up with very high position confidence, the enemy torpedoes so noisy now as they ran at endgame speed. Two Axis fish were still closing in from starboard, one from port, clearly picked up on *Texas*'s side-mounted sonar wide-aperture arrays.

The ASDS tried to raise the *Texas* by underwater telephone, but the message was unintelligible, conditions out there were so bad. Then the minisub started to ping, on maximum power. Taylor realized it was trying to act as a decoy, to protect its more high-value parent. The two men aboard, two good men Taylor knew well and liked and cared about, must know that they'd die: The ASDS was unarmed. One Axis torpedo acquired it; the others pressed on toward *Texas*. Again Taylor had to squelch down his emotions: Around him, man and machine were melded into a conflict that wiped out any possible sense of personal future or past.

Tubes one through four on Taylor's weapons status window flashed green, ready to fire. There was a heavy roar from astern, and the ASDS icon on the mail plot pulsed, then vanished.

There was a pair of distant roars; more shock waves pummeled the ship. Taylor heard several men shouting at once.

"Units from tubes one and three have detonated!"

"Close-in hits on Master One and Master Two, assess both targets destroyed!"

Then from the phone talker: "Flooding aft is worsening, Captain, two feet deep in the bilge!"

The chief of the boat worked his console with tight concentration, trying to preserve neutral buoyancy and maintain level trim. He'd put in his papers to retire just twenty days before the war broke out—forget about that now.

There were still two incoming torpedoes, spaced wide apart off the port and starboard quarters. Taylor ordered tubes one through four fired, more defensive nuclear snap shots. But the inbound weapons were so close now it was a toss-up whether they could be knocked down in time. Even if their proximity fuses were set very tight, buying *Texas* a few extra seconds, the ADCAPs might not reach safe separation quickly enough for survivable preemptive blasts. Again Taylor studied his screens. A week-old image forced its way into his mind, his wife and their two teenage girls, making good-byes on the pier in New London.

"Detonate the weapons," Taylor ordered. He knew it was too damned close.

The explosions, reinforcing each other, knocked him off his feet. His shoulder struck an unyielding corner; an awful pain shot through his chest. Console tubes imploded. The deck shook so hard his vision was blurred, and the air began to fill with pungent smoke.

He saw men dazed, others moving and speaking, then realized he was deafened and he tried to read their lips. The phone talker, bleeding profusely from a flattened nose, mouthed each word carefully. "Flooding in Engineering is out of control." The bilge pumps couldn't keep up.

Taylor turned to the chief of the boat, and commanded an emergency blow. Surfacing into the tons of radioactive steam and fallout topside appalled Taylor, but it was their only chance. The bottom-mapping sonar was useless in such chaotic acoustic conditions, but the inertial nav plot told him enough. The seafloor here went way down past their crush depth.

Compressed air screamed and roared. The helmsman tried to plane up, just like he'd trained. The deck tilted steeply, and the vessel strove for the surface as her ballast tanks were forced to dry. Taylor noticed more blood. One crewman had compound fractures of both forearms, from bracing himself the wrong way. Another man lay on the deck, the stillness of death upon him, his neck badly twisted, broken. Other crewmen donned their emergency air breather masks, before the thickening smoke could kill them all. Fire-fighting teams went to work. Taylor felt a jumble of pride and anguish, at their skill and their courage, their wounds and their dreadful pain. His people—kids, really, most of them—were his surrogate family, and around him they were dying.

Taylor struggled to his console, tried to lift the red handset to Damage Control back aft, and realized his right collarbone was smashed. He grabbed for the phone with his left. Every breath came with agony, He vomited, then almost blacked out.

He made himself go on, of sheer necessity; one-handed, he pulled on his mask. There were a hundred thirty-five people aboard—including the SEALs—all his to lead, to protect; their wives and kiddies collectively totaled twice that. He'd seen them on the pier, too, making *their* good-byes.

Taylor knew the crew needed to stop the flooding very quickly once on the surface, then resubmerge, or they'd be picked off by a nuclear cruise missile. The Axis anti-shipping campaign was conducted with numbing ferocity. As if to emphasize the point, more explosions rumbled in the distance from the now one-sided convoy/U-boat fight.

The *Texas* broached nose first, consummating her sickening upward trajectory, then smashed back flat on the surface, forcing Taylor to his knees. The ship wallowed, rolling heavily, obviously settling fast. The engineer back aft tripped the panic switch, valving shut all sea pipes, which shut down propulsion too, but the water kept roaring in. Vital welds had cracked, in places difficult to find amid the blinding incoming spray. COB had already blown what he could, but the *Texas* was going down.

Taylor knew that if he ordered Abandon Ship, the few men who'd get out would perish horribly. He didn't activate a photonics mast—to see the multiple mushroom clouds would alarm the men to no purpose.

He stared very hard at a digital chart. A few nautical

miles away lay the spur of a jagged seamount peak, an extension of the Azores volcanic chain. The spur's depth was almost seventeen hundred feet, challenging *Virginia*-class crush depth, especially after the beating *Texas* just took. The remainder of the seamount was sheer-sided basalt cliff; if they missed the spur they were doomed. But it was their only hope, to huddle down deep and await a harrowing rescue, and pray their SEAL raid against a crucial German weapons lab could somehow be pulled off before it was too late.

Taylor ordered the sea valves reopened, to get the propulsion shaft turning again. He ordered all non-essential personnel to evacuate the engineering spaces, which were all one giant compartment when it came to truly watertight doors. He knew the men were coming when his aching eardrums crackled and he felt the air get warm; the incoming water was squeezing the atmosphere.

The watertight hatch was closed again, and Taylor told COB to put more high-pressure air in the engine room, help hold back the water. Its influx would only grow stronger as *Texas* drove for the seamount spur, her depth increasing by the minute, all reserve buoyancy lost. American SSN's simply weren't designed to float with one entire compartment flooded.

The XO conveyed by sound-powered phone that he'd stay aft with a handful of seasoned men. He knew that what *Texas* needed the most was speed, and people had to be there to override the safeties as the freezing seawater rose. Taylor authorized the reactor be pushed to one hundred eight percent.

Taylor eyed a depth gauge and watched the vessel's rate of descent, then glanced back at the nav chart. Maybe they'd make it to the spur, and maybe not, and even if they did they might crash-land too hard to live.

In simulator training his crew would have called this scenario grossly unfair. Taylor was fatalistic, staying detached. He tried not to think about the men working aft, who couldn't possibly survive.

The COB and the helmsman fought their controls, as

the main hydraulics failed. The turbogenerators went next, and console systems switched to batteries.

"Rig for reduced electrical," Taylor said, and *Texas* labored her heart out, the propulsor refusing to quit.

The phone talker reported the seawater aft had risen well past the tightly dogged water hatch. It was time to scram the reactor. *Texas* kept going on built-up momentum, sinking like a stone on her glidepath into oblivion.

"Collision alarm," Taylor ordered, as the crucial moment neared. He hoped his inertial nav fix was good and the local bottom charts accurate—with the ceaseless nuclear reverb and swirling bubbles all around, the bottom-mapping sonar only showed meaningless snow. He wished his boat had a gravimeter, which would have removed any doubt, but someone had decided some ten years back that gravimeters were too expensive.

Wincing with every gasping breath, suspecting now he'd also broken some ribs, Taylor ordered an emergency buoy prepared. He had it programmed for a tight-beam laser microburst, and hoped that the satellite due to pass overhead in an hour was still operational. The deeply encrypted message gave his ship's position, his plan for survival, and asked for help. It also reported his two *Rubis* kills, two fewer nuclear subs in the enemy arsenal now; at least if his ship and her people all died, they wouldn't have died for nothing. The buoy was launched. Taylor flashed once more on all those faces on the pier; some were widows and fatherless already.

The surviving men around Taylor braced for impact with the spur. If they missed it they'd keep going until the *Texas*'s hull caved in. They'd know soon enough.

CHAPTER 1

TWO HOURS LATER

SÃO VICENTE ISLAND, REPUBLIC OF CAPE VERDE

Water lapped against the submarine pier. Gulls called, machinery growled, the air stank of dead fish and diesel fumes, and the equatorial sun shown brightly near the zenith in a silvery blue sky. There were no clouds he could watch, nor ships beyond the breakwater, and on this leeward side of the island only minor swell on the sea. Dominating the horizon loomed the next volcanic peak in the Cape Verde chain, seeming indifferent and invulnerable. Lieutenant Commander Jeffrey Fuller fidgeted.

At last, above the sounds of cranes and trucks and urgent, shouting dockworkers and marines, Jeffrey sensed a clattering roar. The Navy courier helicopter swung into view, first above the stuccoed homes sprawling along the parched rocky slopes around Mindelo harbor, then over the drab concrete warehouses of the waterfront itself. The helo flared and hovered by the pier, bringing with it the heady perfume of burnt kerosene exhaust.

Out of the corner of his eye, as she stood next to him, Jeffrey watched the aircraft's prop wash tousle Ilse Reebeck's hair. The engine noise precluded conversation now, but their conversation had already been cut short, back at the hotel. Ilse looked relieved to be coming with Jeffrey, and he was glad, too—the whole thing was very last-minute—but it only complicated matters between them to have her on Jeffrey's ship again. Lord knew in the last two weeks, with their atomic demolition raid on the South African coast, they'd shared enough experiences, and nightmares, to last a lifetime. He told himself it was worth it, for what they'd achieved for the Allied cause, but the personal price was so high. Now, with no chance to catch their breaths or succor in the inner emotional wounds, they were headed right back into the all-consuming maelstrom of tactical nuclear war at sea.

As a marine guard on the pier helped the helo pilot pick his spot to land, Jeffrey glanced at the water. The last of the liberty party was already crammed into USS *Challenger*'s ASDS minisub, moored against the pier—hiding under a special awning that helped mask the goings-on from Berlin-Boer Axis spy birds. Jeffrey knew some crewmen were forced to stand in the mini's swimmer lock-in/lock-out chamber. But the embark was on hold, because of this courier.

"I wish he'd hurry up," Jeffrey said out loud. For most of his life, Jeffrey had wished people and things would hurry up.

As the helo settled on the pier, Jeffrey reviewed what little he knew so far: the *Texas* was down and needed help, and time was of the essence. In this whole big, hot, North Atlantic-wide theater of battle, *Challenger* was the closest thing—the *only* thing—available. Images flashed through Jeffrey's mind, training videos he'd had to watch—ones all U.S. Navy submariners had to watch—of tattered human remains in tortured postures: the men who died on the Russian submarine *Kursk*. Smashed to pulp, drowned slowly, or cremated alive, then soaked in high-pressure seawater—a living medium full of creatures who sought and ate their flesh.

Was that what awaited Jeffrey's eyes, when he got to the *Texas*? His ASDS was supposed to double as a deep-submergence rescue vehicle, to try to dock with the disabled sub once *Challenger* arrived.

Someone stepped from the helo. Like Jeffrey, the courier wore no rank or insignia, for security, but Jeffrey knew him vaguely. He was a lieutenant commander, in fact a rear admiral's aide, and by Navy regulations he spoke for his admiral with equal force. Jeffrey, *Challenger's* executive officer, was now the ship's acting captain. *Challenger* herself was submerged somewhere beyond the breakwater. She was much too high-value a target to bring into port here during this war, and her real captain, Commander Wilson, Jeffrey's boss, was confined at the hotel with a bad concussion.

"Sign, please," the courier said, handing Jeffrey a thick envelope.

Jeffrey eyed the Top Secret markings, the code words RECURVE ARBOR—whatever *that* meant—along with the notation to open only when north of latitude 30 north. "What is this?"

"I don't know," the courier said. "I have other stops to make. This *Texas* thing has everybody stirred up."

Jeffrey scribbled his initials on the courier's clipboard, and did the arithmetic in his head. At *Challenger*'s top quiet speed, twenty-six knots—the fastest she dared go for long in the war zone—it would take more than a day to cross the thirtieth parallel, almost two full days to reach *Texas*.

"Do we know what shape they're in?"

"A lot are still breathing," the man said, "at least so far. They managed to launch another buoy once they crashed. That's why you're being sent."

"Can't you get us a doctor?" *Challenger* would act as a stealthy undersea field ambulance, if and when the survivors from *Texas* were taken aboard.

The courier shook his head. "They're all in surgery, overloaded. A hospital ship put in last night, from Central Africa. . . . Your corpsman will have to do."

"Great." Jeffrey started a mental tally of his ship's medical supplies. His people would be sleeping on the deck, to free their racks for the injured. . . .

"We're not sure yet if the Axis also knows about *Texas*. You may hit opposition en route."

"Terrific." Jeffrey'd transferred on as *Challenger*'s XO well after the start of the fighting six months ago—he'd been more than glad to give up a fast-track planning job at the Naval War College. He'd wanted to get to the front. Now, with no qualified skipper available at this forward base to step in for Commander Wilson, Jeffrey was utterly on his own.

"Good luck," the man called as he ran back to the helo.

Jeffrey turned to Ilse. He saw her read the concern on his face. They were both still so exhausted, her expression seemed to say, and now *this*. Jeffrey shrugged. Ilse was a civilian, a Boer freedom-fighter, but she'd be killed as dead as the rest of the crew if something went badly wrong.

"After you," he said, letting her go first, up the aluminum gangway and down the top hatch of the little submarine. The sixty-five-foot-long ASDS was their undersea taxi today, hopefully too small on its own for someone to waste a nuke, and too stealthy for the enemy to track it to *Challenger*.

Ilse climbed down the top hatch, into the minisub's central hyperbaric sphere, which doubled as entry vestibule. The packed crewmen, all familiar faces, tried to make room for her. She in turn, eased out of the way, so Jeffrey could follow.

Ilse smiled to herself, a bit grimly. Stomach sucked in, elbows close at your sides, watch what you bump into, and respect the other person's personal space—this was how submariners moved about their cramped and self-contained world. Ilse was pleased with how quickly she'd learned these habits during her first trip on the *Challenger*, and how quickly the mindset returned now on this unexpected, hurried second mission. That first time, she'd volunteered; her special skills were badly needed. This time, no one asked; a message from the chain of command had ordered her to go. They were supposed to head for the U.S. East Coast and a needed stint in dry dock—and maybe some leave for Christmas, too—and then this *Texas* rescue came up. Now, Ilse was being swept along in the rush.

Ilse watched Jeffrey reach to close the top hatch. Before he could dog it shut, the heavy door from the minisub's forward control compartment swung open. *Challenger*'s chief of the boat looked into the sphere and made quick eye contact with Ilse.

Ilse smiled back, and her inner tensions died down a bit; it was good to rejoin these people she knew and trusted. They'd help her relieve some of her earlier anger, her barely repressed rage. They were a family of sorts, to replace everything and everyone she'd lost after the Johannesburg coup. Was it worth risking death to be with them again? What was her choice, to languish as a displaced person, utterly alone? Besides, in *this* war nowhere was "safe."

COB winked Ilse a hello, seeming surprised to see her. He was the oldest man in the crew, a salty, somewhat irreverent master chief. He had an amazing charisma, in a tough and blue-collar way, and Ilse had liked him from the moment they first met two weeks ago. Right now COB was acting as pilot of the minisub, with a lieutenant (j.g.) copilot. The last time she'd ridden the mini, it had taken her into combat in her tyranny-ravaged homeland of South Africa. Then a U.S. Navy SEAL chief had been copilot. He didn't come back.

COB called out to Jeffrey, "Sir, another delay. More passengers."

"More?" Jeffrey said. The men standing around him groaned. The youngest, still teenagers really, looked afraid they'd get left behind.

The pressure-proof door to the rear transport compartment was closed, and Ilse wondered how many people were squashed in there already—the official capacity was eight. One of them, she realized, would have to be newcomer Royal Navy Lieutenant Kathy Milgrom; there was nowhere else Kathy could be.

Ilse saw COB glance at his console, as if he were reading a decrypted radio or land-line message. "They're arriving any minute, Captain," COB said.

Jeffrey sighed, handed the courier envelope to COB, and climbed back up the ladder through the top hatch. Out of curiosity and because she liked to be where Jeffrey was, Ilse followed. Past the foot of the pier, beyond the big concrete obstacles and heavy machine-gun emplacements, a local taxi pulled up. Like clowns from a circus car, six big men piled out one after another, all in civilian clothing, as if for disguise. Ilse immediately recognized SEAL Lieutenant Shajo Clayton, his two logistics and backup people, and the three surviving operators from Shajo's blooded boat team. Shajo grinned and waved; he'd been with her and Jeffrey on the South Africa raid.

The men untied several heavy equipment boxes from the cab's roof rack, and pulled more from the vehicle's trunk. Some boxes were black: SEAL combat gear. Some were white with big red crosses: first-aid supplies, presumably for the *Texas*. Jeffrey called for crewmen to help, and everyone started carrying the stuff to the minisub.

Jeffrey shook hands very warmly with Clayton—they'd been through hell together, all too recently, and the resulting bond was tight. "Would somebody please tell me what the heck is going on?" Jeffrey said, smiling with pleasure at this unexpected reunion.

"If they do," Clayton rejoined, "then maybe you can let me know, sir." Then he clapped Jeffrey on the shoulder, equally delighted to see his proven comrade-in-arms again.

"What did they say to you?"

"We're supposed to be, you know, some kind of armed guard. Apparently you're in need of extra muscle."

“”I'm liking this less and less," Jeffrey said, shaking his head.

"I know," Ilse heard Clayton say as they reached the brow to the ASDS. "The base admiral didn't like it too much either."

Under the awning, Clayton gave Ilse a brotherly hug. She'd helped treat one of his mortally wounded men during the raid, and Clayton had brought her back alive; she felt better to know he was coming this time, too. Shajo was in his late twenties, from Atlanta, easy to talk to and even-tempered, with a very hard body. To Ilse his eyes betrayed hints of a persistent sadness that was all too common these days, from the recent loss of friends and teammates in the war, and the loss of innocence.

Jeffrey put down an equipment case and shouted through the mini's top hatch. "COB, how's your trim?" The little sub rode very low in the water, and didn't have a conning tower. With all the crewmen and now the SEALs' gear, keeping the mini stable would be tough.

Ilse heard COB's voice from inside. "Too heavy aft, Captain, and there's nothing left I can pump or counterflood. Any more weight on board and we're gonna have to jettison the anchors."

"Do it," Jeffrey yelled, "right now. And unclip the passenger seats in the back and pass them up to the pier." This was the Jeffrey whom Ilse had quickly gotten to know, and maybe, sort, of, to like; firm but informal, always improvising on the spot, and ruthlessly practical. Jeffrey was driven, coming alive under pressure, though sometimes impetuous or even reckless when in battle. Yet he was oddly hesitant with her—at least when they weren't both being shot at by the enemy. Lonely, too. Ilse had sensed that in Jeffrey quickly. He'd never once mentioned any family.

Clayton's men formed a human chain to pile the seats under the camouflage awning. Ilse couldn't help thinking that all this hubbub, the courier helo and then the taxi with the SEALs, had to get noticed by German or Boer recon assets.

Finally everyone was aboard with their gear, the shore power and mooring lines were stowed, the top hatch secured. Jeffrey went forward to stand behind COB's seat, in the little control room. Ilse started to follow him—she'd stood behind the copilot as they snuck in toward Durban, on the South African coast, the last time.

But Jeffrey held up one hand. "No, I need to talk with Shajo and COB about the rescue plan."

Shajo squeezed past Ilse and into the control compartment. Then Jeffrey closed the door in her face.